NIGHT-LOVER

The room's darkness hid her lover's face.

Who is he? Veronica thought.

The warm hand caressed her breasts, then slid further down. Veronica felt *hot*; her nipples swelled up so much they ached. Desperately she pulled the naked figure atop her.

"I still love you," the figure whispered.

Veronica wrapped her legs around his back, locked her ankles. Moaning, she rolled with each slow thrust. Already, her loins threatened to explode.

"Who are you?" she panted.

Then the moonlight fell across his face . . .

Veronica screamed.

It was a cadaver's face. Clumps of maggots filled its eyesockets, and rotten flesh hung off its cheeks in wet strips. When it smiled, its gray-green lips peeled away.

"I still love you," the corpse said again.

Diamond Books By Edward Lee

COVEN
INCUBI

INCUBI

EDWARD LEE

DIAMOND BOOKS, NEW YORK

INCUBI

A Diamond book / published by arrangement with the author

PRINTING HISTORY
Diamond edition / August 1991

All rights reserved.
Copyright © 1991 by Edward Lee.
This book may not be reproduced in whole or in part, by mimeograph or any other means, without permission.
For information address: The Berkley Publishing Group, 200 Madison Avenue, New York, New York 10016.

ISBN: 1-55773-549-2

Diamond Books are published by The Berkley Publishing Group, 200 Madison Avenue, New York, New York 10016.
The name "DIAMOND" and its logo are trademarks belonging to Charter Communications, Inc.

PRINTED IN THE UNITED STATES OF AMERICA

10 9 8 7 6 5 4 3 2 1

For C.M.

Down the long back street
I roam,
With eight roses in a bag,
and a poem.

PROLOGUE

Aorista, the man thought.

"Did you say something?" the girl asked.

Her breasts were erect chiffon orbs. She lay back on the bed, displaying the trimmed, dark plot of her sex. The man gazed openly, and again he thought: *Aorista.*

"I said you're very beautiful."

"You're beautiful too." Desire drenched her voice, or distilled it. "Don't make me wait," she murmured, and squirmed a little.

The man stood at the foot of the bed. "Let me look at you awhile first. You're beautiful, and I want to look."

She settled back and closed her eyes. She *was* beautiful, and her beauty sang to him. In the room's raw light, her white nakedness poured over his senses like hot wax. He could *consume* this vision, he could lap it up as a famished cat laps milk. It was not lust which exhorted his arousal, it was passion for all that she was, the beauty of her spirit as well as her flesh.

Flesh through blood, his thoughts whispered to him. *Body through spirit.*

She began to touch herself. Her hands slid up her belly, ran over her breasts, then slid back down, ranging over silken, white skin. She was so white—the man felt astounded. *The color of innocence,* he thought. *The color of all colors.* She could be a sculpture of purest marble or a canvas by Rubens. *She could be anything,* he thought.

She opened her legs. "Is this what you want to look at?"

"Yes," he said.

She parted the pink cleft with her fingers. The opening shined like sunlight on a lake. "Please, please," she whimpered.

At once, the man was on his knees, tasting her. She moaned. The man spread the white thighs further and rubbed his mouth over the moist entry, licking. He thought of beauty and creation, avatars and darkness, life and death. He thought of love.

For there could only be one real truth in the world, couldn't there? Love? It had to be love.

He laved her into a fever pitch with his tongue. Her hips flinched and she whined. Her excitement poured out of her.

Then, abruptly, the man stood up. The shadow of his erection played over her breasts, a serpent roving a white vale.

"All the truth that you can bear," he said, "is yours."

Her eyes caressed him. He could see the anguish there, the desperate passion. It filled her breasts. It stuck her big dark nipples out like plugs. Yes, passion. It *beckoned* him.

In each hand now he held a length of cotton rope.

"May I tie you?" he asked.

"Yes," she breathed.

Flesh through blood. Body through spirit.

Yes, the only real truth.

Love.

And it was with love that he next began to open her with the black blade. "I am risen," came the voice, but whose voice was it? His own or his god's? *Father,* he dreamed as he cut. Her flesh parted serenely, like new-churned butter. His erection pulsed down as he extracted the warm organs, kissing each one, then very delicately placing it aside.

Aorista, the man thought. The precious word hung in his mind like the breath of an angel. His arms were glazed red to the elbow. He rejoiced in the word.

He glanced up at his shadow on the wall.

But whose shadow was it? His own?

He smiled with love.

Then he dipped his fingers into the girl's blood and began to write.

CHAPTER 1

Lilacs drooped in the glass of water: doom forthcoming.

Veronica could see the doom in his eyes even before they spoke. *Experience?* he'd shouted at her yesterday. *What are you talking about!* God, didn't he understand anything? Experience wasn't even the issue. The issue was life.

She loved him, but that wasn't the issue either. Jack was just a flatfoot—that's what he always called himself. He had baggage, all right. "You're a terrible dancer," she'd once joked to him. "Baby, I'm terrible at a lot of things," he'd returned, "and damn proud of it." *Paranoid,* she thought. *Insecure.*

Did she need that?

"Well?" he said.

Veronica looked at the dying lilacs on the bar.

"Speak," he said suddenly. "Spit it out. What's going on? I didn't come here to look at the goddamn wall."

So much anger. *Have I caused that?* she wondered.

"I've done a lot of thinking," he said.

Oh, please. Dump me. You do it. Don't make me do it.

"We were meant to be together," he asserted. "I believe that. I don't think we should trash the whole relationship because of a few disagreements."

Whoa, Jackson, she thought. But all she could say back was, "I need a vacation."

"What!"

Veronica looked down at the bar rail.

The Undercroft was their favorite hangout; they were regulars. It was a tavern, really, an under-the-street sort of place made of old brick and mortar and old wood. People came here who didn't want the downtown scene, an interesting mix of art students, journalists, writers, etc. But the 'Croft was just one more fixture in her life that she questioned. She'd met Jack here; she knew everyone. And that made this whole thing so much more unpleasant. Thank God she and Ginny were going on the retreat. Time away. Time heals.

Experience, she thought.

They were both confused; she knew that. At the onset, their problems had bonded them. But now? Jack had had a serious drinking problem after the Longford case. It was before they'd met. Something about a pedophile ring and child pornography. Jack had solved the case, but its aftermath had nearly destroyed him. Veronica sometimes forgot that he had problems too. How many times had her own confusion deluded him? How could he still pursue her when the language of her life clearly stated that now was not the time for her to be in love? It didn't matter that she loved him. Her life was missing something.

"I'm going on a retreat," she said. "This creative thing."

"*Creative* thing? What's that?"

"A forum for artists. We get together and look into ourselves."

Jack closed his eyes as if to nudge something back, rage probably. "Look *into* yourselves? What are you looking f—"

"Hey, gang," Craig cut in. "What can I do you for?"

Craig was the weeknight barkeep. He was notorious. He probably accounted for half the 'Croft's business alone, via women. Ultimate charisma and preposterous good looks. Women had to take a number to go out with Craig.

Veronica and Jack smiled; they always did. Like nothing was wrong. Like, Hey, no problem here, Craig. No, no, we're not having another fight. And if you believe that—

They ordered two Glenfiddich on the rocks . . . and smiled.

When Craig turned away, Veronica repeated, "I need a vacation."

"A *vacation*!" Jack snapped, then lowered his voice. "Fine. We'll go to Ocean City or something. Wherever you want."

Veronica's throat lurched. "I meant a vacation from you."

There. She'd said it.

Jack's eyes strayed down the bartop, then to the lilacs. He absently lit a cigarette and spewed smoke.

Experience, the thought kept coming back. "I need some

time to myself," she said. "Maybe that's why things aren't working. I need time to experience new things. I need—"

"I know. Wild oats," he said. "That's usually the guy's line."

"Artists need to experience new things. I really haven't, and I need to, to be a better artist."

Jack bitterly tapped an ash in the big Spaten tray. "Don't bullshit me. This is about sex, isn't it?"

Be honest! she shouted at herself. "Well, maybe that's part of it," she admitted.

"Getting laid by every swinging dick on the street is not going to make you a better artist, Veronica."

There he went again. Hostility. Sarcasm. Petty jealousy. He didn't even want to know what she meant.

He went on, "You're famous now, and—"

"I'm not famous."

Jack laughed. "TV interviews and news articles mean famous. Hey, *Time* magazine—that's famous. 'The herald of the postmodernist revival.' 'A celebration of the New Womanhood in art.' I know. You're hot stuff now, and I'm old news."

Is that what he thinks? Goddamn him. Why should she feel guilty about being a success?

"Sometimes you're the biggest asshole on earth," she said.

He didn't hesitate. "I know that. But let me tell you something, honey. If you're looking for perfection, good luck. You ain't gonna find it."

Now she wanted to kick him as hard as she could. Were all men this immature, this pitiable?

He slumped at the barstool. Craig put their drinks down, knowing it best to walk away.

Jack's voice sounded ruined and black. "But I still love you."

I love you too, she thought oddly. But she couldn't tell him that, not now. She must be honest. She must move on.

He was trying not to break apart in front of her. "I want us to give it one more shot," he said.

Veronica gulped and said nothing. The pause unreeled like a long rope over a cliff.

"At least tell me this. Have there been other guys since we've been together? Just tell me. I've got to know."

"I—" she said. She felt forged in ice. *The truth, damn it! Tell him the truth!*

"Just one," she said.

Jack's face looked about to slide off his skull.

"It wasn't sexual. It was just, you know—"

"No. No, I don't know. So tell me."

She looked into her drink as if its depths possessed cabalistic answers. "It was rapport or something. He was the one who invited me to the retreat. When I met him . . . sparks flew."

"Sparks flew!" Jack countered too loudly. "Sparks fly when my muffler falls off my car, but I don't fall fucking in love with it!"

Craig looked on forlornly from across the bar; so did several customers. All Veronica could do was close her eyes.

"Our relationship is over, isn't it? Yes or no?"

She looked everywhere but at him. "Yes," she said.

He was nodding slowly, numbly, eyes shut. "So who's the new guy? What's his name?"

Veronica gazed again at the dying lilacs. "Khoronos," she said. "His name is Khoronos."

What was it about the man?

Certainly more than his looks; Veronica never let that sway her. Maybe just timing and place. Success could be obstructive a lot of the time. The show, the praise, the sales that Stewie had made. But that wasn't it either. Something about the man himself. His air, perhaps.

"My name is Khoronos," he'd announced in a faint, attractive accent she couldn't place. "I've long been a voyeur of subjective psychology in modern art."

Subjective psychology? He must be another critic. "Voyeur is a strange way of describing artistic enthusiasm."

"Is it, Ms. Polk? Is it really?"

He stood six feet, dressed in a fine gray suit. Well postured, slender. She could tell he was in good shape by the way the suit fit. He looked late forties, early fifties, and had long grayish blond hair to his shoulders, which added to his dichotomy.

"Besides, Mr . . . Khoronos, I paint objectively."

He smiled like his accent. Faintly. "Of course. Just as Faulkner said he never put himself into his books, and da Vinci never used himself as his own model. It's every artist's right to lie about the motivations of his or her art."

Was he trying to insult her? She *was* lying, but like the man said, it was her right.

There was something about him, though. Just . . . something.

"Your work is brilliant," he said.

The show had gone beautifully. She was used to them by now, and now that she'd broken somewhat into the big time, Stewie got her shows as frequently as possible, if not too frequently. A *Post* critic had shown up; so had someone from *Connoisseur*. The local papers had shown up too. When would they quit with the Local Girl Makes Good stories? But it was all very flattering, especially to a woman who hated to be flattered.

And now this man. This Khoronos.

"I appreciate your compliment," she eventually said.

"Oh, it's not a compliment, it's an observation. If your work wasn't brilliant, I wouldn't say it was."

"What if my work sucked?"

"Then I would summon the necessary gall to tell you. But only if you asked me first, of course."

Veronica liked him. He looked aristocratic, she thought; that or refined through some vast experience. His face was strikingly handsome—perfect hard angles and lines. His eyes were dark, yet she could not discern their color.

Inexplicably, Veronica felt a tingle.

"Why exactly are you interested in subjective psychology in modern art, Mr. Khoronos?"

"The feminine mystique, I suppose."

"What?"

"Your paintings are emblematic of the things men can never understand about women," he answered, half eyeing the canvas she stood before. "It's your camouflage that rouses my . . . curiosities. Not necessarily what your art is saying in general, but what *you* are saying about *yourself*."

"That's fairly rude, Mr. Khoronos."

"I'm sorry. I was just trying to be objective"—he smiled again—"to an *objective* painter."

The canvas he addressed was her least favorite of the new batch. It was called *Vertiginous Red*. A tiny stick figure stood within a murky red terrain while swirls of darker red—blood red—weaved across the background. The figure looked abandoned, which was exactly what she wished to depict. "All right," she challenged. "What does this painting say about me?"

His answer came unhesitantly. "It's an expression of sexual ineptitude, since you asked. Disillusionment in, oh, I'd say a very young mind. This painting is about your very first sexual experience."

Veronica tried not to react. *Is this guy psychic? Vertiginous Red* was her attempt to paint how she felt after her first time. She'd been seventeen. The boy had left her hurt, bleeding, and terribly . . . disillusioned. She'd never felt more unsure of the world.

"Of course, that's only *my* interpretation," Khoronos was prompt to add. "Only *you* can know the painting's true meaning."

"Do you want me to tell you?"

He reacted as if stung. "Heavens, no. Artists must never betray their muse. In fact, I'd be disappointed if you did."

Veronica felt embosomed by some smeary kind of wonder. She didn't know what it was; she only knew that it was definitely sexual.

Khoronos glanced at his watch, a Rolex. "The show's nearly over. I'd like to browse a bit more if you don't mind."

"Please do."

"It was a pleasure meeting you, Ms. Polk."

She nodded as he stepped away.

"Who was that? The man of your dreams?"

Stewie stood beside her now. He was her manager/sales agent, though he liked to refer to himself as her "pimp." He made a point of dressing as ridiculously as possible; this, he claimed, "externalized" his "iconoclasia." Tonight he wore a white jacket over a black "Mapplethorpe at the Corcoran" T-shirt, pink-spotted gray slacks, and leather boots that came up to his knees. His perfectly straight black hair and bangs, plus the boots, made him look like a punk-club Prince Valiant.

"He's just some guy," Veronica answered.

"Just some guy? Looks to me like he put some serious spark into those girlieworks of yours. Quit staring at him."

"His name is Khoronos," she said. "What is that? Greek? He doesn't look Greek."

"No, but I'll tell you what he does look. Rich. Maybe I can milk him. He likes *Vertiginous Red*."

"Oh, Stewie, he does not," she complained. "It's my worst painting in years."

"He likes it. Trust me. I saw it in his eyes."

Several patrons greeted her and thanked them both. The usual compliments were made, which Veronica responded to dazedly. Most of her consciousness remained fixed on Khoronos, across the room.

"I think he's a critic," she said a minute later.

"No way, princess. That guy's suit, it's a 'Drini, a megabuck. Art critics buy their suits at Penney's. And did you see the diamond stickpin on his lapel? He's money walking."

"Shhh! He's coming back."

"Good. Watch Stewie take him to the cleaner's."

Stewie's commercial intuition always hit home, which was why Veronica tolerated his ridiculous wardrobe and haircut. He'd sold twelve of her paintings tonight, one of them—called *Child with Mother,* an inversion of the traditional theme—for $10,000. She felt intimidated now, though. She felt second-rate, even though she knew she wasn't. "Don't ask for more than a thousand," she said.

Stewie laughed.

God, he's good-looking, she thought as he approached. The little tingle worried her. Stewie was right. She was *hot.*

"A most impressive show," Khoronos said in his strange accent.

"Thank you. Would you care for some champagne?"

"Oh, no. Alcohol offends the perceptions. The muse is a temple, Ms. Polk. It must never be reviled. Remember that."

Veronica was close to fidgeting where she stood.

"Hello, sir," Stewie introduced. "I'm Stewart Arlinger, Ms. Polk's sales representative."

"Khoronos," Khoronos said, and declined shaking hands. He viewed Stewie smugly as a hotel owner viewing a bellhop.

"Are you an art critic?" Veronica asked.

Khoronos laughed. "Heaven forbid. I'm nothing like that, nothing like that at all. Nor am I an artist myself."

"What are you, then?"

"I've already told you." The faint, measured smile returned. "I'm a voyeur. And art is what I feast my vision upon." Abruptly he turned to Stewie. "I would like to buy *Vertiginous Red.*"

"I'd be happy to sell it to you, Mr. Khoronos," Stewie answered. "*Vertiginous Red* makes quite a profound and important creative statement, wouldn't you say?"

"I'm aware of the work's artistic significance."

"But I'm afraid the asking price is considerable."

Khoronos frowned. "I didn't ask you how much it was, I told you I wanted to buy it, Mr. . . . Arlinger."

Stewie didn't waver. "Twenty-five thousand dollars."

Veronica almost fainted. *Goddamn you, Stewie! That piece of shit isn't worth twenty-five CENTS!*

Khoronos' face remained unchanging. "My people will be here at eight A.M. sharp. Please see to the painting's proper exchange."

"That's no problem at all, sir."

Khoronos was suddenly peeling bills off a roll of cash, which he then stuffed into an envelope and handed to Stewie. He turned to Veronica, smiled that cryptic smile of his, and said, "Good night, Ms. Polk."

Then he walked out of the gallery.

"Christ on a surfboard!" Stewie frantically counted the money in the envelope. Veronica was too dizzy to think.

"I don't believe this," Stewie muttered. He handed Veronica the envelope. It contained $25,000 in hundred-dollar bills.

Thoughts of Khoronos swam in her head all night; she'd scarcely slept. Late next morning, the phone roused her.

"Hi, Veronica. Long time, no hear."

It was her friend Ginny. "How are things in the novel gig?"

"Not bad. You'll love this, though. My publisher actually had the balls to tell me to make my books shorter because the price of raw paper went up. That's like telling you to use less paint."

"The things we do for art. What're you going to do?"

"Write shorter books. Fuck art. You should see my mortgage."

Ginny wrote grim, deceitful novels which critics condemned as "pornographic vignettes of bleakness which trumpet the utter destruction of the institution of marriage in particular and morality in general." Ginny swore these reviews increased her sales, while the fringe critics hailed her as a genius of the neo-feminist movement. Her themes were all the same: men were good for nothing but sex and could never be trusted. Her last one, *Love Labyrinthine*, had sold a million copies.

"I met the most wonderful man the other day," Ginny said.

"I thought you hated men."

"Except for bed warmers, I do. But this one was different."

"I've heard that before."

"Would you listen! I was doing a book signing at Glen Burnie Mall last week. At signings, most people fawn over you. But this guy spent the whole time talking about the function of prose mechanics, syntactical projection of imagery, creative dynamics, stuff like that. And it was really funny because there wasn't a shred of falseness in him. When was the last time you met a man without a shred of false—"

"Never," Veronica said.

"He was so *enthused,* you know? About literature, about art. When was the last time you met a man who was enthused about—"

"Never," Veronica repeated. "There aren't any." But then her brow rumpled. This man sounded a bit like—

"What did he look like?" she asked.

"Oh, God, Vern. A panty-melter. Tall, slim, great clothes, and a face like Costner or somebody. He was older, though, and really refined, and he's got the most beautiful long gray and blond hair. An accent too, German maybe, or Slavic."

Veronica smirked hard. It sounded just like Khoronos.

"His name is Khoronos," Ginny dreamily added.

The pause which followed seemed endless.

"Vern? You still there?"

"Uh—" This was too much of a coincidence. "I met him last night during my show at the Sarnath. He paid twenty-five grand for one of my canvases, and you're right, he is sexy."

"This is outrageous!" Ginny wailed. "Then he must've invited you to the retreat too, right?"

"What retreat?"

Ginny impassed. "It's a get-together he has every year at his estate, an art-group kind of thing. He called it his 'indulgence,' his chance to be an artistic 'voyeur.'"

Veronica's frown deepened.

"He said he likes to be in proximity to artists, to talk, party, get to know each other. Something like that."

Veronica simmered. Her face felt hot.

"So I told him I'd go. There'll be other people there too. Two guys, a poet and sculptor I've never heard of. Oh, yeah, and Amy Vandersteen's going to be there too."

"You're kidding!" Veronica almost yelled. Amy Vandersteen was one of the biggest feminist directors in Hollywood. All at once, Veronica felt jilted. Why hadn't she been invited?

"Well, I hope you have a good time," she said.

Ginny could tell by the tone of her voice. "You're mad, aren't you? You're mad I got invited and you didn't."

"I'm not mad," Veronica scoffed. She was mad, all right. It made no sense, she realized, but she was madder than hell.

"I didn't mean to gloat, Vern. I won't go if you're mad."

"That's silly. Go. Have fun. Tell Khoronos I said hi."

"I will, Vern. Bye."

Veronica slammed the phone down. But why should she be so riled? It was stupid. Or—

It wasn't just the idea of missing out. It was Khoronos. She wanted his attention, his presence, his shared interest. It was a cryptogram that implied she was less worthy than the other people. Not good enough. *Fuck!* she thought.

Depression assailed her.

She went through the day's mail, to get her mind away. Bills and junk mostly. A renewal for *ARTnews*. But the last letter looked like a wedding invitation, gold letters on fine paper. There was no return address. She opened it and read:

> Dear Ms. Polk:
>
> It was a pleasure to make your acquaintance. In the few moments we spoke, I came away feeling edified; we share many commonalities. I'd like to invite you to my estate for what I think of as an esoteric retreat. Several other area artists will attend. It's something I've been doing for a long time—call it an indulgence. It's a creative get-together where we can look into ourselves and our work. If you'd care to join us, please contact my service number below for directions.
>
> Sincerely,
> Erim Khoronos

Veronica squealed in joy.

When she looked up at the lilacs again, Jack was gone. Ice melted in his empty glass, and he'd left the keys to her apartment on the bartop. How long had she been recounting the events which had led to her invitation? Her eyes were wet; she knew how Jack would take this, but what could she do? She had to be honest.

Craig, the barkeep, brought her another drink. His long look told her he knew exactly what had happened.

"Jack's a great guy," he said.

"I know."

"So you two are finished?"

Experience, she thought, or was she really thinking of Khoronos? "I haven't experienced enough in life," was the only answer she could summon.

"What kind of experience? There are all types," Craig said.

"That's just it. I don't really know."

Craig poured Earthquake shooters for some rowdies at the bar, then drifted back, twirling a shaker glass. Craig and Jack were good friends. This was hard.

"You think I'm a bitch," she suggested. "You think I'm stupid and selfish for dumping Jack."

"No, Veronica. If you don't love him anymore, then you have to move on, and let him move on. It's the only honest way."

Do I still love him? she asked herself. The question was turmoil. She didn't know. She didn't even know if she *wanted* to know. "Maybe I just need some time away. Maybe things could work out for us later."

"Do you think you really want them to?"

"I don't know."

Veronica tried to think of Jack, but all she could see behind her eyes was Khoronos.

CHAPTER 2

The phone sounded like a woman screaming.

I'm dead, he thought.

That's how he felt when he woke. The room's darkness smothered him. He felt entombed. Buried in black.

Veronica, he thought.

The phone screamed on.

"Cordesman. What is it?"

The voice on the other end wavered, as if in reluctance or dread. "Jack, it's me. We've got a bad one."

Me was Randy Eliot, Jack's partner. A "bad one" meant only one thing in shop talk.

"Where?" Jack asked.

"Bayview Landing . . . I mean, it's really bad, Jack."

"I heard you. *How* bad?"

"It looks like something ritual. I don't know what to do."

I'm still half drunk, Jack realized. "Call evidence, call the M.E. Seal the unit and don't let any paper people near the place."

Randy sounded drained. It must be bad, because ordinarily the guy didn't flinch at the tough stuff. The last time they pulled up a floater, Randy was munching chicken gizzards from the Market. He chuckled when the floater burst and spilled fresh maggots onto the pier.

"I've never seen anything like this."

"Just sit tight," Jack said. "I'm on my way."

He hauled on old clothes, grabbed his Smith, and popped six aspirin. He refused to look in the mirror; he knew what he would see. Bloodshot eyes. Pale, thin face and paler body. He'd stopped working out years ago. His hair hung in strings to his shoulders. He drank too much and smoked too much and cared too little. He hadn't always been like that. Was it the job? Or did he simply think too little of himself to cope?

Veronica, he thought.

Jack Cordesman was thirty-three years old. He'd been a county cop since twenty-two, and a homicide detective since twenty-eight. He'd been shot once, decorated four times, and had the highest conviction rate of any homicide investigator in the state. There was a time when he was considered the best cop on the department.

They paid him $36,000 per year to wade in the despair of the world. To protect the good guys and lock the criminals up. By now, though, after so many years, he didn't even know which was which. Crime rates soared while correctional budgets were slashed. These days they were paroling guys for parole violation. One night, Jack delivered a baby in a parking lot. An hour later he gunned down a man who'd raped a thirteen-year-old girl at gunpoint. The baby died three days later in an incubator. The rapist had lived, gotten five years, and was out now on parole. Good behavior.

The truth of what he was condemned him to himself; Jack Cordesman was part of the system, and the system didn't work.

A bad one, he recalled Randy's words. He drove his county unmarked through the city's stillness. They got about half of the city's homicides because the city cops were too bogged down by rapos and crack gangs. He'd seen bad ones before; most were drug-related. Snitches chopped up like cold cuts, dealers machine-gunned for moving on the wrong turf. These crack people didn't fool around. Once they'd firebombed an entire apartment project just to make a point.

Then there was always the ghost of the Longford case. Jack had watched the tapes he bagged as evidence. He thought he'd seen it all until the day he stared at that screen and watched grown men ejaculate into children's faces. One of the scumbags had been chuckling as he rubbed a scoop of Vaseline between a little blond girl's legs. And Longford himself, a millionaire, an esteemed member of the community, sodomizing a five-year-old boy . . .

Jack fired up a Camel and pushed it all out of his head. What was the use? If you didn't shrug, you went nuts. If you let yourself care, you were finished. Those were the rules.

Then the thought crept back: *Veronica.*

It wouldn't leave him alone. Loss? Rejection? He didn't know what it was. He tried to be mad about it, because that seemed the macho way to be. Sad was pitiful. There'd been tears in his eyes on the way home that night. *Yeah, real macho,* he thought. *Just a big crying pussy.*

She was the only girl he'd ever loved.

They'd been friends for nearly a year first. It was almost formality; they'd meet at the Undercroft several times a week, they'd drink, shoot the shit, joke around, talk about their problems, like that. Jack had needed to talk—this was right after the Longford case—and Veronica was always there to listen. He doubted he'd ever have gotten over it without her. But he liked listening to her too. He liked hearing about the joys in her life, the sorrows, the quagmires and triumphs, the ups and downs. Her art isolated her; she'd never been in love, she'd said. She even talked about her scant sex life, which made him secretly jealous. "Nobody understands me," she'd said so many times, her face wan in confusion. *I understand you,* he'd thought as many times. The fact was this: they were both misfits. That was their bond. Jack the reclusive long-haired homicide cop, and Veronica the desolate artist. Their friendship was perfect in its mutuality, but after so many months, Jack realized it was more than friendship. He realized he loved her.

That's when the weeks had begun to pass in slow masochism. His love continued to grow, but so did his certainty that he could never tell her that. If he told her, he might lose it all. "Stewie's always saying that you and I should be lovers," she often joked. Jack didn't laugh. First off, he couldn't stand Stewie ("a silly, stuck-up, fairy-clothes-wearing asshole," he'd once called him) and second, he agreed. Now she was talking about her disgruntled romantic life. "Guys think I'm weird," she'd complained. "They never call me back." What could he say? "There must be something wrong with me," she'd say. "Maybe I'm not attractive. Am I attractive?" Jack assured her she was attractive. But how could he tell her the truth, that she didn't fit into the regular world for the same reasons he didn't? Each night she'd recount her latest broken quest for love, and each night Jack wilted a little more behind his Fiddich and rocks.

And just as he thought his turmoil would tear him apart, the moment exploded. He remembered it very vividly. She'd been sitting there at the bar, right next to him as usual, and out of the blue she'd said, "You know something? All this time I've been looking for something, and it's been sitting right next to me all along." "What?" Jack said. "I love you," she said.

Jack had nearly fallen off his barstool.

It had been a wonderful beginning.

Now it's the end, he thought. His despair hollowed him out as he drove the unmarked down Duke of Gloucester Street. He'd dated more than his share of women in his life; none of them had been anything. Only her. Only Veronica. Her weird uniqueness, her spontaneous passion, her love. All gone now. Had it been all his fault? Had he pressured her? Had he moved too fast? Craig had often suggested that he wasn't giving her enough room to live her life. "She's an artist. Artists are weird." Bartenders knew people better than anyone. Jack wished he'd listened a little harder now.

And now this retreat thing. What the hell was that? *Some candy-ass bippy rap session. Let's drink wine and pooh-pooh about art.* A retreat, for God's sake. She hadn't even said where it was. And now this guy, this . . . What had she said his name was?

Khoronos.

More barkeep philosophy. Long ago, Craig had told him, "No matter how much you love a girl, and no matter how much she loves you, there'll always be some other guy."

Khoronos, Jack thought.

The throbbing lights afar caught his eye. Red and blue. *Don't think about it anymore,* he pleaded with himself. *Just . . . don't . . . think about it.*

The high rises stood like an arrangement of gravestones. In the center lot a pair of county cruisers sat nose-to-nose. One cop stood smoking, staring off. Another was down on one knee with forehead in hand. The red light on an EMT truck throbbed like a heartbeat.

"Put the fucking butt out and put it in your pocket," Jack said. "This is a crime scene. And tuck in your shirt."

"Yes, sir," the cop said. His eyes looked flat.

"Evidence here yet?"

"Upstairs and out back. We're still waiting on the M.E."

Jack pointed to the cop on one knee. "What's his problem?"

"See for yourself. Fifth floor. Lieutenant Eliot's there."

"Any press people show up, tell them it's a domestic. And get yourselves squared away. You're cops, not garbage men."

"Yes, sir."

Jack stalked toward the high rise. He was one to talk: long hair, ragman clothes, unshaven. Uniforms hated brass. You usually had to be a prick to get anything out of them. But these two guys looked like they'd just seen a ghost. *Maybe they have,* Jack thought. He stepped off the elevator onto the fifth floor and headed down the hall.

The familiar scent touched him at once. Faint. Cloying.

Fresh blood.

Randy Eliot leaned off the wall. He always wore good clothes, like a TV detective. But tonight the face didn't match the fine, tailored suit. Randy Eliot's face looked . . . cracked.

"You've never seen anything like it," was all he said.

"Who reported it?" Jack inquired.

"Old guy in the next unit. Said he heard *whining,* and some ruckus. The super unlocked the door for us."

Jack looked at the door frame. The safety chain was broken.

"That's right," Randy confirmed. "Locked from the inside. We broke it to get in. The perp went out the back slider."

Jack eyed the chain, then Randy. "But we're *five stories up*."

"The perp must've rappeled down. He left through the slider, over the balcony. That's all I know."

The apartment was quaint, uncluttered. It made him think of Veronica, and then he knew why. Framed pictures hung all over the walls—pastels and watercolors, originals. *An artist,* Jack realized. A lot of the pictures looked first-rate.

Flashes popped down the short hall. A tech was fuming the handle of the slider, squinting over a Sirchie UV light. He said nothing as Jack stepped onto the balcony.

Five goddamn stories, he thought, peering over the rail. Two more techs mounted field spots below, to check for impressions in the wet ground. It had rained all afternoon. The perp had either worked his way down terrace to terrace or had used a rope and somehow unhooked it afterward. Jack tried to visualize this but drew only shifting blanks.

Randy took him back through the unit. The place had "the feel." Any bad 64 had it, the mystic backwash of atmosphere projected into the investigator's perceptions. Its tightness rose in Jack's gut; he felt something like static on his skin. He knew it before he even saw it. The feel was all over the place.

"In there," Randy said. "I'll wait if you don't mind."

Another stone-faced tech in red overalls was shooting the bedroom with a modified Nikon F. The flash snapped like lightning. New blood swam in the air, and a strangely clean redolence. *Death in here,* the feel itched in Jack's head. *Come on in.*

Jack stepped into the bedroom.

"Aw, Christ," he croaked.

He felt nailed to the wall. The blood shouted at him, bellowed in his face. It was everywhere. He blinked with each pop of the tech's flash, and the image seemed to lurch closer. The bed looked *drenched,* sodden as a sponge in a pail of red paint. This was more than murder, it was a fête. Red shapes, like slashes, adorned the clean white walls. Some looked like words, others like symbols.

Above the headboard, four words stood out:

HERE IS MY LOVE

Love, Jack mused. In slow horror, his eyes moved to the bed.

White rope fastened her wrists and ankles to the posts. She was blindfolded with tape, and gagged—of course, the whining heard by the neighbor. Again, Jack tried to picture the killer, but his instincts, oddly, did not show him a psychopath. Jack could tell the victim had been pretty. The perp had very tenderly gutted her; he'd taken his time. Organs had been teased, caressed, reveled in for their warmth. Ropes of entrails had been reeled out of her sliced gut and adorned about the body like garlands. Her cheeks had been kissed by scarlet lips. Scarlet handprints lingered on her breasts. The epitaph proved the truth: This was not murder. It was an act of love.

Jack swallowed something hard. "Any prints?"

"Plenty," the tech said. "The guy didn't wear gloves. Lots of ridges on her hooters, and in the stuff he wrote on the walls."

"Anything else?"

"Some pubes, definitely not hers. We'll know more once Beck signs her off and gets her into the shop."

Randy stood at the door, looking away. "She was single, lived alone. Cash in her wallet, bunch of jewelry in the drawers, all untouched. The guy next door says he thinks he heard them enter, three-fifteen or so. The whining stopped about three-thirty."

"That's it?"

"'Fraid so for now. Might as well let TSD take it from here."

Jack nodded. He felt dizzy and sick. In his mind all he could see was the girl twitching against her bonds as the blade divided her abdominal wall. He saw the red hands on her breasts, the red lips kissing her.

Randy pointed to the back wall. "Check that shit out."

Jack hadn't even noticed it, too caught up in what lay on the drenched bed. More strange writing emblazoned the white wall, and another design.

"What the fuck is it?"

It was a triangle painted in blood, with a scarlet star drawn at each of its three points.

Written below the design was a single word:

AORISTA

CHAPTER 3

"I wonder what Khoronos is like in bed," Ginny reflected.

Veronica glanced up from her packing.

"Jealous already?"

"Shut up," Veronica said.

Ginny laughed. "I got invited first, you know. But I've always been one to share with my friends."

"You're making some pretty big plans, aren't you? We haven't even left yet. Besides, for all we know, he's married."

"Don't even *think* such a disgusting thing!"

Veronica had confirmed her reservation by the number on the card. A woman, who must've been Khoronos' secretary, had curtly given her directions. She and Ginny decided to drive up together.

"What do you think Amy Vandersteen's like?" Ginny posed.

"I saw her on *Signature* once. She's an asshole."

"Most good directors are."

"And what about these two guys?" Veronica asked, putting panties into her Samsonite. "The poet and sculptor?" ("Two guys picked up the painting," Stewie had told her earlier. "Young but kind of gruff. They gave me a receipt, loaded up *Vertiginous Red,* and drove away." Then Stewie, who made no secret of his bisexuality, flashed his famous grin. "I wouldn't mind going the rounds with them, though. They were what you female types call hunks. Serious baskets, if you know what I mean." "Not only are you a pimp, Stewie," she'd informed him, "you're a horny dog." "Woof, woof," he'd replied.)

"We'll find out when we get there, won't we?" Ginny complained, "but we'll never get there if you don't hurry up and finish packing!"

It was a combination of unconventional tangents that gave Ginny Thiel her attractiveness. She was a little overweight, but in a cute way, not fat, just fleshily robust; she'd always been told that she wore it in the right places. She was about 5′ 5″. A fresh gleam in her face betrayed her age—thirty—such that she often still got carded in bars. Large brown eyes peeked out from under bangs as severe as Stewie's; her hair was black and cut straight at the neckline. She'd been married and divorced twice; she'd dumped her first husband, and her second husband had dumped her, which was about the same time she started to become successful. She often claimed that her failed marriages were the best things to ever happen to her professionally. "If my marriages hadn't turned to shit, what would I write about?" she'd said once. She and Veronica had been friends since junior high.

Stewie came back in, having loaded Veronica's first suitcase into Ginny's 450. "I can't believe you girls are doing this. Talk about spur-of-the-moment."

"It's about identifying our self-actualization," Ginny said, "but you wouldn't know anything about that."

"Oh, is that what it's about?" Stewie laughed, gold chains glittering about his neck. Tails of light shimmered on his knee-high boots. "I think the female sex drive might have a little bit to do with it too."

"That's another thing you don't know about, and Jesus Christ, Stewie, would you please get rid of those ridiculous boots?"

"You two just don't want to admit that you've got the hots for this Khoronos guy."

"I have no problem admitting that," Ginny said.

"Neither do I," Veronica added, then blushed.

Stewie grinned at her. "And what's old Jackie boy say about that?"

"I told you, we broke up—"

"You mean you *dumped* him," Stewie cut in.

Veronica wanted to kick him.

"You ought to at least call him," Stewie suggested. "Let him know you're on your way."

"Stewie, don't be a butthole," Ginny said. "Why should she call him? They *broke up*."

"It just might be nice to give him a call," Stewie addressed Veronica, ignoring Ginny. "He still worries about you."

It was weird the way men were. Jack hated Stewie, and Stewie hated Jack, but as far as their former relationship went, Stewie was all for it. He constantly inferred that Jack was good for her, and she for him. It didn't make much sense, but Veronica knew that's how Stewie felt.

She looked sadly to the phone. *I should call him.*

"Don't," Ginny said. "He's history. He's out of your life now. It's stupid to call him."

"Well, we're still friends," Veronica hemmed.

"Former lovers can never be friends. Get real."

"Don't listen to her," Stewie warned. "She's a bitter, socio-anarchistic feminist nihilist."

"I wish I had a dick so I could tell you to suck it."

"Both of you shut up!" Veronica nearly screamed. She decided not to call. Ginny was probably right. What purpose would it serve now?

They packed the rest of their things into Ginny's car.

"When are you coming back?" Stewie asked.

Veronica looked unassured to Ginny. "I don't really know."

"We'll come back whenever," Ginny grandly answered.

"That tells me a lot," Stewie razzed. "I do have my client's business interests to manage, you know."

"You have your *vanity* to manage, through representing a famous artist," Ginny balked. "That's all you have."

"I'll call you every night," Veronica promised. "Keep working on those Abrams people for the book thing, and push for the show at MFA. I want that one bad."

"Have no fear, O beloved business interest." Stewie jokingly kissed her fingertips. "Your future is in my hands."

"Thank God the rest of her isn't." Ginny started the car. "And lose the boots, Stewie. The Musketeers are dead."

"I'll give them to you for christmas, along with a new vibrator, which you're obviously in need of."

"Would you two *please* stop it?" Veronica pleaded.

"Have fun, girls," Stewie offered.

He watched the car pull out of the lot and disappear. He stared after them for quite some time. It was just a morose feeling, like a sudden shadow on a sunny day. The feeling, for some reason, that he would never see them again.

◆ ◆ ◆

Twice they had to stop for deer. *My God, my God,* was all Veronica could think. She'd never seen deer for real in her life.

Ginny, typically, had forgotten her directions. They used the ones Veronica had gotten from the secretary on the phone. The place was an hour or so out of the city, in the northern part of the county. Long, winding lanes took them up the ridge through forests and orchards and quiet little homes set back off the road. Seeing all this at once, Veronica came to a chilling conclusion—her artist's sanctuary had made her forget that beauty like this existed. What is beauty? the existential instructors had always asked. Beauty is what your work must communicate. Beauty is not what you can see, it's what you feel. In her paintings she'd always tried to find beauty through emotions—through *human* things. But this was different beauty: the trees, the landscape, the blue sky, and all that those things summated visually as a result. Even the silence was beautiful, the air, the spaces between the poplars and pines. Veronica felt lost for a moment, adrift in awe.

"I haven't been laid in two weeks," Ginny announced.

The comment's frankness blew Veronica's muse to bits. Was Ginny making another innuendo? To Khoronos?

"Thank God I brought rubbers," Ginny added.

Her intentions were plain. Veronica's own sex life had been rather shunted before Jack. She'd always felt it inappropriate for a woman to be anticipatory, but now she wondered why. It had been a terrifying decade. Before AIDS it was herpes, and before herpes a dozen different strains of VD. Jack had been the only lover in her life she'd not used condoms with, because the department required drug and STD tests every six months. It wasn't easy for a woman to feel safe nowadays, but it was a pretty safe bet when a guy pulled out five years' worth of negative blood analysis reports from the county health services department. Yes, bringing condoms made Ginny's intentions plain, but Veronica could not help but blush. Secreted into her own suitcase was a twelve-box of Trojan ribbed. This was the first time she'd even admitted it to herself. *Ginny's not the only one with anticipations.*

Ginny was rambling on behind the wheel. "I mean, I can't even sit down without squirming. You know what I'm talking about? I'm . . . mushy."

"And crude."

"Crude? What about you? Isn't that why you broke up with Jack? Because you weren't sexually fulfilled?"

"No, it is n—" But the rest never left her mouth. "It was a bunch of things," she said instead. She didn't dare tell Ginny about her own condoms. "Maybe we're just a pair of sluts and don't know it."

"There's no such thing as a slut, Vern. There are only women who like to come and say so, and women who like to come but don't say so."

"That's pretty thin wisdom from an acclaimed novelist."

"Not thin. Concise. Axiomatic."

Ginny always got the last word, and it was usually a big one.

More of the world passed behind them. Ginny's orange 450SL sucked down onto the blacktop through each winding turn. Then Veronica, without even knowing why, asked, "Have you ever, uh—"

"Have I ever uh what?"

"Have you ever done anything . . . with a girl?"

Ginny's eyes thinned. "Are you making a pass at me?"

"No!" Veronica exclaimed. *Why did I ask that?* "I just—"

"Yes," Ginny said.

Veronica felt her face turn pink. What had compelled her to ask such a personal thing?

"I did once," Ginny continued. "Some girl I met at a mixer in college. I didn't even know her. It was funny. We were doing shots of ouzo and next thing I know we're in bed."

Veronica didn't know how to place the next question, nor did she understand its necessity. "Was it good?"

Ginny's face looked calm. "In a lot of ways it was real good. I didn't really want to do it, but I did it anyway."

"Why?"

"Why do you think? You're an artist. Why do you do things you wouldn't ordinarily do?"

"I don't know," Veronica said.

"Experience. All of life is experience. Isn't that what gives artists—writers, painters, or whatever—their desire to create? It doesn't matter if the experience is good or bad, wise or stupid—that's irrelevant. Without experience, and the curiosity behind it, we'd have nothing to give our art meaning."

Experience. The word echoed in Veronica's head.

"I probably came ten times," Ginny said.

"Any guilt?"

"Why should I feel guilty? It's a free country. People ca do what they want and what they feel."

Veronica fell silent. Suddenly *she* felt guilty. But why? Fo dumping Jack? For flying away from conformity? Or was i more?

"You still love him, don't you?" Ginny asked.

"I don't—"

"Vern, the guy's a washed-up gumshoe. That case he ha last year, that Longford guy, it put a zinger on his head. Yo don't need the frustration of being involved with a guy wh can't cope with his own life."

Was that it? Frustration? *No,* she felt sure.

"He drinks way too much, smokes three packs of Camels day. If he lives to be forty it'll be a miracle of science. Plus he's belligerent and narrow-minded."

Veronica didn't want to hear this, but—

"But you still love him," Ginny said. "It's all over you."

More confusion. *Experience,* was all she could think.

The road wound up. The 450's 5.6-liter V-8 purred. Lat-er Ginny asked, "Why did you ask me if I'd ever been wit a girl?"

More silence. More of the world blurred past. Then Veroni-ca ventured: "Do you believe in premonitions?"

"Oh, God!" Ginny broke up behind the wheel. "You're trip, Vern! A real trip!"

They both laughed the rest of the way to the estate.

It seemed queerly out of place: a white Bauhaus monolith in the middle of the woods. *Dada,* Veronica thought; she hated reactionary architecture. Its lambency blared like an eyesore. Who would build such a thing, here of all places? Rigid geometries and hard ninety-degree angles composed an edifice that appeared dropped from the sky. Gunslit windows and a black door rose like a disparate face as they pulled up the long drive.

"Jesus," Ginny whispered. She slowed to a stop. The house's whiteness seemed to vibrate like blurred vision. As they went to retrieve their bags, the black front door clicked open.

Veronica and Ginny froze.

"Ms. Polk, Ms. Thiel," greeted Erim Khoronos from the front step. He wore a pure white suit that seemed to shimmer with the building's lambent walls.

The faintest smile formed on his lips. "I'm so glad you could come," he said.

CHAPTER 4

"TSD says they've got some doozies for prints," Olsher said. "I gave the whole case number to Beck. She's got the Bureau running the best sets, and she's also doing an n/a/a-scrape. Says she might be able to get a line on the weapon."

Jack Cordesman sighed his best. "Beck's good, but it won't make any difference. The weapon's a knife—big deal. And I can tell you this right now—we're looking at a guy with brains. His prints aren't on file."

"How do you know!"

Deputy Police Commissioner Larrel Olsher's face looked as rigid as a black marble bust of Attila the Hun. He didn't like to be told that his best efforts were futile, especially from a flatfoot drunk who was two steps away from the rubber gun squad. Olsher was black and ugly and bad. Some called him "The Shadow," for his 6′ 2″, 270-pound frame tended to darken any office he saw fit to step into. Beneath the veneer, though, was an unselfish man who cared about people. He cared about Jack, which was probably why he'd been stepping on his tail for the last ten years.

"I know because I know," Jack responded with noteworthy articulation. "The Triangle thing was intricate and premeditated."

"It wasn't premeditated."

"Yes, it was."

Olsher frowned his displeasure. A decade-old bullet scar on his neck looked like a dark zipper. "Why the hard-on for TSD?"

"It's no hard-on," Jack said. It was 2 P.M., and already he wanted a drink. "But this isn't the kind of thing TSD can break. Chromatographs and hair-core indexes won't work on this one."

"What will, smart boy?"

"Competent field investigative work."

"Which you, of course, are an expert on, right?"

"That's right, Larrel." But Jack thought: *What's he hedging?* He had Olsher's psychology down pat; it was easy to tell when this big black golem had something bubbling underneath.

"You still drinking?"

Thar she blows, Jack thought. "Sure. Off duty. So what?"

"A uniform said he smelled booze on your breath last night."

"I wasn't even on the clock. I got the 64 at home."

"You hung over?"

"Sure," Jack said. "You ever been?"

"That's not the point, Jack."

"I can't predict when someone's gonna get 64'd."

"That's not the point either, and you know it."

Yeah, I guess I do.

Olsher sat down and lit an El Producto. Gobs of smoke obscured his face, which Jack was grateful for.

"Word's going around, Jack."

"Okay, so I wear a little lingerie on weekends."

"Word's going around that Veronica dumped you and you're falling apart, and that you're hitting the booze worse than you did after the Longford case."

"That's bullshit," Jack said.

Olsher adjusted his paunch in the chair. "County exec's office calls me today. They say it might be 'prudent' to 'extract' you from the Triangle case. They don't want any 'incongruities' that might 'impoverish' the stature of the department. Then the comm's liaison calls and says, 'If that shitfaced walking lawsuit fucks up this case, I'll have his goddamn balls hanging from my rearview mirror like sponge dice.'"

That's what I call confidence, Jack thought.

"They want the Triangle case solved quick and clean."

Jack's heart slowed. "Don't take me off it, Larrel."

"Give me one reason why I shouldn't."

"I'll give you three. One, I'm a Yankees fan. Two, I drink *good* Scotch, not rail brands. And three, I'm the best homicide investigator on your fucking department."

"You gonna get this guy?"

"Probably not, but I've got a better shot than TSD or the rest of your homicide apes. Christ, Larrel, most of those guys couldn't investigate their own bowel movements."

Olsher toked further. Creases in his big, dark face looked like corded suet. "I like you, Jack. Did you know that?"

"Yeah. You wanna hold hands? Kiss, maybe?"

"You've crashed in the last year and a half. I think you're letting the job get to you, and I think this shit with Veronica blew your last seal. I think maybe you should see the shrink."

"Give me a break," Jack groaned. He doodled triangles on his blotter. "Why does everyone think I'm a basket case because of a girl?"

"You tell me. And furthermore, you look like shit. You're paler than a trout belly."

"Can I help it I wasn't born black?"

"And your clothes—Christ, Jack. Are wrinkles the new fashion or do you sleep in a cement mixer?"

"I sleep in a cement mixer," Jack said. "That's between us."

"You look worse than some of the skell we lock up."

"I work the street, Larrel. I work with snitches. How effective would I be with a whitewall and black shoes and white socks?" But then he thought *Oops*, noting Olsher's black shoes and white socks.

"You're not even the same guy anymore," the DPC went on. "You used to have spark, enthusiasm, and a sense of humor. I just don't want to see you go down. Everything about you says 'I don't give a shit anymore.'"

This was getting too close to home. Jack felt like a cordon stake being hammered into soil. *I'm getting my ass gnawed by my boss, I'm one hair away from reassignment and two away from early retirement, I've got a killer who just carved a girl up like lunch meat, and all I can think about is Veronica. Maybe I am a basket case.*

Olsher let the moment pass. "What have you got so far?"

"The girl's not even cold yet," Jack said. "Give me some time. Eliot's squad is doing the make, but I don't think it'll amount to much. I think she was random."

"You just told me it was premeditated."

"The murder, not the victim. The guy's been planning this. For him, it's the *act*. That's why I think the latents'll be useless. He left them because he *knows* they're not on file. This guy's not a delusional psychopath or a psychotic. Psychopaths tend to think they'll never make a mistake, but they always do. This guy won't."

"You think he'll do it again?"

"Probably. It depends on the nature of his delusion."

"You just got done telling me he's *not* delusional."

"That's not what I meant. He's delusional, but the crime scene shows someone who's not psychopathic; he's what a crime shrink would probably call 'tripolar.' He executes his crimes according to his delusion but *without* losing sight of reality. He's afraid of getting caught." Jack paused to light a Camel. "I want to fork my strategies, let Eliot and his guys follow the normal SOPs while I—"

"Go off on the other fork in the road?" Olsher said.

"Right. It works. Remember the Jamake hitter we had a couple years ago? Or the guy at the CES convention who ripped those three hookers? And there's always the Longford case . . ."

"I remember. You don't have to blow your horn for me."

"Good. I'll need slush money for consulting fees—"

Olsher winced like gas pains.

"I'll need a researcher and a forensic shrink, maybe that woman from Perkins. But what I need more than any of that is for you to trust me."

Olsher rose. No DPC enjoyed the headache of cash authorization; getting it was like standing before a Senate subcommittee. Nevertheless, Olsher said, "You've been thinking about this all day, haven't you? Maybe you do give a shit. So get on it."

"You're giving me the case?"

"What do you think, Jack? You're a ragass. You're a longhair. You're probably a drunk. You can't handle the psychological pressure of the job anymore, and you're letting a busted romance pull you to pieces. The Yankees suck, and I've seen you drink house booze many times. But you probably *are* the best homicide investigator on my fucking department."

Jack smiled.

"But don't make a dick of me on this, or you'll be the best *unemployed* homicide investigator . . ."

"Loud and clear, boss." Jack crushed out his Camel and lit another. "If I'm lucky—and sometimes I am—I can get a line on this fucker. To catch a killer, you have to know him before you can find him. He can be the smartest killer in the world, but no matter how well he covers his tracks, there's always one little thing he always leaves behind."

"What's that?" Olsher asked.

"His soul." Jack drew smoke deep into his chest. *Red,* he thought. In his mind he saw red. "This guy left his soul *all over* the walls of that girl's bedroom."

It stuck in his mind—a memory more persistent than the others. He didn't know why then, but he thought he did now. Perhaps it had been the present telling him something about the future, an eager specter whispering in his ear, saying, *Listen, Jack. It's really you they're talking about. Listen. Listen . . .*

A month ago? Two? He wasn't sure. They'd gone out to eat somewhere—McGarvey's, he thought—and then had stopped for a drink at the Undercroft. Veronica seemed particularly content; she was used to their relationship now, comfortable with it. She accepted it as part of her.

Jack, too, was very happy that night. It was a combination of complacencies. He'd just gotten a raise and a letter of commendation. Veronica had just sold two more paintings and had been interviewed by *Vanity Fair*. Their lives, together, were stable. They were happy, and they were in love.

That was the sum of the combination: love. It was his love that made him happy.

Romantic affection sometimes seemed silly, but that made him happy too. Just holding her hand, or the easy way their knees touched when they sat. How she unconsciously touched him when she talked. These were subtleties, yet they were also anchors, weren't they? Verifiers. More little pieces of their love.

There'd been many nights like this, but this one stuck out because of something that happened later. As the evening wound down, some guy from the state film institute came in and introduced himself to Veronica. His name—if Jack remembered right—was Ian. He was young and had just graduated from film school; he was currently directing an independent movie, some avant-garde sort of thing. Very quickly Ian and Veronica got into a very heavy discussion. It didn't bother Jack, giving some of his time with her to someone else; it seemed important. Instead, he yacked with Craig about beer, women, and the Steelers.

But something bothered him. He found he couldn't help keeping an ear on Veronica's conversation. She and this Ian guy seemed to be talking about the function of *fear* in art.

What's fear got to do with art? Jack wondered.

"Like Argento and Bava," Ian was saying, "it's all a system of psychological symbols."

"And Munch and Benton," Veronica said, sipping a Sapporo.

"Exactly! Using objective structural standards as a method of subjective conduction."

"Looking in the mirror and seeing someone else's face."

"Or no face at all," Ian postulated.

"Ah, so you're an existentialist," Veronica assumed.

"No, I'm just a director. The only honest creative philosophy is no philosophy. Truth is all that motivates me—*human* truth."

Sounds like a bunch of gorilla shit to me, Jack thought.

"And you view truth through its correlation to human fears," Veronica stated rather than asked.

"Yes," Ian said. "Our fears make us what we are. Every action generates a *re*action. Fear makes us react more than anything else."

"Wait a minute, pal," Jack interrupted. "You're saying that fear is the only truth in life?"

Ian's eyes sparkled. "Yes, I think I am. Fear is the base for everything else we want to be truth. Even our joys are created out of inversions of our fears."

"That's a load of shit."

"Jack!" Veronica snapped.

"But he's just proved it himself. His reaction to our discussion has created a denial. His fear that we might be right."

Jack felt fuddled.

"For a short time in my life," Ian explained, "I went on a hiatus. I knew I could never be creatively complete until I had identified my greatest fears. So that's what I did, I went looking for the things that scared me the most."

"What were the things?" Veronica asked.

"There were only three," Ian said. "Drugs, greed, and love."

Love, Jack thought. Cigarette smoke smeared the sunlight in his office window. The sudden recognition numbed him. *Fear. Love.* Was one really based upon the other? Now he knew why that night stuck in his mind. It was a portent, a mirror to the disheveled future he was sitting in right now. Ian had been right. Jack's love—now that he no longer had Veronica to give it to—scared him to death.

Fear is the base for everything else we want to be truth, Ian had said.

Love, Jack thought.

Then he saw another, closer memory. In red:

HERE IS MY LOVE

"I just talked to Beck in Millersville," Randy Eliot said.

Jack hadn't even noticed the entrance of his partner. Randy, in a sharp gray suit, was helping himself to Jack's coffee. When he turned, he stopped. "Christ, Jack. You look like—"

"Like I slept in a cement mixer. I know. Olsher just got done doing the plunger on my ass. Thinks I'll fuck up the case."

Randy stayed comment and sat down.

"Let me ask you something, as a friend," Jack said. "Do you think I'm slipping?"

"Anybody who brews coffee this bad must be good for something." Randy dropped his cup in the trash. "You want the truth? You drink way too much, and you're too impressionable."

"Impressionable? What's that supposed to mean?"

"You don't let go of things. Like Veronica."

Jack smirked. "Who asked you anyway?"

"You did."

"Well, next time I ask, don't answer. What's that about Beck? I thought you were running down the Bayview girl."

"I am, and we've dug up plenty of shit. Name's Shanna Barrington, thirty-two, single, no roommates. Got an art degree from St. John's, worked for an ad agency off the Circle, one of the big ones. She started in the business as a commercial artist . . ."

Jack remembered the pastels and watercolors on the walls.

"Got promoted to senior art director last year, pulling almost fifty K. Good job record, good credit . . ."

"But?"

"Mary Poppins she wasn't."

"Guys, you mean?"

"All kinds. She was a dance-club queen. Neighbors say she'd come home with a different guy every night. Hung out at a lot of the ritzier places downtown. The resident manager got tons of complaints about her; she was a screamer. A few of the downtown barkeeps gave us the same story. She'd meet a guy, tag him in the sack the first night, then—"

"Next day she's sick of him," Jack finished. "She's out looking for someone new. It's a common cycle. Lotta girls that age get that way because they're afraid they're losing it . . ." Then he paused, thinking. What? *Afraid. Fear.* Again, he thought of Ian. "They go hypersexual because they never get the kind of emotional attention they need. So they replace it with physical attention. It gets to be a compulsion. They don't feel real unless they're getting laid by a different guy every night."

"A girl can make a lot of enemies doing that. All she's got to do is burn the wrong guy . . ."

No, Jack thought. *Not this one.* The feel was all wrong, and so was the evidence. Shanna Barrington was not murdered as a result of her promiscuity. She was chosen *because of it.*

"What were you saying about Beck? She find something?"

Randy nodded, then patted his hair, which was his own compulsion. "The victim had an address book in her nightstand. There were over a hundred names and numbers in it."

"Big deal."

"Beck ninned it, and you know what?"

"Let me guess. It was wiped down."

"Right," Randy said. "But Beck found a single ridgeprint on the *edge* of the book. It was intact, but it wasn't big enough to tag to the killer. So Beck—"

"Let me guess again." Jack knew Jan Beck well. "She fumed the friction ridge, 'scoped it, and determined it was the killer's by comparing the pore schemes."

Randy looked disgruntled. "Yeah, exactly."

"Which means the killer removed the book and opened it. And you think he was looking for his own name."

"Well, wasn't he?"

"No. He was either looking at it out of curiosity or to see if it contained anyone he knew. Shanna Barrington and the killer *did not* know each other. She was *picked* for precisely that reason. The killer's name isn't in that book."

These were the mechanics of their professional relationship: Randy making speculations, and Jack picking them apart. Randy was perceptive; however, Jack was more perceptive. In the long run it made for an effective method of teamwork.

In the short run, though, it pissed Randy off. "Then why the fuck did he pick the book up, look at it, and put it back!"

"Simple," Jack said. "He wants you to think that his name *is* in it."

"Why?"

"To run your ass off for nothing. To waste your time."

The sharp seam of Randy's lips made no secret of his mood. "So you're telling me not to check the names in the book?"

"That's not what I'm saying at all. I could be wrong, I just don't think I am. You're the protocol man; follow protocol. Check out every conceivable lead you've got. That's your job."

"Oh, I see. I pound every sidewalk in town getting a line on over a hundred guys, and you sit in your office and drink coffee. You're really trying to piss me off, aren't you?"

"Sure," Jack said, and sipped his coffee. "You work better when you're pissed off. What else did Beck say?"

"Said she found some pubes that were 'funny.' And she's sure the girl got it repeatedly—the killer left a lot of wax. There's also some problem with the wounds but she didn't say what."

"I'll talk to her," Jack said. "Meantime, you shag ass out of my office and go earn your pay."

"What are you, privileged? Why can't you help out with some of the shit work?"

Jack shook his head. "The shit work's all yours, partner. Wear your galoshes." In his mind he saw the triangle. He saw the red. "I'll be busy checking out some other angles."

CHAPTER 5

"Don't worry about your bags," Khoronos said. "Gilles and Marzen will bring them up later. Let me show you around."

Veronica and Ginny followed their host in. Further contrast dismayed them: the interior couldn't have been more opposite of what one would expect. Khoronos was obviously a man who saw some principal purpose in contrast. The inside looked more colonial than anything else, or antiquarian. Lots of heavy paneling and stained, ornate trim. Lots of antiques. In the living room was the largest fireplace Veronica had ever seen.

Khoronos' white suit seemed to project luminescence into the dark room. "The locals, I'm afraid, think that I'm quite eccentric," he regarded.

"We're all eccentric," Ginny said.

Khoronos half smiled. "Perhaps, but maybe we're *dismissed* as eccentrics only because others lack the courage to follow their hearts. We are not understood; therefore we are condemned. In truth, we're not eccentrics at all."

"What are we, then?" Veronica inquired.

"Superior."

This rather pompous conclusion hung like static before them, as did Khoronos' wraithlike smile.

"The will to create is what made the world, not logic, not reason," he said. "Without the will—and the challenge—to create, free of the structure of what we call conformity, there would be nothing. Don't you agree?"

"Yes," Ginny said.

"I don't know," Veronica said.

An equally large colonial kitchen came next on the tour, a pantry, and a palatial dining room. All these things compelled Veronica to continue to wonder. *This huge place, all this room—what's it for?* They stepped through French doors onto a deck which overlooked the backyard. Trimmed topiary and hanging plants surrounded a large swimming pool. A tall fence and outer trees filled the entire yard with shade and quiet. Ginny was stunned, but Veronica remained more curious than impressed.

"Are you married?" she asked.

Khoronos laughed. "Heavens, no."

"I only meant that—"

"What does a single man need all this space for?" Khoronos finished. "I don't *need* it, but I can afford it. 'Faith bestows treasure upon the faithful.'"

"Old Testament?" Ginny guessed.

"Indeed."

"You're saying *faith* made you rich?" Veronica couldn't resist.

"Faith in my broker, Ms. Polk." He laughed again. "I was being facetious. I don't feel guilty about being rich."

More pomposity. At least he was being honest.

Up the heavily banistered staircase, a single long hall seemed to be all that composed the upstairs. Poshly framed paintings lined the walls, but Veronica didn't recognize any of them, nor their styles. Had Khoronos painted them? Maybe he pursued an interest in artists out of an artistic failure on his own part. That would explain a lot.

"Your bedrooms are sparse, but you'll find them comfortable."

Hers and Ginny's were identical and side by side. A small bed, a nightstand, and a tiny dresser. Bare white walls and drab green curtains. Each contained a bayed morning room and balcony. In Ginny's was a desk and a Smith Corona typewriter. In Veronica's was a painting table, some blank canvases, and a box of supplies.

Veronica and Ginny only looked at each other.

"My only requirement is that, during your stay, you create something," Khoronos informed them, "on a day-to-day basis."

So that was it. Khoronos was just a proverbial patron of the arts. At once Veronica felt like a unique prostitute.

"But I don't mean that you must create something for me,"

the man countered. "Quite the opposite. I want you to create something solely for yourself."

"That'll be easy," Ginny said. "I'll write a porn story."

"As you wish. Create whatever your heart compels. Passion is born of the heart, correct? That's what thrills me. Particularly what is born of a *woman's* heart."

Is this guy for real? Veronica thought.

"But there's one thing else, it's very important. Whatever you create, I must ask that you show it to no one until it is finished." Khoronos extended his hand. "And now I'd like to reveal a bit of my own heart."

He took them into the last room.

Jesus, Veronica thought.

The room was windowless. Its walls, ceiling, and floor were heavy plate mirrors, projecting their images infinitely into a bright silver demesne. A wire chair faced a TV and VCR. Several tapes sat atop: *The Lamia, The Seeker, The Woman in Black*—all films by Amy Vandersteen. A wire stand contained all of Ginny's novels. Veronica gasped when she looked up. Hanging on the front mirrored wall was *Vertiginous Red.*

"This is where I pursue *my* compulsions," Khoronos said.

Veronica felt a sudden heat rush to her head—like mild shock. Khoronos stood in the center of the silver room, vivid in his white suit. His long grayish hair seemed to sift, and the gleam in his eyes revealed him now as something more than a rich man with misguided interests. He was a preceptor, a guide. He looked messiahlike in his thousand reflections.

Veronica and Ginny could only stare.

"I'm certain we will have an enlightening time together," the man bid. His hands splayed before him. "We all have our quests, am I right? We're looking for something that is greater than what we actually are. That is the reason I've asked you here. To help me find what I'm looking for and, hence, what I am. In return, I will do the same for you. I will help you discover what you really are—what you were really meant to be."

CHAPTER 6

After the rain, the sun drew steam up Main Street's bricks. Past the City Dock, boats rocked idly in their slips as the bay reflected clean light like slivers of shaved metal. Jack parked up by Church Circle, electing to walk.

He hoped the walk might clear his head. The after-storm air and salt breezes often revitalized him; that's why he lived here. Every place he saw, though, and every place he passed reminded him of Veronica. He should've known. He should've driven.

There was the second-floor crab house he'd taken her to. That had been their first date, hadn't it? Up ahead, he eyed Fran's, which had been their last. He stared into the window of Pendragon's, remembering the silver locket he'd bought for her there, then across the street to the art supply store where he'd bought her a bunch of pastels and things for her birthday. Two stores down was the record exchange where he'd found some obscure tape she'd mentioned—Cocteau Twins, a group he'd never heard of. Later they'd made love for hours to the layers of sedate, shifting music.

He felt digusted with himself, a little boy pining over a first crush. Everywhere he looked, he saw Veronica.

He wondered about this guy Khoronos, and this retreat thing. He wondered when he'd see her again, and what seeing her again would be like. Strained smiles. False greetings . . .

A car horn blared, and a voice. "Is that pig I smell?"

Jack turned. *Who the f—*

"Hop in."

It was Craig, grinning behind the wheel of a white Alfa Romeo Spider, a convertible. Vanity plates ALLINYT, and

Sinatra crooning "Summer Wind" from the in-dash CD. Flawless white lacquer made the car look made of ice.

The door clicked shut like a well-oiled lock. "I see barkeeps in this town do pretty well. That or you're a gigolo on the side."

"Me? A kept man?" Craig shifted up to the light. "Haven't met a woman yet who can afford to even *look* at the price tag."

Jack shook his head, bemused. But oddly Craig went on, "You look like something's bugging you."

"What makes you think—"

"Yeah, something's bugging you. Veronica, right?"

Now Jack frowned. "Since when do barkeeps read minds?"

"It's part of the job, man."

Veronica, Jack thought. *It shows that much?*

"Tell me if my keep's wisdom is on the mark. You've been busted up with her for a couple weeks now, right? You're depressed because she got over it quick, and you haven't gotten over it at all. Right?"

Jack showed him a lackadaisical middle finger.

"You think she's forgotten all about you. Right? And that makes it worse because you still love her. Right?"

Shut up, Jack wanted to say. "Yes," he said. "How can you tell all that just by looking at me?"

"I'm a bartender. When you see things from the other side of the counter long enough, you know them at a glance. Trust me."

"Fine. I'm impressed. What do I do?"

"Put yourself above it. If you don't, you're putting yourself *down,* and that's a waste. You have to look at it this way: 'I'm better than that. I'm better than her, and I'm better than whoever she's balling now.' You don't have to have faith in other people, Jack. You only have to have faith in yourself."

Faith in yourself. This sounded like good advice, but right now Jack didn't feel *better* than anybody. "That's kind of selfish, isn't it?"

"Sure," Craig said. The light changed, and the Spider jumped past the light. "But isn't it more selfish to feel that your whole life's falling apart because of a girl?"

Jack tried to assess the question. "I don't get you."

"We think we've got it tough? Shit, we don't know what tough is. Ask people in Siberia about tough, ask people in

India, in Africa. Ask all the poor fuckers who're starving, or blind, or quadraplegic. They'll tell you what tough is. What I'm saying is we shouldn't take things for granted. My tuition just got hiked, and I'm pissed. You think your whole life's shit because Veronica dumped you for some other guy. Poor us, huh? In Cuba you've got to save three months to buy a pair of shoes that'll fall apart in three weeks. In Chile they torture people with power tools. Kids in Africa have to eat tree bark and dirt. And we think *we've* got it bad? Shit."

Jack felt slimed in guilt. "I get you now."

"When we take life for granted, we're assholes. Every day we wake up and the world's still turning—that's a great day."

Craig was right. Jack was taking things for granted. He was forgetting how lucky he was simply to be living in a free state. Usually simple things were the answers to the most complex questions.

The Spider's engine hummed. Now Main Street came alive in the after-storm glitter. "So where you headed?" Craig asked.

"The Emerald Room. I'm meeting someone."

"That's the spirit. The best way to get over one girl is to go out with another."

"Drop me off here is fine," Jack said, indicating the corner of Calvert Street. "This isn't what I'd call a hot date."

"Who are you meeting?"

Jack began to get out. "Thanks for the pep talk, Craig. I'll see you later tonight at the 'Croft."

Craig's sunglasses reflected duplicates of Jack's face. "Don't bullshit me, man. Who are you meeting?"

"A forensic psychiatrist whose specialty is criminal insanity."

Of the city's many outstanding restaurants, the Emerald Room was the best, and it had class without being stuck up, unlike certain other restaurants down on the Square. Immediately a stunning hostess smiled despite Jack's attire, then noticed the shield clipped to his belt. He wore faded ink-stained jeans and a ratty dark raincoat through which his Smith .38 could easily be seen. "I'm here to meet a Ms. Panzram."

"She's right over here. Follow me, please."

Jack had never actually met Karla W. W. Panzram, though he'd spoken to her many times on the phone. She was chief psychiatric consultant at the Clifford T. Perkins Evaluation Center. This was where all state criminals were evaluated for psychological profiles; whether they would be considered criminals or mental patients was decided here, and Karla Panzram was the one who did the deciding. She also consulted on the side for many outside police departments. Jack had couriered the TSD summary (of which there was very little) and the Barrington case file (of which there was even less) to Perkins that morning. On a psycho case, moving very quickly was very important, even when there was little to move with.

The voice on the phone had always showed him a large, even Amazonish woman. Reality showed him the opposite: delicate, if not frail, a petite woman. She had coiffed, steelish blond hair, and looked about forty. She wore a plain gray skirt and white blouse.

"Captain Cordesman, we finally meet," she said, rising to shake hands. Her hand was cool, dry. "You don't look like a cop."

"I know. I look like a hippie who sleeps in a cement mixer."

"Oh, but you could never do that. You're a claustrophobe."

Jack flinched. This was true. "How did—"

Her smile showed small even white teeth. "The way you walked to the table. As though something were hovering over you."

She's psychoanalyzing me before I can even sit down.

"You're also sad about something," she said.

Jack sat down. He was tired of everyone telling him about himself. "I appreciate you doing this for me on such short notice."

"And whatever it is you're sad about, confronting it, to yourself, or to others, makes you feel insecure."

Jack laughed feebly. "Tell me about my killer, not me."

"I think I can do that, Captain."

"I know a little bit about the *ins* of these kinds of things, but you know the ins and *outs*."

"You'll probably never catch him," Karla Panzram offered. "*And* you won't luck out with a reactive suicide or a guilt-reversion."

"You're telling me he's stable, right? And smart?"

"He's very smart. Very ordered thought patterns, high IQ, and an attention for detail. He's logical, and he's a planner."

Lots of sex killers had high IQs, well past genius levels. But this was ritual, and Jack knew nothing about that. "He's not psychotic," he said more than asked.

"No, and he's not paranoid, psychopathic, or unsystematized. He's not even acting like a sociopath."

Jack let that one sit. The Emerald Room was not only known for the best food in town but also the best service. When their waitress arrived, a beautiful redhead in black pants and white blouse, Jack said, "Order whatever you want. Tab's on the county." This was a lie, however; Jack was picking this one up himself. Olsher could justify consulting fees but not dinners. Dr. Panzram ordered steamed mussels, crabmeat flan, and grilled Muscovy duck for appetizers, and blackened prime rib. *Where's she going to put it all?* Jack wondered. He ordered a dozen oysters.

"Cocktails?" the waitress asked.

"I never drink on d—" He beamed at his watch: 4:01 P.M. "Fiddich, rocks. Dr. Panzram?"

"Just a Coke," she said.

When the waitress left, Karla Panzram added, "You drink too much."

Jack gritted his teeth. First Olsher, then Randy, then Craig, and now this woman. They knew more about him than he knew himself. "I haven't even had one yet, and you've pegged me as—"

"Retraction of the mimetic muscle groups and lid margins, fluctuation of the frontalis and lateral pterygoid, and the usual facial inflections. It's the best lie detector. It's also a wonderful way to gauge subconscious excitement. Your face lit up like a pinball machine when you looked at your watch and saw you were off duty."

This depressed him, but what else was new? When the waitress brought his drink he had to fight not to touch it.

"Let's call him Charlie," Karla Panzram said. "Let's make him human instead of a shadow. Charlie is erotomanic but not in the same way as your usual sex killer. He's not a sadist, a sexual sociopath, or some horny nutcase with the wrong levels of FSH and LH in the brain. Charlie's compulsions are not founded by cerebral defect or biogenic deviations. He's very . . . passionate. Passion, I think, is a key word here. He's also deflectional."

"I don't know what that means."

"It means he didn't *want* to kill the girl."

"He did it for an outward reason, you mean? The ritual angle?"

"Yes, and whatever the ritual is, it's not an unsystematized symbol or an idea of reference. Charlie's very level-headed. The only way he'll fuck up is if he lets his *passion* get in the way."

Hearing this delicate woman use the word *fuck* unnerved Jack, like knocking over a vase in a crystal shop.

"Passion," she repeated. "Remember that. It was his passion that allowed him to go through with the murder."

Passion, Jack thought. He lit a Camel. *Here is my love.*

"It's not the ritual itself, but his *association* with the ritual that's important. It involves some personal belief mechanism that allows him to vent his passion. Did you run the M.O. through III?"

"Yeah. Nothing yet, but they're working on it."

"What about Interpol CCCS?"

Jack raised a brow. "I didn't bother. You think he could've done this in another country?"

"Sure. Look where we are."

"A seaport," Jack acknowledged. He felt instantly stupid.

"If I were you, I'd be calling every port city on the coast. And run the M.O. with Interpol too."

"Good idea. I'm also getting a researcher to try and get a line on the ritual." But as Jack spoke, his eyes kept flicking to his drink.

"It's calling you, Captain."

Up your ass, he thought. He liked this woman, but he didn't like the truths she made a point of rubbing his face in. The aroma of the Scotch was almost erotic. He took a sip, then sighed.

"Charlie is very conative; there's something in his life that's turned a hesitant impulse into a free act. He's probably never even come close to a reality break. He knows right from wrong as clearly as you do. His passion is purposive."

Jack wasn't sure if he got that. "You mean the impetus, right? And you're saying it's objective?"

"Yes, er, at least to Charlie it is. And that's the funny part. Heavy purposive fantasies generally have roots in a very deep delusion. But Charlie's not deeply delusional."

"Neither are sociopaths, but you say he's *not* sociopathic."

"You know a lot more about these cases than most cops, but you should also know that a sociopath wouldn't have drawn the symbols, and he would've terrorized the girl. Charlie didn't. He even blindfolded her so she wouldn't see what was coming. Sociopaths like to see the terror in their victims' eyes. They have no feeling for them, but Charlie did. I may be wrong about some of this, but I'm not wrong about that. Plus, a sociopath would've turned the place upside down for valuables, and he would've taken her money. Whatever Charlie's delusion is, he's got it under complete control."

Jack sneaked another sip, thinking. His long hair kept falling in front of his face.

"Charlie's also persuasive, a magnetic personality. He's probably very attractive. The victim was willing from the start, and that too is a key word. The bondage wasn't forced. Otherwise the wrist and ankle lacerations would've been more severe. Most girls don't let a man they just met tie them up. There was something special about him, something that made her trust him instantly. Girls with andro-compulsive desires have a tendency to fall for guys fast. It never lasts, but that doesn't matter."

This definitely didn't last, Jack thought.

"Willingness. Remember that," Karla Panzram induced. "You're looking for a charmer with a knack for making girls sexually willing in situations that would normally project reluctance on the part of the female. Lots of male erotopaths are like that—the only difference is they don't kill the girls afterward. One question: Did the girl have a drug history?"

"No, but her tox screen'll be in today."

"Have your tech check for cocaine, and also the usual synthetic morphine derivatives. There's a lot of Demerol and Dilaudid going around now that the coke prices are up. He may have enticed her with something to make her less inhibited, and if so, you've got another string to diddle with, someone with drug connections."

"What about Charlie himself? Do you think he's a drugger?"

"I doubt it," Karla Panzram said. "The act is very important to him—there's no way he'd round off any of the corners of the experience with drugs. The way he wrote the stuff on the walls shows me someone with a clear head. We TAT drug users all the time and what they come up with is completely different. I know this may all sound very obscure to you, but I still assert that the major keystones here are passion and willingness."

"But there was blood in the vagina. Not much, but still. I'm thinking vaginal abrasions."

"She must've been on her period, then; ask your tech. Charlie is not the type of personality to commit rape. It's a priority that his victim be *willing*. I even think that if one of Charlie's prospects turned out to not be willing, he'd leave. He wouldn't go through with it. Charlie is not a hostile person."

Jack almost winced. "Not hostile? Shanna Barrington looked like a botched autopsy. He tore her up."

"He tore her up out of passion, Captain, via the ritual delusion. Not hostility, passion."

Some leads, Jack thought, smoking. His drink kept beckoning him. He felt Dr. Panzram was right about Charlie, and she was probably right about Jack. He'd like nothing more than to down the rest of his Fiddich and order another—no, two more at once—but to do so would make him afraid of what she'd conclude of him. Without pretense, then, the words tolled: *I'm an alcoholic.*

"If I didn't feel secure in what I've told you, then I *wouldn't* tell you," she said over her mussels. Each one she delicately removed with her fork, inspected, then consumed. The shelled mussels looked like little vaginas. "I've seen all kinds, for the last twenty-two years. Charlie's definitely different, but he's just as easy to type as a hebephrenic or hallucinotic. You can trust my speculations. The majority of my conclusions, though, are graphological."

"You mean the writing on the walls," Jack said.

"Not the writing itself, but how he wrote it. You can tell as much about someone from one writing sample as six months of psychotherapy. I'm sure you've deduced from the bloodfall and entrance wounds that Charlie is left-handed."

"Sure. A majority of sex killers are. So what?"

"You can also tell he's left-handed by *how* he inscribed the symbols, the letters, and the triangle. You'd be surprised how objective the human mind can be when analyzed comparatively. Different types of people tend to do the same types of things when they externalize themselves. Our graphological references are quite accurate. Tell a patient to draw a house, and what he's really drawing is an aspect of his subconscious. Have a patient write the alphabet, and you see the insides of all his feelings, what he loves, what he hates, and so on. I can't drop Charlie into a neat psych category for you, but I can tell you all about him, comparatively, simply by the way he draws and writes."

"I'm all ears," Jack said. *And all mouth too, which I'd really like to fill with Scotch.*

"Writing is an equiposture of consciousness, subconsciousness, and mental structure. And that's the most important part from your end—his creative revelations."

"Huh?"

"The letters and symbols aren't as much written as *formed.* They were applied quickly but with great accuracy. The angles of the symbols, and especially the triangle, are almost perfect, as though he used a compass to outline them. Would you like some?"

"Huh?"

She pushed the plate of mussels toward him. A dozen little vaginas peered up through their shells. Some even had tiny beards.

"No thanks," Jack said. "I gotta drive."

Karla Panzram smiled. "That's interesting, Captain. Something about mussels distresses you. Hmm. I wonder what that could be."

"Fear of female genitals, right? I'm not afraid of women, if that's what you're implying."

"Oh, but you are, Captain. Women terrify you, because you get lost in them. You're very passionate too."

"Like Charlie?"

"Oh, no. Your sense of passion is much more primitive—"

"Thanks."

"—but much more real. However, you're afraid to let your passion out, because you're afraid it will disorient you. You're afraid of rejection. You've been recently rejected, haven't you?"

Jack lit another Camel and sighed smoke. "I like you, Dr.

Panzram. You're smart, and I admire you. But I hate it—and pardon my French—I fucking hate it when people try to analyze me."

"I know you do, Captain." She forked another mussel, daintily plucking its bread with her fingers.

"You were saying something about the structure of the symbols and the triangle. Accuracy."

"Oh, yes. It could be of no investigative significance at all, but Charlie's very creatively inclined. He may be an artist."

He's an artist, all right, Jack added. *And that was a hell of a piece of artwork he left in that apartment.*

"That's all I have for you now," she said. "When you get more, send it to me. I'll do whatever I can to help you out."

"I appreciate that."

Karla Panzram was tapped out. She was a very strong woman; dealing with people who didn't want to help themselves wasn't as bad as dealing with people who couldn't. It made Jack think again of what Craig had said, about taking things for granted.

When the meal—which she'd consumed completely, double-baked potato included—was done, Jack reached for the check, but she snatched it up first. "This is not a county tab, Captain. Shame on you for lying to me."

"Hey, I lie to women all the time."

"You feel emasculated when a woman pays?"

"Pay the goddamn tab, Dr. Panzram. You can pay my phone bill too, if you want, but that wouldn't make my balls feel any smaller."

Karla Panzram laughed out loud. As they were leaving, she said, "Forgive me for toying with you, Captain. You're a moving target. Did you know that?"

Jack lit another Camel. "A moving target for what?"

"A woman's psychology. We're all devils on the inside."

"Do you hear me arguing?"

But on West Street she turned serious. She looked at him almost dolefully. "I'm worried about you, Captain Cordesman. If you decide you need some help—and I don't mean with the Triangle case—please call me."

She left him at the corner walk, disappearing like an angel—or like a ghost—into the glare of midday sun.

CHAPTER 7

"Meat racks!" Ginny whispered.

"Shhh!"

The two figures stepped through the foyer. "Ah," Erim Khoronos said. "Here they are now." He turned from the bar, pouring glasses of spring water. "Marzen, Gilles, it's my pleasure to introduce our guests, Ms. Virginia Thiel and Ms. Veronica Polk."

Veronica felt an itch of rage. *Why didn't he introduce me first?* she thought as a child might. But Ginny was right. These guys were . . . *gorgeous*.

Standing before them were two tall handsome young men in identical baggy white slacks and sleeveless T-shirts. Marzen had long blond hair; Gilles' was black and cut like a marine's. Veronica's gaze felt immobile on them, and she could sense Ginny's dopey man-grin. Both men were well muscled and well tanned.

"It's very nice to meet you," Marzen said, shaking hands. His hand was large, rough. His accent sounded German.

"We're happy you can be with us," Gilles added. A French accent, obviously. His hand was softer, more delicate.

Veronica raced for something to say but found nothing.

"See to their bags," Khoronos said.

Marzen and Gilles left.

Shit! Veronica thought.

"Shit!" Ginny whispered.

"Marzen and Gilles are my charges," Khoronos said. "I think of them as sons."

"They seem very nice," Ginny said. "How did you meet them?"

"Through my dealings abroad, over time," Khoronos answered, but it wasn't much of an answer. Veronica felt certain it wasn't meant to be. "They're masterful men, as you'll soon see," he went on. "They look upon me as their pundit, so to speak. I'd like to think that much of their aesthetic insight comes from me."

As you you'll soon see? Veronica thought. What did that mean?

"I must tend to some things now. Dinner will be at seven."

Abruptly, Khoronos left them alone in the great room.

"This is really strange," Veronica said, and sat back down on the couch. She jiggled her ice in the spring water.

"I think it's fun. It's mysterious." Ginny grinned. "And we're definitely going to get laid."

"Ginny, we're not here to *get laid.*"

"What, you took all that stuff he said seriously? Come on, Vern, it's all a game to him. He's rich and bored and he likes games."

"Keep your voice down," Veronica suggested.

"He thinks of himself as some artistic seer or something. It makes him feel good to invite artists up here and pretend he's teaching us something. All this whole thing is leading to is an orgy. The decadence of the idle rich."

"You're rich."

"Yeah, but I'm not idle. This whole thing's a party, so I'm gonna make the best of it. I'm gonna party my face off."

Some party. Veronica looked at her spring water. Khoronos had informed them that no alcohol was allowed in the house. No tobacco either, and no drugs, not that Veronica did them. "True artists must maintain immaculate spirits," their host had said. "Any substance which taints the *spiritus* is forbidden in my home."

Eventually she and Ginny went out on the balcony off the kitchen, a huge deck which overlooked the pool. A faint breeze rustled through the trees, and a scent of pine. "You sure changed your tune about Khoronos," Veronica said.

"Just because I know what makes him tick doesn't mean I don't want to get into his pants anymore." Ginny closed her eyes, turned her face to the sun. "I do and I will. And

Marzen, Gilles—I'll ride their brains out too. Everyone's got to cut loose sometime."

"Cut loose, huh? That's what life's all about?"

"You want to know what life's all about? First I'll tell you what it's *not* about. It's not about babies, two-car garages, a dog in the yard, and a station wagon in the driveway."

Ginny hated domesticity, but Veronica didn't know how she felt about that herself. Jack had never actually proposed to her, but the implication of marriage was clear. Had that been what scared Veronica off?

"It's about independence, Vern," Ginny continued. "That's the only way a woman can be free."

Veronica wanted to say something mean, like *You're only saying that because it's the only way you can rationalize two failed marriages*. "Freedom and sexual abandon are synonymous?"

"Sexual *liberty*, smartass. If you don't do what you want, you're actually doing what someone else wants. Whether it's a person or society doesn't matter. It's subjugation. If a guy fucks everything that moves, that's okay because it's an accepted trend. But when a woman does it, she's a slut. Men can be free but women can't. It's a bunch of sexist bullshit. My rebellion is my right of protest. I will not allow myself to be subjugated. I'll do anything I want, anytime I want."

Sometimes Veronica forgot she was talking to a notorious feminist. She wanted to agree with Ginny but couldn't. Veronica had thought that being in love was her freedom, but freedom had its price, didn't it? *Experience*, she thought. Being in love had kept her from experiencing what she felt she had to as an artist. Either way, she was torn between ideals.

Ginny lit a cigarette.

"Khoronos said no smoking," Veronica reminded.

"No smoking in the house; this is the balcony. And . . ." Ginny paused, peering down. "Well, what have we here?"

Marzen and Gilles walked across the backyard. Off one of the pool decks stood a rack of weights and a bench.

"See?" Ginny observed. "Men are such vain assholes. Without their muscles and their cocks they have no identities."

But Veronica remained looking on. Marzen and Gilles each peeled off their T-shirts and began curling dumbbells of formidable size. They seemed bored, curling the weights and speaking casually. They seemed to be speaking French.

"But I still love 'em," Ginny went on. "Check out the beef-cake."

Veronica couldn't help not. In moments, their rippled backs shined, muscles flexing beneath their tanned skin. It was erotic, earthy, the way their sweat sheened their flesh. Veronica caught herself in a secret image: running her hands over those slick pectorals, exploring. At once she felt dizzy, like the first time she'd met Khoronos. She felt trickly.

"They know we're watching," Ginny said.

"They do not," Veronica objected. Or did they? Her throat felt thick. Next image: herself naked, squirming atop Marzen . . .

"And you're trying to tell me you don't want to cut loose?" Ginny continued to goad. "That's subjugation too. You're afraid to release your inhibitions. Is that freedom?"

Veronica felt lost in her imaginings.

Ginny crushed her cigarette and dropped it into the bushes below. "You know," she said, "men have been using women for the last fifty centuries. It's high time we started using them back."

Veronica imagined Marzen poised nude above her. His sweat was dripping off his chest onto hers, hot, like hot wax.

"They like to show off?" Ginny was saying. "I'll show them some showing off."

Veronica gasped within the frame of the vivid image. Marzen penetrated her. Her eyes closed, the image cocooned her. She could picture Marzen's penis sliding in and out . . .

Oh, for God's sake!

The fantasy was ridiculous, a useless breach of reality. She was like a high school girl dreaming of the quarterback.

"What the—" Veronica turned, breaking her muse. "Ginny!"

"Hey, I'm showing off." Ginny had removed her blouse, braless beneath. She waved the blouse in the air, in circles. "Save your strength, fellas! You're gonna need it!"

"Ginny, are you nuts!"

Below, Gilles looked up at the spectacle and chuckled.

"That one's mine," Ginny said.

But Marzen's face remained plain. He was not looking at Ginny. Instead, his eyes bored directly into Veronica's.

◆ ◆ ◆

Jack owned a century-old row house on Main Street, which he'd inherited from his father. The equity was preposterous. It had been purchased in the late fifties for $15,000; today he could sell it for three hundred grand, and it wasn't even in very good shape. Jack lived in the upstairs and rented the downstairs to a couple of college kids. The row house was essentially the only thing he had of real value.

He didn't sell because he liked it here. He liked the city's ambience—or the persona, perhaps, of its age and its history. His bedroom window showed him the City Dock; the bright vanishing point of Main Street to the sea looked surreal. He loved the faint salt scents off the bay, and the city's lights when it was late. He liked being lulled to sleep by the ghostly chimes of sail lines striking the masts of countless boats in the docks. The sound was indescribable.

He showered and dressed without really knowing what for. *Never drink alone,* Craig had once philosophized. Jack refused to keep liquor in the house, his only gesture of constraint. He could see himself in ten years, or even five—a holed-in drunk, empty bottles piled high in the kitchen. At least in bars, someone else worried about the bottles.

Light classical issued from the dilapidated stereo; it was all he could listen to without being distracted. Distraction was any investigator's enemy. He wondered if love was too. How many marriages had exploded because of The Job?

Here is my love, he thought. He closed his eyes, to see it in his head, the neat red letters.

HERE IS MY LOVE

And the great star-pointed triangle.

Not an act of murder, an act of love. He remembered thinking that the instant he'd stepped into Shanna Barrington's bedroom. Karla Panzram had verified this, but with trimmings he couldn't imagine. The killer had taped her eyes so she couldn't see what was coming, had tied her up so she couldn't move. He'd *adored* her as he extracted her entrails.

Shanna Barrington had been sacrificed, but to what? What madness? *Aorista,* Jack mused. He'd looked it up in his paperback Webster's but found nothing. The FBI's Triple-I interservice link had reported back this afternoon: nothing.

And nothing yet from Randy's good squad. The Interpol run would take weeks, and even though Auxiliary Procurements had authorized his request for a researcher, there was nothing more on that either. Most murders were solved within forty-eight hours. After that, the apprehension statistics plummeted.

Suddenly he was staring at the portrait of himself. Veronica had painted it, an abstract mash of wedges and smears, the pieces of which formed his face. The likeness, now, was distressing—it looked like a man falling apart. He wondered whose face she was painting now.

When the phone rang, he jumped. The word *Veronica* echoed somewhere deep. *Don't be an asshole,* he told himself. What reason would Veronica have to call him now?

"Cordesman," Jack said.

"Hi, Captain. Your man's jiz won't type. He's no secretor."

Jack's brow creased. No, it definitely wasn't Veronica, it was Jan Beck from the Technical Services Division. "The killer's you mean?" he asked.

"I'm not talking about Bullwinkle's sperm, sir. And I'll tell you something, this guy's got a lot of love."

Jan Beck's voice was ashy, soft, which never fit with the way she talked. Talking to her was like talking to one of the guys, or worse.

"What do you mean, Jan?"

"He gave it to her like it was going out of style. Cum City up there. Only thing that doesn't jibe is the timing."

"He wasn't in there long enough to do her a bunch of times."

"Then your estimations are wrong, or he's the fastest draw in the East. Average ejaculation's four to six milliliters, up to ten after a long dry spell. This guy left more than thirty hung up past the minus ridge, and that's not counting the wetspot, which looked about as big as the state of Alaska. My estimation, this guy blew eighty mils of the joy juice, probably more. I'd say she had ten guys in there with her, but the cum's all morphologically identical. And this girl was ready for it. This was no aggravated rape."

Willingness, Jack remembered, snapping a Camel. Karla Panzram said that willingness was a key word for Charlie. "You're saying that the victim was willing, right?"

"She was definitely willing, Captain. Her lube glands were

drained. Average girl doesn't dry up till she's been getting it steady for a couple of hours."

"But there was blood in the vagina. Was it her period?"

"That was a cervical bleed," Jan Beck said. "Not a rape-related abrasion. Last night Shanna Barrington was the best-lubricated woman in the county. You can't argue with a chromatograph."

"Maybe he—"

"No artificial lubes either; they would've been obvious on the source spectrum. And he didn't use spit. It was all her up there."

Jack gulped. This was getting gross, and, knowing Jan Beck, it would probably get a lot grosser.

"The blood was a capillary trauma. Ready for why?"

"No, Jan, but I have a feeling you're going to tell me anyway."

"The guy's hung, and I mean hung serious. Average girl's got about seven inches of loveway; Shanna Barrington had eight. Your man popped her cervix—I've only seen that a couple of times. This kind of bleed's minor because of the nature of the capillary structures of the cervical cap. It's common with girls who make these porno videos. They get all coked up, can't feel a thing, then some guy rams his schlong up her cooze—he's got more schlong than she's got loveway—and force-dilates the cervical cap. Tears some minor vessels. Like I said, it happens sometimes, but what doesn't happen is the rest. Your man's rod was in her cap when he *came;* he blew his steam right up into her ampullae, and that's something I've *never* seen. The cervical channel is about a mil wide unless the girl's preggers, and the uterine line is essentially microscopic. Both were filled with his stuff. We're talking about a tremendous ejaculator. Dilating her cervix with his cock is rare, but this kind of seminal presence is downright *unreal*. Most pathologists would tell you it's impossible. This guy blew his load all the way up her repro tract. He came so much even her infundibula were distended. The fucker filled this poor girl up like you fill your unmarked at the motor pool."

Jack's stomach was beginning to sink.

"Average erection's about six inches. We're looking for someone with more than twice that, and that's *very* uncommon. I looked it up. We're talking about less than one tenth of one percent of the male pop. Your killer's a walking smokehouse, sir."

"You have a lovely way with words, Jan," Jack said. "Is the tox screen in yet?"

"Yes, sir. BAC was .01, she was buzzed but not shitfaced."

"Drugs?"

"Zip. No coke, pot, PCP, skag, no nothing."

What else did Panzram say? he tried to recall. "Did you run her blood for any synthetic morphine derivatives?"

"Of course. Zero. My spec is the girl wasn't into drugs and never has been. Even recreational users have a pot history, and one look at the brain tells all. Lipofusial rancidity, we call it. Shanna Barrington didn't have it. She had a clean brain."

A clean brain, Jack thought. He could easily picture Jan Beck removing the victim's cranial cap with a Stryker orbital saw, looking down, and saying, *Yep, a clean brain.*

"But there was one thing, sir." Beck's unearthly voice seemed to shimmer through a pause. "Was she a health nut?"

"I don't know. We don't know that much about her yet."

"I mean her place. You find any vitamins, herbs, health stuff?"

"No," Jack said.

"Her blood says she's pretty healthy, except for the booze. Her liver looks like a moderate drinker. The only real deficient blood levels were B6, C, and magnesium, which is common for anyone who drinks regular."

I better start taking vitamins, Jack supposed.

"We found something in her blood that's not CDS. It looks like an herbal extract or something."

"Maybe a designer drug."

"No way, wrong chain. It's something organic."

From his seat on the bed Jack expertly flicked his butt out the window. "Work on it. Anything you got. There's a real deadline on this." *What else?* Olsher, yes. "Olsher said you were doing an n/a/a-scrape."

"I'm in the middle of that now, I'm going to work all night. The resilience lines and entry patterns worry me. He's using a funny shank, I mean. The scrape-spectrum'll be in by morning. Come and see me."

"Okay, Jan. Thanks."

"Good night, sir."

Jack hung up, sputtering. In the mirror, he could not conceive that the reflection was his own: a pale stick-man sitting on a bed, smoking a Camel, long hair a wet mop in his face. *Pretty as a picture,* he thought.

He went to his dresser for socks. Beneath the socks was a picture of Veronica. He knew he should not be thinking about this now. He should be immersed in the Triangle case—but the picture catalyzed him. It kicked his spirit back in time. Veronica was sticking her tongue out at the camera, holding a big cup of Guinness, her arm around Jack. Craig had taken the picture at the 'Croft last St. Patrick's Day. It was the day after Veronica had told Jack that she loved him.

One time she'd gone to Atlantic City with Ginny. She'd called long-distance just to tell him she loved him. Another time they'd been downtown with Randy and his girlfriend, having a good time, talking innocuously about innocuous things, and Veronica had inexplicably passed Jack a bar napkin on which she'd penned *I love you.*

These were just a few. How could something once so bright have turned so black? Now he could view the past as only a dead providence.

He shoved the picture back in the drawer.

He dawdled about the flat, kept glancing at the phone. *You're an idiot,* he concluded an hour later. *She is not going to call you. Why should she call you? She* broke up *with you.*

. . . *his passion is purposive,* Karla Panzram had said. *He's very passionate.*

I love you, the bar napkin read.

HERE IS MY LOVE, the wall read.

This guy blew his load all the way up her repro tract.

Jack stared at the dresser mirror. "I am a very fucked-up person," he stated to it. His reflection looked like a stranger. There was a loose cannon in his town, cutting up girls alive, yet all Jack could think about was Veronica.

He looked deadpan at the phone.

She's never going to call you again. She's too busy with what's his name. Khoronos.

He left the flat. Dusk was descending; it was warm out, pretty. Main Street was alive with lovers and clean salt air. The purity of the vision depressed him. His long hair was still wet. He walked up toward Church Circle, toward the Undercroft—

—but at the corner he stopped. Was he sick? He felt dizzy at once; he backed up against a MOST machine to keep from falling. When he closed his eyes he thought he saw fire.

Something skittered across his mind. Something—a thought. A red thought.

No, a word.

Aorista.

"I knew I should've locked the door," Craig said.

"What, and keep out your best tipper?"

"I'm not into coin collecting, Jack. I've told you dozens of times."

"Just keep hocking in my Scotch like you've been doing for the last five years. I'll get the message eventually." Jack took his usual stool at the end. Several regulars raised their glasses in greeting. Jack liked the bar's appointment. The rafters bore hundreds of beer coasters from around the world. Banners from breweries as obscure as Felinfoel, Tennent's, and Tucher covered the front wall. Craig piped Fine Young Cannibals through the sound system while an Orioles game with the sound turned down progressed from the high TV. Jack was happy to see that the Yankees were using the O's for toilet paper.

"What do you call three cops up to their necks in sand?"

"What, Craig?"

"Not enough sand." Craig twirled a shaker cup full of ice perfectly over his shoulder, then poured equal volumes from four bottles at the same time, holding two in each hand. Bar tricks were something he'd honed to an art.

"Poor man's Tom Cruise," Jack commented.

"What that make you? Poor man's Columbo?"

"I'll drink to that. And speaking of drinks, do I have to fire warning shots to get one in this joint?"

"Keep your liver on." Craig put a shooter before him. "Try that. It's a tin roof."

"What?"

Craig rolled his eyes. "It's on the house. I call it the Piss Shooter."

It looked like urine. "If your fly was open, I'd be leery." Jack downed the shooter. "Not bad. You're learning."

Craig ejected the shaker's ice over his shoulder. The ice landed directly in the sink. Craig was famous for never missing. "Couple of your boys were in today, giving me the business."

Randy's men, Jack deduced. "They show you pictures?"

Craig nodded and grabbed the Glenfiddich bottle without looking at it. He had the exact location of every bottle memorized.

"You know her?"

"I've seen her around, but I didn't know her. Shanna something. She's got a rep downtown as a monster rack."

Craig's terminology never ceased to amuse, along with such gems as Mr. Meat Missile, Killer Mammalian Carriage, Body by Fisher, Brains by Mack Truck. Craig also had the ultimate last call: *Everybody get the fuck out of the bar!* A "monster rack" was a girl with whom not much effort was required to get into bed.

"You know anyone who ever jammed her?"

"No one by name. I've seen lots of guys pick her up at Fran's and the Map Room. Sounds like something heavy went down."

"I'll spare you the details. Ever see her in here?"

Craig shook his head. "She only hangs out at dance places."

Not hangs, hung. And she ain't dancing now.

Craig brought him a Fiddich on the rocks, then raised a brow a few minutes later when the glass was empty. "First one always goes fast," Jack excused himself.

"I'll bet that's what you tell all the women."

"Just your girlfriend."

Craig guffawed. "I don't have *a girlfriend*. I have a *harem*."

Jack had to fake going along with the jokes; the first drink was already bringing him down. "Another, Craig." *Watch it, don't get shitfaced again.* Then the latent fact hit him like a fist. This was the same stool he'd been sitting on the night he met Veronica.

Khoronos, of course, would be strikingly handsome, older, mysterious. He would be *different*. He would be the kind of guy who could offer her a different experience.

Experience, she'd told Jack that last night.

The second drink went nearly as fast. "Riding the black train again, huh?" Craig asked.

Jack lit up, slouching already. "I'm its favorite passenger these days." The alcohol and memory formed a whirlpool. He was flotsam in it, wreckage. He was going down.

"Let me tell you something." Craig flipped a Marlboro in the air and caught it in his mouth. "You're not the first guy in the world to get sacked by a girl."

"I know," Jack said.

"You gotta tighten up the bootstraps and move on. Remember what we were talking about today? Every day you spend boohooing about it is another day down the drain."

Jack shrugged. He didn't need lectures.

"Here's another way of looking at it, and stop me if I'm getting on your nerves."

"You're getting on my nerves."

Craig grinned. "First, look at yourself. You're drinking too much, you feel dismal, and you're depressed. Since the minute Veronica broke up with you, you've been *miserable*."

"I don't need to hear this, Craig."

"Yes, you do. Okay, we've established that *you're* miserable." Craig paused, probably for dramatic effect. "Is Veronica miserable?"

The question sunk deep. Was Craig trying to make him feel *worse*? The answer was obvious.

Veronica is not miserable. Right now she's partying it up with Khoronos. I'm miserable and she's probably having the time of her life. She's happier . . . without me.

"See?" Craig said, pouring a Betsy Bomber and Bloody Mary at the same time. "It hurts, sure. It's the last thing in the world you want to think. But you have to face it, and get on with your life."

"I know," Jack whispered.

"And you're better than all that shit."

Craig walked away, taking beer lists to some newcomers. *Am I really?* Jack thought.

He went upstairs to the men's room, where the walls proved more of the Undercroft's diversity. No phone numbers or cuss words—the 'Croft sported highbrow graffiti only. "Loss of love equals loss of self," someone had written. Jack frowned as he whizzed. "The sleep of reason breeds monsters." *Better,* he thought. "The test of will is man's ultimate power," read another.

I don't feel very powerful today. He went back down with full intention of ordering another drink.

"Captain Cordesman?" Craig was inquiring. "See that guy

there, with the long hair and off-duty gun in his pocket? That's him."

A girl, either timid or annoyed, came around the bar. There was some kind of *plainness* about her; she was attractive through no overt kind of beauty. Her roundish face lent her a cast of frayed innocence; her gray eyes seemed extant. She was neither fat nor skinny in simple faded jeans. A plain print blouse accommodated a plenteous bosom, and a straw-colored ponytail hung nearly to her waist. She was carrying a briefcase.

"Captain Cordesman?"

"At your service."

"I'm Faye Rowland. Lieutenant Eliot said I might find you here."

"Jack lives here," Craig cut in. "He sleeps on the bar after we close. We let him shave in the men's room."

Faye Rowland frowned at the jokes. "I'm an information systems technician for the state public service commission."

"Oh, you must be my researcher."

"That's right. Someone named Olsher made the arrangements with my department head. I'm on loan for as long as you need me."

Jack had hoped for an associate prof or at least a T.A. from the university. Instead they'd sent him a systems jockey.

"All I know about your case is what your office faxed me this morning," she went on. "They said there's a big rush on it so I thought maybe you could brief me tonight. Save time."

Jack wasn't used to people hunting him down in bars on business. At least she was dedicated. He took her to a corner table. From her briefcase she withdrew color dot-matrix prints of Shanna Barrington's walls, and Jack's initial 64 summary.

"The very first thing you have to do is find out what *aorista* means," he told her. "That's the—"

"*Aorista* is an exclamatory form of the noun *aorist*. It indicates an intransitive verb tense. It's in the Oxford Dictionary."

Jack felt dumbly impressed.

"Denotatively, it's a grammatical inflection from Greek and Sanskrit, a set of inflectional verb forms which denotes action without specific reference to duration. In this case, though, I think you're probably looking for the common *con*notation."

"Which is?"

"A process which doesn't end."

The possibilities pricked him at once. He ordered another drink and a pint of Wild Goose for the girl. *The girl,* he thought. *What did she say her name was? Faye? Faye something?*

"A process," he said. "Could it be a *ritual* that doesn't end?"

"Sure. It's a connotation. It could apply to anything."

A ritual that doesn't end, Jack pondered.

"How was the girl murdered?" Faye Rowland asked.

"You don't want to know."

No, but I *need* to know once I start digging into current U.S. cult activities. Any detail you can give me might help make a tie."

Jack hesitated. It was one image he'd never cleanse from his head. "She was eviscerated," he said.

Faye Rowland didn't flinch. "Was her heart missing?"

"No," Jack replied with raised brow.

"Were any of her organs missing?"

"No. Some of her organs were removed and placed around her on the bed. But none of them were taken."

"What about her head? Was her head missing?"

Jesus. "No. Nothing was missing. Why?"

"Organs and heads are big with several devil-worship cults in this country, particularly heads. They believe the heads of their adversaries give them power. Was the murder victim baptized?"

"I don't know. What difference does it make?"

"Unsanctified sacrifices are big too. There was one group in Texas a few years ago—they murdered six unbaptized babies before the FBI busted them. They'd make good-luck charms out of their fingers and toes. Severed pudenda, particularly those of infants, were considered a supreme protection from enemies."

Jack ordered another drink. He had a feeling it was going to be a long night.

CHAPTER 8

"What *is* this shit?" Ginny whispered.

Veronica didn't know. Gilles and Marzen served "dinner" at the long linened table. Khoronos sat appropriately at the head.

"It's sashimi," he said.

Plates of pale strips of meat were placed before them, white pieces, reddish pieces, and yellow lumps. A smell wafted up.

"This is raw fish," Veronica whispered.

Ginny nearly spat out her Evian. "I refuse to eat r—"

"Optimum sustenance for the artist," Khoronos explained. "*Eka, toro,* and *uni*—rich in nutrients, amino acids, and omega lipids. Recent studies have concluded that sashimi increases intelligence, memory, and creative thought."

"Yeah, but it's raw fish," Ginny complained aloud.

"Try it. The *ika,* the squid, is particularly good."

Squid, Veronica thought. *Jolly.*

Marzen and Gilles began to eat, wielding chopsticks like experts. The servings were huge. Veronica plucked at her pieces, then chose a red slab, looked at it leerily, and ate it.

"*Toro,*" Khoronos told her. "Fatty tuna belly. Good *toro* costs hundreds of dollars per pound."

"Tuna *shit* could cost hundreds of dollars per pound too, but I wouldn't eat it," Ginny said under her breath.

"Be polite," Veronica whispered. "Actually it's not bad."

"Sashimi increases the sex drive," Gilles pointed out, then inserted two pieces at once into his mouth.

Marzen looked at Veronica. "Increasing zah ability to orgasm."

Veronica blushed.

"In that case," Ginny ventured. She fumbled with her chopsticks and raised one of the yellow collops. It looked like a lump of snot.

Khoronos smiled. "Go ahead."

Ginny ate it, paused, then swallowed. "It's kind of mushy but not bad." Then she put another piece in her mouth.

"What you are eating," Marzen defined, "iss called *uni*."

Gilles: "It is the raw gonad of the sea urchin."

Ginny wailed close-mouthed. She transferred the *uni* from her mouth to a napkin, then fled the table.

Khoronos, Marzen, and Gilles laughed. "Not adventurous," Khoronos concluded. "The human aesthete must never falter at a new experience."

What does raw sea urchin gonad have to do with the human aesthete? Veronica wondered. She tried a piece herself. It tasted . . . funny.

"Tell us about love, Ms. Polk," Khoronos abruptly bid.

"Pardon me?"

"Love."

All eyes turned to her. She could not fathom an answer.

"What is truth?" Khoronos asked next. "What is truth really?"

"I don't understand," Veronica said.

"It's love, isn't it?" Khoronos suggested.

"I've never thought of it that way."

"Love iss in zah heart," Marzen offered.

Khoronos again: "Real creativity is rooted in the heart. Be transitive."

Right, Veronica thought. *These people are nuts*. "Okay. Real creativity is rooted in the heart. Truth is love. Therefore, creativity is truth."

"Exactly." Khoronos turned to the Frenchman. "Gilles, go and see if Ms. Thiel is all right."

Gilles left the table. Khoronos went on, "Creativity is all we can be; that is, if we want to be real. Those below us are too subject to the frail *externi* of the world."

"You're saying that most people are false?"

"Yes. Indeed. It's only the artists who preserve the real truth of humanity."

"Vee are zah heralds," Marzen added. "Vee are zah portents."

Then a pause, as finely placed as a brick in a vast wall. Khoronos asked: "Ms. Polk, have you ever been in love?"

Heralds, she thought. *Portents.* She sensed a point, but Khoronos' last question bushwhacked her. "I was once," she answered. "At least I think I was."

"You confuse physicality with spirit," Marzen said.

"To know love, you must bring them together. One without the other is a lie, isn't it?"

"I guess," Veronica said. Already the conversation darkened her. It brought up ghosts of Jack.

"You don't love yourself enough to love someone else."

God, he was rude. "How do you know?" she challenged.

"I'm merely being substantive. It's clear, though, that you lack something within yourself."

"What about you?" she dared. "Have you ever been in love?"

Khoronos' piercing eyes seemed to float before the question. "Many times," he said in a lowered voice.

All the while, Marzen, the German, had been eating, as if he'd heard this discussion repeatedly in the past. A brief glance from Khoronos, then, commanded him to leave the room.

Now Veronica felt more on guard. She tried to change the subject. "Isn't Amy Vandersteen coming?"

"In the morning," Khoronos said. "Don't change the subject."

"I'm uncomfortable with the subject."

"Why?"

"Because you make me feel like I've made a mistake."

"In coming here?"

"No."

"Why, then?"

He was putting her against herself, making her fight her own twin. Where the hell had Ginny gone? Why couldn't she come back and save her from this . . . interrogation?

Instead of responding, Veronica stared Khoronos down.

"I love anyone who is true," he said. "I want you to be true."

What did *that* mean? He must know of the power he had over her. Was it really truth that compelled him, or cruelty?

"Why are you sad?" he asked.

She felt limp in her seat. "I used to be in love with this guy, but I ended the relationship, and now I'm not sure if I did the right thing."

"Only you can decide if you did the right thing. How do you propose to do that?"

Veronica stared.

Khoronos rose at the end of the table, his face clement in some kind of boundless— what? Wisdom? Or was it truth, the sum of wisdom? That's what Veronica sensed in him now—an utter lack of falsehood. Here was a man who truly did love.

Here was a man who *knew*.

"I'm sorry to have upset you," he said through a voice that issued like smoke."You are a great artist."

"I'm not a—"

"And once you are able to see yourself, and your desires, in a more truthful light, you will be even greater."

"I—" she muttered.

"You will be timeless, Ms. Polk." The subtle, incised smile touched her like a caress. "You will be immortal."

The Mitchell's Brewery clock ticked toward midnight.

"I better get going," Faye Rowland said. "I live in Tylersville—that's fifty miles away—and I've got to drive to the LOC in the morning."

Jack, somehow, had stayed sober. Getting plowed in front of the girl would not make for much of a professional first impression. He admired her perseverance; she'd suffered an hour's drive just to get briefed early and save time.

"You can stay at my place if you want," he offered, then regretted it. *She probably thinks I'm putting the make on her*. "I've got several extra rooms, and I live a bit closer than Tylersville."

"How close?"

"About a quarter of a mile."

"Okay," she said. "I mean, if it's no trouble. I'd get an earlier start in the morning if I stayed tonight."

"No problem." Jack motioned for the check.

"Is the clock two hours fast?" Craig asked in disbelief.

"Lately I've been turning into a Scotch-filled pumpkin at midnight." Jack paid up, and when the girl was out of earshot, he whispered, "It's not what it looks like."

"Sure," Craig said. "And I'm a virgin. Later."

Jack took Faye up the short steps to the street. A used-book store across the street had a poster in the window: "Big Brother is watching you." Lately, Jack felt watched everywhere he went, overlooked by his own doubts in himself. But tonight he was impressed; this was the first night in a while he'd left the Undercroft sober.

They drove in Faye's car, a big red Chevy clunker that sounded like a Russian tank. He showed her into his row house and flicked on the lights. "I got three rooms downstairs. Two I rent to college kids, but they're on break." He showed her the spare. "Linen closet's there, shower's there. I'm upstairs if you need anything. And thanks for doing this for us."

She kicked off her shoes. "Researching a ritual murder is a bit more interesting than running state unemployment fluctuations all day. I'm happy for the change." But when she set her briefcase down, Jack noticed the wedding ring on her hand. How could he have missed that?

He tried not to act surprised. "Oh, and feel free to use the phone if you want to let your husband know where you are."

She looked remiss, then laughed. "Oh, this?" she said, and held up her hand. "I'm not married, I just hate being pestered. I only wear it to keep the predators away."

Jack gave a sad smile. The comment swept him, and his mood crashed. *Honey,* he thought, *you're gonna need a lot more than that to protect you from the predators in this town. Just ask Shanna Barrington.*

"Good night," he said.

CHAPTER 9

"Good night," Khoronos said.

Veronica turned at her bedroom door. "See you in the morning."

"Remember, Ms. Polk, you're also here to create. Start giving your project some thought."

They'd sat up for hours after dinner, discussing only artistic formalities. Their conversation was harmless, but this, she knew, was part of Khoronos' tactic. He'd sown his psychological seeds at dinner; now was time to let them grow. What did he want of her? Just a painting? Formalistic chitchat? The man, and his cryptic motives, distracted her. She had no idea what to paint.

"Dreams," Khoronos remarked now. He was a shadow on the landing, faceless.

"What?" Veronica asked.

"Pleasant dreams." He drifted back downstairs.

Dreams, she thought, and closed her door. Had he meant that she should use her dreams as her models? She'd painted many of her dreams in the past, but lately she'd stopped that. It seemed indulgent, selfish even. *Love iss in zah heart,* Marzen had said. *Creativity is rooted in the heart,* Khoronos had added. Was it really an indulgence, then? Dreams were manifestations wholly of one's self—in a sense, of the heart. Khoronos had even implied that all true art had its corms in the indulgence of the artist. Seeing, and the intricacies through which one saw, meant everything. *Indulgence is vision,* she thought, and giggled. She liked the sound of that.

She felt odd somehow. She turned off the lamp and let the moonlight seep in. The open French doors admitted a warm breeze. A moment later, she was taking off her clothes.

What am I doing? she asked herself. She stood nude before the doors. Anyone who might be out back could look up and see her. But the impression appealed to her: being viewed in secret. *Indulgence is vision. I'm just being indulgent.* She giggled again. Then she stepped out onto the veranda.

It felt good here—nude in the open air of night. She parted her legs and let the faint breeze touch her sex. That felt good too. Now she was symbologizing: the night was her lover, the moon its eyes, the breeze its hands which traced up and down her body. Yes, that's what she wanted—a faceless lover, a stranger full of primordial desire. No formalities, no bogus social games or strained inhibitions. Her mind at once filled with raw images of sex. Rough but seeking hands ranging her skin, male weight atop her body, a mouth sucking her nipples till they hurt. She tried to put a face on the lover, but it didn't work, as though a *lack* of identity was what made the fantasy truth. It didn't need a face to be real. All it needed was a heart and a cock, a hot curved cock stuck in her up to the balls. Here was vision, all right—turning fantasy to an inner truth. Khoronos *had* helped her see herself more honestly. That's how she felt just then: being fucked by a new sense of truth.

Next she was whining softly. When enough of her consciousness leaked out of the muse, she discovered her finger burrowed deep into her sex. *What am I doing!* she screamed in thought.

She slipped back into the bedroom, her sweat now a bath of embarrassment. What if someone *had* seen? *I must be nuts!*

When she clicked the French doors shut, she heard the bedroom door click open. A gasp froze in her chest, and she whirled.

The figure stood in the faint spilled light of the hall. It was a shadow, it was faceless. Veronica just stared. The figure closed the door and stepped forward.

"I vill go back aus if you like," it said. It was Marzen, obviously. Closer now, she could see he was naked in the blocks of moonlight, though the room's high shadow hid his face.

"Do you vahnt me to leave?"

Her stare locked forward. "No," she said.

"Zen close your eyes."

Veronica did so with no hesitation. This was the last appendage of any fantasy: reality. She wanted her eyes closed, to keep him faceless. She could sense each of his steps as precisely as if she were seeing him. She didn't even flinch when he took her hand.

He brought her hand to his mouth and sucked the finger she'd been masturbating with.

"Get down now," came the clipped whisper. "Down on zah floor."

Veronica lay back on the carpet, spreading her legs. She pulled her knees back to her chin, showing it all to him without scruple. She felt wicked, lewd. *I'm a slut,* she thought, stifling a giggle. She parted her thighs as widely as she could, her feet in the air. Her sex felt like a pot of warm oil.

At once Marzen began to lick it. He licked slowly and hard. The sensation, as well as the crude immediacy of the act, jolted her. It felt delicious and wild. Then the tongue bore down over the opening and penetrated her. She wished it could be huge; she was being invaded in a trespass that made her want more, that begged for a deeper and more meticulous inquest. Her bare feet clenched in the air when he began to suck her clitoris.

This promptitude and complete lack of ceremony drove the pleasure deeper. There was no falseness here—just guileless lust. It was what she wanted, wasn't it? Marzen the faceless phantom, the night caller—her selfish fantasy enfleshed.

Oh, no, she thought. She was ready to go off already. Something began to crest, something huge in her that *demanded* exit. Her breasts ached, her sex and belly and inner thighs felt aflame. Just as her orgasm would break, Marzen stopped.

Her eyes slitted open. Marzen was kneeling between her legs; she could see the shadow of his erection in the moonlight. All she wanted in the world just then was for him to sink it all into her at once. *Just get on top of me and fuck me,* she was dying to say. *Put your cock in me and fuck me right into the floor.*

His big blue eyes roved from her sex to her face. "Love iss metamorphosiss," he said.

What was he talking about? She reached forward to take hold of his penis, but he slapped her hands away. When she leaned up, his big open hand landed between her breasts and shoved her back down. It was not a gentle gesture. It was nearly violent.

Yet his voice remained serene. "Love iss transposition," he whispered. "You are not yet ready to transpose."

Veronica's fascination played with her rage.

"Before you can love another person in truth, and be loved by another, you must first learn to love yourself."

She wasn't sure what he meant.

"Do it," he said. "Don't think about it, or vunder. Do it."

"Do what!" she exclaimed.

He pushed her legs further apart and looked at her sex.

Oh, my Lord, she thought. Somehow he *had* seen her on the balcony. He'd probably been watching from the door. Strangely, though, she felt no embarrassment. Just frustration colliding with her lust.

She brought her fingers to her herself and began to masturbate. Marzen remained knelt in attendance between her legs. His erect penis pulsed almost directly above her moving hand. She glided her other hand up and down over her body. Somehow this combination of sensations felt even better than Marzen's oral ministrations.

Her sex felt burning now; it was thumping against the careful succor of her fingers. She looked up at Marzen, at his shining muscles, at his erection, thinking that seeing him would give the experience more spark. But it didn't. *Transposition,* she thought. *I am not yet ready to transpose*. She didn't even know what that meant, yet it clearly worked within the structure of this bizarre, self-investigating liturgy. So she closed her eyes and thought about nothing. She fought to banish the image of other men from her mind. Her moisture continued to well. Instead, she thought about herself. She pictured herself touching herself, loving herself, and then she began to come.

She moaned beneath the shadow. Marzen's silence gave evidence to a poignant supervision, and this, for some reason, made it feel better. Frantically her fingers teased repeated orgasms out of her sex, her buttocks flexing. Her fluids seemed to throb out of her sex, a tapped cask of flesh and pleasure. She'd never come this hard and this many times in her life.

Soon she could go no further; the jolts left her sex so sensitive another touch would make her scream. As her fingers came away, she felt the sudden hot spurts land across her stomach and breasts. She knew what he was doing, and it even pleased her; it *sated* her, being dampened by the fluids of his own orgasm. The last of his ejaculation dripped warmly onto her belly.

She lay panting for a time. Her body turned to rubber. She opened her eyes and saw his penis limpening in the dark.

"Now zat we have loved ourselves, next time we can love each other, *ja*?"

Next time? "Just give me a minute," she pleaded. "I'll be ready again in a minute."

Her disappointment gaped. Marzen got up and left the room. Before he closed the door, he said very quietly, "Pleasant dreams."

Veronica sighed. She had no energy left to reply, or even move. Then the door clicked shut—finality.

The long lines of his semen began to cool. She ran her hands over them, thinking of body lotion, and covered herself as much as she could. It dried quickly to starchiness—more finality. She wasn't wearing his semen as much as she was wearing *him,* and that idea consoled her. Even though Marzen was gone, she still had him all over her.

She fell asleep on the carpet, curled up as a warm ball. The scent of him mixed with her musk, and the joyous exhaustion, rocked her consciousness away.

She dreamed all night.

She was standing naked in the deepest grotto. A figure ascended—a figure composed entirely of flame. The figure was caressing her. Beneath its fiery skin, eloquent shapes moved, the suggestion of flesh. Hands of fire kneaded her body. A mouth of fire kissed her lips. The fiery shaft of the figure's penis entered her sex and ejaculated endless spurts of flame.

She knew that the fire was love.

It didn't burn her. It didn't hurt.

All she felt, as the fire devoured her, was ecstasy.

CHAPTER 10

"It's not metal," Jan Beck said the instant Jack Cordesman walked into her lab, which occupied half the basement of the county's HQ. Myriad junk filled the workup section, shelves of glassware and chemicals, rows of fuming cabinets, comparison microscopes, and squat machines. Jan Beck looked tiny amid all this, for she was tiny herself. She looked deviantly thin in her lab coat. Her hair was flat ashen brown and frizzy, and she wore huge spectacles. In her hand she tapped a fat camel's-hair brush.

"You want a Coke, sir?"

"Sure. And what's not metal?"

She opened a refrigerator and got two sodas. Jack had time to glimpse a clear-plastic evidence bag containing one human foot. Then the fridge door sucked shut. "I worked up the n/a/a-scrape," she said, handing him a bottle. "The weapon that opened Shanna Barrington is not composed of metal."

"An airplane knife or something? One of those polycarb jobs?"

Jan Beck shook her frizzled head. "Plastic composites would be easier to ID. It's some kind of stone, I think. Our spec-indexes don't provide reference for stone-cutting objects, so it'll take me a while to ID."

He guessed she was about forty. She'd worked for the state police for years, and had come to the county for more money and because "county gets better homicides," she'd told him once. Jack often wondered exactly what constituted a "better" homicide.

"Stone," he said after her.

"Something brittle. It shredded well against the ribs and sternum. Some of the particulate residue I could actually gander fucking bare-eyed."

Jack loved this woman's sense of terminology.

"—but it's also something that takes a mean edge. Flint, maybe, or obsidian. Some of the initial incisions could've passed for scalpelwork."

A stone knife, Jack contemplated. He'd have to inform Faye Rowland as soon as possible. The instruments of the ritual could lead to the ritual itself.

"And your killer's blood is B neg," Jan Beck said.

This was a bombshell. "How the hell . . . ? Her fingernails were clean. And you said his semen didn't type."

"They were, and it didn't. I salined random bloodstains and malachited them. Shanna Barrington's type was A pos. One of my malachite samples gave a different hue, so I factored it. All that shit the killer left on the walls, the triangle and the symbols, was done in the victim's blood. All except one."

"Aorista?" Jack speculated.

"Good guess, sir. That word was written in B neg. What's it mean, by the way?"

"A process that doesn't end," Jack muttered.

"That's a kick from your end." Jan Beck's cynical grin looked vulpine. It was her way of saying, *You've got a real winner here, sir*. A killer whose buzzword indicated an unending process was the same as saying *I will not stop*. But Jack was thinking about the blood. *The fucker cut himself,* he thought. *Why?*

"We've got a hair problem too," Jan Beck went on. She led Jack to a labtop piled high with red hardcover field texts. *Morphological Differentiation of Human Hair,* one title read. And another: *Microchemical Cortex Analysis*. Several large CRP slide frames hung from a glowing lightboard. Jack saw that they contained long kinky hairs.

"Can I ask you a personal question, sir?"

"Sure," Jack said.

"Have you ever seen fit to measure your pubic hair?"

Jack stared. "Well . . . no, I haven't, Jan."

"I didn't think so. We in the trade call it 'crotch-hair morpholistics.' Can you guess the average length of a dick hair?"

"To tell you the truth, Jan, the average length of dick hairs is not something I've given a whole lot of thought."

"It's four inches. Some get as long as seven before they fall out. Most people probably don't think they get that long."

"I'm astounded by this new knowledge."

She pointed her fingerprint brush to the slide frames. "Those are eleven inches long."

Jack's face pinched up. "Those are *pubic* hairs?"

"Yes, sir. It's easy to tell auxiliary body hairs from one another. Standard microscopic inspection of the sheath wall and medulla verifies that these are pubes. Only problem is they're about twice as long as the average."

Jack's gaze held fast to the kinky hairs in the frame.

"Here's another thing most people don't realize." Jan Beck seemed to gauge his dismay. "Female pubic hair is thicker than male. But your killer's pubes are the thickest I've ever seen."

"You're not going to tell me the killer's a woman, are you?"

Jan Beck laughed beneath her breath. A silly question deserved a silly answer. "Not unless you know any women who can blow eighty to a hundred milliliters of sperm. You know any women like that, sir? You know any women with penises bigger than rolling pins?"

Jack nodded his stupidity. "Go on."

"This guy's core diameter is four hundred microns plus. Average is one fifty. It's just really odd, you know?"

"Yeah," Jack said. He wanted a drink. Bad. "Maybe it's a growth-hormone disorder or something."

"Good point. But there's one more thing. The field boys brought in several other hairs located high on the spread outline. They were straight and black. And they weren't ancillaries."

"Head hairs, in other words."

"Correct. Thing is, head hairs and ancillaries from the same person are always microscopically matching through fusiformal comparison and thermal analysis of the scale count."

"You're losing me, Jan. I'm a stupid flatfoot, remember?"

"The pubes and the head hairs did not come from the same person. The black hairs had a different pigment lineament, and they were cut. They lacked root-cell sheaths. And let me ask you this. Do you know what dihydrotestosterone is?"

Jack thumbed his brow. "No, Jan, I don't."

"It's a hormone secretion from the human scalp. This substance is *microscopically ever present* on the shaft cuticle of any human head hair. But these black hairs didn't have it."

Jack was getting tired of this. "Let me put it this way, Jan. What the fuck are you fucking talking about, for fuck's sake?"

"The killer wore a wig."

Jack sat down on a lab stool, though he dearly wished it were a barstool. He needed a drink. Even more, and quite suddenly, he needed normality. The memory hung before him in color: Shanna Barrington butchered on the blood-drenched bed, her flesh opened up like a book. Jack wanted his world back—no, he wanted a different world, a world where people loved, not butchered, each other. Was that too much to ask for? Suddenly he felt so sick he wanted to bend over and vomit right there on Jan Beck's shiny linoleum lab floor. It would all come up, not just his breakfast, but everything, his broken dreams and short-changed love, his spirit and his psyche. His heart.

"Are you okay, sir?"

Then he saw Longford, which was as bad. There'd been so many videotapes . . . Jack would never stop seeing the faces. It was evil. That was the only explanation. You could blame environment and upbringing and personality disorders only for so long. There came a point when it simply didn't wash. Grown men, with wives and children of their own, hugely successful businesses. *Having sex with abducted kids,* he thought. *What is wrong with the world?*

"Captain Cordesman, are you all right?"

"Yes," he said quietly. He took a deep breath and closed his eyes. Eventually the moment, with all its blackness, lifted.

Jan Beck was looking at him funny.

"What about the impressions?" he asked.

"You sure you're okay, sir?"

Jack felt his temper shudder, a bad spirit devouring his heart, his mind. *Get your act together,* he pleaded to himself. "I was just having a bad moment, Jan. But I'm okay."

The pause checked. Now Jan Beck looked uncharacteristically solemn. "There isn't much more. We can talk about it later if you want." A longer pause. "I kind of heard through the grapevine—"

"You heard that my girlfriend dumped me and I'm a drunk and I've been cracking up ever since the Longford case, right?"

"Well . . ."

She was too polite to answer. Jack knew he was slipping, but why? Why now? Even after Longford he hadn't slipped this bad. He felt impotent. He remembered the graffito he'd read last night: "Loss of love equals loss of self." Was Veronica the catalyst?

"Tell me about the impressions, Jan."

"The techs didn't bother pouring any. That whole ring of high rises sits real close to the bay, and there's a bad water table. The ground back there gets real mucky when it rains. We were able to establish a walking pattern, though. Forceful gait, long strides. The footspreads indicate someone who's tall, and he's probably heavy too, a big guy. What was left of the impressions was pretty deep. And we know he didn't rappel down the back. I found his prints on the terrace rails below Barrington's flat."

"So he climbed down with his bare hands?" Jack asked.

Jan Beck nodded. "Terrace to terrace, to the ground. Maybe the guy's ex-military or something."

What have I got? Jack asked himself. *I've got a sex killer with eleven-inch pubic hairs and a dick bigger than a camshaft. Does he use a regular knife? No, he uses a stone knife. Does he kill girls to get his rocks off? No, he kills them as part of a ritual. He leaves his prints all over the place because he knows they're not on file. He even cuts himself. He leaves enough semen in the victim to indicate repeated intercourse but we know he wasn't in the apartment more than a few minutes. Last but not least, he wears a wig and he has the physical ability to climb down five floors with his bare hands. Do I have a typical killer? No, lucky me. I have an absolutely extraordinary one.*

"Last night you said you found some herb extract in her blood."

"I ran the chain through the NADDIS landline-link. Whatever it is it's not in their index," Jan Beck said.

NADDIS was an interservice narcotic catalog that the DEA provided for outside agencies. The molecular constituents of an unknown substance were transcribed digitally and coded into their data-storage system via telephone. NADDIS kept thousands of mole chains on file. "If it's not in their file, how long will it take you to ID?" Jack asked.

"Who knows?" Jan Beck said. She set her Coke down on the lid of an Abbott Industries Vision Series blood analyzer. "I was sure it wasn't CDS, and it's not pharmaceutical either. Now I won't have to waste time finding out what it isn't. I'll let you know."

"Anything else?"

"That's it, sir."

Jack stood up, looked absently about the lab. He could not identify the impulse which came to him then. For years the job had stripped him of his feelings. Now those feelings were coming back like a flock of mad birds. Perhaps he needed to immerse himself now—*drench* himself in feelings. Perhaps he needed more.

"Where's the body?" he asked.

"Still in storage. Unfortunately there's no next of kin to release it to. It's kind of sad."

Kind of sad, his mind repeated. "What'll happen to it?"

"The state takes them after sixty days."

Jack nodded, attempted to distract himself. "I need to see it."

Jan Beck's eyes thinned behind huge glasses. "The corpse?"

"That's right. The corpse."

"There's nothing to see, sir. She's sewn up and bagged. She's—"

Jack held up a hand to silence her objection. *She thinks I'm a nut,* he realized. "Just show me the corpse, Jan."

Her expression constricted. She took him down the hall. TSD had its own autopsy facilities; the corpora delicti of the more excruciating homicides were brought here rather than the county hospital, to speed up evidence procurement. Jack had been here many times. They called it the Body Shop.

The shiny black door was labeled merely "Storage." There were no slide-out drawers or such, just metal tables which hosted bulky black plastic bags. A stringent odor filled the cool room, a combination of formalin and iodine wash.

One of the bags was tiny: a baby, Jack realized. Another table contained several smaller bags. Pieces. Jan Beck approached the center table. There was no expected zipper but big metal snaps instead. The bag shimmered in fluorescent light.

Jack needed to see; that's why he was here. He needed a sense of reaction to smash him in the face. Jan Beck unsnapped the bag, then opened the inner clear-plastic shroud.

Then she stepped away.

Silence seemed to rage in Jack's ears—the silence of chasms, or of the highest places of the earth. He wasn't *looking* nearly as much as he was *being shown*. But whose show was it? God's? Fate's? *This is what the world does to people,* whispered a voice that was not his own. *This is what we do when we're bored.*

Shanna Barrington's head had been shaved; metal staples—not stitches—reseated the skullcap. She looked like a bad mannequin. The notorious Y-incision—pathology's universal signature—ran from clavicles to pubis, the black seam held together by big black stitches. Her organs had been weighed, histologized, and replaced. Jack thought of a grocery store turkey restuffed with its own innards.

Yes, this was what the world did to you sometimes—for kicks. The world didn't care. Stone-still, he stared at the corpse. What a cosmic rip-off. The corpse's white skin almost glowed. If this was what the world gave you for being innocent, then the world ate shit. Suddenly Shanna Barrington became Jack's sibling, a sister of conception. It didn't matter that he didn't know her. He knew her by what she represented. Here was her reward for daring to dream: cold storage in a Parke-Davis cadaver bag. All she ever wanted was to be loved, and this was what the world had given her instead. Good and evil weren't opposites—they were the same, they were twins. Horror was as much a monarch as God.

You are my sister now, he thought in a fever of blood to his head. He didn't know what he wanted to do more: laugh or cry.

He grinned through gritted teeth. What he stood in now—a human meat locker—formed the answer to all his life's questions at once. The answer was this: There are no answers to anything. Jan Beck appraised him from aside, the funkiest of looks, as Jack continued to appraise the corpse. The blue nipples had once been pink with desire. The blue lips had once kissed in a quest for love. Somewhere beneath the black-stitched seam was a heart that had once beat with dreams.

I will avenge you, Shanna Barrington. When I catch the motherfucker who did this to you, I'm gonna bury him with my bare hands and piss on his grave. I'm gonna feed him piece by piece back to the evil shit-stinking world that made him.

He stepped closer, through the vertigo of a thousand cruel truths. With the tip of his finger he touched the cadaver's hand. *Oh, yeah,* he promised her. *I'm gonna make him pay.*

CHAPTER 11

The subway took Faye Rowland to Capitol South Metro in about twenty minutes. Late morning had thinned the crowds; it was a pleasant, sedate ride which urged unimposing thoughts. Her coming tasks at the Library of Congress didn't worry her. If there was information to be found, she would find it. Simple. She thought instead of Jack Cordesman. What was wrong with him? She knew little of police procedure and even less of police. Something shattered seemed to brood behind the man's eyes, a drowned vitality. Something, or a combination of things, had left him standing on the edge of some oblique ruin. She could name no specific reason for feeling this; she knew it was pointless to care about every sad person in the world. But Jack Cordesman had passed that point. He wasn't sad, he was *crushed*. He was a crushed man, yet somehow he prevailed.

Faye Rowland had prevailed too. The broken pieces she saw in Jack Cordesman's eyes she often saw in her own. She'd been in love once in her life. Once was enough. He'd run out two weeks before the wedding. "I'm sorry," was all he'd said. Perhaps love was indeed blind; her reaction made no sense. Faye blamed herself. She hadn't been considerate enough. She'd failed to compromise. She'd pressured him, she'd been lousy in bed. She'd spent a year asking him to forgive her for flaws that hadn't existed. She'd later learned that he'd been sleeping with other women for most of their relationship, but that was Faye's fault too. She reasoned that she must've failed to meet his sexual needs and had left him no choice. Self-pity often bred self-indictment.

A year later, she finally came to see the truth. Her only

flaw had been in trusting someone who was not trustworthy. The real thing seldom ever turned out to be real.

Once is enough, she thought, stepping off the car into the subway's bowels. Here was where her real failing came. What scared her most of all was the risk of being hurt again. Faye Rowland would avoid that at all costs, even if it meant being alone for the rest of her life.

So why was she thinking so intently of Jack Cordesman?

He was a slob. He was skinny, pale, out of shape. He had long hair—which Faye hated on men—and he was probably an alcoholic. It was something inside that attracted her. Prevalence, perhaps, or shared negations. Jack Cordesman had prevailed and so had she. They both knew the bottom line because they'd both been at the bottom.

The escalator lifted her from darkness to light. First Street stretched on as a crush of dirty sunlight and harried pedestrians. Black limos roved past ranks of bums in rotted clothes. Pigeons excreted en masse on pristine white government buildings. To Faye's left stood the Supreme Court. To her right stood a hatchet-faced black who asked, "Cokesmoke, frog, ice? I got whatcha need."

The Adams Building loomed over Second Street, a cluttered, ugly edifice. Getting started always took a while; there was a text limit and a half-hour wait on book requests. The reference index ran on a data base now, which was quite simple to use. She punched up the subject file, then punched in *O*.

O, for *Occult*.

"Where did you disappear to last night?" Veronica complained, walking barefoot through the plush backyard grass.

Ginny looked remote, or tired. She wore white shorts and an orange halter, and sat poolside with her feet in the water.

"I was with Gilles," she said.

Veronica joined her. Morning blazed through the trees. "What happened?" she asked, and lazily rowed her feet in the water.

"After dinner, if you can call that disgusting shit dinner, Gilles took me for a walk. The estate is huge. He took me along all these paths in the woods. I didn't get to bed till two."

Veronica remembered what *she'd* been doing at two. The whole thing now seemed dreamlike. What Marzen had done, and had made her do, confused her. She wanted to tell Ginny but it seemed too weird to communicate.

"I don't even remember how it started," Ginny was going on. "He took me to this kiosk at the end of the main path. He said I looked beautiful in the moonlight—Christ, what a line. I knew what he was planning. Next thing I know I'm bare-assed on the floor of this kiosk, the moon in my eyes. I never saw his face."

Veronica chewed her lip. She hadn't seen Marzen's face either. "What happened next?"

"He went down on me," Ginny said bluntly. "Pretty good technique, I can tell you that. Average guy doesn't know what he's doing. Anyway, I'm just about to get off, and Gilles stops."

Veronica didn't have to ask the rest. "I got the same treatment from Marzen," she admitted. "He told me I had to love myself before I could love someone else."

"Gilles said the exact same thing to me!"

"Transposition," Veronica mumbled.

Ginny laughed. "Boy, are we a couple of dopes. At least I don't feel so silly now."

Veronica watched the pulse of ripples in the water. Then she thought of her orgasms, their ferocity, the raw wildness of their release. "I wonder what kind of game they're playing."

"I told you. They're trying to mystify us. Men think women are impressed by shit like that, the idiots. But . . ."

Ginny's eyes beseeched her. Ginny was the most straightforward person Veronica knew, yet now there was only confluence in her expression, utter doubt. "I think I could fall in love with the guy," she said.

"That's the dumbest thing I've ever heard come out of your mouth. Some French musclehead goes down on you, and you're ready to fall in love? You? The literary destroyer of love?"

Ginny didn't answer. She returned her gaze to the water. Eventually she said, "I started my story. Did you start your painting?"

"Sort of," Veronica said, remembering Khoronos' request that they create while they were here. She hadn't put anything on canvas yet, but she knew she would paint her dream. *The Ecstasy of the Flames*, she might call it. Or *The Flame Lover*.

"My story's going to be about—"

"Don't tell me!" Veronica insisted. "Khoronos said we weren't supposed to talk about our projects till they're done."

"Speak of the dilettante," Ginny said. "Here he comes now."

They stood up quickly. Khoronos was crossing the yard with someone. "I wonder who he respects more, artistically," Ginny ventured with some resentment. "Us or her?"

"I couldn't care less," Veronica claimed, yet she admitted a little resentment of her own. The woman Khoronos led across the yard was Amy Vandersteen, who seemed to have achieved the best of both worlds: the only thing bigger than her bank account was her critical acclaim. Veronica liked most of her movies—psychologic sojourns of womanhood insinuated through a dark Polanskiesque eye.

Khoronos approached them, in gray Italian slacks and a black silk shirt. "It's my pleasure to introduce Amy Vandersteen," he said. "This is novelist Virginia Thiel and expressionist painter Veronica Polk, both quite well received in their fields."

They exchanged smug handshakes. Amy Vandersteen wore clothes that reminded Veronica of Stewie: white leather pants, black boots, and a Day-Glo red cardigan over a bright blue T-shirt which read "Birdsongs of the Mesozoic." *New-wave Cleopatra,* Veronica thought. The woman's hair hung perfectly straight, with high straight bangs, and was dyed snow white. Designer contacts made her eyes purple.

"I've seen your books in the stores," she told Ginny. She had a cool, nasally voice. "I'll have to read one sometime."

"Don't hesitate to buy film rights," Ginny joked.

"Unlikely." Amy Vandersteen wasn't joking. "I write all my own scripts." She turned to Veronica. "I haven't heard of you."

"You will," Veronica said.

Then she turned back to Khoronos. "I'd really love to see the rest of the estate, Erim. You have impeccable taste."

Khoronos led her back toward the house.

"Jesus," was all Veronica could comment.

"You were right," Ginny said. "She is an asshole."

"Stewie!" Jeri blurted over the line. Some unnamed excitement raged in her voice. He'd hired her from St. John's as a secretary. "You got a call on line one! It's the—"

"Calm down," Stewie replied. He felt disaffected today, depressed or something. "Who is it?"

"It's the Corcoran!"

The C—. This sounded funny. "What do they want? A donation?"

"They want you, Stewie! They want—"

"I got it," he mumbled. He punched the extension. "Stewart Arlinger here."

"Mr. Arlinger," came a dry and rather sexless voice. "This is D. F. Pheeters. I am the director of the schedule of events for the Corcoran Gallery of Art." The voice pronounced *schedule* as *shed-yule*. "You are the agent of Veronica Polk, the expressionist?"

"Yes," Stewie perked up, "not that I'd label her as an expressionist. I believe my client's work transcends categorization."

"Yes, of course."

It was true, Veronica had gained some notoriety over the last year. Making waves was the name of the art game. But had she made enough waves for the Corcoran?

"We'd like to do a show," the voice told him.

This statement, coldly conveyed, locked Stewie up at his desk. "You mean a joint show, a filler or something?"

"No. We'd like to show Ms. Polk's work exclusively."

"Uh, when?"

"First week of next month. We have a cancellation, Mitterteich, the abstractionist. We want your client in that slot."

This was difficult to believe so abruptly.

"Mr. Arlinger? Are you there?"

"Uh, yes, yes, I was just thinking."

Now the voice seemed impatient. "Well, are you interested or not?"

"Yes, uh, yes, we are—" How should he address the genderless voice? Sir? Ma'am? Director? "There's a minor probl—"

"Mr. Arlinger. Surely you're aware of your own client's schedule. She is either available or not. Which is it, Mr. Arlinger? If you're not interested at showing your client at the Corcoran, I'm rather certain I can find someone who is."

"We are interested," Stewie said, but what else could he say without sounding incompetent? "My client is out of town for a short time. I'm expecting a call from her very soon."

"Is your client prepared to show new work?"

"I—" *I don't fucking know!* he wanted to yell, *because I don't know where she is, and I have no idea how to reach her!* "I'm not sure to what extent, and I apologize for this inconvenience. She wanted to get away for a little while. I'm certain she'll be in touch very soon."

"Very soon, you said that twice, Mr. Arlinger. How soon?"

"I'm not sure," Stewie confessed. "It wouldn't be wise for me to make a commitment before talking to her first. She's very secretive about what she's got ready to go. But I'll get back to you the minute I hear from her. I just need a little time."

"A week is all the time I can give you, Mr. Arlinger. If I don't hear from you by then, I'll presume you are not interested in showing your client at the Corcoran Gallery of Art."

"I understand," Stewie said. "And thank you very m—"

When the line went dead, he yelled, "Goddamn it to *hell*!"

Jeri's college-girl face appeared at the door. "Stewie, w—"

"*Get out!*" he bellowed. He threw the phone at the wall and knocked out a chunk of Sheetrock. Jeri disappeared in terror.

How the hell could he manage Veronica's career when he didn't even know where she was? She hadn't left Khoronos' address or number. She'd promised to call him every day, but he had yet to hear from her since she left with goddamn Ginny three days ago!

This was the third gallery bid he'd gotten since she left. The first two were smaller, and he'd dogged them easily. But the Corcoran was a different matter. The Corcoran meant nationwide credibility, higher sales values, even fame. An art agent dogging the Corcoran was like an unpublished novelist dogging Random House. Professional suicide.

She's my life, he realized, looking at the prints of hers in the office. Stewie had been two-bit before Veronica. Without her, he'd be two-bit again. But was that all of it?

He knew it wasn't. Veronica was also his friend. He felt protective of her, like a brother. She went off on tangents; she was a confused girl with a lot of confused ideals. This Khoronos thing was a prime example. Veronica's reclusion as an artist made her vulnerable as a person. There were a lot of sharks out there; Veronica, on her own, wouldn't stand a chance against them. Just who was this Khoronos guy anyway? What did he want?

He stared out his office window. A cop car driving by reminded him of Jack. Stewie and Jack were polar opposites, but Stewie was honest enough to realize that Jack was Veronica's best protection against her vulnerabilities. She'd been content with him, and she'd worked better; on the same hand, Jack's own problems diminished. They were good for each other, and Stewie could see that. He could also see that, apart, Veronica was all alone with her confusions. *Experience*, she'd said a million times. But experience had many faces, some very ugly. Stewie had seen a lot of them.

Complete strangers. That's what Khoronos and his two friends were. Art eccentrics, rich, good-looking. Veronica would be putty in their hands.

Stop worrying, he thought, quite uselessly. What could he do? *Nothing*. She'd either call or she wouldn't.

Maybe he'd go out tonight. Yeah. Dress up, grab a handful of rubbers, and a head for the singles' bars. Get drunk, get laid, get his mind off it. One good thing about bisexuality was you always had twice as many prospects to choose from. But as he thought about it now, staring out the window, nothing could've seemed more remote.

"Stewie?" Jeri's voice peeped from behind. "You okay?"

"Yeah," Stewie said.

"Don't worry about Veronica. You know how she is, she just forgot. She'll call soon."

Nice try, Stewie thought.

"See you tomorrow. And stop worrying!"

"Sure. Good night, Jer."

Stop worrying, he thought when she left. But that was it. Stewie was worried, all right. He was worried to death.

"I wonder what she dug up," Jack said. He looked out his office window. The moon was rising in the rim of dusk.

"Probably nothing. It's been that kind of day," Randy Eliot said. "The harder we bust our humps, the less we get."

That much was true. After meeting with Jan Beck, Jack had spent the rest of the day helping Randy interview Shanna Barrington's "acquaintances." They'd all recounted similar stories: I met her at the club. She came onto me, so I went with it. We had a few drinks, danced a few dances, then she wants to go back to her place. You have sex with her? Sure. How long were you there? Most of the night. You ever call her again? Most had not. She knew the score, a one-night thing, no big deal. She seem level headed to you? Sure, she wasn't a nut, if that's what you mean. You have sex with her more than once that night? Most had. Several repeatedly. One guy said, "Six, seven times. The usual." She do drugs, coke, anything like that? No way. You use rubbers with her? Of course, I ain't crazy. She into kinky stuff? Kinky like what? Kinky like maybe she wants you to tie her up, gag her, blindfold her? No way, man.

Nearly half of Shanna Barrington's address book had been interviewed. Randy put tails on the few weirdos in the bunch, but Jack knew these were strikeouts too. He could tell by looking at them: they were weirdos, but they weren't murderers.

"Those things'll kill you," Randy said when Jack lit a Camel.

"Are you my mother?" Jack's mother, by the way, had died of oat-cell lung cancer. "Cigarettes help me think," he said.

"Great. I'll ask you what you're thinking on the respirator."

On the wall hung a layout of the Bayview complex, and blowups of Shanna Barrington's walls. The bizarre red glyphs seemed three-dimensional, the star-pointed triangle seemed to hover in space, with its proclamation in blood.

"The Triangle case is going nowhere fast," Randy concluded. A sip of Jack's coffee made his lips pucker.

"I already told you, the only way we're going to nail this guy is by taking apart his M.O. Rome wasn't built in a day."

"You're right. It took fifteen hundred years, and I don't think Olsher plans on giving us that much time."

"We know plenty more than we did yesterday." Jack was trying to sound confident, and failing, he supposed. "We know his blood group, gait, approximate height and weight, probable hair color. We know he's hung, and we know he wears a wig. And Beck thinks he's a foreigner, Slavic or East European."

"How'd she get that?"

"She indexed the scale count of his public hair. And that jibes with what Panzram suggested. He's probably from abroad, a mover."

"What about this researcher?"

"She's green, but she seems pretty squared away." Jack glanced at his watch. "And she's late. Maybe that's a good sign."

"Rumor has it she's staying at your place."

Jack quickly smirked. *Fucking grapevine*. "I offered her one of my spare rooms to cut down on her drive time. And I'm *not*—"

"I know you're not," Randy said. "It just might not look too cool—a thirty-three-year-old captain and a twenty-two-year-old state employee."

"She's only twenty-two?"

"That's what Olsher said. Graduated early, got a double major in library science and Latin. Anyway, she's young, and she's been subcontracted from the state. The C.E.'s office might not like the idea of her staying at a county captain's place."

"Bugger them," Jack said. He knew what Randy meant, though. The people upstairs were axmen. Don't give them a reason to chop off your head.

A few minutes later, Faye Rowland straggled in, briefcase in tow. She looked disheveled and tired. Jack introduced her to Randy, then cleared room for her at his desk. "Well?" he said, and put a cup of coffee in her hand.

She took one sip and pushed it away. "I identified the term *aorista* and its applications to the occult. I took all day."

"Is that good or bad?" Jack asked.

"Let's just say your killer is into something very authentic."

"You identified the ritual?" Randy asked.

"Aorista denotes a process that doesn't end." Then she said to Jack, "You were right to apply the term directly to the ritual, you were exactly right. The word is a general reference to a *type* of sect, cult, or schismatic religious unit that practices a specific ritual in a manner that is philosophically indefinite. Just think of it as a general term—an aorist sect. They were big in the Middle Ages; in those days the ruling classes were unduly influenced by the Catholic Church, so if you weren't in the Church, and if you weren't nobility, you were peasant. Witchcraft and demon worship grew out of a rebellion to organized Christianity. Devil worship was the social counterculture of the times, the poor man's way of striking back against his oppressors, and the aorist sects were the most extreme mode of this rebellion. While the average peasant was saying Black Mass, the aorists were killing priests, burning churches, and sacrificing children. They were the transitive component of a belief that was largely intransitive."

"Action instead of words," Jack speculated.

"Right. The aorists sects were to satanism what the Jesuits are to the Catholics."

Randy loosened his tie. "What about the sacrifice angle?"

"Mankind has been making sacrifices for the last thirty thousand years. The only way I can identify this specific ritual is if I'm lucky enough to match its protocol or emblemation to your crime scene."

"What do you figure your chances are?" Jack asked.

"Not good," Faye Rowland admitted. "The fund of information is too obscure. There aren't any reference books I can just whip open and identify your sect. It's like a needle in a haystack."

Jack crushed out his Camel and lit another. He was thinking, thumbing his eyebrows. "Protocol . . . Ritual . . . Our forensic tech determined that the knife used on Shanna Barrington was made of some kind of brittle stone. Flint maybe, or obsidian."

Faye looked at him baldly. "Many civilizations, once they'd begun to develop organized religious systems, believed that fire was a gift from the gods. Flint sparks. So they used flint for their sacrificial implements. The Toltecs are the best example, and the Seleucids of Asia Minor. And a lot of the aorist sects used knives chipped out of volcanic glass—"

"Obsidian," Jack muttered.

"—for a similar symbolic reason. They worshiped demons, which they believed lived deep in the earth, so they crafted their tools out of materials that came from the same place. They were using what they'd been given to exalt the giver. Gifts of the devil to the people of the devil."

Jack felt a weird chill run up his back, the same chill he felt anytime he asked himself how far madness could go. Madness could have order, couldn't it? It was a creepy thought.

"They were called *dolches,*" Faye added. "Not knives. Dolches."

Randy looked disgruntled. "We were hoping it was just some crackpot or a random nutcase who's into the occult."

"Oh, no," she assured. "Whatever your killer is into, it's not something he read in some paperback occult manual. It's very deep and very intricate. The aorist sects were the ultimate form of religious sedition in the Middle Ages. They butchered babies, roasted virgins on solstice feasts, gutted priests like deer."

"Great," Jack sputtered.

The pale lamplight made black punch holes of Faye Rowland's tired eyes. "This guy's no crackpot, Captain. He's the real McCoy."

CHAPTER 12

Becky reread the lines she'd scribbled in her book:

Evil kisses, or angelic sendings?
I want to be in a bed of beginnings,
Not endings.

She turned her nose up at it. Here was the next one:

THE GHOST

Remnants never vanish
but give spawn to loss
and banish all I care for
on the earth. Does this
last ghost give birth to a
new me, or another
impassioned catastrophe?

The things I do to make things
rhyme—Jesus!—what a crime to
time and art and the cooling ashes
of the broken heart. But it should
be fun at least to see what
midnight passion beckons me next
to the next caress of faith.

Becky knew her poetry wasn't very good, not from a poet's standpoint anyway. She didn't care, though. She wrote poetry for herself. She'd picked up a guy last week who wanted to know about it. This was unusual because guys generally didn't care about aspects of her that didn't involve coitus. "You should try to get it published," he'd said. "That would be unthinkable," she'd returned. "Why write it if other people can't read it?" "Because it's not for other people. It's for me. Poetry is how I define myself." What a moron. He hadn't even come close to understanding. At least he understood how to put his penis into her. That's all she'd wanted him for in the first place.

The mirror reflected back her thirty-one years like an inner eye of all that her past had led to. Becky Black assayed herself nude. Minuscule bikini marks resembled white satin underthings against the dark tan. She worked hard to keep trim; she stood 5′ 6″ and weighed 107. She was lithe, not skinny. Long sleek legs ascended to a sculpted contour of hourglass curves. A thought from the past lingered when she looked at her breasts. *Cupcakes*. They were firm as lemons, with soft-pink areolae. Philip had referred to them as cupcakes during his efforts in the bedroom. He'd used all kinds of silly, adoring little pet names for her body parts. Her breasts were "cupcakes." Her navel was her "Becky button," and her vagina was her "little lamb." This aspect of his adoration amused her. Philip was arcane and very loving, but little else. "I love you more than you ever have been loved or ever will be loved," he often cryptically remarked. This was probably true, but so what? Their one-year marriage left her bored and unimpressed. His love did not scratch her itches, so why should she feel guilty? She'd cheated on him like a she-demon at the merest turn of his inept back, the poor fool. Frequently she called him at work while handsome strangers put the blocks to her. Marriage seemed a silly—even embarrassing—blight that too many people let crawl over their lives. It seemed like a mistake. Philip's love did not change the way she viewed her desires. Love did not give her *completeness;* adventure, risk, and physical diversity did. Once she'd been talking to her friend Debbie, and said, "Marriage is like going to McDonald's every day and eating a fish sandwich. Sometimes a girl wants a Big Mac," which may have been the first time in history that fast food assumed a philosophical application. Philip was a fish sandwich. The marriage fell apart in a year.

Release! She thought of birds soaring from the prisons of

their cages. She was free. Without the millstone of marriage about her neck, society became her own private playground. It amazed her how easily the lure of sex transformed mature, capable men into mindless marionettes with erections. She could walk into any bar at any time and leave with another pinch of the spice her life needed. She picked up all manner of men: young, old, rich, poor, conventional, eccentric. The McDonald's theorem held true; it was variety that fulfilled her, not complacency. Becky Black didn't want love. She wanted fireworks every night, a new Roman candle to explode in her, and catherine wheels of flesh to light the fuse of her lust.

She didn't care how shallow her plight might truly be.

The night seemed to ripple with waves of energy, charging the City Dock into a carnival. Becky parked across from the Harbour Square Shops. Frolic droves of revelers moved from one bar to the next. Pedicabs carried lovers away under the moon, and music beat in the air. Becky's sheer, clinging dress inspired a periodic whistle; four midshipmen in summer whites leered as her long legs carried her across Randall Street, high heels clicking. A new place called the Map Room beckoned her with cubistic neon squiggles in the window; she entered into a crush of young lawyers and upper-class floozies. Another clique bar, where people came to pretend to be chic and paid five dollars for a mixed drink. New Order beat bleakly from high speakers; more neon lights flashed. At the long black marble bar, men stood leaving their Porsche and Jag keys in plain view, while their dates perched alertly on Art Deco stools, laughing at jokes they didn't get. The waitresses looked like a Robert Palmer video, and the barkeeps looked like genetic hybrids of Mickey Rourke and Morrissey. False pretenses raged; Becky liked the place.

"Excuse me, miss—"

The sparsest of accents, sexy in reservation.

She turned around.

"May I buy you a drink?"

She stared through the utter failure of trying not to. The urge was a summons.

He was beautiful.

"Yes, you may," Becky replied as the clock struck midnight.

◆ ◆ ◆

Veronica sat up late in the vast living room, sharing her company with Amy Vandersteen. Very little in life came easily, Veronica reasoned, but disliking Amy Vandersteen was an exception. She was arrogance, pride, and ego all wrapped up in one.

"I'm doing a short screenplay, a mélange," Amy said. She stretched rudely on the couch with her feet up. "I'm not clear yet as to the *Leitmotiv,* but Erim suggested I use my dreams as the basic thematic premise."

Erim, Veronica thought. She still didn't know how to assess Khoronos; her initial physical attraction seemed to be restructuring itself into something more complex. Yet whatever the attraction, she still had to confess an incontrovertible jealousy.

She didn't, for instance, like the way Amy said *Erim.* The lax, easy tone implied they'd known each other for years, which she undoubtedly wanted everyone to think. "So what do you think of . . . *Erim*?" Veronica finally asked.

"Oh, he's absolutely awesome," Amy replied, wriggling her toes in the plush couch upholstery. "He's the most aesthetically sagacious person I've ever met, and that's saying something, considering my own creative status. He and I get along famously."

Veronica's frown menaced her face. "Famously, huh? How long have you known him?"

"Oh, just a few weeks. He came to my latest opening, *Princess Sex and Death.* It doesn't matter that we haven't known each other long. Truly great relationships often begin spontaneously."

Veronica wanted to howl. Relationship! All she wanted to do just then was dump her iced tea right into this silly woman's lap.

"He told me he's from Yugoslavia," Amy went on. Her face was a smugly content mask within the frame of ridiculous white-dyed hair. "I don't know about the other two, but who cares, you know?"

"What do you mean?"

"Gilles, Marzen—they're babies. You can have them, you and your novelist friend. Me, I prefer an older man, more mature and sophisticated. I'm gunning for Erim."

Veronica, hot not to scowl, reserved comment, though several rather articulate ones came to mind. This "retreat"—the entire idea of it—perplexed her more and more. So far it was a bust. They'd had a few communal meals together, a few conversations, and that was it. In fact, Veronica hadn't seen Khoronos and his two protégés all day. She hadn't seen Ginny either, not since morning.

She picked at a tray of cold hors d'oeuvres they'd found in the refrigerator: handmade Korean egg rolls and spiced cabbage. No dinner had been prepared tonight, which made her wonder further. Khoronos might be mysterious and intellectual, but as a host he was striking out. With her fingers, she ate several pieces of cabbage.

"This stuff's not bad," she remarked. "You should try it."

Amy Vandersteen grimaced at the tray. She dug in a pocket, extricating a tiny steel pipe, a lighter, and a vial.

"You've got to be out of your mind," Veronica groaned.

"Why? It's a free country."

"Someone could walk in."

"Who? Just your novelist friend, and I haven't seen her. Erim left with Marzen and Gilles hours ago. He has a beautifully restored Fleetwood, all black. He said they won't be back till morning."

This, too, puzzled Veronica. "Where did they go?"

Ms. Vandersteen tapped white powder from the vial into the steel pipe. "Business, he said."

Business? At midnight? Just what kind of business was Khoronos in? "Did he give you that shit?" she asked.

Amy laughed chidingly. "No, he did not give me this *shit*. Frankly, I don't think Erim uses coke, none of them do."

"You should take an example."

Another dismissive laugh. "A prude, are you, Veronica?"

"I'm not a prude. I just don't think it's too cool to come into a man's home and smoke cocaine without his knowledge."

Amy Vandersteen was heating up the pipe. "It's not Erim's house, it's a friend's, some investor who's out of the country for a while. Didn't you know that?"

Apparently there was a lot Veronica didn't know. Hadn't Khoronos implied it was *his* house?

"Erim vacations here a lot. That's what he told me."

"Where does he live, then?"

"All over—he told me that too. Kind of strange."

"Yes, it was. Suddenly Veronica felt steeped in questions, and this made her jealousy worse. Amy Vandersteen seemed to know everything about Khoronos. What made her so privileged? "Do you know what he does for money?" she finally summoned the nerve to ask. Rich friends. Living from place to place. Business at midnight. And what had he said their first day here? Faith bestows treasure upon the faithful? "Is he involved with drugs?"

"You're *so* paranoid. Erim is not involved with drugs. He's independently wealthy—old, old family money."

Veronica watched in loathsomeness. Amy brought the tiny pipe to her lips and sucked until the flame sublimated the cocaine. Then she relaxed back on the couch, grinning dopily. "Class A," she said.

"Jesus Christ."

"You want some?"

"No thanks. I'd prefer not to contribute to the denegration of our society."

Amy Vandersteen chuckled tightly, eyes closed in the sudden infusion of bliss. "You're unique, Veronica. A conservative artist."

"I'm not a conservative, I just don't break the law."

"But laws are only for the inferior minority."

"Is that so?"

"Because I'm superior enough to handle it."

"Tell that to the two million cocaine addicts in this country. They thought they could handle it too. The same people you buy that shit from are the same people who sell crack to elementary school kids. It's all part of the same machine."

"Other people's weaknesses aren't my problem."

"That garbage ruins people's lives, and it's shitheads like you who lend a helping hand every time you buy it. Maybe you'll have kids someday, Amy. Maybe the same slobs you buy from will get them hooked. See how you feel about it then."

"Don't worry, I'll never have kids. And I'll ignore those remarks. You know why? Because I like you, Veronica. You have conviction, and I like that." She sat up again, to prepare the pipe. "I even think you and I could be friends."

"Don't hold your breath," Veronica replied. She got up and headed for the stairs.

◆ ◆ ◆

His name was Fraus, which sounded German. He was dreamy and handsome; he was *different*. He carried an air of the genteel—a lost prince—yet his first kiss had shown her a robust and very fervid passion. The kiss had *taken* her, and that's what Becky wanted. To be taken.

At the Map Room they'd talked about poetry, which he seemed to know a lot about. His favorites were Shelley, Jarrell, and Seymour. But Becky didn't dare tell him that she was a poet—he might ask to see her work. He had rather short black hair, slightly mussed, which added to the image of the lost prince. His body must be magnificent beneath the tailored Italian suit. And he must have money—which always helped. The suit looked expensive, and he'd thought nothing of ordering a bottle of Perrier-Jouet for $125. "Like sipping rainbows," he'd metaphored. Strange, though, that he'd consumed none himself.

Her attraction to this man had put a caul around them, closing out the Map Room's din. Fraus gestured his words with periodic touches. He told her with his hands what he wanted, and Becky liked that too. His hands transcended words—they told her he needed to touch.

Of course he'd agreed to the "nightcap" at her place. Becky maintained her front, letting him in, locking the door, getting the drinks. She chatted about her job as he surveyed her abode. But that was where the game ended.

They broke at the same time, sensing each other. His kiss was first delicate, then explosive. His big hand gripped the back of her head, and his mouth devoured hers. A great finesse enabled him to continue kissing her as he stripped her right there in the living room, shedding his own garments alternately.

All he left on were her stockings.

The brashness of his desire excited her. When the door closes, the masks come off. The closed door left them to be what they really were: night creatures pursuing their own lusts. What was wrong with that? This was the nineties, the age of assertions, and she could tell, stripped bare by a perfect stranger, that her little lost prince was a very assertive man. She was already thinking of the poem she would write: "The Lost Prince."

His flesh felt hot and firm. He was as beautiful as she'd expected. His tongue invaded her mouth, pursued her lips and teeth. She liked it when he placed her hand on his testicles, which felt large as eggs. She rubbed them gently, held them as coveted prizes as his mouth sucked her tongue. She felt steamy, light. Her horniness began to trample her—she felt drenched in herself.

They kissed and touched and fondled their way to the bedroom. His penis throbbed between their pressed bellies; his large hand parted her buttocks and squeezed. A finger slipped into her sex from behind, and that was about all she could take. His attentions focused her awareness of herself to a pinpoint, which filled her head with dirty pictures. *Do anything you want to me,* she thought.

He lay her down on the bed. She fought not to fidget; she needed this beautiful human thing on her right now, and in her. But he just stood there. Looking at her.

"Turn off the lights," she whispered.

"No, please." His gaze traipsed down. His erect penis throbbed as if counting off seconds. "You're beautiful. I want to *see* you."

Why was he so hesitant? Was he worried about protection? Becky ordinarily insisted upon it—she even had a box of condoms in her nightstand for the inconsiderate assholes who didn't bring their own. But in a moment she saw she was wrong . . .

It wasn't hesitation at all. Somehow, she sensed that very openly. He wasn't hesitating, he was *pondering*. He was pondering *her*.

He leaned over and stripped her stockings off.

Now her desire imbued every nerve. Suddenly Becky wasn't concerned about anything, not protection or morality, what he was like or what he thought of her, not her job, her friends, her future. She felt drugged with her own lust, and the need which itched at the passage between her legs.

He stood before her in the light, a stocking in each hand.

"May I tie you?" he asked.

She extended her arms, crucifixion on the bed.

"Yes, you may," she said.

CHAPTER 13

The darkness damped the room to perfect silence. Her lover, unknown as yet, slid beside her into bed.

Veronica gasped, in passion.

His hand gently molded the contours of her breasts, then slid to her sex. It touched her with such precision she thought she might come at once; the hand seemed to know her. A blurred face lowered, lips touched her lips and kissed. The room's dark hid her lover's face like a veil.

What's . . . happening? she thought lamely. A tightness spired at her loins like an overtorqued spring. The hand continued to play with the tender groove of her sex, investigating.

Who was this man in her bed? Veronica moaned, short of breath. *Marzen,* she concluded. *Or Gilles.* She pulled the naked figure atop her, felt a warm, hardened penis slide across her belly. Her nipples swelled up so much they ached; she felt the veins beat in her breasts. She sensed an earthy purgation, the preliminary release of feelings that demanded to be loosed. "Who are you?" she panted, adjusting herself. She felt frenzied, desperate to be penetrated.

"Darling," whispered the voice.

Now Veronica gasped, in shock. A cloud passed, letting moonlight fall into the room. She knew the voice, she knew it was all wrong, all impossible. The moonlight now revealed his face.

Jack's.

Impossible.

Yet it was him. She looked up and saw beyond doubt the face of the man she used to love. His long hair hung down in strings. The clean sweat of passion made his flesh shine, and his big forlorn eyes gazed directly back into hers.

It was. It was Jack.

"Oh, Veronica . . ."

She felt locked in heat and incomprehension. Jack reached down, put the end of his penis into her vulva.

"Jack, I—"

"I still love you," he cut off.

He eased into her and slowly began to thrust. The feel of the entry, and its immediacy, robbed her voice. It robbed her sensibilities too. At once she didn't care that this could not be explained. She was with Jack now, and he was making love to her. That's all she needed to know.

His thrusts gained rhythm. She looked down and saw his penis appearing and disappearing into her flesh below the tuft of fur. Her impending orgasm seemed to chase her, cutting distance.

"Do you remember?" he asked. The strings of his long hair dangled. He seemed sad.

"What, Jack?"

"Do you remember when we were together, what it was like?"

Her voice shredded the word. "Yes."

"Do you remember the plans we made?"

Veronica couldn't speak now; her throat felt shivered shut. It was true. They'd made lots of plans—all ashes now. Suddenly tears welled and blurred with memory like blood in water.

He leaned down, still slowly stroking. He licked the tears out of her eyes. "What happened? Why did it all fall apart?"

The question crushed her. She could never answer it.

"We could have it all back again," he whispered like a plea. "We could start over. It would be better this time, I promise."

What could she say, even if she could not speak?

His head drooped between his shoulders. The deep sadness darkened his words. "We were meant to be together."

The same sadness beat into her with his thrusts.

"Sweetheart," he began to whimper. Soon his thrusts raced. Their loins slapped. He collapsed onto her as he came, shivering. She could feel the repeated, hot spurts.

She didn't want him to be sad, but what could she do? Their relationship had trapped her, robbed her of the experience she felt convinced she needed to be whole. Maybe she did still love him—she didn't know. But what she did know was that she wasn't ready to resume anything.

"I still love you," he groaned. The last of his orgasm leaked out, trickling in her.

She rubbed his back, his face in the crook of her neck. Her ankles unhooked. All she could see in her mind was what he must see every day in his loss—all his love that now had no place to go.

"I'm sorry, Jack," she said.

"Forget it."

"I'm sorry I can't tell you what you want to hear. I can't lie to you. I'm not sure what I want, or what I need."

"I know," he said.

God, this was awful. How had it happened? He must have found out where Khoronos lived, and come here in desperation. But then she thought, *What the . . . ?* She could still feel his semen in her, but it felt . . . lumpy. No, it felt *moving*.

Then the sudden impact: the stench. She hacked, gagging, at the sudden stench like a fish market dumpster in the sun.

Bile began to pulse up her throat.

Her horror smothered her scream. Jack leaned up on his arms, but it was not Jack now who lay between her legs—it was a raddled corpse. Perforated slabs of flesh hung off vermiculated bones. Its skin was green-hued gray, its eyes were holes. Veronica pushed up at the gray meat of the cadaver's face—

—then half its face slid off its skull.

The corroded mouth struggled to form words but only voiced a deep, phlegmy rattle. It tenderly touched her face, bones showing. When it tried to talk again, out poured a slew of pus and putrefactive slop onto her breasts. She flailed under the thing's diminished weight. Rot-warm skin slid away everywhere she pushed up. She pulled on an ear and the ear came off. When she shoved up against its bloated belly, her hands sunk into a substance like raw warm hamburger.

"Please, don't . . . ," the thing finally managed. More corpse-vomit urped onto her chest. Small things twitched amid the rank slush—maggots—and at once Veronica realized exactly what the cadaver had ejaculated into her with its semen.

Grue lay splattered on her: a chunky, stinking porridge of parasites. She bucked again, heaving up, and flipped the cadaver off the bed.

It feebled to hands and knees. Steam rose off its dilapidated flesh as maggots squirmed their way through hot gray skin. Eventually the thing rose to its feet in wet crunching movements and turned its head to her. Veronica crawled back on the bed. The cadaver beseeched her in its loss, holding out worm-riddled hands as if to divulge a crucial wisdom.

"There's me in you now," it gargled. "Me. In you. Forever."

She knew what it meant when she dared look between its rack-thin legs. No penis remained—

"My gift, my love."

—and if it wasn't between its legs anymore, it could only be—

Oh . . . my . . . God, the thought poured in her mind. She choked back vomit and parted her legs. With thumb and forefinger, she extracted the soft, rot-sodden penis from her vagina. It swung, dripping, off her fingers; a white grave-worm squiggled out of the tiny peehole. Veronica shrieked and flung the organ away.

"This is what," Jack's corpse grated, "all love comes to. It falls to pieces in our hands."

His scalp and the rest of his face slid off his skull, but only after the peeling lips uttered the final testament: "I . . . still . . . love you, Veronica."

Then the cadaver collapsed to a pile of steaming rot.

Veronica rolled off the bed. She was naked, beslimed, crawling for the door. *The door! The door!* was the only thing in the world she could think.

Then the door burst open.

Heat and intense orange light filled the hall, and next the figure of flame stepped into the doorway.

The heat beat down on her. The figure's penis burned white-blue like a blowtorch flame. It hissed. Slowly, then, the burning man extended its fiery hand, as if to invite her away.

Hands were on her, shaking her then, shaking her awake as she screamed and screamed, impossibly, in bliss.

"Jack? Jack?"

He sensed smothered light, and heard his name reach down as though he were hearing it through a closed coffin lid.

His eyes snapped open.

"Are you all right?"

Faye Rowland leaned over him, squinting in worry.

"What?" he said.

"You were screaming."

Screaming? He tried to clear his mind. He was in bed. The nightstand lamp had been turned on, and the clock read 3:37 A.M.

"You were having a nightmare," Faye Rowland said.

He felt stupid looking up at her. His mind felt like a spilled puzzle. Then he thought: *Jeeeeeeesus.* He remembered the dream.

He'd been standing in Jan Beck's morgue. The steel door had slammed shut behind him. Before him lay Shanna Barrington's naked, white corpse. He pounded on the door, but it wouldn't open. When he turned, of course, Shanna Barrington's corpse was getting up off the morgue slab. She stood, looking down, and began to pick the stitches out of her autopsy section as if unbuttoning a blouse. The seam came apart. Bagged organs fell onto the floor.

She looked at him again, sunken-eyed. Her blue lips smiled.

Jack screamed.

The corpse's face had changed. To Veronica's.

"I had a nightmare, all right," Jack said now. "A doozie."

Faye Rowland sat down on the bed. "You were screaming bloody murder up here. It's funny, though. I had a nightmare too."

Jack lit a cigarette. "I'll tell mine if you tell yours."

Faye Rowland laughed and pushed her long hair back. All she wore as a nightgown was a large T-shirt that came down to her hips. "I used to be engaged to this guy. A couple weeks before we were supposed to get married, he called it off."

"Bummer," Jack said.

"I dreamed that he was lowering me into a hole full of fire."

"And?"

"That's all. That was my nightmare."

"Aw, shit," Jack scoffed. "Mine was much better than that." But when he told it, it sounded silly.

"That's the name you were screaming," Faye said. "Veronica."

Great. Jack smirked and blew smoke at the ceiling.

"We all have our wounds." Her large breasts showed through the big T-shirt. "But at least they make life interesting."

"Sure," Jack said.

"Can I ask you a personal question?"

"Sure, why not?"

She only half looked at him. "Do you still love her?"

What a question. "Yes," he said.

He stared past her, seeing nothing.

"I'm sorry," she said. "I shouldn't have asked that. I don't know why I did. I guess I'm just curious about you."

"Forget it. At least we know we have something in common."

She laughed again slightly. "Yeah, we've both been dumped."

"My friend Craig—you met him, the keep at the bar—he says that getting dumped only means you're better than the other person."

"Typical male rationalization. No offense, but men have a tendency to change the truth to suit them."

Her quickness to dispute him was admirable. *Is that what I've done?* he wondered. *Made my own truth?* "Women rationalize too, you know."

"No, we don't," she said. "We *adapt*."

He looked at her more closely, and at this entire situation. He was naked beneath the sheets, and here sitting on his bed, was a girl he'd met yesterday. Her big T-shirt made a relief of her own nakedness. Her body looked plush, soft. He wondered what it would feel like to just lie down with her and hold her. The idea of sex with her was too alien. Images of Veronica would come back. Jack wasn't the purest person in the world, but he hoped he was honest enough not to *use* someone for the sake of a dead fantasy. He liked Faye Rowland. She was truthful and straightforward. She was a survivor.

The complete inappropriateness of this was what made it appropriate. He wasn't even surprised. She stood up and turned off the light. In the darkness he saw her skim off the nightshirt. He held the sheet up for her, and she got in. He put his arm around her.

"It's been a long time for me," she said.

"Me too."

Her hair smelled faintly of soap. She lay right up next to him. "We can if you want to," she said. "But—"

"Let's just sleep. I think that would be better."

"Yeah, we'll just sleep. It's nice, you know, to just sleep with someone."

"Yes, it is."

"I like you."

"I like you too."

"I guess I just—"

"Shh," he whispered. "I know."

She lay her head on his chest, her breasts pressing. Her body felt so warm; the gentle heat lulled him. "Thank you," she said.

"For what?"

She was asleep. Jack drifted off a minute later, caressed by the softness of her body and her heat.

Their dreams would be better this time around.

CHAPTER 14

The mirror was a wall, proffering a thousand reflections of himself and things greater than himself.

The mirror was more than a wall. It was more than a mirror.

The mirror was the future and the past. It was the whisperer of insuperable truths and the face of all man's lies. It was uteri and bones, incubators and coffins, semen and grave dirt. The mirror was the open arms of history, and he, its son, gazed back in wait of its hallowed embrace.

Again, he thought. *Again.*

The mirror opened. He stepped into black, descending.

He held a candle in one hand, and a black silk bag in the other. In moments, the narrow steps emptied into the nave.

He moved slowly, lighting each candle with his own. Soon the nave came alive in flickering light. There were one hundred candles in all.

Below, the floor bore the sign: the starred trine. He mused a moment, and thought of the beauty that awaited the faithful. *Father of the Earth,* he thought. *Carry me away.*

Suddenly the man was very tired. Wisdom had a price. So did the truth of real spirit. He was a strong man made stronger by the truths that the world had buried eons ago.

He approached the chancel and bowed.

Black candles stood on either side of the altar. Their tiny flames looked back like the Father's eyes. *So close,* he thought. He was nearly sobbing. The distance between two worlds reduced to a kiss. He felt joyously light, buoyant.

He picked up the *jarra,* a stone cup. *My love,* he thought obscurely. *I give thee my love.* Then he opened the silk bag.

He removed the dolch.

It gleamed in the dancing light: long, sharp. Beautiful.

Father of the Earth, we do as you have bidden. We give you flesh through blood, we give you body through spirit.

He raised the dolch as if in offering.

Flesh through blood, body through spirit.

He closed his eyes. Tears streamed down his cheeks.

Walk with us, O Father of the Earth. We beseech thee.

He placed the dolch upon the altar.

To thee I bid my faith forever.

He stepped back. He opened his eyes.

Baalzephon, hail! he, Erim Khoronos, thought.

"Aorista!" he whispered aloud.

CHAPTER 15

"You should've heard yourself," Amy Vandersteen said.

And Ginny: "Yeah, we thought someone was murdering you."

The entire account made Veronica feel foolish. They were seated now at the big breakfast table by the pool deck. Last night Ginny and Amy had shaken her awake; she'd been screaming. Even now the nightmare lay like bilge in the bottom of her mind: Jack's corpse making love to her, ejaculating maggots into her sex. At once she felt pale, and pushed her breakfast away.

Ginny delved into her plate of cantaloupe, pineapple chunks, and cottage cheese. Amy Vandersteen picked at hers. "This stuff tastes awful," she remarked of her carrot juice. Veronica agreed.

"But you know," Ginny commented, "we've only been here a few days, and I feel a thousand times more creative. Don't you?"

"Not really," Veronica said.

"I'm always creative," Amy Vandersteen asserted.

Ginny ignored her. "It's the environment, I think. Good food, clean air, serenity. It purifies the soul."

"Where were you all day yesterday?" Veronica asked.

"That's what I mean. Creativity. I was just making some notes for my story, but all of a sudden I felt—I don't know—elevated, I guess. I just started writing. Next thing I know it's midnight. I'd wound up writing the entire first draft."

"I did some sketches," Veronica said lamely. Two nights in a row she'd dreamed of the fire-figure, and she was determined to paint the mood it evoked, the emotion that the figure courted. Passion—pure, unadulterated. It was this same figure of flame, in fact, that had saved her from the nightmare of Jack. She hadn't been able to tell Ginny and Amy that those final screams, just as the figure had touched her, were not screams of horror but of ecstasy. She felt driven now, as an artist, to translate that ecstasy onto the canvas. But how?

The Ecstasy of the Flames, she thought. The project enthralled her. So why couldn't she get started?

She decided she'd talk to Khoronos about it.

"I'm not hungry," Amy Vandersteen complained. Abruptly she stood and slipped out of her terry robe. The white bikini against her white flesh made her look nude. Immediately she dove into the pool. The tiny splash swallowed her.

"Asshole," Ginny muttered.

"Last night she was freebasing coke," Veronica recalled.

"I did it a few times several years ago until a med student I was balling showed me all these research articles on it. Long-term use deregulates your sex drive, sometimes permanently. If there's one thing I can't live without, it's my sex drive."

"She said Khoronos doesn't own the house; it's some friend's of his. Oh, and she said he's from Yugoslavia."

Ginny grinned. "I wonder if he's hung."

"I'm *serious.* Isn't this whole thing a little funny to you?"

"Funny like how?"

"I don't know. He invites us to this *retreat,* but we barely ever see him. Yesterday he and his two sidekicks were out on 'business.' They didn't get back till past midnight. *Business,* till *midnight*? Don't you think that's strange?"

"No. He's an eccentric."

"And where does he sleep?" Veronica kept on. "I only counted five bedrooms. Me, you, Amy, Marzen, and Gilles."

"Oooo, what intrigue," Ginny mocked. "Five bedrooms, six people. I could write a best-seller. Hasn't it occurred to you that this is a very big house and that there are probably other bedrooms in it? Or do you suppose Khoronos sleeps in a coffin?"

"Shut up, Ginny," Veronica suggested.

"You're just frustrated 'cause you're not getting any work done. It happens to me all the time. I'll get a block and my mind wanders. But the best way to cure a creative block is to work your way out of it. Forget about things that don't matter. Forget about the bedrooms, for God's sake. Just get to work."

Veronica didn't know whether to be mad or concessive. Ginny was probably right.

"And now that I've said that," Ginny added, wiping her mouth with a napkin, "I must get back to my typewriter."

"How are things going with you and Gilles?"

Ginny shrugged. "I haven't seen him. And that's good, because I'm too busy with my work right now."

"Too busy?" Now Veronica could've laughed. "Yesterday you said you might be in love with the guy. Today you're too busy?"

"Art is the ultimate conceit, Vern. When people become more important to you than what you create, you're a phony."

Veronica glared.

"Later, kid," Ginny said, and walked away.

The impression left her steaming. More guilt? More jealousy? Ginny was in control of her creative life. Veronica, suddenly, was not. *Why?* she questioned herself. Was it true that selfishness was prerequisite to true art?

"Hey, Amy," she abruptly called out. "Can I ask you something?"

Amy Vandersteen's wet, white head bobbed in the water. She swam enfeebled, dog-paddling. That's what she looked like just then, a skinny wet dog in the water. "Sure, sweetheart."

"Is selfishness prerequisite to true art?"

Amy stood up in the low end. Her wet bikini top clung to her small breasts like tissue, showing dark, puckered nipples. "Honey, let me tell you something. True art *is* selfishness."

"That's the most egotistical shit I've ever heard," Veronica countered.

"Of course it is." Amy Vandersteen grinned like a cat, hip-deep in the water. "And that's my point. You're either a real artist with real creative focus, or you're a fake."

Veronica's fuddled stare fought to stray but couldn't. Her eyes stayed fixed on the slim, sneering figure in the water.

"Which are you, Veronica? Real or fake?"

Veronica stomped off. The worst question of all followed her like a buzzard: Was she more infuriated with Amy Vandersteen or herself? Behind her, the snide woman began to clutzily backstroke across the pool, laughing.

Passion, the word popped oddly into Veronica's head. *The heart.* Khoronos' words. *Real creativity is rooted in the heart.*

She jogged back to the house, to look for Khoronos.

The alarm clock clattered in Jack's head. He turned, groped about the covers. Faye was gone, but her scent lingered on the pillow.

He got up, showered, and dressed, amazed as well as baffled that he had no hangover. Hangovers had gotten to be something he could count on—not having one nearly made him feel estranged. And now that he thought of it, he hadn't had a drink in over a day.

Downstairs, he chugged orange juice, grimacing. A fruit magnet pinned a note to the fridge door. *Gone to LOC, call you later at your office. Faye.* Short and sweet. He wondered how she felt about things now. *I slept with her last night,* he fully realized. They'd kept their promise, they'd just slept. Did she regret it now, post fact? Jack hoped not. It had been nice sleeping with her, it had been soothing and unstrained and very nice. He'd wakened several times to find themselves entwined in one another. She'd murmured things in her sleep, nuzzling him.

He drove the unmarked to the station, whelmed in thought. Yes, he liked Faye Rowland a lot, and he was attracted to her. Yet the idea of sex with her almost terrified him. He thought of the proverbial bull in the china shop; having sex with Faye would shatter whatever strange bond existed between them. Jack liked that bond.

Besides, sex would remind him of Veronica.

The substation's clean, tiled floors led him to his unclean, cluttered office. But before he could enter, the black mammoth bulk of Deputy Police Commissioner Larrel Olsher rounded the corner. "How you coming on the Triangle case, Jack?"

"Making some progress," Jack said.

"Well, make *more* progress. You ever heard that shit runs downhill?"

"The axiom rings a bell, Larrel."

"Let me just say that the people upstairs eat *a lot.* Pretty soon I'm gonna have to carry an umbrella, if you catch my drift."

"Noted," Jack said.

"How's the state researcher working out?"

"Good. She's only been on it a day and she's already digging up a lot of stuff. She's trying to get a line on the ritual."

Olsher's eyes thinned in the frame of the great black face. "How come you don't look hung over?"

"Because I'm not."

"Keep it that way, Jack. And get a haircut."

"Which one?"

"That joke's older than my grandmother."

"Yeah, but it's not as close to retirement as you. Har-har."

"You look like something that walked out of Woodstock."

"My hair is my strength, Larrel. You know, like Samson."

"Samson doesn't work for this department, and if you don't bust the Triangle case, you won't have to worry about hair regulations anymore. If you catch my drift."

"Noted," Jack repeated. *Who tinkled in his cornflakes?* he wondered.

Olsher began to thump off. "Oh, and you have a visitor."

Jack went into his office. Dr. Karla Panzram sat primly before his desk, her nose crinkled above a Styrofoam cup. "I helped myself to your coffee," she said. "It's terrible."

"Bad coffee fortifies the soul." Jack poured himself a cup. "I'm living proof, right?"

Karla Panzram offered the most indecipherable of smiles. "I just stopped by to tell you I finished checking the recent psych releases and background profiles. Nothing."

"I figured as much," Jack said, and sat down.

"I'm getting some feedback from some of the out-of-state wards and lockups, too. But don't get your hopes up."

"I *never* get my hopes up, Doctor. It's always the outer angles that let us into a case like this. But at least we know more about our man, thanks to you and TSD, and we're getting closer to the ritual element. Knock on wood."

"That's Druidic."

"What?"

"Knocking on wood. The Druids believed that knocking on wood appeased the gods and brought luck to the faithful."

"I better start carrying a two-by-four around. No wonder things haven't been going well."

Karla Panzram crossed her legs. "How are the *other things* going?"

Jack wanted to frown. "What do you mean?"

"I think you know. You've been in the office several minutes already and you haven't even lit a cigarette."

"Thanks for reminding me," Jack said, and lit a cigarette. "But believe it or not, I haven't had a drink in over a day."

"Good. You've decided to quit?"

"No. I've just been too busy to drink. Besides, my liver is like the Rock of Gibraltar."

"Oh? A healthy male liver weighs three pounds. The average alcoholic's liver weighs fifteen. Alcohol clogs the hepatic veins with cholesterol; the liver distends from overwork."

"I'll keep that in mind when I order my next Fiddich." Jack snorted smoke. He didn't like the idea of having a fifteen-pound liver. "Did you come here just to tell me about livers?"

"No. I have an additional speculation about Charlie. It didn't occur to me until last night."

"I'm ready," Jack said.

"Charlie probably has a magnificent physique. We know he's attractive in a general sense; Shanna Barrington was an attractive woman. But I also suspect he's obsessed with his own physique."

"What makes you think so?"

"Charlie's obsessed with female beauty. Seeing is as important to him as doing. This is a commonplace trait for sex killers on a fantasy borderline. It's called *bellamania* or *beau-idée-fixe*. He's seeking an *ideal* of female beauty in his victims. Therefore, he must be beautiful himself or else he won't be worthy to offer—and to sacrifice—his *victim's* beauty to whatever structural basis his ritual exists in. Physical beauty is what propels him. His victim's and his own."

Jack stubbed his butt. "Sounds pretty complicated."

"Actually it's not. Like I said, it's a commonplace trait. It's something to consider, at least."

Magnificent physique, Jack pondered. *At least no one will be accusing* me *of the murders*.

The phone shrilled, like a sudden alarm.

"Cordesman. City District Homicide," Jack answered. But he felt sinking even before the voice replied.

"Jack?" It was Randy. The pause told Jack everything, its emptiness fielding a root of dread. *Aw, Jesus, Jesus . . .*

"We've got another one," Randy said.

Jack scribbled down the address. "I'll be there in ten," he said. He hung up. All he could see for a moment was red.

"Come on," he said to Karla Panzram.

"I know," Khoronos claimed. "I heard you screaming too."

But how could he have? Veronica knew he hadn't been in the house when she had her nightmare. He *couldn't* have heard.

"But it's something else that's bothering you," he observed.

She'd come in after leaving Amy at the pool. Instead of finding Khoronos, he'd found her in the library. She hadn't asked where he'd been all night, though her curiosity still itched. "You look . . . discomposed," he'd said almost immediately. "You look separated from yourself. Why?"

The living room was quiet, dark. Khoronos' presence made her feel sequestered. "I can't work," she said.

"Before you can be one with your art, you must become one with yourself."

Why did he always suggest her spiritual self was not intact? It seemed like a distant insult. "Tell me what to do," she said half sarcastically. "You have all the answers."

"The answers are within yourself, Ms. Polk, but to reveal them you must realize the full weight of the questions. You haven't done that, you *never* do. You have profound convictions about your art, but you haven't applied that same profundity to yourself. This, I believe, is your greatest failure."

She felt like shouting at him, or giving him the finger. Who the hell was he to imply her failures?

"Your sense of creation runs deep, so why does your sense of self remain so impoverished? Synergy, Ms. Polk, must exist between the two. What you create comes from you, yet if you don't know yourself, how can you expect to create anything of worth?"

Veronica couldn't decide if that made sense.

Then he said: "What are you running from?"

She sat back in the couch and frowned.

"Synergy is balance," he continued. "It's equanimity between what we are and what we create. Do you understand that?"

"No," she said.

"All right. Creation is born of desire. Do you agree?"

She shrugged. "I guess."

"To know ourselves as artists, we must know our desires first. Any desire, even potential ones. Desire is the ultimate stimulus of what we are creatively, and the authenticity of the impetus can only dawn on us through an unyielding love of ourselves."

Veronica contemplated this, then thought of what Amy Vandersteen and Ginny had said at the pool. They were all saying the same things. Suddenly Veronica felt like the child among them.

"But the root." Khoronos lifted a finger. "We must now reveal the root of the impediment."

"Fine," she muttered. She felt stupid, inept.

"Tell me about the nightmare you had."

Her face blanked. At once the images lurched back, and when she squeezed her eyes shut the nightmare only came more precisely into focus. She saw it all again, razor-sharp, searing imagery.

"Tell me everything," Khoronos said.

She spoke in the darkest monotone. The voice she heard didn't even sound like her own; it was someone else's, some dark confessor removed from her. The voice recounted everything, every detail of the dream, like sludge pouring out of her mind into the blackest fosse. The confession—and that's what it was, really—seemed to gnaw the flesh off hours.

At the monologue's end, Khoronos smiled, or seemed to. "Dreams are the mirrors of our souls. They tell us what we don't realize about ourselves, and often what we *don't want* to realize. Dreams make us confront what we refuse to confront." His eyes assayed her. "You feel guilty. That's what's obstructing your work. That's what you're running from. Guilt."

"Bullshit," Veronica replied.

"You don't know what to do," he professed. "So your dream has told you. Your dream has shown you the answer."

"The dream hasn't shown me anything," she dissented. Her temper seemed to pulse, testing itself.

"The dream is the answer, Veronica. The figure of Jack isn't really Jack; it's a symbol of the love of your past, a death symbol."

"Meaning my past is dead," she stated rather than asked, to emphasize her sarcasm.

"Exactly," he said.

Veronica smirked.

"But you don't want to confront that. It makes you feel guilty, because when you ended your relationship with him, you hurt him. Society teaches us not to hurt people. When we hurt people we produce a negative reflection of ourselves. You feel that selfishness is what compelled you to break up with Jack. Am I right or wrong?"

Veronica gulped. "You're right."

"You've been taught that selfishness is bad. You ended your relationship because of selfishness. Therefore, you are bad. That is your conscious conception of the entire ordeal."

"All right, maybe it is!" She now succeeded in raising her voice. "Maybe I am bad! Maybe I'm nothing but a selfish bitch who shits all over people! So what?"

Khoronos sat back and smiled. "Now we're getting somewhere."

But Veronica wouldn't hear of it. She stood up quickly, pointed her finger like a gun. "I know what you're going to tell me, goddamn it! You're going to tell me some egotistical garbage like the true artist must be selfish in order to produce true art! You're going to tell me that art is the pinnacle of culture and the only way to achieve it is to completely disregard other people, and it's okay to disregard other people because art is more important!"

Total silence distended the wake of her outburst. She trembled before him, heat reddening her face.

"It's not my intention to tell you any such thing," he responded. He seemed lackadaisical, even amused. "Sit back down, Ms. Polk. Collect yourself, and we can go on."

Veronica retook her opposing seat. Her heart slowed back down.

"What we're really talking about here, Ms. Polk, is conception and misconception. Art is the ultimate proof of mankind's superiority, not politics, not feeding the poor and disarming the world of its nuclear weapons. Those are but mechanics. The sum of the parts of all mankind, all that we have risen to since we crafted the first wheel, is what we create to symbolize what we are."

"What's that got to do with conception?" Veronica objected.

"Everything," he said. "What you conceive of as selfishness isn't selfishness at all. It's truth."

"*Truth?*" she queried.

"You ended your relationship with Jack in pursuit of your inner sense of truth. You only think it was selfishness because you don't fully understand yourself. It's truth, Ms. Polk, not selfishness."

She felt exhausted now, as her mind strayed over his epigrams. She felt like something taken apart in error and reassembled.

"You did exactly what you had to do to preserve the most vital aspect of truth. You destroyed something that was false. That is what your dream was trying to tell you."

Veronica gazed at him, damped.

"When the figure of flame entered your dream," Khoronos went on, "you felt at first afraid. When it touched you, you screamed, yet you admit that those screams were screams of ecstasy. I'll even dare to say that upon the fire-figure's touch, you climaxed. Am I right or wrong?"

"You're right," she admitted, and this admission came with no reluctance. The fire-lover's presence had drenched her in sexual anticipation, both times she'd dreamed of it. And when it touched her, she came.

"So what have we revealed?" he asked. "That you're not selfish but devoted to truth. And in the dream, Jack existed as a symbol of your past." Khoronos rose from his seat. "The figure of flame is the symbol of your future."

She felt enlightened now, yet enmeshed with confusion. Suddenly she wanted to plead with him, this doctrinaire, this pundit who had dug into the tumult of her psyche and shown her the most promising image of herself. She groped, speechless, helpless.

"Your future begs your final awakening, Ms. Polk. It begs you to reembark upon your quest and become what you were put on earth to be. It begs you to discover yourself as completely as you can be discovered."

"But *how*?" she pleaded, looking up at him. "I don't know what to do!"

"As I've said, and as you have agreed, creation is born of desire. And what is desire in the uttermost sense?"

"What?" she begged.

"Passion," came the flat, granite answer.

"Passion for *what*?"

"Passion for everything." Khoronos began to walk away, shrinking silently within the room's enfeebled light. "Delve into your passion, Ms. Polk, and you will discover at last what you really are."

CHAPTER 16

"Same M.O., same guy," Randy said. "Front door locked, nothing ripped off, no signs of struggle. He went out the back."

Jack walked into the living room. TSD was all over the place, stolid automatons dusting door frames and snapping common areas. Gorgeous morning sunlight poured in through fleckless windows, a mocking affront. Places like this should be dark, sullen, as any place of the dead.

"What's her—"

"Rebecca Black, thirty-one," Randy answered. His face told all, a mask cracked by terrible witness. "Paralegal for one of the big firms on the Circle. Good work record, no rap sheet, no trouble. Pest control was doing the complex this morning. They came in with the passkey from condo maintenance and found her."

Jack's gaze imagined the killer's trek, bedroom hall, across the living room, to the slider. "Any TOD?" he asked.

"Beck's here now. Oh, and the victim's divorced. We're gonna—"

"It ain't the husband," Jack stated. "We know that." He made no further inquiries, heading for the bedroom. Karla Panzram followed him in silence.

"You'll have to bootie up, sir," a young, brawny uniform told him at the door. "Hair and Fiber's still working." Jack nodded. The cop doled them Sirchie plastic foot bags—"booties," they were called—and two hairnets. Jan Beck did not want her crime scene contaminated by irrelevant hairs and clothing fibers or shoe debris. Jack and Karla put on their booties. *If only Dad could see me now,* Jack considered, stuffing his long hair into his net.

Karla Panzram was smiling. "Do hairnets make you feel emasculated, Captain Cordesman?"

"Shut up, Doctor," Jack replied."As long as they don't make me wear panties, I'll be fine."

What they stepped into then was not a bedroom. Bedrooms were where people slept, dreamed, made love, got dressed in the morning and undressed at night—bedrooms were where people *lived*. They walked, instead, into a charnel house. Jack's vision swam in red; he needed to look at nothing in particular to see it. It was simply there—the *red*—enveiled and hovering. The red figure lay within red walls, red wrists and ankles lashed to the red bed.

Karla Panzram said nothing, made no reaction, and Jan Beck, too, tended to her grisly business denuded of emotion. The spindly woman jotted down ITDs—incremental temperature drop—every five seconds at the sound of a beep, reading digital figures off a Putfor Mark II contact thermometer which had been adhered just below Rebecca Black's smudged throat. The device, zeroed at a mean of 98.6, gauged how quickly the epidermal temperature decayed.

"Hello, sir," Jan Beck said without looking up. She wore red polyester utilities, foot bags, acetate gloves, and a hairnet. So did the two techs who roamed the floor on hands and knees with illuminated CRP magnifiers. Polyester was less inclined to drop fibers, but on occasions when that happened the bright red material was easily spotted and rejected as fiberfall. "Feel free to look around," Jan Beck invited. "But please do not approach the contact perimeter."

Jack was staring at the back wall. "I need TOD, Jan."

"Give me a sec." She punched a thirty-second drop-reading into an integrated field thermometer/barometer made by the same company. The figures were accurate to within 1/100 of a degree. Then she said, "Ballpark, between twelve-thirty and two-thirty A.M. I'll have a better number for you once I get her into the shop."

Jack nodded, thinking of the tedious protocol that awaited. Canvass the complex. Check taxi logs and newspaper vehicles. Interview every neighbor. The same thing all over again.

Lampblack and anthracene smudged the door frame, drawer lips, dresser tops, even the toilet seat. The sink drain in the bathroom had been removed; so had the toilet and sink and bathtub handles. The toilet roll and tissue box lay in evidence bags, awaiting iodine fuming. Everything in the wastebasket had also been bagged. Essentially, TSD had dusted, bagged, fumed, or removed all the sundries of this woman's life. Soon the woman herself would be in a bag.

Jack lowered his gaze and looked at what lay on the bed.

Who knew what she'd looked like in life? In death, she was a red mannequin, tied up, gutted. Her belly had been riven, organs teased out and arranged about her on the mattress. Duct tape covered her eyes, sealed her mouth. Again the scarlet ghosts of the killer's affections remained: lip prints about her throat, fingermarks about her breasts. Blood had been smoothed adoringly over the inner thighs and down the sleek legs. There were even lip prints on her hands and feet, under her arms, along her sides—myriad red smudges. Rebecca Black had been dressed in kisses of blood.

A massive wet spot darkened the red-stained sheet between her legs. Jack thought of a great fleeing spirit.

Then Karla Panzram muttered: "Oh, no."

Jack turned. It was just like Shanna Barrington. Odd prismoid configurations muraled the walls in hand with jagged red glyphs. The three-starred triangle had been drawn above the headboard.

Above it were the words HERE IS MY LOVE.

And below it: AORISTA!

There was something else, on the opposite wall:

PATER TERRAE, PER ME TERRAM AMBULA!

But Karla Panzram was squinting at the red glyphs, moving from one to the other, scrutinizing them.

"What?" Jack asked.

The psychiatrist's voice echoed flatly in the cramped room. "This is a different killer," she said.

"Bullshit!" Jack yelled.

"Look at the juncture angles, and the stress marks in the strokes. You can see the delineations where the blood dried."

"So what!" Jack yelled.

"The person who did Shanna Barrington was left-handed," Karla Panzram said. "The guy who did this is right-handed. There's no doubt whatsoever. You've got two killers executing the same M.O."

◆ ◆ ◆

The book, entitled *Ordinall of Demonocracy*, bore a printing date of 1830, published privately in London by a supposed mystic named, oddly, Priest. Faye Rowland scanned half the tome before she found:

> fornication in the name of Lucifer, Black Mass, and human sacrifice. Sacrifice in particular was thought not only to appease the higher demons but also spiritually and physically fortify the activists themselves. Most offensive of such blasphemous activism were the Cotari and the Aorists.

Faye had prowled the lower levels with her stack permit and stumbled upon several more obscure tomes. Many titles in the listing weren't there, and some that weren't in the listings surprised her. Next she checked a reasonable translation called *Dictionnaire de Dieu,* by someone named Christoff Villars. The pub date was 1792, yet the translation date was 1950. She looked up *aorist* and found nothing. Then she looked up *cotari:*

> COTARIUS: A nomenclatic title referring to the covenhead or sect leaders of any particular anti-Christian faction. The cotarius was the denominational clergy of Satan's worshipers. Its most powerful members were supposedly blessed by the demons themselves.

Hmm, Faye thought. It would not be topics that would lead her toward specifics, but words, terms. What she'd found out yesterday about the aorist sects was all general. She needed exactitudes. Next she opened the *Annotative Supplement to the Morakis References*. These were a series of texts on all manner of the occult, and though the source was untraceable—no one, for instance, knew who Morakis was or when he lived—the information had been deftly translated and was surprisingly well maintained. Faye wanted the other volumes of the regimen but so far she'd only found this supplement. She looked up *cults* and found:

> CULTUS OF LUCIFER: Religious sectarianism, diabolism, and organized counter-Christian worship revolving around

the devil or devils. Such activities predate modern records; little specific is known of their origins. All religions since earliest times have had their counter-religions. Satanism was the peasant's religion, a reaction to the oppression of the Roman Catholic Church. Regrettably, most literary viewpoints up until the last century are clearly Catholic viewpoints and, hence, misleading as to true sociological objective. We do know, however, that the furthest extremities of such satanic culti—known as *aorism*—

Paydirt, Faye thought.

—proved a formidable revolutionary foe to Christian thesis in the Middle Ages; the aoristae burned churches, murdered priests, sacrificed children, etc., without reservation, under the acceptance that the worst atrocities they could commit against God would better commend their favor in the eyes of Satan. Aorist activity rose to epidemic proportions in the fourteenth century, particularly in France and the Balkan provinces. Aoristae frequently operated covertly, planting "spies" among the apprentice clergy, who would secretly defile consecrates before Mass. Holy vessels were purloined at night for demonic rituals and replaced by morning, especially chalices and fonts. Raiments, likewise, were secreted out of the church and worn by high sect members during orgiastic rites, and hung back up for the priest for the next day's services. One such agent, posing as a verger in Mauléon-Soule, confessed to performing acts of bestiality in the nave at night, reciting satanic incantations before the Cross, raping and strangling prostitutes upon the altar, and sacrificing children to a demon called Alocer. He was said to have taken a particular pride in impurifying consecrates with semen and replacing blessed Mass candles with candles made of baby fat.

Faye rubbed her eyes. This was not what she would call light reading.

Demonic aorism demonstrated an impressive organizational structure. Each sect was governed by a prelate or mastrum, one said of formidable psychic and magical powers. Several apostates operated under the prelate, and from there the rank structure descended to various grades of underlings who carried out insurgent duties. Prelates were thought to be immortal through reincarnation, and purified by each life, while lower members were promised favorable positions in Satan's eternal congregation. Church desecration often served as initiation for new members; as vassals rose in status, assignations rose in extremity: the abduction of children for sacrifice [usually young girls from prominent religious families], the murder of priests and clergy members [priests were routinely sodomized or forced to have sex with sect odalisques before execution], and innumerable other grievous sacrilegious activity—archival documentation proves quite exhaustive and grueling. Poisoning was another activity of choice; aorist "operatives" frequently contaminated consecrants with toxins, sickening and sometimes killing whole congregations during Mass. Catholic records, in fact, indicate a surprisingly intricate use of toxins and narcotics by aorist sects. Pharmacological knowledge during these times was scant; however, one sect vassal apprehended by the Holy Inquisition near Florence told his confessors that prelates possessed "the divine wisdoms of the Lords of the Earth," and that a demon named Deittueze "gifted mastri [prelates] with sacred knowledge of holy elixirs which blind, kill, corrupt the body, arouse the chaste, or cause to become mad." Deittueze bears a striking resemblance to an Assyrian demon called Deitzu, the malformed half-son of Ea [the god of the underworld]. Deitzu was a despoiler, an incarnate, and himself "Lord of Amasha," or cultivator of the flowers of Hell. [See NARCOTICS, RITUAL USE OF]

Aorism, like Babylonian mythology, presents an interesting demographics of worship. Sects worshiped an assemblage of patron anti-saints or lesser demons, and it is through such demons that the aoristae engaged in their most active oblation. In 1390, aoristic activity became so rampant that the Congregation of the Holy Office began to plant its own spies. These attempts failed miserably and with embarrassing promptitude, though a handful of successful infiltrations did help to corroborate the records. One interesting account from the Archives of the Holy Office tells of a young deacon named Michael Bari, who was sent to imposture himself within a sect operating out of Vasr, a large township in what is now western Hungary. Though questionably translated and obviously recounted from a strong Church viewpoint, Bari's narrative tells of a shocking scene indeed. "The Praeta [prelate] dressed in cope, cassock, and mitre, stood before the Holy Altar, bloody handed in mock profference. Beside him stood two surrogoti [probably higher ranking vassals], naked, betranced, and aroused. Upon the floor they had fashioned their most damnable emblem, the trine, formed of the ground bones of priests, and severed hands of abbots served as the emblem's stars. They drank gustily of the cup—the Holy Chalice!—which they'd filled with the blood of a prostitute, and then of the paten consumed collops of her sullied privates. The blasphemous communion had then been passed to the rest of their evil congregants, the Praeta incanting divinations in the guttering light, of which I had been blessedly spared for I with a few others bore aside their luciferic black candles, reciting to myself the Prayer of Our Lord . . . To the Altar, a girl of her teens had been fettered, stripped of all garb, and she lay not in horror but in arousal forced into her blood by their demonian elixirs. Then the detestable Praeta intoned words I'd unthus heard—the Devil's tongue—erecting his red hands. The navis grew hot though it was a chill night, and the air thickened as fevered blood. Then, and most horribly, one surrogot mounted the bliss-shrieking odalisque [one who is abducted for sexual purposes] of which he immediately penetrated her privates right upon the Altar, and the other surrogot fornicated unto her mouth. Here the black congregation, so too entranced by their noxious rootmash [an aphrodisiac, probably a cantharidin extract], began to partake of each other in all manner of indecorousness, laving upon each and other's privates, and fornicating all manner of orifice, as they called out the name of their most vile Baalzephon. For much time mine eyes remained upon this carnal fête of flesh and profanation; these blasphemers, through the abuse of their bodies and the utterance of the most iniquitous words, rejoiced in the ultimate offense against our Lord—the most unspeakable acts. The vision shall never leave my memory! But later the festivities abated, the offenders exhausted in their Devil's bliss. Many of the women rose naked in the sordid light, some with bosoms bloodied having offered the men to drink, and men crawling off those ignoble companions now too ravaged by sin to rise of their own. I looked again upon the Altar. The drugged odalisque had been taken down and lain within the trine. Now the votaries stood in full attention and silence as the Preata faced them, whispering further abyssal praise to their horrible master. The words, though I did not know them, seemed to arrogate some physical form that I cannot metaphor, and, as the thickened black words emanated from his lips, the two surrogoti . . . changed. They'd become something more or less than men—hideous misshaped things that could be born only of Hell's most tenebrous chasms, and released guttural moans from their gnarled and hirsute throats sounds not of men or of anything of the earth. The battered odalisque lay still beneath the monstrous things, the joy of Satan on her dying face. Much blood pulsed awfully from betwixt her splayed legs, and then the first surrogot knelt, its chest like hillocks and its member stout and large as a man's forearm, and it raised the black dolch up and plunged it down into the young girl's belly. "Hail, Father!" proclamated the Praeta, and came the response of the nefarious congregation: "Baalzephon, hail!" thus repeated in cadence as the surrogoti completed their evil work. They tore out the girl's innards and held them ahigh, they beslickened their bodies with her blood, and about their thick necks and members looped her entrails in monstrous glee as the Praeta raised his hands above and exclaimed: "Aorista, Father! Aorista!" Sickened in body and poisoned of mind, I blinked, and in the passing of that blink, the girl had vanished. Three nights later I fled their evil fold and escaped to the Rectory of Maijvo in the west.

"Aorista," Faye muttered, and pushed the book away. *A ritual that does not end.* The young deacon's account made her eyes hurt, despite its obvious overstatement. It depressed her, though; much of it was probably true. She thought about the convolutions of madness and realized that it was all the same through the ages, then and now, a rite of changing masks over the same face.

She looked up Prelate in the same text:

PRELATE [also prelatus, or mastrum]: The liturgical leaders of activistic sects, predominant among the aorists. Prelates were thought to be reincarnatible, psychic, and wise. They were also inexplicably wealthy, supposedly financing their aorist activities through treasure granted via Satan or apostate demons. One prelate, apprehended near Paris in 1399, confessed to inquisitors: "He bestows treasure upon the faithful." *He*, in this case, was not Satan but a demon called Gaziel, a lower demon said to preside over underground treasure, namely gold. Soldiers of the Holy Office found a fortune in gold and currency buried in the prelate's château. Additionally, prelates were said to be clairvoyant, and possessed the ability to trance-channel at will.

Next, Faye looked up *Baalzephon:*

BAALZEPHON: A demon of higher orders. He reigns over fertility, passion, and creativity. European sects, between the eleventh and fifteenth centuries, according to the Church registry, knew Baalzephon as the "Father of the Earth," or "He who stands closest to the earth," and is said, due to this proximity, to encourage his worshipers to incarnation rites. Baalzephon's appearance is not known. His sign is the triad, or trine, of black stars.

Lame, Faye thought. She needed *details*. This grim stuff was actually starting to get interesting. Next she looked up the name in a much older text translated from French, called *Demonomanie Pharmacopae*. It read, simply:

BAALZEPHON: An incubus.

CHAPTER 17

Faye nearly gasped when she stepped into Jack's office at 9 P.M.; he looked wrung out, and his looks did not improve when she explained what her day's research had divulged. His own disclosures of the latest murder did not surprise her. She knew quite a bit now about the protocol of the aorist sects. Earlier, TSD had verified Karla Panzram's graphological conclusions; the latents from the Barrington murder were different from the Black murder, which meant that two killers were executing the same modi. Faye easily translated the Latin left on the wall: *Pater terrae, per me terram ambula* meant "Father of the Earth, walk the earth through me."

"It's a specific reference to the demon they're worshiping," she told him now. "His name is—"

"Baalzephon," he muttered when he spotted the name highlighted several times in the material she'd photocopied.

"An incubus," she added.

"What the hell is an incubus?"

"A male sex-spirit or incarnate. It comes from the Latin *incubare,* which means to lie down upon, or to lie with. Incubi were said to have sexual relations with sleeping women, supposedly using sexual pleasure to incline a woman away from Christianity toward evil. Satanic incarnation was a chief belief among aorist covens for about five hundred years. Sufficient supplication and ritual homage was thought to bring the devils closer to the earth. Sacrifice was considered the best way to achieve a complete incarnation, the full bringing of a devil into the coven's midst, which they called *onmiddan.* Think of it as an objectification of a spiritual realm, the putting of flesh upon spirit. That's what *incarnate* means in Latin. To make flesh."

"In other words these psychos thought that cutting people up on altars would bring real devils into their presence?"

"For a time, yes, but not necessarily on altars. The aorists' rituals were *occulic,* which means interstitial. In fact, the impresa for Baalzephon—the triad of black stars—was thought to be an actual occulus."

"You're losing me, Faye," Jack complained.

"An occulus—a doorway. The impresa was—"

"What's an impresa!" Jack half shouted.

Faye half smiled. "The emblem, the triangle that the killers left on the walls. It was supposed to be a gap between the domain of the demons and the real world. The deacon's story indicates this pretty clearly; not only did the two surrogates become incarnations of incubi, but the girl, after she was sacrificed, *disappeared* through the impresa on the church floor."

"She went to hell, you mean."

"Yes, or I should say she was *given* to hell through the rite. She was given, in body and spirit, to the demon. To Baalzephon."

"And Baalzephon is the same demon that is being worshiped by the murderers of Shanna Barrington and Rebecca Black?"

"It seems so," Faye said. "The methodology of the ritual is the same, and the impresa is the same. Then there's the Latin on the wall. Pater Terrae—Father of the Earth. Baalzephon was known by many nicknames like this. Father of Passion, Father of Art, and Father of the Earth."

Jack slouched. "I don't know about you, Faye, but I could sure use a drink."

Jack drove them in his unmarked straight to the Undercroft. Faye could tell he'd had a bad day. He smoked three cigarettes on the way and said almost nothing.

Inside was a typical weeknight crowd. Jack and Faye pulled up stools as Craig poured from three taps at once behind the bar. "I want something with some kick," Faye said.

"I think that can be arranged," Jack remarked. "Craig, the young lady here would like something with some kick. We'll leave it to your professional discretion. As for me—"

"The usual," Craig finished. He poured Jack a Fiddich and got Faye a bottle of Tucher Maibock. "By the way," he said, "one of your least favorite people in the world was in earlier looking for you."

Jack opened his mouth but stalled. "Whoever it was, don't tell me. The way I feel right now I don't even want to hear about it." He held up his glass in the bar light. In a few moments it was empty.

"You drink too much," Faye said, "but I have a feeling you've heard that before."

"Once or twice. Alcohol brings out the best in me."

"I can see that." Coming here, Faye saw now, was a mistake. By consenting to come here she was allowing him to be fed upon by his problems. She knew that she liked this man, but right now she didn't like the part of him she was seeing. Yesterday she'd vaguely entertained the idea of getting involved with him, and last night, they'd slept together. Now, though . . . she didn't know. Jack's voraciousness for drink unsettled her. Did she really need the headache? Jack drank because he couldn't handle his problems, and if he couldn't handle them, then that wasn't her problem. *I've got my own problems,* she thought. *I can't worry about his.* And this presented another problem. She didn't know if that's how she really felt, or if that's how she thought she *was supposed* to feel.

"Ninety percent of all homicides are either domestics or drug-related," Jack said when his next drink was poured. "Those are easy. Why do I get all the winners?"

Now he was feeling sorry for himself, which Faye couldn't stand in a man. "Maybe it's because you're a good investigator."

Jack looked at her. "I doubt it. This case is sinking. Maybe the people upstairs know that, and they're letting me have it because they think I'll screw it up. Then they can get rid of me."

"Poor little you."

"Why are you so sarcastic tonight?"

"Self-pity brings out the best in me."

"Sarcasm is your best trait?"

"Keep talking like you're talking, and you'll find out."

Now Jack smiled genuinely for the first time tonight. "You're doing very good work."

"Please don't patronize me."

"I'm not. You're doing good work, but I need you to do *better* work. Now I want you to identify the *geographics* of the ritual."

"I don't think I can; it's too diffuse."

"Give it a try, though."

"Okay. What else?"

"You're the researcher, not me. I'm too busy with the mechanics of the case. You decide what research avenues would be the most productive, then give me what you've got."

No, he wasn't patronizing her at all, he was putting his faith in her, and she guessed she liked that. She liked the beer too; it was smooth and malty, and they weren't kidding when they said it had kick. She was beginning to feel a buzz already.

"Do you think any of it's true?" Jack pondered.

"What, the stuff the aorists did? Sure."

"No, I mean the supernatural stuff."

Faye squinted at his meaning. "Are you asking me if I believe that human beings became incarnate of devils, and that sacrifice victims were ritually transported out of the real world?"

"Yeah, I guess that's what I'm asking."

"Of course I don't believe it."

"But they believed it. There must've been a reason."

"Oh, there was a reason. They were peasants reacting to a *tremendous* oppression. Oppressed people become fanatical in their belief systems. All of history is a pretty good example."

"So the guy was lying?"

"Michael Bari, the deacon spy? No, he wasn't lying. He was living in the middle of a delusion he didn't understand, that's all. He was intimidated to believe by a simple but repetitive exposure to an antithetical force. The Catholic Church believed in demons; it still does. That's one part of Christian thesis that never changes: to believe in God, one must also believe in the devil. It's also pretty likely that Michael Bari was under the influence of narcotics; the aorists routinely used drugs to heighten their religious experiences. Bari could never have maintained his credibility as a sect member without taking part. I have no doubt that he *believed* he witnessed an incarnation. And as for the sacrifices, the rituals and desecrations—all that stuff was definitely true."

"It makes me think about how much mankind has progressed."

"Or hasn't progressed," Faye said.

"God, you're pessimistic."

"Am I really? Michael Bari's account of the aorist ritual is six hundred years old. You've got people practicing the exact same ritual, in this city, right now."

"I guess you got me on that one." Jack slugged back the rest of his Fiddich and flagged Craig for another. "That reminds me—what you were saying about drugs. My TSD chief found an herbal extract of some kind in the first victim's blood, but it's not in the books. Find out everything you can about drug use among the aorists. And find out more about . . . what's his name?"

"Baalzephon," Faye replied.

Even Craig winced when Jack put his empty up for a refill. He'd just downed two drinks like they were shooters. *Great,* Faye thought. She'd need a wheelbarrow to get him out of here. Again, she began to revert to the lack of compassion she always felt when she was disappointed.

"Haven't you had enough?" she suggested.

"There's never enough, and there's an old saying by a very famous person that I subscribe to wholeheartedly. 'If I don't drink it, someone else will.'"

"We got here less than a half hour ago and you're already ordering your *third drink*!"

"I like odd numbers," Jack said.

"Jack's favorite number, by the way, is thirteen," Craig joked.

But before Faye could further complain, Jack said, "Be right back," and excused himself for the obvious.

"He tries," Craig said when Jack went up the stairs.

"Tries? He's ruining himself."

"Why don't you give him a break? He's got some problems."

"Everybody's got problems, *Craig*. Getting drunk is the weakest way to deal with them."

"Well, *Faye,* you must care about him despite his weaknesses, otherwise you wouldn't be here."

"I work for him, that's all," Faye insisted.

"You sure that's all?"

Even if it wasn't, what business was it of his? "Are you trying to piss me off on purpose?"

Craig grinned, chewing on a bar straw. "Only for the sake of practicality. Offhand, I can't think of anyone who's perfect. Can you? I mean, besides yourself, of course."

Faye glared at him. She had a mind to slap him but didn't for fear that he would probably slap back a lot harder.

"He used to be famous, sort of—I mean locally. Couple of years ago he solved a bunch of really bad murders."

"What's that got to do with what we're talking about?" Faye said.

"A lot. Jack's devoted his career to helping people in need and making the world a little bit better. He always got the worst murder cases because he was the best investigator in the county. Every day he was neck-deep in the worst crimes you could imagine. He had to look at all that—all that tragedy, all that evil—and somehow hold up enough to get the job done. Could you, Faye? Could you work on a case where some slob is raping kids to death and burying them in his basement? Could you work on a case where crackheads are kidnaping babies for ransom and then killing the babies? Could you do that and hold up, year after year?"

"No," Faye said.

"Jack did, and there are a lot of people alive today because of it, and there are a lot of scumbags and murderers sitting in the can because Jack had the strength to hold up."

Faye didn't know what to say. If Craig was trying to make her feel like shit, he was doing a fine job. "So what happened?"

"He burned out, used himself up. About a year ago he was working on a pedophile case. He followed up a bunch of long-shot leads and got a line on a suspect, some rich guy, president of some big company. Jack's superiors told him to lay off or else. But Jack didn't lay off. He bamboozled a warrant to search the guy's house. He found dozens of videotapes of the rich guy and his friends sodomizing little kids. The guy's doing life in the state pen now. But that was it for Jack. He was never the same."

Faye felt a lump in her throat. "And now you think I'm a shitty person for not taking Jack's problems to heart."

"I wouldn't say you're a *shitty* person, Faye. Just not a very considerate one." With that, then, Craig loaded up a tray of Heinekens and Rocks and took them to a table.

I guess he's right, Faye thought, though she didn't like the idea of being outpsychologized by a brash, cocky bartender. When Jack came back from the men's room, Faye tried to smile but it didn't come off. *I'm sorry, Jack,* she thought.

"Baalzephon," he muttered, jiggling the ice in his glass. She watched this blank and tragic futility—fleeing one form of hell through the inundation of another. She felt helpless.

He was getting drunk already, but his eyes looked keen, or ruminant in some displaced wisdom. "Baalzephon," he muttered again. He signaled Craig for drink number four.

Baalzephon, Faye thought. *Madness. Devils. He's right. They gave him a real winner this time.*

And for the next hour she watched Jack Cordesman disappear into his own impresa, not one of triads or satanic rites, but the universal impresa: alcohol.

CHAPTER 18

Passion for everything, the strange words seemed to lilt in her head; they were like a shadow peering over her shoulder as she sketched. Veronica looked at the clock now for the first time since noon and saw that it was midnight. She'd worked twelve hours without even being aware of it.

Delve into your passion, whispered Khoronos' words.

Veronica felt stunned.

She rubbed her eyes and stretched. Prototypical sketches lay all over her worktable. She pictured herself sitting here all day and night, a blonde oblivione maniacally wearing out one charc pencil after the next. The block was gone; Khoronos' wisdoms had inspired her into a creative tempest. At last, Veronica had begun to see her passion.

She examined her work in the bleary lamplight. Most of the sketches failed to convey the eye of her dream. They seemed compressed by structure; she knew the failure at once. True art must never be bound by structure. The dream, the fire-lover, was an image, not a concept. It was up to her to give the image meaning, to *release* it from structure into aesthetic truth.

Blake and Klimt had advised that the artist must always work until he or she dropped. Faulkner had recommended stopping when the going got good, to protect the creative élan from becoming famished. She tried again, reconstructing the fire-lover on a fresh sheet of Lanaquarelle pH-neutral paper. The figure must make the viewer feel the same impassioned heat that Veronica felt in the dreams. She gave it a new poise and put it further back in the jagged dreamscape, but she still couldn't quite make it work. She decided, then, that it was time to take Faulkner's advice.

Hunger gnawed at her belly like a taloned paw. She went immediately down to the dark kitchen and opened the fridge. Someone prepared snacks for them every night—Marzen or Gilles, she guessed. Rolls of smoked Nova salmon, a creamy nougat on tiny bread pieces, and bowls of various spiced kimchi. Veronica ate insatiably.

Then she heard a splash.

It was a tiny sound, a secret. She looked abruptly out the window, then just as abruptly withdrew.

People were in the pool.

Next she carefully cracked the French doors and peeked out. Ginny and Amy Vandersteen, their shed clothes on the pool ledge, backpedaled in the luscious water before two onlookers—Marzen and Gilles. Dressed only in white slacks, they were staring, smiling at Ginny and Amy. *Voyeurs,* Veronica thought. *Like Khoronos.* But Khoronos wasn't with them. A moment later, Marzen and Gilles had stripped too, and were lowering themselves into the pool.

Thanks a lot for inviting me, Veronica thought in complaint.

The four frolicked in the water amid tails of moonlight. Veronica felt something like jealousy bubble—she felt left out even though skinny dipping wasn't her style. Amy Vandersteen was giggling like a high school girl as Gilles cornered her and splashed water in her face. Marzen hoisted Ginny up and heaved her headfirst into the deep end. Then the frolic quieted.

Damn!

Veronica wished she could see more. The moonlight reduced them to pale forms in the water; they'd paired off in opposite corners. Amy and Gilles were more visible—they were kissing. The director's arms wrapped intently about the Frenchman's muscled neck, hanging on. What burned Veronica more was the certainty that Marzen and Ginny were doing the same thing.

Damn! she thought again. Her breath thinned. Decency told her to leave. This was not what good girls did. Good girls did not spy on people. *Go back upstairs,* she ordered herself. *Go to bed, forget about this.* Of course, she didn't. It was fun, doing something her upbringing had taught her not to do. Just as she thought she'd like to see more, she got her wish. Gilles sat Amy Vandersteen up on the pool ledge. The woman parted her thighs and lay back, paddling her feet languidly in the water as Gilles brought his face between her legs.

Who's the voyeur now? Veronica thought.

Soon the images conspired: the dark, the quiet yard, moans enlaced with cricket trills. Veronica felt hypnotized. Could Khoronos' admonishments apply here? He'd told her she must examine herself, to pursue truths of her self-identity. Society would condemn this as voyeuristic, perverse. *So why am I doing this?*

She contemplated the answer, the truth.

Because it excites me.

She let herself . . . what? Immerse? Confront? No, she *injected* herself into the fantasy.

She put herself where Amy Vandersteen lay, her legs draped over Gilles' shoulders. She wondered if Gilles was as deft of tongue as Marzen. Her imagination said yes. It was her mind that lay back in substitute of her body, and brought Gilles' mouth to her sex. The visualization made her wet at once.

Delve into your passion, Khoronos' words drifted up again.

When she blinked, they were getting out, standing naked in the moonlit grass; they were drying themselves with big white towels. Marzen's physique seemed even more magnificent than Veronica remembered, all sculpted muscles and tapered lines, and Gilles too, a more delicate version. Gilles dried Amy, and Marzen dried Ginny, then they switched. Both women looked dizzy in wantonness.

Then they were coming in.

Shit! She dashed through the kitchen entrance just as the swimmers entered. The entire house was dark save for the hall light upstairs. Giggles rose, bare feet padded across the carpet. Veronica hid just out of sight behind the kitchen entry. Eventually naked shapes rounded the lower landing. But there were only three. Ginny and Gilles scampered up the stairs first, followed by Amy Vandersteen. But where was Marzen?

"*Ja,* here she is," came the accented voice. "Our beautiful little peeper."

Veronica whirled. "Jesus Chr—"

Marzen had sneaked up behind her.

"You like vahtching, *ja?* You like to see."

Veronica could only gaze back. He was a nude shadow, he was huge. Beads of water glittered on his broad chest. This sudden sexual presence overwhelmed her; she doubted she could even speak. The sudden truth relit in her mind: she wanted him again. All of him this time.

"You must join us, Veronica."

No, she started to say. She knew what he meant—an orgy. He wanted her to be a piece of furniture in a game of sexual musical chairs. She couldn't think of anything less sincere. So why didn't she protest when he approached?

His hands pulled up her sundress and skimmed it off. He turned her around, popped her bra, and threw it aside. All this deepened her excitement, the rough yet exacting quickness with which he'd stripped her. Then he knelt and skimmed her panties off.

He picked her up and carried her toward the stairs.

She could think of nothing to say to him. She put her arm around his shoulder, felt the hard muscles, the heat of his solid flesh. She felt drifting as he ascended a step at a time.

When he took her to Ginny's room, he set her down. She could barely stand, she could barely think past her anticipation. Marzen went to the window, next to Gilles. Ginny and Amy Vandersteen sat on the edge of the bed.

Khoronos had told Veronica she must delve into her passions, even potential ones. But group sex? Her mind fought with the impulse, and lost. Right now she knew she would do anything for any manner of sexual release. She didn't know why, she just knew. Anything. Even a five-way orgy.

"Transposition," Gilles said.

"*Mein Herz,*" Marzen said. "*Mein Geliebte.*"

The men seemed very serious. They stood with their arms crossed, staring. Veronica, Ginny, and Amy stared back.

Ginny moaned. Amy, whose wet white hair looked like a swim cap, discreetly touched herself. Veronica managed to mutter, "What the hell is this? What's going on?"

The men were waiting for something. But what?

"Are you guys gonna stand there all night," Amy Vandersteen finally said, "or are you gonna fuck us?"

Both men seemed to frown at the expletive, as though it soiled whatever was taking place here. Veronica could not help but stare at them, at their penises, at their grandiose physiques.

"None of you are ready yet," Gilles answered.

"Not yet ready to transpose," Marzen added.

But Veronica knew already, a subtle hot shock in her chest. Self-identity. Discovering oneself as completely as possible. Passion. Even potential ones. Her horniness felt like a trapped animal raging to escape its snare.

"Before you can learn to love us," Marzen said.

"You must learn to love each other," Gilles finished.

The two men walked out of the room and closed the door.

Veronica felt a jolt: a touch. Amy Vandersteen pushed her back on the bed and kissed her on the mouth. Veronica paused, shivered—then she gave in and kissed her back.

CHAPTER 19

To Jack Cordesman, hangovers were a familiarity. His head quaked when he leaned up in bed. Sunlight through the blinds cut into his vision like a razor wheel. He lumbered to the bathroom, thrust his mouth under the faucet, and gulped tap water.

Then he threw up, another familiarity.

He could tell by looking at the bed that Faye hadn't slept with him. *What the fuck happened?* he wondered. He stumbled downstairs in his shorts, guzzled some orange juice, and threw up again. It was 8:30; he was going to be late. No note had been left on the fridge, and Faye wasn't here. He tried to think, but he could remember nothing of last night past his sixth drink.

Birds chirped cheerily on the window ledge. *Shut up,* he thought. First he called work. "Running a little late." He tried to sound nonchalant. The desk sergeant didn't sound surprised. Then he called Craig.

"Everybody do me," Craig said.

"Hey, Craig, it's Jack. Did I wake you up?"

"No, I always get up at eight-thirty when I go to bed at four."

"Sorry. Look, I need to know what happened last night."

Craig serviced a bemused pause. "You got faced. Bad."

"How many did I have?"

"I don't know. Ten, twelve. I tried to stop serving you but you threatened to shit on the floor and close us down on a health violation."

What could he say? *Nothing,* he thought. Nothing he hadn't said before. "What happened with the girl?"

"Faye? Oh, she sat it out—she's a good girl. At last call you passed out. We stuffed you in the car, drove you home, and dragged you upstairs."

"Did she stay? At my place, I mean."

"Yeah, in one of the downstairs rooms, I think."

"I guess she was pretty pissed," Jack lamented.

"If she was pissed she would've walked out hours before. Like I said, she's a good girl."

Don't remind me, Jack thought. "You were saying something before I got tanked. Something about someone looking for me?"

"Yeah, what's his name. The guy with the Ivanhoe haircut."

"Stewie," Jack said, like the name was phlegm in his throat.

"Yeah, that guy."

"What did he want?"

"He said he was looking for you, I said you hadn't been in. He drank up and left. That was a few hours before you and Faye came in. The candyass left me a nickel tip."

That's Stewie, all right. But what did he want that was so important he actually came looking for Jack?

Now what? Jack held the phone, his head thumping through silence. "Look, Craig, I'm really sorry about—"

"I know. You're really sorry about getting fucked up and making an ass of yourself in public."

"I guess by now it goes without saying."

"Of course it does, so don't worry about it."

Jack was grateful for Craig's barman's couth—breaking Jack's balls and being a good guy about it at the same time. "And thanks for helping Faye get my drunk ass home."

"Forget it," Craig said. "Before I go back to sleep, you want some friendly advice?"

"Quit drinking," Jack guessed.

"Hit the nail on the head. And the girl, Faye—she's a decent kid, and I think she really likes you."

"So what's Craig's divine advice?"

"Don't fuck it up."

Jack reflected on the words through the dial tone. He was beginning to wonder what in his life he *hadn't* fucked up, and his present hangover only amplified the question. He went up to the shower, not just wondering what the future might hold, but wondering if he even had one.

NARCOTICS, RITUAL USE OF: Medieval counter-worship displays a vast utilization of narcotic substances.

> In fact, many pre-Christian-era belief systems revered particular entities who supposedly presided over the existence of narcotic properties and pharmacological knowledge, and it is through such demonographies that similar influences probably became insinuated into later Christian counter-worship.

Boring, Faye thought in her study cubicle. She skimmed down the text, eyeing only for key words of significance:

> known as *elixirists,* of special note with the aoristic orders of the late 1200s. Here we find an astounding logistic of narcotic manufacture. Drugs were generally used communally, during group rites of Mass, mostly root and botanical derivatives. Prelates often spiked thuribles with a preparation they called "cavernsmoke," which was said to "fortify the spirit for the service of our lords." What it really did was extend the initiate's susceptibility to hypnotic suggestion, increasing the likelihood of the commission of a crime. Cavernsmoke, as it turns out, was a tuber extract of a butyrophenone chemical chain which when induced affects a CNS depression and lowers a subject's conscious resistance to suggestion. Its chemical constituents are nearly identical to a modern psychiatric drug called Raxidol, which is still used to this day as a therapeutic hypnotic and involves a complicated synthesis process. This is just one example of a long series of sophisticated pharmacologies that included hypermanic drugs, psychostimulants, amphetamines, and opiate-based hydromorphinic pain killers and euphorics used today. One may find this premise very interesting: how did such cults, composed primarily of ignorant peasants living a thousand years ago, develop such a pervasive and comprehensive knowledge of pharmacological science?

You're right, Faye rejoined. *It is an interesting premise.* The aorists were using narcotic technologies that hadn't even been invented. It explained quite a bit, though—how the prelates were able to influence their subjects so effectively: drug addiction and hypnosis. She skimmed down further:

> to the extent that any ritual occasion demanded the antithetical gesture of sexual sin, which was viewed as a paramount

affront to God, the more perverse in nature the greater the homage to Lucifer and his appellate demons. Orgies *en masse* were common from the earliest times, covenheads making liberal use of crude aphrodisiacs in order to provoke rampant sexual behavior among the congregants. Such substances were largely physical in mechanism, and often quite dangerous: harsh astringents such as bergamot and distilled tarweed roots which irritate mucous membrane linings—such as those of the vagina, the anus, and the urethra—and hence affect an accelerated urge to stimulate the irritated areas via intercourse. The aorists, however, whose pharmacological prowess is aforementioned, used much more sophisticated aphrodisiac substances, which might help to explain the ease with which the aorists executed such excruciating sexual acts as bestiality and necrophilia. Somehow, sect prelates managed to isolate narcotic substances that directly affected desired dopaminergic mechanisms in the brain. One chief aphrodisiac compound was know as "rootmash" or "loveroot," whose formulation required a complex series of distillation syntheses of the tubercore of the stalky pod-bearing blackapple plant, or *Taxodium lyrata*, exclusive to lower Europe. Properly processed, the distilled aggregant when taken internally stimulates an overproduction of certain biogenic amines that regulate sex drive, causing hypersexual impulses, abnormal excitation states, and an aberrant willingness to partake in acts which would otherwise seem unappealing or extreme. This particular extract is classified today as a cantharadine, which is, in pharmacological terms, a cervical-channel dilator and libidinal stimulant.

Faye reread the passage, then photocopied it. Jack might be very interested in this. *Willingness,* she thought.

Her eyes were beginning to blur—too much squinting at too much fine print and intaglio. She went outside for some air, taking a bench amid the hustle of the city. Two blocks past the Capitol she could see an adult bookstore. *Skin flicks and politics,* she mused. There were five hundred murders per year in this city, most drug-related. *The Cultus of Crack, the Cultus of Lucifer,* she considered. She wondered how much different the two were when you got right down to relativity. *Evil for evil. It's all the same, just different colors.*

Then she wondered about Jack. Evil wasn't just relative, it was far-reaching, obscure. Jack was a good man, and these same evils—regardless of face—were destroying him. Part of Jack infuriated her, the zeal with which he pursued his own ruin. Another part of him she thought she could love.

A trash can bore a black sign: *Silence=Death,* a maxim of the gay world. Under it someone had markered, *The sodomites are being judged.* Faye wondered about her own cosmic verdict, when she herself would be judged. *Who will judge me?* she asked no one in particular. *Where will I go? To the grave? To hell? Reborn as a centipede?*

She was not religious, despite a vigorous upbringing in the Church. "People were meant to be together in the eyes of God," she remembered from the last sermon she attended about a decade ago. She also remembered her mother once saying: "Not being truthful is the worst sin."

There was good and there was evil, Faye simplified. People were meant to be together in the eyes of God. But who was God? An idea? A serene-faced man with flowing white hair and beard in the sky? It didn't matter who or what He was. He was proof that the body of mankind sought to reject evil. Faye wondered where that left her.

The fresh air did not enliven her. It made her, in fact, feel keenly sullen. If not being truthful was the worst sin, what in her life had she failed to be truthful about?

She went back into Adams Building and reread the entries she'd circled on her latest bib printout:

James I of England, *Daemonologie*, Edinburgh, 1597.
Murray, M., *The Witchcult of Western Europe*, London, 1921.
Morakis, D., *The Synod of the Aorists* [place and date of reprint and translation unknown. Pamphlet format; rare].

"That's my baby," she whispered, eyeing the last entry.

She stared for a moment, chilled. It was more than these tomes that awaited her, she knew. It was evil too.

It was Baalzephon.

CHAPTER 20

Was it a dream?

A slit of sunlight through the curtain gap bisected Veronica's face in a nearly perfect state of congruity. She opened her eyes, looked to either side, and gasped.

The three of them lay entangled, nude, in Ginny's bed. Amy Vandersteen hugged Veronica's hips. Ginny slept higher, with an arm and leg draped. Very slowly, then, Veronica remembered . . .

Holy shit, she thought.

She tried to chronologize. She'd worked late into the night. She'd gone downstairs and eaten. She'd spied on Ginny and Amy in the pool with Marzen and Gilles. Then . . .

Holy shit, she thought again.

The two men had instigated the whole thing; they'd seduced them, then left them alone with their desires. It was the intensity of the desire that Veronica remembered most. She'd been dizzied by it, driven, and so had Ginny and Amy. They'd made love to each other all night. They'd done everything conceivable to each other, and some things not. They'd drawn each other's passions out to scintillating threads, each a probe of desire and real flesh exploring every facet of every sensation. They'd opened up their passions and *delved.*

Veronica couldn't have felt more confused. Was it honesty that had compelled her to participate, or subversion? But she didn't feel subversive. She thought about what Khoronos had said. In a sense, all of life was an experiment of revelation, of experience.

Of passion, she added.

Should she feel dirty for having embarked on this adventure, or should she feel blessed?

The erstwhile images replayed in her mind, a vivid assemblage of diced sights, sounds, sensations. The overall memory lost all basis of order; the night had passed frenetically in a meld of moving bodies, moans and caresses, breasts in her face and legs wrapped around her head. Veronica had made a terrain of herself for the others to investigate, and they'd made the same of themselves for her. Their time together had been measured not in minutes, but in human scents and flavors, the heat and weight of flesh, and one orgasm after the next.

Lust, she thought now, in bed with her two new lovers. But lust hadn't been behind any of it. Lust was greed, using another person's body for a singular gratification. Passion was the difference—mutuality. Veronica had found as much pleasure in giving as taking. That fact, and its irrevocability, made her feel purified.

Amy Vandersteen stirred. Veronica closed her eyes, pretending to be asleep. The director quietly slid out of bed. The door clicked open, then clicked shut.

The notion was difficult to pinpoint, but it almost seemed as though Amy had been *summoned* awake.

Summoned by what?

Veronica slid out from Ginny's embrace, careful not to wake her. She cracked the bedroom door and peeked out. Amy was tiptoeing naked down the dark stairs. Veronica slipped on Ginny's robe, wondering. Then she edged out toward the landing.

First light had not yet worked its way inside; downstairs was filled with soft, grainy dark. The house was so silent Veronica could hear herself blink. Amy Vandersteen seemed to be kneeling, searching for something under the couch downstairs. Her pale nakedness made a ghost of her in the murk.

What is she doing? Veronica thought, peering down.

Seconds later, she knew.

It was a tragic sight. The orange glow of the lighter gave it all away. It tinted the room and cast a desperate halo about Amy's coiffed head. Her face looked pinched shut as she sucked on the tiny pipe, answering the summons, the call of her curse.

Veronica could not remember the last time she felt this sad. *Addict,* croaked an unholy voice in her head. In the slender woman's desperation, Veronica glimpsed all the woe of the world.

Amy sucked the pipe dry, then lay back. If she'd been oblivious, that would've made it more reckonable. But the look on the woman's face told the whole truth. Hers was a countenance not of euphoria, but of slowly creeping horror. Tears ran down her cheeks as she rode the wave of her high. The glint in her wide-open eyes shone with pure ruin.

Veronica's heart felt squeezed up into her throat.

She went back to the bedroom and looked out the window. What could she do to help Amy? *Nothing,* she answered. The image remained, an equally sad truth.

Sunlight struggled to reach above the treetops. It was as though this remote pocket of the earth were flinching against the sun, quailing to keep its veil of night. *Did I dream?* she wondered. Her memory flinched too, against splinters of images, colors, heat. Yes, she had dreamed . . .

The fire-lover had come yet again, her suitor of sleep. It had caressed her with its flames, kissed her, penetrated her. In her sleep she'd wrapped her legs about its blazing torso and . . .

The memory scalded her. Bliss. Sheer erotic bliss.

Goose bumps slid across her skin. She glanced about, hunting for a distraction, when her gaze plopped onto Ginny's little desk.

Scribbled notes and correction tapes cluttered around the typewriter. A small stack of sheets had been turned upside down—Ginny's work in progress. One sheet hung out of the typewriter's platen in plain sight. Impulse, not premeditation, urged her to read:

> a harrowing spangle of moisture and muse. His gaze swept her away to lush, uncharted planes, chasing her like a sleek bird—

"Get away from that!"

Oops. Shamed she turned slowly around, looking down.

"It's creative respect, you know." Ginny was sitting up in bed, glaring. Somehow anger prettied her face. "It's an unwritten code. One artist never looks at another artist's work without permission. You *know* that."

"I know," Veronica peeped. "Sorry."

"Then why did you do it?"

"It was just sitting there. My eyes kind of fell on it. I only read a little."

"How would you like it if I went into your room and looked at your stuff without you knowing? Huh?"

"I said I was sorry. Jesus."

Ginny glanced away. Her hair lay tangled about her face in strings. "Where's Amy?" she asked.

"Downstairs. She's freebasing again."

"That's too bad." Ginny's sharp smirk saddened. "She's an asshole, sure, but she's got a lot of talent and a lot of good ideas. What a waste."

It was a cold way to abridge a human life, but it was true. It *was* a waste. How many great artists had destroyed themselves with drugs?

"A waste of a lot of passion too."

Veronica glanced up. "What?"

"She's a wonderful lover."

She looked back down again, too quickly. She knew Ginny would get around to it eventually.

"Well?" Ginny asked.

"Well what?"

"Observations, comments . . . conclusions?"

"About last night, you mean?"

"No, Vern, about last Fourth of July. You know what I mean."

Veronica refaced the window, anything to avoid Ginny's prying gaze. What should she say? What *could* she say, in truth?

"Did you like it?"

"Yes," Veronica said.

"Do you regret any of it?"

"No, but it still bothers me. The whole thing was premeditated. Those guys manipulated the hell out of us."

"Bullshit, Vern." Now Ginny sat on the bed's edge, uninhibitedly naked. "That's a cop-out. We can't blame others for what *we* do."

"It's not a cop-out," Veronica objected. But why did she feel so defensive? "You've got to admit—"

"Be real. No one forced you to do what you did last night. No one *manipulated* you. What happened, happened because we allowed it to. You're repressing yourself, Vern, which is exactly what Khoronos is trying to teach you not to do."

Veronica's anger began to unreel. "I'm *repressing* myself? I spent most of the night with my face between your legs, and you call that *repression*?"

"It's repression because you don't have the courage to admit your own motives for doing it."

"Oh, I see. I'm a lesbian but I'm just not admitting it."

Ginny shook her head; she smiled dismally. "You really can be stupid when you try hard. Sex has nothing to do with any of this. Don't you listen to anything Khoronos says?"

"What is he saying, Ginny? Since I'm so stupid, tell me."

"He's saying that we have to shed our repressions in order to maximize ourselves as artists. Not just sexual repressions, but every repression in regard to every aspect of our lives. To be everything we can be as artists, as creators, we must—"

"I know," Veronica sniped. "We must delve into our passions."

"Right. And it's true. Because that's all that creativity is founded in. Passion."

Passion for everything, Veronica finished in thought. Her petty anger was gone, spirited away. She looked down at her shadow thrown across the floor. She thought of herself as two separate entities, one of flesh, the other of shadow—her id, perhaps. That was where her passions lay, in her shadows, and that's what Khoronos meant yesterday when he'd spoken of her failures. She was keeping her passions in shadow. She must illuminate them to become real.

"Come back to bed," Ginny said.

"I—" Veronica faltered. "I'm not tired."

"Neither am I."

Veronica let the robe slide off her shoulders. Then she was getting back into bed with her friend.

Jan Beck handed Jack a strip of multicolored paper—the source spectrum from a mass photospectrometer. Under it Jan had written:

3-[-3-(p-hydrophenyl)-4-chloroxyiphone]-3'-disodium-edetate.

"That's the stuff," Jan said. "The chemical designation."

"And you found it in the bloodstreams of both girls?"

"Yep. Too bad it's meaningless."

It was 7 P.M. now; Jack and Faye stood in the TSD main lab, where they'd arranged to meet after Faye got out of the LOC. Neither had mentioned Jack's drunken foray of the night before.

"Meaningless?" Jack countered. "It's our biggest lead. Once you identify it by name, we can nail down a geographic scheme. Whoever's making it or selling it can lead us to the killer."

"Killer*s*," Jan Beck reminded. "And that's the problem. I don't know if I *can* identify it by name."

"You said it's not in the CDS and pharmaceutical indexes, right?" Jack asked. "That knocks out about ten thousand possibilities."

"So what? They're U.S. indexes. It could be a foreign pharmaceutic. It could be homemade."

These revelations did not enthuse Jack. He tried to sort his thoughts, smoking. "How much time, Jan?"

"Cold? Weeks."

"I don't have weeks."

Jan Beck laughed. "Captain, unless you can give me something to go on, I'll have to catalog every index one at a time."

"Here's something you might be able to use," Faye Rowland interrupted. "I found a bunch of stuff today about drug use among the aorist sects." She riffled through a sheaf of Xerox sheets. "They used lots of drugs during their rituals; one of them was an aphrodisiac called rootmash. They made it by distilling the pods of a plant called blackapple." She scanned her underscores. "*Taxodium lyrata* is the botanical name. The book said it was a cantharadine, whatever that is."

"Cantharadine," Jan said to herself.

"Sounds like you've heard of it," Jack said.

"It rings a bell. Give me that." Jan took Faye's papers and began to walk away toward her index library.

"Where are you going?"

"You gave me something to go on, so now I'm going to go on it."

Jack got the message. "Let's get out of here," he said to Faye. "Jan likes to be left alone when she works."

Faye followed him up the stairs of the county HQ. He seemed remote, or distracted. Then he said, "Sorry about last night."

"You won't last long, drinking like that," Faye replied.

I'm gonna quit." Jack smiled at the excuse. "I know, that's what they all say. But I'm really going to do it."

Faye kept quiet.

As they were about to exit, an ancient sergeant at the main desk stopped them. "Hey, Captain, you got a call from City District."

"Thanks." Jack took the phone. "Cordesman."

"Jack, it's Randy."

"How you coming on the interviews?"

"It's like what you predicted. Rebecca Black had as many pickups as Shanna Barrington. And we struck out on the ex-husband. He was verifiably out of state during the murder."

"Just keep plugging."

"Sure, but that's not why I called. Some guy keeps calling your office, says he knows you. Sounds like a real prick."

Stewie, Jack guessed.

"I've got him on the line right now," Randy said. "How about taking it and getting the guy off my back."

"Switch me over," Jack said. The line transferred, hummed, and clicked. "What do you want, Stewie?"

"Jackie boy! How's it going?"

"Fine until you called. What do you want?"

"I need to rap with you, paisan."

"Well, I don't want to *rap* with you, Stewie. I've had a taxing day, and talking to you would only make it more taxing."

Stewie guffawed. "You never did like me, did you?"

"No, Stewie, I never did. And I still don't."

"I need to talk to you about Veronica."

The name seemed to give Jack an abrupt *shove*. "What about her?"

"I think she's in trouble."

"What kind of trouble? I'm listening."

"Better if we meet, you know, man-to-man."

But what could he mean? What kind of trouble could Veronica be in? "All right, Stewie. Man-to-man."

"Or, hell, let's be honest. Libertine to drunk."

"How about assailant to assault victim?"

"Aw, Jackie, that's so sad. Are you threatening a law-abiding citizen over a police line? Is that wise?"

"Where and when, Stewie?"

"How about the Undercroft? In your constant inebriation, it's probably the only place in town you can find without a map."

"I would really love to kick your ass, Stewie, and if this is a bunch of bullshit, I will."

"Come on, Jack. An alcoholic wreck like you? You couldn't even kick your own ass. Now, are we going to bicker like a pair of *bêtes noires,* or are we going to rap?"

"I'll be there in a half hour."

Jack hung up. He looked stolid, vexed.

"You'll be where in a half hour?" Faye asked him.

"I—" *Shit,* he thought. "The bar."

"That's great, Jack. A minute ago you told me you were going to quit drinking. Now you're going to the bar. Great."

"I'm not going there to drink, Faye."

"Of course not. You're going there to play racquetball. Why else do people go to bars?"

"It's something personal. I gotta talk to someone, that's all. You can come too, if you don't believe me."

"I have better things to do than sit in bars, Jack." She turned, was walking away. "I have a bunch of material to go over for *your* murder case, remember? Have fun at the bar."

He trotted after her into the parking lot. "Why are you always pissed off at me? I won't get drunk, I promise."

"Don't promise me, Jack. What do I matter?"

"You . . . you matter a lot."

"Don't promise me. Promise yourself." Faye slammed her car door shut, then drove off.

Jack watched her big Malibu turn out of the lot. *Boy, I could use a drink,* he thought, and got into his own car. That was the unique thing about the power of promises. They always dared to be broken.

"All right, Stewie. I'm here."

It was not easy for Jack to pull up a stool next to Stewart K. Arlinger. It demanded a placation he didn't feel capable of. Stewie wore a slate-blue Smiths T-shirt that read "You handsome devil." He'd recently stylized his black, banged hair with a streak of silver, and most of his white jeans evaded visibility for the cuffed black boots which rose up past mid-thigh. A yellow clove cigarette burned in one hand. Before him stood a tall glass of gin.

"Good to see you, Jack," he said through a snide smile.

Jack sat down. Craig spun a bottle of Seagram's over his shoulder and caught it behind his back. "The usual, Jack?"

"No. Soda water. Put a piece of lime in it to make it look like I'm drinking something."

"Soda water. Hmm," Craig remarked. His brow arched, as did the brows of several patrons. *I will not break my promise,* Jack thought.

"Graduating to the hard stuff, huh?" Stewie commented.

"Believe me, Stewie. It's very difficult for me to be in the same room with you and be sober at the same time."

"Let's just get to business before we get into a fight."

"Fine," Jack said. "I don't have time to drive you to the emergency room. I'd miss *Wheel of Fortune* reruns."

"You know, Jack, I like you, even in spite of your rampant aggression and alcoholic ill-will. But let me ask you something. Why exactly do you hate my guts?"

"Plenty of reasons," Jack was quick to respond. "You're selfish, greedy, pompous, you make a living off my ex-girlfriend's work, and you wear boots that come up to your crotch."

"All of the above are true, Jack, but let's try real hard to be adults for a minute—a trying task, in your case. I'm really worried about Veronica."

"You said she might be in trouble. How so?"

"I'm not sure. She's never been one to shirk her professional responsibilities. Shows, galleries, interviews—all that kind of stuff's very important to her, the business end of her art. That's why she has me to manage her career."

"Get to the point."

"I haven't heard from her all week."

Jack set his drink down and thought about that. Stewie was right. Veronica would never remain out of touch with her manager for so long a time. There had to be a reason.

"That's why I'm worried. She's close to the big time, which is great because she deserves it. But it's real easy for an artist to fuck up. All you have to do is snub a few important people, and that can mean the end of a career. She's got a lot of things in the fire right now. *Art Times* wants to interview her. Two major publishers want to do books of her work. I got galleries all over the country who want to put her up. Yesterday the fucking Corcoran calls, they want to do a show too. I don't know what to tell any of these people. Some of them are *important* people, Jack. All week long I've been telling them I'll get back to them once Veronica has contacted me. I can't jerk them off forever. When the fucking Corcoran Gallery calls, you don't say, 'I'll get back to ya, bub.'"

This didn't sound right, none of it did.

"I've got to get ahold of her, Jack. I've got to know what she's got ready to go. If I can't get back to these galleries with some kind of commitment soon, they'll write her off. That would be really bad for her future. You got to help me out here, Jackie. My bread and butter's on the line, and so is hers."

"What can I do?" Jack queried.

"Tell me about this thing she went on with Ginny. She hates my guts too, by the way."

"I don't know anything about it," Jack said. "She said it was a creative retreat of some sort, said she wanted to 'find' herself. And she said some rich guy was putting her up."

"Khoronos," Stewie said.

"Yeah. Khoronos. If you ask me, the whole thing sounds pretty fucked up."

"We finally agree on something. Do you know where Khoronos lives?"

"She wouldn't tell me. I think she was afraid I'd hound her or something. She hit me with all this the night we broke up."

Stewie stirred his gin with his finger. He'd grown his pinky nail long and painted it white. "I met him once," he said.

Khoronos, Jack thought. Already the rats were coming home to feast, jealousies and the blackest thoughts, all to remind him of what he had lost. "What's he like?" he asked.

"Pompous but refined," Stewie answered. "Something awesome about the way he carries himself and the way he talked. The word 'scintillating' comes to mind."

Awesome, Jack thought. *Scintillating. Excuse me while I puke.*

"And real good-looking," Stewie was kind enough to continue. He ordered another Sapphire from Craig. "Sharp dresser, tall, well proportioned. *Fantastic* body."

Jack frowned.

"Human beauty's a wondrous thing, whether you're a man r a woman. Too bad you can't relate to that, Jackie."

"Yeah, too bad," Jack muttered. "Go on."

"What I'm saying is this guy Khoronos is a real hot number. /eronica fell for him the instant she met him."

Each word of Stewie's revelation made Jack sink further. Ie remembered what Craig had said. No matter how much 'ou love a girl, there was always someone around the next orner waiting to ruin it all. There was always a Khoronos. 'What else do you know about him?"

"He bought one of Vern's paintings. The guy was carry- ng twenty-five large in cash. Tell me that's not weird. He ent a couple of guys around the next morning to pick up the icture."

"Delivery men? Big deal."

"These guys weren't delivery men. They almost acted like ervants. Heartbreakers, Jackie. Musclemen with class."

Now Jack's head spun with the most terrible images. "Crea- ive retreat, my ass," he mumbled under his breath.

"I know what you're thinking. We both know there's a side o Veronica that's very susceptible to outside influences. In a ot of ways, she's very vulnerable."

"What are you saying?"

Stewie put a good dent in his Sapphire. "Come, Jackie. Guys ike that, rich, sexy, art enthusiasts . . . Veronica will be putty n their hands, and you know it."

"Ginny'll keep an eye on her," Jack lamely suggested.

Stewie threw his head back and laughed, a bit too loudly. Ginny protecting Veronica is like a vampire in a fucking lood bank. Wake up, Jackie. She's a feminist existentialist, or Christ's sake. Read her books. They're all about women reaking free of relationships, sexual independence, doing vhatever they feel like to find actualization."

Jack didn't know what actualization meant, but it didn't ound good.

Stewie ordered yet another gin. "I've always believed that ove between two people is a holy thing. Two people together re stronger than when they're on their own. There're a lot of ad people in the world, Jackie. Users, liars, con men, and very other kind of motherfucker who'll take advantage of vulnerable people for their own kicks. But love protects u from people like that."

"You're the last person I'd expect to hear that from."

"We all have our fronts, Jackie. You do, I do. You thin my only interest in Veronica is financial."

"As a matter of fact, Stewie, I do. Veronica's your onl important client. Without her, you'd be washed up."

"That's true. But she's also my friend, and I care about her."

This was very bizarre. Stewie was showing a side of him self Jack didn't think existed. Could it be possible that Stewi was something more than a self-centered art pimp? Beneath th new-wave clothes and hairdo, and the decadent pretenses, wa there really a decent human being?

"You still care about her too, Jackie."

Jack stared at him. *Yeah, I do,* he thought. *And I can't d shit about it, can I?*

"All I mean is that Veronica could be in a bad situation, an goddamn Ginny isn't going to be any help at all. Veronica's no a decisive person, and as far as this retreat thing goes, Ginny' be right there to help her make all the wrong decisions."

"Which makes Veronica even more vulnerable."

"You got it. This Khoronos guy, he's slick, he's a smoot operator. He knew all the right things to say to impress Vern and all the right ways to say them. It took him all of fiv fucking minutes to make her completely oblivious to com mon sense, and it was almost like he had the whole retrea thing planned in advance. The fact is he's a perfect stranger Khoronos and his two pretty boys? They could be nuts, for a we know."

Jack began to foment. Stewie was right. Who knew wh these guys were, and what their game was?

"I saw them off, Vern and Ginny. Vern promised to kee in touch on what was going on with the gallery bids. I hav en't heard one word from her." Stewie drained another gin "You've got to take care of this, Jack."

"I don't know where he is," Jack countered. "I don't kno anything about any of it."

"Don't you give a shit at all, man?"

"Of course I do, you asshole."

"Then do something about it, shithead."

"What?"

"Come on, Jackie. You're a cop. You can get a line on this Khoronos clown. Just do whatever it is you cops do when you want to know something."

"I could run his last name if he's got a criminal record, but that would take a while. I could try MVA too. If I had his date of birth or his S.S. number, it'd be a lot faster, but we don't have any of that shit. You say he bought a painting with cash? Were they big bills, small bills?"

"Big bills, man. C-notes."

"You still have the money?"

"Fuck no, I deposited it the same day."

"Shit," Jack muttered. Banks kept serial number records of large withdrawals. "He give it to you in anything? An envelope?"

"No, he gave it to me in a fucking toolbox. Of course there was an envelope. But there was nothing on it."

"You still have the envelope?"

"I threw it out."

Jack frowned. "All right. You said these two guys picked up the painting Khoronos bought. What kind of vehicle?"

"A step van. White."

"Make, model, year?"

"I don't know, man. Do I look like a car dealer?"

"You see the tag number?"

"No, I had no reason to look."

"Did you notice the state, even the *color* of the plates?"

"No," Stewie said.

Jack tapped the bar. What else was there? "These two guys? You must've given them a receipt for the painting."

"Yeah, a standard exchange receipt. I have our copy. The smaller guy signed it, but I can't make out shit for the signature."

"I'll need to see it anyway," Jack said. "I'll also need the day you made the deposit, and what bank you use. The bank'll log a cash deposit that big and the serial numbers of the bills if they're consecutive. If they're not consecutive, they'll record sample numbers."

"What good would that do?"

"I might be able to link your deposit to Khoronos' withdrawal. If I can locate his bank, I can locate him. The only problem is bank records are protected information. Unless I have probable cause to convince a magistrate that Khoronos has committed a crime, which I don't, then they won't show me the transaction records."

"Talk to me, Jackie. You guys have ways around that shit."

"I might be able to go under the table, but I doubt it. I'll give it a shot. After that, there's nothing."

Stewie got up, a little stumbly. "There are other things you can do, Jackie, and you know what I'm talking about. Excuse me."

Yeah, there are a few other things, Jack agreed. He was already thinking about them.

While Stewie utilized the men's room, Jack began to feel edgy. Just seeing people drink goaded him, just seeing the bottles lined up on the wall. Craig was shaking up some shooters for a pair of local cuties. A goateed guy and an area writer were drinking a toast: "To darker days and evil women," the goateed guy proposed. Everybody was drinking, having a good time. *Just one,* Jack considered, but he knew it was a lie. For men like Jack there was no such thing as one drink. He'd made a promise tonight, and he resolved to keep it. He might break it tomorrow. But . . . *Not tonight,* he thought.

"Another soda water, Jack?" Craig asked. He flipped a lit cigarette and caught it in his mouth. The two cuties applauded.

"I, uh—" Jack groaned. *Fiddich, rocks,* he wanted to say. "I made a promise that I wouldn't drink tonight."

Craig ejected a shaker of ice behind his back into the sink. "My view on promises is thus: A man can only be as good as his promise. When we break our promises, we break ourselves."

"Another soda water, Craig," Jack validated. The wisdom of barkeeps, again, amazed. *When we break our promises, we break ourselves.* He should have it tattooed on his wrist, a constant reminder. "With lime *and* lemon this time," he added.

"Where were we?" Stewie retook his stool and ordered another Sapphire. His eyes looked bloodshot.

"Hey, Stewie," Jack began. "How come you're getting tanked?"

"*You're* lecturing *me*? That's balls, Jackie. You're the A.A. candidate, not me."

"I'm not lecturing you, I just—"

"I told you, I'm worried about her, I'm concerned."

"I used to be in love with her, remember? I'm concerned about her too. More than you."

"Bullshit, Jackie." Stewie swigged, wincing. "You've never been concerned about anyone in your life."

Jack gaped at the insult.

"And if anything bad happens to her," Stewie ranted on, "it'll be your fault."

Jack gaped at that one too. "Since you're drunk I'll pretend I didn't hear that."

"No, Jackie, since I'm drunk, I'll tell you what I really think. You wanna hear it?"

"Sure. I listen to crap every day. Yours is no different from anyone else's."

"Here's what I think, Jackie boy. I think you were the best thing to ever happen to Veronica."

Jack's mouth fell open. Of all the things he might expect Stewie to say, this was the least imaginable.

"Before she got involved with you, she didn't have anything but her work. She was confused, disillusioned, and unhappy. But you gave her direction—"

Jack was confused too, thoroughly. "Stewie, how come all of a sudden you're saying good things about me?"

"—and then you failed," Stewie, ran on. "You gave her the promise of something good, and then you let her down."

Jack roused. "How the fuck did I let her down! She dumped me, remember? *She* ended the relationship, not me!"

Stewie shrugged. "You dangled happiness in front of her face, but you never let her have it. All you did was moan and groan about your own problems without ever considering hers. It broke her heart, Jackie. You never even tried to care about the things that were important to her."

"Oh, yeah? What? What things?"

"The things that make her tick. Her desire to create, her visions and her insights. Her art, Jackie. Her art."

Jack's mouth felt frozen, an immobile hole.

"She loved you so much, more than you could probably ever know. You led her on, but you never came through. You were too selfish."

Could all this be true? Could Jack have been so blind that he didn't see any of this?

"You left her with no alternative, Jackie."

Jack felt dried up in the aftermath of Stewie's dissertation. His first impulse was to deny it all, to dismiss it, but that would only be evasion. Why would Stewie make up so detailed a condemnation?

"I didn't know," Jack said. "I didn't realize . . ."

"Yeah, right." Stewie slapped some cash down on the bar, and also the date of the deposit and the name of Veronica's bank. "Are your excuses always so sophisticated? With Veronica, you could have had everything. Look what you get instead."

Jack didn't know what he meant.

"I gotta go now, Jackie. Enjoy the view." Stewie shoved his wallet back into his pants and walked out of the bar.

Enjoy the view, Jack repeated in his mind. He looked up. In the mirrored bar wall, behind rows and rows of bottles, he saw his own face staring back at him.

"Hey, Craig. Dump the soda water and pour me a Fiddich."

"What about your promise?" Craig asked, stacking some pint glasses with Oxford Class emblems on them.

"Fuck the promise. Get me a drink."

"With all due respect, Jack, I don't think that's such a hot idea. Why not just play it cool tonight?"

"I don't need a counseling session, Craig, I need a drink. Just pour me a fucking drink, or I'll find a bar that will."

CHAPTER 21

"Father of the Earth," spoke the Prelate, "we live to serve your will."

"Hail, Father, hail," responded the Surrogoti.

"We give you flesh through blood, we give you body through spirit."

"Flesh through blood," came the antiphon. "Body through spirit."

The Prelate kissed the dolch. The cloaked Surrogoti stood at opposite points of the Trine. The Prelate turned to face them. They joined hands. They looked down and they prayed.

"Walk with us, Father."

"Protect us."

"Bless us, Father, and deliver us. Give us strength to do your will in this holy time, we your unworthy servants. Let us walk unseen and speak unheard so that we may give to you again. Bless us and come among us, Father."

"Flesh through blood."

"Body through spirit."

The Prelate felt risen. He closed his eyes and looked. *Show me,* he prayed. *I beseech thee.* He saw black like onyx and endless chasms of flesh and loss. The sky was red beyond the stygian terrascape; lattices of distant fires pulsed slowly through the chasms' rough clefts like glowing veins, and the merged black mutterings of chaos deafened the endless gorge. It was beautiful. The Prelate swept down into the abyss, no longer a man but a great svelte bird. Down and down, into lovely chaos, into the grace of the tumult. Visions soared past, dark blood colors and movements of things barely seen. Each crevice of the vale wound through oozing slabs of rock, escarpments and catacombs, riven earthworks and bottomless pits. *Carry me away,* thought the Prelate upon gorgeous black wings. The void's screams flooded his bead-black eyes with tears of joy, the fury of truth, its quickness and its infinity. The gorge descended further into tenebrae, leading him to some inverted pinnacle older than history. A mile or a thousand miles off he could see the blessed summit, but below the chasm's gushing black, movement began to reveal itself beneath the sheen of sulphurous smoke. Beaked scavengers picked through piles of twitching bodies; sluglike excrement-dwellers sloughed flesh off bones. Gaping holes in rock disgorged corpses charred to sticks, billowing smoke sooty with human fat. *Beautiful,* dreamed the Prelate. Figures less than human emerged from gaseous cracks: faceless, indescribable ushers that pawed at the pitiable human horde, drinking up their screams, inhaling their blood. Naked shapes in swarms struggled through slime and shit only to be trod upon by the chuckling attendants of this place. Bodies squirmed with vigor as skulls were cracked apart and plucked of their pink meat. Limbs were torqued out of sockets, spines were yanked out of backs, bodies were slowly and methodically squashed and gazed upon as bones snapped and organs burst. One usher sunk huge genitals into a squirming woman's rectum while another curiously twisted her head around and around till it came off. Other bodies were skillfully flensed by nimble claw-hands, dismantled piece by piece. Faces were shorn off living heads, fingers and toes were nibbled as tidbits. Grotesque genitals rose to plunder any orifice in reach. Inhuman hands pulled open scrotums to expose raw testicles to flames. Needle teeth sunk into glans, bit off nipples and breasts, hands and feet, ears, noses, scalps. The ushers rejoiced in their determined work, peerless in their execution. There was no end to the workings of their beauty. One of the ushers forced a man to eat parts of himself; others directed children to dissect their mothers alive, then themselves. Whole tangles of writhing human bodies were submerged into pits of steaming excrement, held under until they drowned, and huge, misshapen feet plodded systematically upon carpets of pregnant women till their wombs disbirthed. Placentae and fetuses were set aside upon hot rocks, to cook.

Here was recompense. Here was truth.

The Prelate looked for the day when he, too, would join the ushers in their holy onus.

The earthworks led on. The Prelate glided serenely over turning fire and smoldering pits. The screams like beautiful music faded behind. Plinths studded the precipice, black cenotaphs and dolmens old as the world. Higher and higher the Prelate sailed, and down and down until soon there was no sound at all, only the serenity of this lightless, ancient place. He could feel the beauty of its presence, he could almost *touch* it, for it was coming . . .

Closer, closer . . .

The Prelate stopped.

He hovered in infinity, staring.

Before him stood the Father's obsidian throne, and in it:

The Father.

The Father of the Earth.

"Aorista!" wept the Prelate.

"To you we give our faith forever," wept the Prelate down into the Trine.

"Flesh through blood," chorused the Surrogoti. "Body through spirit."

The Prelate turned and held up the *jarra*. "My love, Father. My gift to thee." He held up the dolch. "And your gift to us."

The Surrogoti raised their arms.

"Give us grace, O Father, to fulfill your destiny."

"Baalzephon, hail!"

"Aorista!"

The cement floor, around the Trine, grew warm.

CHAPTER 22

Veronica looked up from her worktable. She heard footsteps. But when she peeked into the hall, the stairwell was empty.

The footsteps had sounded misplaced. They hadn't even sounded like they were coming from the stairs.

It must be my brain thumping, she thought. Her work lay before her. The basic sketch was done. Yesterday's sketches had lacked something, but today she realized what.

The sketches had lacked *her*.

Last night's dream of the burning man had been the most detailed yet. *The Ecstasy of the Flames,* she thought. *The Fire-Lover*. The vacant space at the flame-lover's side needed to be filled. Veronica had filled that space with herself.

Thus far her only attempts at self-portrait had been deeply expressionistic. This would have to be different, though; she would need to paint herself not in abstraction, but in a physical reality. She'd never done that before. The prospect excited her, but it was also a little bit scary.

What if she failed?

Sudden voices distracted her. Now she was sure people were in the hall. How could she have missed them when she looked a moment ago? The voices spoke in French. Marzen and Gilles were easy to tell apart. She got up again and listened through the door.

Jibberish composed the entire exchange. Then a third voice spoke, in English. It was Khoronos.

"She is tainted. I made a serious error."

"*Ja,*" Marzen agreed. "Vut do vee do?"

"It was my error," Khoronos said. "I will assume my state of accountability."

"Tomorrow?" Gilles asked.

"Tomorrow night," Khoronos instructed. "But don't worry about it now. You must go."

Gilles and Marzen departed down the hall. Veronica peeked out the door. Both men were dressed in sleek, dark suits. Marzen seemed to be carrying something. A black pouch?

A door clicked shut to her right. That's where they'd been, in the room made of mirrors. Khoronos had called it his "muse room." What did he do in there? Veronica could picture him sitting in the silver room all alone, contemplating his wisdoms.

She heard Marzen and Gilles leave out the front door. Then a car started up and pulled off.

What had Khoronos said? *She is tainted.* Who did he mean? She shrugged it off. "Who cares?" she muttered, and meandered back to her table. It had been another blurred day. She'd sketched obliviously from noon, and now it was 10 P.M. Time seemed to have no meaning here, no weight.

Now her mind wandered. Ginny and Amy must have worked the day away too; Veronica hadn't seen or heard them. She wondered if she would sleep with them again tonight but immediately answered *No*. She was finished with exploratory sex. The next person she slept with would be a man.

What now?

The sketch was finished. She used sketches only as outlines, much like a novelist. The sketch would not be part of the actual creative product. Khoronos had provided several sizes of canvas frames—a good brand too, Anthes Universal, which was double-primed and suitable for any paint base. She chose a 24″x34″; she hated easels, preferring a Trident brace-frame, which Khoronos had also surprisingly provided. And he'd provided equally good paints, Gamblin oils, among the best in the world, and Pearl brushes.

It was all here, but she still didn't feel ready to start. She still had not yet figured something out completely.

Me, she thought.

That was it. She didn't feel ready to paint her own likeness.

The sketch looked all right, but it was just a sketch, a rudiment. It wasn't her. Suddenly she felt frustrated.

I know, she thought just as suddenly.

She rushed to the hall. Khoronos was here for them, wasn't

he? Would he be mad if she disturbed him now, at this hour? She stood for a moment before his door, paused, then knocked.

"Come in."

"I'm sorry to dis—" but then she stopped just inside. Khoronos sat shirtless in a lotus position. He was meditating.

"I'll come back later," she said.

"No, stay." He raised a finger, eyes closed. "Just a moment."

Standing there, behind his back, discomfited her. She felt like an intrusion. Then he stood up and turned. The mirror-walled room was full of him, a thousand reflections at myriad angles.

"It may seem wildly eccentric, or even exaggerated."

"What?" she asked.

"This room."

"No, but . . ." She glanced around. "It's a little weird."

"This room helps me think. It inspires me. When I'm here, alone, I feel as though I'm sitting in the lap of infinity."

Veronica looked up and down. She saw her upturned face. She saw herself looking at herself between her feet. Even the ceiling and floor were mirrors.

"I didn't mean to disturb you."

"You're not. I'm here for you."

Now she looked at him. He was slim yet crisply muscled, well tanned. He wore white slacks and powder-blue shoes. His silver-blond hair hung like fine tinsel to his shoulders.

"Your work is going well. I can see it. Am I right?"

"Yes. Well, sort of."

"But you've come upon a stumbling block."

Veronica nodded. All that remained in the room now was the single chair made of chrome wire. Khoronos sat down in it and looked at her.

"Tell me."

How could she start without sounding stupid? "I'm painting my dream," she said. "I've got it all worked out now, but—"

"You are in the dream, correct?" he asked.

"Yes."

"And you don't know how to render yourself?"

"No, I don't. I have no idea. It's scary."

"That you might not paint yourself well? Or is it merely the *idea* of painting yourself that scares you?"

"The latter, I think."

Khoronos subtly smiled. "Re-creation is often scary, particularly when we must re-create ourselves with our own hands. The possibility always exists that we may falter, and hence—"

"Destroy ourselves," Veronica finished.

"Exactly." Suddenly he looked stern. "But had artists never dared to challenge themselves, then there would be no art."

Veronica glanced down. "You're disappointed with me."

"No," he said.

"I don't know what to do. I don't think I've ever been this excited about a painting before. I want it to be good."

"Then you must look into the face of your fear, grab it by the teeth, and accept the challenge."

The room nettled her nerves. There was nowhere she could look without seeing herself look back. Each wall extended as a vanishing point of her own doubt. "I don't think I'm looking at myself right."

"You are correct," Khoronos said.

"Sometimes . . ." Her voice diminished. "Sometimes I don't think I've ever really seen myself at all."

"But the impetus of all art, Ms. Polk, is seeing. You've learned to see many things. You merely have not yet extended your perceptions to the necessary extreme."

"What's the trick?"

"Transcension," he said.

She thought about that, aware of the mirror-faces watching her. The faces seemed hopeful, expectant.

Then Khoronos said, "Define art."

Her expression confessed her desperation.

Khoronos laughed. "Not an easy question, I know."

"But you have the answer," she felt sure. "What?"

"Art is transcension. There can be no other answer in the end. Art redefines all that we see, and without that redefinition, nothing has meaning, Ms. Polk. Nothing. To the entire realm of creation, the artist is but a vehicle of redefinition. Creation, in truth, is *re*-creation. Do you understand?"

"I guess so," she said, but she didn't really.

"Art is nothing more than the act of transcending the physical into the spiritual. That may sound cold, but it's also the greatest power on earth. We each assume our place in life, and the artist assumes his or her place too, merely in an exalted relativity."

What is your place? she wanted to ask.

He smiled as though he'd heard the thought. "The level of the success of any art depends on the success of the artist's power of perception. The power . . . to *see*."

Now Veronica felt swamped. She felt drowning in a lake of riddles, reaching out for something to hold on to.

"Do you understand now? Everything is meaningless until we give it meaning. Including ourselves."

Veronica stared not only at him but at what he'd said.

"But there's one more function, one more piece that makes art ultimate."

"What?"

"Transposition."

The word buried her at once. *None of you are ready yet,* Gilles had told them last night. And Marzen: *Not yet ready to transpose.*

She repeated the word in her mind. *Transposition.* It sounded echoic and vast, like a word spoken by a spirit.

"There," Khoronos said. "Art is transcension, and transcension, ultimately, is transposition. Art transposes something small with something great. It *becomes* something else *of* itself, something more than what it was."

Transposition, she thought again. The word now made her whole life, and all that she'd created in life, insignificant.

"Now." Khoronos rubbed his palms together. "You are creating a specific work, a definition of your dream. But you can't move on for one obstruction. The obstruction is yourself. Do I have it right so far?"

"Yes," Veronica said.

"The dream is the paradigm of the project, and you are an ingredient of the dream, which means that you must not only redefine the dream, but you must also redefine *yourself* as a component of the dream. You must turn your creative instincts upon yourself."

"How?"

"By looking at yourself."

"I don't know how! I told you!"

"By looking at yourself more completely than you ever have. Truth is the veil, Ms. Polk. You must look at yourself in *truth*."

She felt sweat begin to trickle under her arms. It was what he'd said earlier that scared her most of all—the challenge. It was easy to challenge ideals, it was easy to challenge concepts, insights, and politics. But it was not easy to challenge oneself in the same light.

"Look now," Khoronos commanded.

She turned to a mirror panel and looked. She must look at herself as more than a woman; as an object of transposition. She knew that now, and that was how she tried to see.

But . . . *Nothing,* she thought.

"Tell me what you see."

"Nothing."

It was just a reflection, a simple, physical replication in glass of nothing more than she was in life.

"Take off your clothes," Khoronos said.

In the mirror, her eyes widened at the brash request. Khoronos stood up. "I'll leave if you're modest," he said.

"No," she whispered.

She stripped quickly, casting each garment aside like pieces of things no longer wanted. She tried to avert her eyes but couldn't. No matter where she looked, her own face was there, looking back.

Naked, she stood up straight. The reflection showed Khoronos appraising her in the silver background. He wasn't appraising her body, though. He was looking straight into her eyes.

"You are a beautiful woman," he said.

Veronica tried not to gulp. She wanted to winnow her thoughts but she found his gaze too distracting; she couldn't concentrate on the matter at hand. Ingots of sweat formed between her breasts. Others broke and ran down her back. Was this Khoronos' way of seducing her? Was this how art preceptors made passes?

She almost hoped it was, for that she could deal with. She hoped he would remove his slacks in the reflection, come up behind her, and start. Then she could relate.

But none of that ever happened.

"Look at yourself, first, as though you were an object," he said. "Say you're painting a still life—you're painting an apple. Don't think of what you see in the mirror as a reflection, it's an *object.* Assess that object now, with your eyes, and transpose the objectivity of that object through your artistic muse."

The reflection isn't me, she convinced herself. *It's an object. It's an apple that I'm going to paint.* The mirror created a sudden intense clarity, surfacing the details of her body to razor sharpness. She could see each detail of her nipples, her navel, the shine on each strand of public hair. The profuse sweat made her flesh look shellacked. Soon she felt close to blushing; seeing herself through such extreme lucidity began to excite her, or perhaps it was the hope that Khoronos was seeing her the same way. Her sex began to moisten. Her nipples swelled.

"Now," Khoronos said, "Close your eyes and continue to look. Retain the visualization, and examine it with your mind."

When she closed her eyes, the image did indeed remain. Only the background changed, from bright mirror-silver to utter black.

No, it didn't *change*. It transposed.

"The mirrors are gone now," he said. "You are standing in the grotto of your dream. You are no longer an object, you are a *woman*. You are the most creative, and most beautiful . . . *woman* . . . on earth."

Veronica saw. She was standing identically—naked, sweating—in the hot, dark place of her dream. She seemed to be waiting for something.

Or someone.

"Go on," he said, perturbed. "You're not looking closely enough."

She stood in limbo, in black, staring through closed eyes.

"If you don't look closely enough, you will *fail*."

Now she whimpered. She could feel her mind exert upon the image, squeeze it like squeezing juice from a pulpy fruit.

"Imagine your passion," he said.

Her mind scurried. What *was* her passion? She imagined herself masturbating on the terrace, the moon watching her. She imagined Marzen deftly knelt between her legs as his mouth tended her clitoris. She imagined her bacchanal night with Ginny and Amy, and the glut of lavish sensation, their hands and tongues investigating every inch of her flesh.

But nothing happened. The image remained unenriched.

What about fantasies, or passions that had not yet occurred? She imagined Marzen's penis in her mouth, his testicles warm and large in her small hand. She imagined Gilles pushing her knees back to her shoulders and penetrating her, flooding the moist purse of her sex. She imagined Khoronos—

The disappointment was thick in his throat. "You're failing, Ms. Polk. I guess I was wrong about you."

He must see the anguish on her face. She could think of nothing else that might allow the image of herself to transpose. She would never be able to do the painting now. *Quit,* she thought. *You're a failure, so quit. You're not an artist, you're only pretending to be—you're a fake. You can't see, you can't even see yourself. Quit the whole business. Go back to Jack, get a normal job, lead a normal life. What good is an artist who can't see past her own nose?*

"Try again," Khoronos said more softly. "Look deeper. If you visualize your rightful place in the dream, the image will transpose into what it must be in order to create it. Try again."

She remained standing, her head back and her eyes squeezed shut. She wanted to bolt. She wanted to grab her clothes, find Ginny, and get the hell out of this crackpot madhouse of foreign studs, carnival mirrors, and art-weirdo philosophy.

But—*Try again,* she thought.

The dream is black, but she is bright within it; she is almost luminous in the explicit clarity of her flesh. It's a black grotto, some subterranean fissure of her id. She is waiting for someone. That is the key. Whoever she is waiting for will make the image transpose. She will find her transposition through the acknowledgment of her passion—not fantasies or past sexual experiences. Real passion. Passion which transcends. She knows one thing: whoever is waiting for her is her passion.

The grotto's empty black space thickens with heat. The rough pocked walls begin to tint, tongues of wavering orange light growing bright. Out of nothing, the burning man rises, the man made of flames. The fire-lover.

She sees him. His body is beautiful and sculpted of millions of tiny points of flame. He is hissing. His large, delineated genitals are pulsing for her, rousing. In his fire-eyes, she sees all the passion of history.

Then she sees herself. She is more than herself. The splendor of her passion transcends her flesh. In this bright, hot unreality, she is now more real than she ever has been or ever could be. Her spirit now transposes with her flesh. It has made her greater, more beautiful, truthful, and real than all the sum of her worldly parts.

She is arching back. Her arms are rising as tears are squeezed out of her eyes.

"I can see it!" she whimpers.

"Yes."

The burning man approaches her. The proximity of all that passion burns her into a state of ecstasy. She is coming, reeling, nearly screaming in bliss.

The fire-lover takes her hand and leads her away forever.

Veronica's knees went out; she collapsed to the smooth mirror floor. Sweat ran off her in rivulets, and her sex was throbbing down. She tried to rise to her hands and knees but collapsed again. Seeing herself transposed into the dream siphoned off all that remained of her strength. Her sweat left a print of herself on the glass.

She rolled over on her back. Her wet hands reached up for Khoronos.

Khoronos was no longer in the room.

CHAPTER 23

Susan lay back in her plush bed and stretched like a cat. Desire existed for a reason—to be sated—so why should she feel bad? The two young men administered to her from either side; she felt like a dynast on a bed of feathers, with these two as her sex slaves. They were irresistible. She had no inhibitions about leaving the lights on. "We want to *see* you, Susan," the short-haired one had said. "Fine," she'd said. She wanted to *see* them too. The best sex must slake every sense, like the best poetry.

They'd come on to her at the Undercroft. She'd shot the shit awhile with Craig, who she'd been putting the make on for months. As usual he'd politely declined her rather forward suggestion. "Know any good plumbers, handsome?" she'd asked. "I have a drain that needs to be snaked." Craig had very kindly given her the local number for Roto-Rooter. It didn't matter, though. Perseverance always paid off. She'd have his gorgeous ass in bed one of these days, and then she'd show him what a *real* woman could do. Yes, sir, she'd suck his balls right out the hole in his knob.

Then there was that lush cop—Jack something. The poor fucker had been plowing one Scotch after the next. She'd heard he was a county homicide cop on the skids. He looked like drift: crushed slacks, coffee-stained shirt and tie, and hair longer than Jesus. At eleven o'clock sharp he went facedown on the bar. Craig and another keep had carried him out.

That's when Susan had been just about to leave. *Damn good thing I didn't,* she thought now, and giggled as a pinky slipped up her anus. Because that's when Fraus and Philippe had walked in.

Where'd guys this young get money for suits like that? These two were dressed to the max. *Rich European daddy's boys,* Susan had concluded from their accents and mannerisms. By now Susan had heard every bar come-on line in the book. These guys, though, they had it down. "Miss," the bigger one had said, "you may find this hard to believe, but I have psychic tendencies." They stood on either side of her, smiling and beautiful in their crisp Italian suits. "Oh, yeah?" she challenged. "Tell me something about my life." "You are a poet," he said.

She'd been taken aback. It was true. She'd dabbled in poetry since college, had even had some published. Most of her stuff was clearly derivative of Anne Sexton (Susan preferred to think of it as *emulation*), descanting stanzas of free verse which depicted the finding of oneself through sexuality. Sex, she believed, was power, and her poetry detailed that power, often quite explicitly. Her favorite thus far was called "Female Utilitarian Coronation in Knowledge," which had been published with some others in *The Tait Literary Review.*

"I am Fraus," he said. "And this is my friend Philippe. He is also a poet."

Susan found them immediately fascinating, these two beautiful suave boys. They'd talked for two hours, about theology, poetical dynamics, and the philosophy of sex. Philippe claimed to be published in *Métal Urbain* and *Disharmonisch,* renowned European art journals.

"What do you write about?" Susan had asked.

"*La beauté des femmes.*"

"What?"

"The beauty of women."

Hmm, she thought. "And you? What do you do?"

"I sculpt," Fraus said. "On the same theme."

"Do women pose for you?"

"Not in the traditional sense. I do not sculpt by looking at a model. My models must be women I have loved. I sculpt by the memory of touch, from what my hands have touched in passion."

Their approach refreshed her. So what if it was phony? It was different and unique. She drank Cardinals through their trialogue of creative innuendos. They drank beer called Patrizier Z.A., which was nonalcoholic. When she asked about it, Fraus replied, "Neither of us partakes in alcohol. The creative spirit is quickly corrupted through the flesh."

"Drink is not a very edifying pursuit," Philippe added. "There are better things to do than drink."

Now you're talking, Susan thought. But this proposed a problem. Who would she go home with? Philippe or Fraus? Unless they were roommates, she couldn't very well go home with both of them.

"Hurry up, please, it's time," Craig quoted T. S. Eliot to announce last call. "Or to put it more eloquently, everybody get the fuck out of the bar!"

Susan finished her Cardinal. Immediately she felt even more aroused—her panties must be soaked. Perhaps the pressure of choice spurred her libido further. They paid her tab and theirs, and looked at her, their faces forlorn, beautiful.

Which one do I want? she struggled.

Then came the simplest answer of all.

Both.

"Follow me," she said. "The blue Miata convertible."

She hadn't quite made out their car. It was big and black, like a Caddy. The headlights behind her could've been the light of their expectations, which was fine with her. Her own expectations were beginning to drench her. She hoped she didn't soak through her dress to the suede seat. Once on a whim she'd picked up a middie at the Rocks, whose own rocks hadn't lasted long enough for her to get it in her mouth. *Kids,* she thought. *They never last.* The nut stain on her seat would last, though. For sure.

The complex was dark. In the elevator they'd assailed her, kissing both sides of her neck. Philippe played with her breasts while Fraus stuck his hand up her skirt. She giggled almost embarrassingly as her hands drifted to their crotches, then she giggled again. The elevator wasn't the only thing going up.

None of them had wasted time on preliminaries. She'd never done two at once before, but as horny as she felt right now, she thought she'd do just about anything.

And that had been that.

Philippe's pinky slipped out of her anus; she flinched. They bathed her with their tongues. Fraus went down on her like a famished animal brought to a full trough. She gasped at the abrupt avalanche of sensation. Her first orgasm went off like a bomb in her loins, and she shrieked.

"Shh," Philippe whispered. He straddled her chest as Fraus kissed circles of afterglow around her sex.

The first one always flattened her; it made her feel run over. She lay back in descending bliss. She'd only need a little time to be ready again, and this thrilled her. Most guys would've been finished by now, but these two were just starting. Refraction, the sex books called it. After a first big bang she could start having multiples. And Philippe's penis between her breasts would give her something to do in the interim.

Then, for the first time, the question occurred to her. "How did you guys know I was a poet?"

"Your aura," Philippe said, gently pinching her nipples.

Fraus kissed the nest of trimmed black hair. "Creative people give off a light, like a halo. You have a beautiful halo."

What lovely bullshit this was. Of course, she didn't believe they were psychic. They'd obviously read some of her local poetry, and someone had pointed her out to them downtown somewhere.

"If you were for real," she said to Philippe, "you'd write a poem about me."

"I will. I'll call it 'Lady of the Halo.'"

"And I will do a sculpture," Fraus added.

"Of me?"

"Of this." His hand cupped her pubis. A finger ran gently up the groove. "I will call it 'Adoration.'"

"And I'll write a poem about you guys," she said. "I'll call it 'Bullshit Artists with Style.'"

All three of them laughed.

Soon it would be time to play sandwich. *They'll be the bread, and I'll be the cheese.* She'd seen it in a movie once, *Room for Two,* not exactly an Oscar winner, but the idea had always titillated her. Many things did, in fact. She felt alight with lust; nothing occurred to her then but her desire, not condoms or morality, not danger. Just the pinpoint, knife-sharp edge of the sensations that demanded to be loosed.

She pressed her breasts together and let Philippe stroke between them. "I'm a little disappointed, though," she joked. "I was hoping you guys really were psychic."

"Are you ready to go on?" Philippe asked.

"We'll be the bread," Fraus said. "You'll be the cheese."

CHAPTER 24

Jack woke up in his clothes. *Aw, Jesus, not again.* He staggered to the bathroom, groaning, and threw up. Only when he staggered back did he notice Faye sitting there.

"I'm sorry," he said.

Her detached gaze was the worst response he could fathom.

"I broke my promise."

"You sure did," she concurred.

"Something happened. I . . ." Only shreds of memory flitted back. He sat down on the bed and rubbed his eyes. "Somebody told me something about someone. I guess I couldn't handle it, and I got drunk."

"It's that girl, isn't it? Veronica?"

Jack nodded.

"You were calling out her name in your sleep."

When Jack Cordesman fucks up, he thought, *there are no half measures.* How could he explain this? "I'm an alcoholic, Faye. I have been for a while, I guess. When I'm faced with something I can't deal with, I drink."

"That's supposed to be an excuse? How long do you think you can go on like this? This was the second night in a row you've had to be *brought* home. You're not in control of your own life."

"I know, I can't help it," he said. "I'm a drunk."

"If that's what you think, then that's all you'll ever be." Faye got up and walked out of the bedroom.

He followed after her. "Why don't you give me a chance!"

She turned at the door with her briefcase. "A chance for what?"

"You know."

"No, I don't know. What are you saying?"

What *was* he saying? "I thought that when this Triangle thing is over, we might, you know—"

"Don't even say it, Jack. Three nights ago you told me you still loved Veronica. Now you're saying you don't?"

Jack sat down in the middle of the stairs. "I guess I don't know what I'm saying. I'm trying to get over it, that's all."

"So what am I? The consolation prize?"

"That's not what I mean at all, and you fucking know it. You ever been in love, Faye, and have it not work?"

"Yeah," she said. "Once."

"And all you had to do was blink and you were over it?"

"No, of course not."

"How long did it take you?"

She looked at him. Her anger fizzed away. "A year," she said.

"And if something happened to that person, say he disappeared, say he got in some kind of trouble, wouldn't you still be concerned about him, even if it happened after the relationship fell apart?"

Her pause drew out. "Yeah, I'd still be concerned."

"All right, fine. That's what's happening with me right now. So why don't you cut me a little—"

Faye left and slammed the door. *Outstanding*, he thought, chin in his palm. He went down to the kitchen, drank some orange juice, and threw up again. Then he dialed Craig's number, to find out what he'd forgotten about last night. Craig's roommate answered.

"Craig there?"

"No," she said. Jack could never remember her name; all he knew was that she rented him a room up the street. She sounded distressed. "The police took him," she said.

"The *police*? What for? He get in trouble or something?"

"No, they just took him. For questioning, they said."

"Questioning about what?"

"I don't know!"

"Calm down, will you. I'm a cop myself. I might be able to help him out. But I need to know *who* took him."

"I told you! Police!"

"What kind of police? City cops, state? County?"

"It was those county assholes."

Jack frowned. "All right, I'll—"

She hung up. *Questioning?* he wondered. But before he could make another call, the phone rang.

"Jack? Randy. We got another one."

"Holy mother of shit," Jack muttered. He felt faint, sick, and enraged all at once.

"And we've also got something else," Randy added.

"What?"

"Two witnesses."

"That's it!" Jan Beck shouted nasally. "There's too many people in here! Everybody out!" Jack and Randy stood behind three uniforms at the door. She pointed at the uniforms. "Out!" She pointed at Randy."Out! You too, Captain. Out!"

"You heard the lady," Jack said. "Everybody out."

It was a cramped sixth-floor apartment, one bedroom, but nice, in a nice location. Jan Beck needed room to do her thing; Jack had only glimpsed the bedroom, but that's all he'd needed to show him what he'd already seen twice this week. A room vibrant in red streaks, redecorated in blood, the pale victim lashed to the drenched bed. Red everywhere. Red.

Everything was the same, Randy had informed him upon arrival. No forced entry, exit off the balcony. Neighbors on either side had reported hearing a commotion at about 2:15 A.M.

"Susan Lynn," Randy said in the living room. "Real estate broker, thirty-five. She owns the place."

"Same kind of rep as the other two?"

"Yeah, only she got around more." Randy flashed Jack a promo picture the brokerage had given him. Elegant face, short black hair. Big crystal-blue eyes and a pretty mouth.

"I've seen this girl," Jack said.

"Everybody has. She hangs out a lot in the local bars. Every single keep we showed this to has seen her. She made the circuit. Couple places—'Dillo's, McGuffy's, Middleton's—have barred her."

"For what?"

"Slutting around. It's bad for business. One night she got plastered at McGuffy's and started taking off her clothes. Bunch of other places caught her blowing guys in the men's room."

"She comes to the Undercroft every now and then."

"We know, and that's where we hit pay dirt. She was in the Undercroft last night."

Very slowly Jack said, "I was there last night too."

"So we heard. Your pal Craig is down at the station for questioning. He says he saw her leave with two guys after last call."

"*Two* guys?"

Randy nodded. "You remember seeing her, Jack?"

Did he? *I don't remember seeing anything last night.* "I got fucked up. I don't even remember what time I left."

The look on Randy's face told all. *Drunk again,* it said. "We should have a good composite in a couple hours."

"You find out anything about her background?"

"We're working on it. All we know right now is she's a local."

"Same as the other two."

"Right. And something else—she was a poet."

A poet? Jack thought. "We found poetry at Rebecca Black's too."

"Yeah, some coincidence, huh? Susan Lynn was a bit more serious, though. She'd had some published, local literary mags."

Jack rubbed a hand over his face. He'd forgotten to shave. "Maybe a coincidence, maybe not. We'll have to check out what schools they went to, literature courses, poetry classes. It's all a mutual interest."

"But Shanna Barrington didn't write poetry."

"No, but take a look at what she did do."

Randy shrugged. "She worked for an advertising firm."

"Right, and don't you see a commonality there? Shanna Barrington was the director of the—"

"Art department," Randy remembered. "I still don't—"

"Karla Panzram says the killers have some very definite artistic inclinations. So far they've murdered three women, and all three also had definite artistic inclinations."

"I don't know, Jack. Sounds like you're digging in shit to me."

"Maybe," Jack said. "You dig in shit long enough, though, sometimes you find gold."

"Make way!" someone shouted. Two techs rushed out bearing a stretcher. On the stretcher lay the familiar dark green transport bag full of the remnants of one Susan Lynn. Jack watched the woman leave her home for the last time. Several more techs came out next, holding boxes of relevant evidence. Last was Jan Beck, in bright red TSD utilities, walking briskly as she snapped off rubber gloves. The gloves were dark scarlet.

"This one looks different," she said.

"How so?"

"I'm not quite sure yet, sir. Stop by the shop later; I'll know more then." She brushed by the uniforms at the door and left.

"Come on," Randy invited. "Let's talk to our witnesses."

But Jack stood spacily in the dark apartment, his eyes wandering. This place didn't feel like someone's home at all. It felt like a robbed grave.

Craig looked haggard as he sat beside the composite artist in interview room no. 1. The artist herself, a heavyset woman with a dark ponytail, looked flustered.

"How's it coming?" Jack asked.

Craig sputtered. The artist said, "It's not."

"What's the problem?"

"Can't get anything down," Craig said, laxing back at the table. "I saw them, but I can't remember what I saw."

"Come on," Randy said. "A small bar like the 'Croft, two well-dressed white males sitting with a regular?"

"They pay cash?" Jack asked.

"Yeah. Their tab came to about forty bucks. They paid with small stuff, left a double-saw for tip."

"They pay hers too?"

Craig nodded.

"What did they drink?"

"The guys drank Patriziers, three apiece. Susan was drinking Cardinals, her usual. She had four of them, and a sandwich."

"Were any of them smoking? They leave any butts?"

"None of them were smoking. In fact, they were the only group sitting up at the bar that didn't use their ashtray."

"How about glasses? Did the guys pour their beers or did they drink out of the bottles?"

"Bottles," Craig said.

Randy was smirking. "For someone who doesn't remember anything, you sure remember a lot."

"I told you, the thing I don't remember is what they looked like."

"Come on, they were sitting right up front at the bar. You were serving them for two hours, looking right at them. Did you know her at all?"

"Yeah," Craig said, tapping a Marlboro. "I knew her pretty well."

"How well?" Randy interjected.

"Not *that* well. She'd come in a lot and put the make on me, you know, flirt around."

"She'd make herself available to you, in other words."

"Yeah, you could say that. But I never—"

"Right, you never took her up on it, huh? A good-looking woman like that? Never?"

"Never," Craig said. "I'm just saying I knew her. People come in on a regular basis, you get to know them, you talk to them, you know?"

"Sure," Randy said. "You talk to her last night?"

"Yeah, I said hello to her."

"What did she say?"

"The usual shit, how ya doin', what's new, that sort of thing."

"And the two guys were with her then?"

"Yeah." Craig lit his cigarette, sighing smoke. "And you're gonna love this. She even introduced me to them."

Jack and Randy leaned over the table at the same time. Jack said, "You mean you *met* these two guys?"

"Yeah."

"She introduce you to them by their names?"

"Yeah."

"Craig, what were their names?"

"I don't remember."

"Jesus Christ!" Randy slammed his fist down on the table. "You saw them but you don't remember what they looked like! She told you their names but you don't remember what they were!"

"I remember Susan introducing me to them. I remember shaking their hands and saying nice to meet ya, or something like that."

"And what did they say?"

Craig slouched. "I don't remember, man."

Randy's face looked pressurized. Jack shifted the angle to cool him off. "Does the 'Croft throw away the empty bottles?"

"We take them twice a week to the recycling plant. All the downtown restaurants and bars do."

"You still have last night's bottles?"

"They're still downstairs, boxed up. We haven't taken them out yet."

"Did many other people order Patrizier last night?"

"No, just the two guys with Susan. It's zero-alcohol beer; not many people buy it. Tastes like German lager, but no buzz."

"I'll need those bottles for our evidence people. The prints'll tell us if we're dealing with the same two killers, or two new ones. How hard will it be to retrieve those bottles?"

"Easy. They'd be in the last box we stacked last night."

"Good, I want you to go down to the 'Croft right now with one of our techs. Give him the bottles. Then go home, get some rest."

"Get some rest?" Randy objected. "We need a composite!"

"Get some rest," Jack repeated, "think about what you saw, and maybe it'll come back to you. We're looking for any details you can give us. Hair color, eye color, moles, scars, anything. Two of the guys we're looking for are probably tall, well built, and attractive. We know from pubic hair analysis that one is dark blond, the other's got darker hair. We also know that the same black wig was worn by each of the first two killers. Go home and give it some thought. Maybe some of that will ring some bells."

Dejected, Craig nodded.

Jack led him out and arranged for TSD to meet him at the 'Croft for the Patrizier bottles. But out in the parking lot, before Craig got into his Alfa, Jack asked, "Was I in the bar last night when the two guys were there?"

"No," Craig said. "You passed out. I had the cook fill in while I took you home. The two guys came in sometime after that." Craig donned his shades and looked up. "But . . .

"Yeah?"

"I do remember one thing. It was just when I was leaving to take you home. As I was pulling out of the lot, another car was pulling in. The only reason I remember is that it looked like a classy set of wheels, high-buck stuff."

"Is there any detail you can give me about that vehicle?"

"Just that it was big and black. It could've been a limo."

"I hope you've got a sense of humor," Randy said.

"In this business? What do you think?"

Randy opened the door to interview room no. 2. "And I hope you brought plenty of cigarettes," he added.

What Jack saw sitting at the table made him think of the word "emaciation." They called them "dock bums," any port city's equivalent to an alley denizen. Health Services did a good job of taking care of them in this state—shelters, doctors, food—but there was a percentage of this human detritus that simply refused assistance. These people wore their homes on their backs, slept under boat tarps, and ate out of dumpsters. According to statistics, more than fifty percent were chronic schizophrenics.

"Mr. Carlson, this is Captain Cordesman. I'd like you to tell him what you told me a little while ago. Okay?"

The man at the table wore rotten tennis shoes, an oil-smudged dress shirt, and a crinkled black tie with an embroidered half-moon on it. Folded over the next chair was a tattered gray overcoat. The man's hair, a dull steel-gray, was neatly combed back and longer than Jack's. The lined, weather-beaten face captured some vague impression of lost power, a Lear of the streets, a proud exile. His teeth were rotten. His left eye showed only cloudy white.

"Do you believe in gods?" Carlson looked up and asked.

"God or gods?" Jack specified.

"It makes no difference."

"Well, I'm really not sure, Mr. Carlson. But I think so."

"I would like a cigarette, please."

Jack slid the man his lighter and a pack of Camels. Carlson removed a cigarette, examined it, then tapped it down. "You should always light the imprinted end when you're smoking a filterless. The blank end is the end you put in your mouth."

"Why is that, Mr. Carlson?"

"So if the enemy finds the butts, they won't know what brand it is. They won't know if it's their own people or yours. I know of men who've died because they lit the wrong end. The enemy finds the butts, then they know what direction you're headed.

You ever thought of that? That you can give your position away with a cigarette?"

"No, Mr. Carlson, but it's an interesting point. Were you in the war?"

"I was one of the gods." Carlson lighted the Camel savoringly, sucking deep. "We rescued twenty-two thousand people one day. I T.C.'d an Easy Eight. We thought it was all over by then, but we were wrong. I was a captain too."

This was not going to be easy, Jack realized, but then Randy offered, "Mr. Carlson was a tank commander in World War II. He won the Distinguished Service Cross."

"Me and my boys had twenty-seven kills. Tigers and Panthers. The Tigers were tough to open, had over a foot of armor up front. Only way you could get them was to hit the turret ring. The Panthers were easy; they were diesel and always leaked at the lines. All you had to do was put one phosphorus round on the back deck."

"Mr. Carlson was in the unit that liberated Buchenwald," Randy said.

Jesus, Jack thought. *No wonder he's so screwy.*

"It goes back to what I was saying, about gods."

Gods? "Mr. Carlson, tell me what you saw last night."

"We're all points of force," Carlson answered, smoke drifting smoothly from his nostrils. "Everybody. We got bodies, sure, but inside, we're all points of force. You can define a point of force as a unit of will. Do you follow me, Captain? What is all of life about? Why are we here? There is a reason; it's not just an accident, even though that's what most folks think these days."

"All right," Jack ventured. "Why are we here?"

"To prove the nature of our will."

There was something haunting about this man. He spoke softly but with intense deliberation. There was belief glowing deep behind the tattered features and racked body. Jack felt a chill; Carlson seemed to be looking at him with the dead left eye, and seeing something.

"The world is a passion play," Carlson said, "an eternal drama where each actor represents either graciousness or corruption. Bet that sounds silly to you."

"No, Mr. Carlson. It doesn't sound silly at all."

"Gods," Carlson repeated.

Randy leaned against the wall. Carlson was crazy, obviously, but why did his madness seem so effervescent? Jack very much wanted to know. He wanted to see this man's heart, not just the blasted face and blind white eye.

"You got a head here?"

"Sure, Mr. Carlson. Down the hall to the left."

Carlson got up, joints ticking. *Yes,* Jack thought. *He looks like a conquered king.* A corporal at the door led the old man to the rest room.

"He's been in Crownsville a bunch of times," Randy explained. "City cops pick him up wandering the docks at night. Carlson gives them the spiel about gods and points of force and all that, so they check him in for a standard psych evaluation. He doesn't take Social Security and he turned down a disability pension from the Army. I kind of admire him."

"Me too," Jack concurred.

"Too bad he's incompetent to testify."

Jack lit up and blew smoke. "I don't care about that. I just want to know what he saw. No word salad, no pink elephants or aliens in his pocket. He doesn't seem to be story-mixing, and he doesn't seem schizo, does he?"

"No. And that's what ticks me."

"Why?"

"Listen to the rest of his story, Jack."

Carlson teetered back in, his head held up beneath old flowing hair like a mane: pride in ruins.

"Mr. Carlson, when was the last time you ate?"

"I eat three times a day, son. Be surprised what the downtown restaurants toss out. I probably eat better than you."

Jack recalled his last TV dinner and was inclined to agree. "How about shelter, Mr. Carlson? We have state and county departments that can find a place for you to live."

"I got a place to live, son. A fine, fine place."

"Where?"

"The world," Carlson said with the vaguest half-smile. He lit another of Jack's Camels and smoked it very methodically.

Jack looked hard at this human wreck, and the only important thing finally hit him. Carlson, though completely destitute, was completely and honestly happy.

"Let's get back to what you were saying, about gods."

Carlson nodded as objectively as a cop talking about a bust. 'Gods made the world, gave it to us as a gift. Worst thing is nost people don't care; they think *they're* the gifts. Makes ne feel bad that folks can be so selfish, take all the beauty or granted, everything. Me, I love it."

"What, Mr. Carlson?"

"The beauty, the joy. It's all over the place, everywhere you ook. Thing is, when you stop looking, you're finished."

Jack wanted to ask what this had to do with anything, but e quickly realized that was Carlson's point. "I think maybe I now what you mean, Mr. Carlson."

"Hope so, and your friend there too. All of you. I get to valking. Probably walked thousands of miles in my life. And very step I take"— Carlson looked right at Jack with his dead ye—"every single step is a celebration. Every time I put my oot down in graciousness, that's like saying thank you."

"Thank you to who? To the gods?"

"Yes, son, to the gods. It's acknowledgment of the gift. Me, walk mostly at night 'cause night is better, clearer. I gotta ee it all to keep my graciousness real. I gotta *be in it*—the eauty, the gift. The stars, the sky, the way the water sounds lapping the piers, all that. And especially the moon. Somemes I think the gods put the moon up there so we'd never orget the gift."

"So you like to walk the docks at night?"

"That's right. Where the sea meets the land and all that. Vhere one gift joins another under the light of the moon." Carlon stubbed out the butt. "Big things, dark. They had no faces."

Jack's forehead crinkled. "What?"

"You believe in the gods, right? Isn't that what you said?"

"Yes," Jack told him for lack of anything else.

"And if you believe in the gods, you have to believe in their ounterparts, right? Can't have one without the other. That's ie way it is. Reckoning. A point of force is a unit of will. 'ou believe in one, you believe in both. You believe in the ods, you believe in the devils too."

"Sure, Mr. Carlson," Jack said, but he thought: *What the ell is this guy talking about?*

"That's what I been trying to tell you, son. That's what I aw coming down that building last night." Carlson's dead eye tared. "I saw devils."

CHAPTER 25

Faye found two more good sources in the lower levels, but still not the one text she wanted most of all. Her attention, though, as she bent over her desk, kept wandering off. She'd read whole passages of *Das Grimoire* and could remember none of it.

> of calling upon Satan himself to obfuscate detection. Lucifer, as does God, protects the faithful.

The study coves were abandoned; she felt astray down here, abandoned herself in silence. She could guess what it was: her unpleasant scene with Jack. Had she been too hard on him, or not hard enough? Did he know how badly it hurt her to see him like that? He'd said a lot this morning, things that ordinarily would have overjoyed her. He'd asked for a *chance*, hadn't he? But circumstance had ruined it all. It always did.

Always, she thought.

The fact was, it hurt too much to care. By now she knew that she loved him—disheveled drunk that he was—but she didn't know what to do. There was logic and there was hope. Why was it that the two could never meet on common ground?

She closed *Das Grimoire;* it was either poorly translated or just unreadable. The second text, *The Morakis Compendium of Demonology*, was apparently an annotation of an earlier text. The printing date was 1957.

> SURROGATISM, SATANIC: The process, usually in Black Mass, of the substitution of spirits, not to be confused with invoked possession. This was sometimes sacrificial. It is

derived from the Middle Latin *sub*, in place of + *rogare*, elect, which implies a discretionary selection of participants. There is some suggestion, according to recent subtranslations of the *shelta thari* manuscripts recovered in the St. Gall Monastery, that pre-Druidic magi, called Ur-Locs, practiced deitic surrogatism as early as 2500 B.C. The Occupation Registry of Caesar, too, hints suspiciously of similar activity, that seminarial hierophytes [apostate priests] "offered up themselves to the devils so that they may come to the Earth and see the new nemesis with their own eyes." Most notorious, however, was the subrogatic process of the mid-era aorists of lower Europe, where, according to Catholic transcriptions, *praelytes* [highest-order priests or prelates] used well-trained surrogates to "give spirit and flesh to the lords of the dark." Unfortunately, like the Druids, the aorists left no written record of themselves, practicing exclusively *sub rosa*, and therefore the actual ritual designs of satanic surrogatism remain mostly speculative. [See INCARNATION, RITES OF]

"Okay," Faye muttered. "Progress." The stout binding crackled as she turned to the *I*'s.

INCARNATION, RITES OF: The ritual practice of the physical supplantation or substitution of deities and humans. [From the Late Latin *incarnare*, to make flesh.] Ritual incarnation seems to be surprisingly widespread yet strangely difficult to trace with much detail. However, most forms of counter-worship have always employed verifiable rites for the incarnation of their gods—

Faye skimmed down; it was a large—and decidedly grim—entry. Many cults supposedly brought demons forth for short periods, to eat. Faye did not need to be advised of the menu. Much evidence suggested that the famous cenotes of Assyrian and Mayan cultures were actually incarnation temples, where Ashipu and Toltec priests would surrogate themselves with demons and attempt to inseminate human women. Female bangomas of the African Bantu tribes allegedly incarnated war demons into the bodies of soldiers during battles with hostile tribes, and the Dandis of ancient India used incarnation rites to give flesh to the legion of Asura, demons of vampirism and lycanthropy. Apparently demons, regardless of geography, liked to have a little walking-around time on earth. But, *Come on,* Faye thought impatiently. *What about the aorists?* A little more skimming and she found:

> numerous records attest that aorists near what is now Erlangen routinely incarnated Narazel with apostate surrogoti, to oversee Black Mass, witness the murder of priests, and participate in orgiastic rites. A Slavic sect regularly incarnated the demon Baalzephon, an incubus, who yearly took a human wife. Baalzephon, who closely parallels many demons of passion and creativity [see SAKTA, Hindu; TII, Polynesia; LUR, American Indian], was known as "The Father of the Earth." Here the student will discern ritual incarnation at its greatest extremity. The Sect of Baalzephon existed solely to surfeit the demon's thirst for 1) creative stimuli, 2) the visualization of the beauty of women, and 3) intercourse. Baalzephon's passion was apparently unlimited. His impresa, the starred trine, or triangle, was said to serve as a lacuna, or physical ingress, which opened annually via a series of precursory sacrifices. Generally three such sacrifices (one for each point of the trine) were implemented as prelude to the final rite, all of which were discharged by Baalzephon himself, incarnated through trained surrogates. Baalzephon could even be incarnated multiply, to increase his stimulus. A fourth sacrifice was later executed upon the trine itself, which allegedly effected a bodily supplantation and granted Baalzephon an actual moment of nonsurrogated existence on earth. This rite, the ultimate form of incarnation, was known to the aorists as transposition.

Faye felt mentally washed out; all this demon stuff was beginning to get under her skin. *Precursory sacrifices,* she thought, depressed. *Transposition.* The aorists believed that their rituals were never-ending. How many people had they murdered through the ages? Probably thousands. It was madness.

She went up to the small cafeteria and got a cup of strong coffee, trying to free her mind of the undertow of her reading. The librarians still hadn't found the one book she wanted most,

The Synod of the Aorists, which had evidently been misplaced during recent renovations. It was the only book on file devoted solely to the practice of aorism, and hence probably the only title of its kind in the world. Thus far, though, all this dark stuff—murder, sacrifice, incarnation—made her feel like a mop in a wringer. Part of her hoped the librarians never found that last book.

Patterns, Jack pondered.

The vital element in solving any unusual homicide was pattern. A pattern must be established in order to pursue the perpetrator. Two types of patterns seemed the most viable. Patterns of modus and patterns of psychology. They'd examined the patterns of modus in the Triangle case and had gotten nowhere. The psychological pattern he found much more useful; when you understood the killer, it was easier to get on his tracks. *But I've got two killers,* he thought at the desk. *Maybe four. Maybe more than that.* And they all seemed to be committing the same crime not only through the same modus pattern but also through the same psychological pattern. Intuition was important too, but actually all intuitions were preformed through their own pattern of assessment. Jack was good at assessing things; that's the only reason he wasn't still driving a sector beat and shooting five with the other uniforms at Mister Donut. He could maturate a workable pattern of intuition out of the assessment of facts.

But neither pattern was working here. *What about victim patterns?* In his mind he saw triangles, glyphs, and the scarlet word *Aorista.* The victims had patterns too. Unstructured moral behavior, promiscuity, erotomania, as Dr. Panzram called it—sexual patterns. All three 64s were successful, well-educated single women. And still another: they were all looking for the same thing when they died, which meant they *lacked* the same thing.

Passion. They had everything in their lives but passion.

Now a new pattern had alighted. Susan Lynn wrote poetry. Rebecca Black wrote poetry. Shanna Barrington was an art director. *A creative pattern. A general artistic pattern of shared interest.* And stranger, the evidence proved that none of them had ever worked together, gone to school together, or knew the same people. Nor at any time had they ever known each other. Yet the patterns remained.

Bizarre words occurred to him. Similitude. Homology. Parity.

Parallelism, he thought. The patterns of the perpetrators adjoined with the patterns of the victims. Karla Panzram's graphological diagnoses indicated a general artistic pattern motivating the killers. All of a sudden Jack felt inhumed by patterns.

Gods, he thought next. *Devils.* He wondered what the old dock bum Carlson had really seen last night. Two *things* scaling down a six-story condo. Large and naked but not human. Many dock bums were alcoholics, many hallucinated. "Faceless things," he'd told Jack and Randy. "Nothing on their faces but eyes, big yellow eyes. Stubby little horns too." "Horns?" Jack had asked. "Yeah, son. Horns, little horns in their heads. Like I told you. Devils." Jack thought it would've been too rude to ask if they'd also had pronged tails.

Give yourself a breather. Brainstorming and hangovers did not mix well. His head felt like a jammed computer. Overload. Thinking too much could often be worse than thinking too little. The perceptions fizzed out. A pink Post-It on his desk lamp flagged his eye. *Farmer's National Bank,* he'd written on it. He'd stopped by during lunch to talk to the assistant branch manager, a beautiful green-eyed redhead. "All cash deposits over ten thousand dollars are serialed," she'd told him. "It's part of the new DEA laundering bill. We have a machine called a serial scanner. You stack the cash in the bin and the serial numbers are photographed and entered into the deposit computer automatically. Size of the bills doesn't matter." "Can you trace the bills to the point of withdrawal?" he'd inquired. "Sure. That's what the system exists for. It takes five minutes if the withdrawal came from one of our branches, a couple of hours for a different bank." "What about a foreign exchange bank?" "Couple of days." He'd handed her Stewie's deposit date. "Will you trace this for me?" "I'd be happy to, Captain, but first you have to either bring in a records warrant from the state magistrate, or subpoena the bank registrar with a writ of *duces tecum.*"

Jack had walked out, swearing under his breath.

Should he even be worrying about Veronica now? *Does Veronica worry about me?* He retrieved a mental picture of her from the past and tried to insert it into the present. Where was she? What was she doing, what was she thinking? *When was the last time she thought about me?*

"Jack," came a morose voice. Randy appeared in the doorway. "Larrel wants us in his office."

"What for?"

Randy only gave a shrug.

"Anyone told him that we're a little busy today?"

"IAD's here," Randy said. "And someone from the comm's office."

I haven't taken any pad money lately, have I? Jack tried to joke to himself. But this was no joke. IAD was the department ball-cutting crew; they didn't fool around. Jack put on a tie and sports jacket, and groaned when he looked in the mirror.

"Too bad there's not a barbershop on the way," Randy commented as they went down the hall. "Comb your hair or something, man."

"I could use a dry cleaner too," Jack said, combing frantically, "and an electric razor."

"I got a bad feeling, Jack. Sometimes you can smell the shit *before* it hits the fan, you know what I mean?"

"Tell me about it. Why do you think I've been wearing a clothespin on my nose for the last ten years? What could IAD want with us?"

"We'll find out in about two seconds."

Larrel Olsher's office felt cramped, like a smoking room at a funeral home. Olsher, the black golem, sat stolid and huge behind his desk. To his right sat Deputy Commissioner Joseph Gentzel, fiftyish, lean face, short graying hair, and a smirk like he'd just taken a swig of lemon juice. Beside him stood a meticulously dressed stuffed shirt, young, with reptile eyes and a pursed mouth, pure Type A.

Jack nodded to Olsher and the deputy comm. Then the kid stepped forward and said, "Captain Cordesman, my name is Lieutenant Noyle. I'm the field investigations supervisor for Internal Affairs."

"Delighted to meet you," Jack said. "What's this all about?"

Gentzel answered. "Someone leaked details of the Triangle case to the press, Captain."

Then Noyle: "The *Evening Sun* is doing a front page today, and tomorrow the story will be in the *Post* and the *Capital*."

Deputy Commissioner Gentzel stood up. "This is inexcusable. Do you have any idea how this will make the department look?"

"Sir, I didn't leak the story to them," Jack said.

"Perhaps you didn't. But the zero progress you've made on the case will only make us look worse."

Jack and Randy stared at him. Randy said, "Sir, it was probably somebody in admin; every police department has a mole to the press. It's impossible to keep a lid on *any* case for long."

"That's not the point." Gentzel sat back down. He looked at Jack. "I've examined your paperwork regarding the Triangle case, Captain, and I'm not impressed. Three ritual murders in a week, and you're no further along today than when you started."

"That's not true, sir—"

"We didn't want you on this case in the first place, but your superiors assured us you were the best man for the job." Gentzel shot Olsher a blank stare. "Your superiors, obviously, were wrong, which leaves me to wonder about the efficiency of this entire squad."

"With all due respect, sir, that's not a fair conclusion."

"And from what I can see, your active participation on the case is all but nonexistent. Lieutenant Eliot seems to be carrying most of the investigative load."

"I'm very close to identifying the specific ritual," Jack asserted. "If I can—"

"The ritual is a dead end. The perpetrators are obviously psychopaths."

"That's not true either, sir. We have plenty of evidence to suggest that the—"

"I know all about you, Captain, you and your radical investigative avenues. I don't want to hear about psychiatric profiles and satanic rituals. A homicide should be pursued through *proven* methods, not investigative quackeries."

"Let me remind you, sir, that my past performance record—"

"And I don't want to hear about your success rate, and your awards and decorations. In my view many of your operations were of questionable legality, and your search and seizure warrant in the Henry Longford case was barely constitutional."

"I beg your pardon, sir, but—"

"And furthermore—"

Jack, finally, exploded. "Would you at least let me talk for a minute, goddamn it, sir!" he shouted.

The silence in the wake of the shout felt thick as wet cement. Darrel Olsher and Randy averted their eyes to the floor. Noyle remained standing stiffly, hands behind his back. He was smiling.

"And there's another disturbing matter," Gentzel went on after the pause. "Lieutenant Noyle?"

Noyle stepped forward. "Clearly, your conduct in general is bad enough, and it only proves to disservice your own professional integrity, and the integrity of the department in general. I've never witnessed such irresponsibility on the part of a rank officer, not in all my time on the department."

Jack could bear no more of this. "All your *time*?" he objected. "What's that, about six months? I've been on this department for ten years, kid. I was busting dope dealers when you were still playing with G.I. Joes. And in case you haven't noticed, I outrank you."

But Noyle went on, cold as stone. "And in case *you* haven't noticed, Captain, Internal Affairs operates under the direct authority of the county executive's office. When we hear things within the department, we investigate. That's our job. And we've heard quite a bit about you."

"Okay, sure," Jack said. His only tactic was to beat this punk to the punch. "I went a little batty after the Longford case, and I've had a few personal problems, and sometimes I drink a little too much, but I've never consumed alcohol on duty."

"Were you drunk last night, Captain?"

Jack didn't answer.

"Were you drunk two nights ago?"

The motherfucker put watchdogs on me, Jack realized.

"On those two nights did you drink liquor in the Undercroft Tavern?"

"Yeah, I drank liquor," Jack admitted. "I'm pretty sure that Prohibition was repealed a couple of years ago."

"Did you not in fact drink to the point of complete inebriation, Captain? Isn't it true that you drank so much that you lost consciousness at the bar and had to be physically carried out?"

Jack was seething. It was all spelled out for him now, so there was no reason to restrain himself. "You suck-face little fairy. You put tails on me."

"It's my job to investigate the public behavior of any officer whose professional reliability is in question. Based on its documentation, Internal Affairs is satisfied that you have a serious alcohol-abuse problem, and it has been recommended to the commissioner's office that you submit yourself to the county alcohol-rehabilitation program, posthaste."

Posthaste, Jack thought. *Only a pussy would use a word like "posthaste."* Suddenly he felt his entire career in the hands of this prim, anal-retentive little brownnose. "I will," he said.

"Additionally, it has been recommended that you be suspended from active duty, with pay, until you have successfully completed said program. Please know that you have the right to contest IAD's recommendations. I would strongly advise against that, though."

"Please don't take me off the Triangle case," Jack said.

"Do you have a hearing problem too, Captain?" Gentzel asked. "You are suspended from all investigative operations as of now. Whether you consent or not, you're off the Triangle case."

"Please, sir. Suspend me later, I'll do the rehab thing later. I just need a little more time. I'm really close."

"Captain, the only thing you're really close to that I can see are insubordination charges and a mental breakdown. It would be derelict for us to allow an unstable alcoholic to remain in charge of a critical homicide investigation. You've expended valuable time and money, yet have produced no positive results. I'm reassigning the case to Lieutenant Eliot, who will work under the direct supervision of Lieutenant Noyle."

Jack was aghast. "*Noyle?* You've got to be shitting me, sir! He's an IAD buttprobe, he's not a *cop*! You can't let this stuffed punk take charge of a ritual murder investigation!"

"That's enough, Jack," Larrel Olsher advised.

"No, it's not enough!"

"Lieutenant Noyle is a competent investigator," Gentzel said.

"He's a candyass creamcake who couldn't investigate the back of his own hand!" Jack yelled. Randy was grabbing him, trying to nudge him toward the door. Noyle's stiff posture and irreducible smile highlighted his triumph. As Randy edged Jack into the hall, Jack continued to shout, "He'll run this case into he ground, Gentzel! He'll fuck it up so bad you'll never catch hese guys!"

The door slammed. Randy held Jack off. "Are you out of our mind? You can't talk to a deputy comm like that."

"Fuck him," Jack said. He shook loose. "And that asshole Joyle, fuck him double." His rage, like a puff of smoke, suddenly reverted to a physical weight of defeat.

"Forget it, man," Randy offered. "You did your best."

"Then I guess my best isn't good enough."

"Quit feeling sorry for yourself, and let me tell you something, as a friend. Those two shitheads in there are right about one thing. You got some serious problems, and if you don't tart taking care of them, you'll be through as a cop."

I already am, he thought slowly. He brushed his hair out of his eyes and left the station.

I've failed, he thought. *Myself, and everyone.*

CHAPTER 26

Voices. Words.

White light like mist oozed through black like onyx.

Was she dreaming?

Transposition.—You are not yet ready to transpose.—Imagine your passion.—Which are you, Veronica? Real or fake?—Let the image transpose . . . Tainted-tainted-tainted . . .

Veronica roused. *Aw, God.* She'd fallen asleep at her work desk. Her mouth and eyes felt sealed shut; they opened stickily. She'd worked all day and all night, hadn't she? Again, she could not remember at first. After Khoronos' guidance in the room of mirrors, she'd worked until 4:30 A.M. and had fallen asleep.

What strange dreams, if they'd been dreams at all. They'd been more like fragments of dreams tossed haphazardly into her head. Transposition. Awake or asleep, the word haunted her. Though she believed she understood its artistic meaning now, she couldn't escape the suspicion that more of its meaning lay hidden, and that Khoronos wanted it that way. Why should she think such a thing, though? Khoronos had revived her, had given her a creative vision she hadn't thought herself capable of. In three days she'd developed more as an artist than she had in the last three years.

Then the final mutterings of the dream idled back. *Tainted-tainted-tainted. She is tainted.* Who had Khoronos been talking about? *Who* was tainted?

Did he mean me?

She hadn't dreamed of the burning man, though. Perhaps the vision had completed itself in the mirrored room, had shown itself fully, leaving her to paint it without distraction.

She rubbed her eyes, stood up. *I'm a mess,* she thought. She was flecked, spotted, and smudged with paint. She reeked of linseed oil. When she glanced down at her work, her breath froze.

The background was done. Every detail of the dreamscape lay before her on the tight, primed canvas. The grotto's pits and rabbets, the rough curvature of its black rock walls. Each pointillistic feature melded to convey the background's subterraneous dimension. Veronica could *feel* the transcension of the colors, and the image of the bottomless infinitude.

She'd never delved into such techniques before, utilizing impressionistic strokes and devices to communicate an expressionistic vision, an intercourse of opposites. Yet here she had used those opposites . . . perfectly.

Yes. *This . . . is . . . perfect,* she realized.

The rush of joy flooded her, exhilaration like soaring heavenward. Perfect denoted the unachievable, yet that's what she felt she achieved. The background was perfect.

And now it was time to unleash the theme. It was time to paint herself in hand with the burning man.

As she sat back down to work, she felt as though she were being watched from above, or looked upon by gods.

Devils, Jack thought. It was not what the old man had said as much as how he'd said it. It just . . . bothered him, like a jag of déjà vu. *Why the hell should I care, anyway?* he reminded himself. He was off the case.

"Shooter, Jack?"

"I'd love one," Jack admitted, "but I'm through with booze, for good. How many times you heard guys say that?"

"Hundreds," Craig said. Jack didn't know if he was joking or serious. The Undercroft was empty in its post-happy-hour lull. Craig stacked glasses in the rack, whistling something by Elvis Costello. At this moment, just the two of them there, the bar felt haunted. *Devils,* Jack thought again.

"I got suspended today," he finally said.

"Suspended?" Craig questioned. "Why?"

"Drinking. Fucking up the case." He shrugged.

"Well, sometimes fucking up is the best thing we can do.

When we see how stupid we can get, we keep ourselves in check."

"Good point. Too bad I still want a drink."

"Here you go." Craig set down a shooter. "A virgin Mary. That's tomato juice and vodka, without the vodka."

Jack shot it back. "Thanks, I needed that."

He thumbed through a local magazine called *The Critique*, one of several TSD had found in Susan Lynn's bedroom. It contained a poem called "Love-Epitaph," which seemed grimly fitting. It was the last poem Susan Lynn would ever have published.

"But I'll tell you, Jack," Craig continued. "A bar isn't the place to be if you're trying to quit."

"The test of will is man's ultimate power. It's true, I read it on the bathroom wall the other night."

"Try this." Craig set down a brown bottle. "Drink like a killer, think like a killer."

It was Patrizier, the nonalcoholic stuff that Susan Lynn's murderers had ordered. "Not bad," he said after a sip. "Know what it tastes like?"

"Beer without alcohol."

"Right."

Craig went down into the pit to load the reach-ins. Jack turned to the page of the magazine that carried Susan Lynn's poem.

This bar is my grave and my power. Amid it even my own demons cower to these wan nights which slaver and devour like the strange faceless men who come and pluck me like a flower.

You hit a homer with this one, honey, Jack thought. Had she been writing about the Undercroft? *Power. Demons. Faceless.* He closed the magazine and slid it away.

"Would you cheer up!" Craig yelled, coming back up. "Every day above ground is a good day. It's true, I read it on the bathroom wall."

Jack knew he was putting off the question. Through his pants pocket he could feel the print of his HPCs. "I also read your phone number on the bathroom wall, didn't I?"

"You must've put it there after the last time you fucked me."

"I'm a cop, I fuck people every day. It's my job," Jack said. *But it probably won't be for long,* he reminded himself. "Actually I need your advice. I need some more of that barkeeper's wisdom."

Craig flipped a Marlboro Light into the air and caught the filter end in his mouth. "Shoot."

"When does an ethical person know when it's time to do something unethical?"

"Since when are you ethical?"

"Funny."

"Are we talking legal or illegal?"

"Let's just say that my intentions do not fully conform to the parameters of the law."

"I don't know if I should hear this, Jack. Isn't there a little something in the books about accessory foreknowledge? Failure to report the knowledge of a second party's criminal intent?"

"Are you a bartender or a fucking lawyer? Call it creepery with intent to mope."

"Is that anything like balling with intent to hold hands?"

Jack laughed. "Now you've got it."

"Here's the best advice I can give you." Craig struck a book match one-handed and lit up. "Ready? This is deep."

"I'm ready."

"A man's got to do what he's got to do."

The statement's bald unoriginality felt like a mental impact. *To hell with ethics,* Jack decided. *What have I got to lose except a career that's probably lost already?* "Thanks for the advice," he said. "See ya around."

He hopped off his stool and went out of the bar.

What would he get if he got caught? A fine? Probation before judgment? They wouldn't put a *cop* in jail, for God's sake. Not for a first offense illegal entry.

Nevertheless, illegal entry it was, just as shit by any other name was still shit. Jack had never been very good at this. Once he'd picked an apartment utility room to get at the phone box. There'd been this cowboy dealing crack through the Jamakes, so Jack had bugged his ringer and listened in long enough to tag the next pickup time and place. Later the deal went down, and the county narcs had been waiting, presto. Breaking the law to bust lawbreakers was only fair. Unethical? Definitely. But so were crack dealers and killers.

He'd given Veronica's keys back the night they broke up. He remembered the dying lilacs on the bar, and how cold she'd looked as she sat there on the stool waiting for him, how shivery. He remembered how gray her voice had sounded, and how desperate he'd felt to plead with her, to beg her to give the relationship one more chance as he watched it all fall to pieces in front of his face.

Jack remembered everything.

She had a little condo off Forest Drive, quiet neighbors, no skell buzzing around. *Look normal,* he reminded himself. He approached the door as though it were his own. The dead bolt was tricky; he had to maintain a perfectly even pressure on the tension wrench as he stroked the 18mm keyway with his double-hook. It took several restrokes before the pins gave. The knob lock opened as swiftly as if he'd had the key.

He thought of a vault opening as he opened the door. Veronica's only windows faced the woods in back; turning on the lights wouldn't give him away. The place seemed smaller, less airy, and the silence seemed amplified. At once Jack felt like exactly what he was: a trespasser, a burglar. He could see himself being cuffed and hauled away by city cops.

First he checked the pad she kept beside the kitchen phone. *Eggs,* it read. *Milk, tomato paste,* and *Call Stewie about Abrams contract.* "Shit," he mumbled. He went into the bedroom.

More memories here. More ghosts. *Just leave,* he told himself, but he couldn't now. Here was the bed in which he slept with her, and had made love to her. Here was the shower they'd bathed in together, and the mirror in which he'd dressed himself so quietly in the mornings so he wouldn't wake her. He would see her sleeping in the reflection as he knotted his tie. How many times had he stood in this selfsame spot? How many times had he told her he loved her in this selfsame room?

His trespassing rubbed his face in loss. It was part of his past that he stood in now, another dead providence. *What am I doing?* he logically wondered for the first time. This was crazy, pointless, masochistic. He'd come here simply for a clue to Veronica's whereabouts, and now he felt inundated in the blood of a love relationship that was dead. *It's dead,* he thought, staring. *Dead, dead, dead. She doesn't love you anymore. Her love for you is dead.*

"Dead," he muttered.

The memories soon converged to crush him. She had loved him once, he was sure of that. Why had she stopped? What had happened that her feelings had so suddenly changed? It wasn't fair, because his feelings *hadn't* changed, had they? *Why can't you just let go?* he didn't ask as much as plead with himself. *Veronica doesn't love you anymore, so why can't you forget about it?*

The past was indeed a ghost, and so was his love—a cruel specter feeding on him, sucking his blood out.

He forced himself to commence with his search. The bedroom, the kitchen, the spare room in back—none contained anything that might hint as to where she was.

He sat down at the kitchen table, hoping that the images would drain away. He was too confused now to concentrate on anything. *Ghosts,* he thought. *Ghosts in every room.* Even here. How many times had he eaten with her at this table? He'd even made love to her on it once, himself standing as Veronica lay back. "The bedroom's too far away," she'd said, and dragged him over. "I want you right here, right now." "One the *kitchen table*?" he'd exclaimed. "That's right. The kitchen table."

Every image scavenged him now; he felt helpless. *Get off it!* If he didn't settle himself down, he felt like he might fall apart.

Think.

You came here to—

But he'd found nothing that might reveal her location. He'd checked everywhere for anything, a note, a phone number, directions. She'd said that Khoronos had *invited* her to this retreat thing. She must've written down *something* with regard to it.

He thought of Poe's famous purloined letter. *Sometimes the things we search the hardest for are in plain sight.*

A stack of letters lay on the kitchen table. An electric bill, a renewal notice for *ARTnews,* and some junk mail. But right atop the stack was exactly what he'd come in search of.

It looked like a wedding invitation, a fancy white card with a gilt border:

Dear Ms. Polk:

It was a pleasure to make your acquaintance. In the few moments we spoke, I came away feeling edified; we share many commonalities. I'd like to invite you to my estate for what I think of as an esoteric retreat. Several other area artists will attend. It's something I've been doing for a long time—call it an indulgence. It's a creative get-together where we can look into ourselves and our work. If you'd care to join us, please contact my service number below for directions.

Sincerely,
Erim Khoronos

Jack wrote the phone number down. *Service number?* he wondered. No return address on the envelope, but the postmark was local. There were no directions. She must've written the directions down when she'd confirmed by phone.

Jack went to the phone and dialed. *Have something ready,* he warned himself. *I'll just tell her Stewie needs to talk to her. If she asks how I got the number, I'll lie. Easy.*

"Message center?"

"What?" Jack brilliantly answered.

"Church Circle Message Center," a woman told him.

A message center? "Oh, I'm sorry." *Message centers transfer calls to specific customer accounts.* "Would you please switch me over to Mr. Khoronos' account?"

"Hold, please."

Why would Khoronos hire a message center to relay his calls? *Maybe he's a doctor or something. Maybe he travels a lot.*

The operator came back on line. "I'm sorry, sir, but Mr. Khoronos' account was canceled last week."

"Is the transfer number still in your file?"

"Well, yes, but I'm not allowed to give that out."

Think! "My name is Peter Hertz," Jack said. "I'm Mr. Khoronos' investment broker. His stocks jumped today, and I really need to get ahold of him. It's very important."

"You're his broker but you don't have his number?"

Shit! Stupid! Think! "I only have his office number, I'm afraid, and he's left for the night. This really is very important."

The operator paused. Then: "991-0199."

"Thank you very much." Jack hung up and dialed again. There was a strange, distant ticking. Then: "The Bell Atlantic portable cellular phone you have dialed is not in service at this time. Please call again later."

Jack slowly hung up. *This is some bizarre shit.* Why would Khoronos relay calls through a message center to a portable phone? There would always be an alternate number for when the phone was turned off. Now Jack was in the same trick bag as the bank. He could contact Bell Atlantic and ask for the customer service address but they'd never give it to him without a warrant or subpoena.

All this hassle for squat, he thought. He'd run out of alternatives.

Or had he?

He checked to make sure everything he'd touched was in its proper place and turned off all the lights. Then he left.

And as he turned onto Forest Drive and drove away, he considered his final alternative.

You've already illegally entered one apartment tonight. So why not make it an even two?

CHAPTER 27

"Sacred Father, Father of the Earth."

"Enrich us."

"Your will is our blessing, your spirit our flesh."

"Mortal as we are, sanctify us."

"Our love is to serve you. Accept our love and give us grace."

"Unto you, we pray. Deliver us."

"Receive our prayer, O Father of the Earth. Carry us away from the hands of our enemies, and protect us. Give us strength to do your will, and smile upon us." The aorist held up the *jarra*. "Accept our sacrifices as a sign of our love." The aorist held up the dolch. "Accept our gifts as a sign of our faith." The aorist set the objects back on the altar and raised his hands.

The surrogoti also raised their hands.

"To you we give our faith forever, Father."

"*Pater terrae*—"

"—*per me terram ambula*."

"Baalzephon, hail!"

"Aorista!"

The Prelate's black raiments billowed in the nave. Hooded, his face wavered in candlelight. He felt risen, radiant in love.

"Go!" he whispered.

The surrogoti, nude and drenched in sweat, stepped off the points of the holy Trine, their heads bowed in reverence. The fresh cuts on their chests—their own blood offerings—glimmered red as slivers of rubies. They turned and hurried out of the nave.

The Prelate dropped to his knees at the Trine's high star. He lowered and kissed the star, his lips coming away whitened by the powder of crushed bones of priests murdered eons ago.

"Soon, Father," he whispered. The floor felt hot. The candlelight danced like gossamer veils, or lit faces in the air—

"Soon," the Prelate whispered. "Again."

—and back into the earthworks his god took him, the sleek beautiful black bird sailing down and down into the impossible inverted heights rimmed by ramparts of obelisks and ancient dolmens and thrones of kings, ever downward floating in deafening silence and the lovely music of screams over chasms of blood and roasted flesh and heap upon heap of squirming corpses as ushers peeled away living faces and pried open heads and split bellies to reveal the soft, hot treasure of their eternal feast.

Ever downward, yes, over the sweet, sweet black of chaos.

CHAPTER 28

"Has Jack been in?" Faye asked, briefcase in tow. "He's not at his office, and he's not home."

Craig was crafting a perfect shamrock shape into the head of a pint of Guinness. "He was in earlier, but he left. Didn't say where he was going."

It was still early, not much of a crowd. Faye sat down at the end of the bar and sighed.

"Jack's not on the case anymore," Craig said.

"What?"

"They suspended him today."

Faye felt incredulous, shocked. "Sus—*why?*"

Craig pointed to the TV. "Just watch. Here it comes again."

It was the six o'clock news. "The Triangle case," the newscaster kept saying. "Three ritual murders in a week." The case had blown, and it had blown *bad.* The news made it look like it was the police department's fault the murders had been committed, and now some man named Gentzel was passing the buck to Jack. "Captain Cordesman has been suspended from active duty," the man said as they flashed a picture of Jack, "pending successful completion of the county alcohol program. Unfortunately he was assigned the case before his superiors knew he had a problem."

"Pretty low-rent, huh?" Craig suggested.

"It's awful. He was doing the best he could."

"Those guys don't care. They needed a fall guy for when the news found out, and Jack was right there."

Faye could imagine how bad Jack felt. *He's probably getting plastered right now.* But what could she do? She didn't even know where he was. "Was he drinking when you saw him?"

"Nope. Said he was going to quit. His whole career's on the line now. This time I think he'll do it."

Faye hoped so. And where did this leave her? Was *she* still on the case? Who was she to give her research to?

"Have a drink."

"No, really, I—" She thought about it. "Sure," she decided. "One of those big bottles I had last time." After this, in addition to all the horrible stuff she'd read today, she figured she was entitled to a good drunk.

Next, a couple strolled in. Before Craig could take their order, they were sitting at a corner table, kissing. "You kids drinking tonight, or just here to eat face?" Craig inquired. The couple laughed, snuggling. Faye tried to remember the last time she'd been kissed. *A year*, she thought. *A year.*

"Tell me about this girl Jack used to see," she asked when Craig returned from the floor. "Veronica."

"Haven't you ever heard of male confidentiality?"

"No. Just tell me about the girl."

"Ask him."

"He won't talk about it."

"It's not my place to talk about his business."

Faye laughed snidely. "Bartenders talk about *everybody's* business, and don't give me that male confidentiality crap."

"Since you put it that way . . . He knew her for a while before they got involved. The relationship lasted about six months."

"What broke them up?"

"Usually people break up because they find out they're not compatible, or don't have the same ideas about things. But that's not how it was with them. I think it was confusion."

"Confusion?"

"Sure. Veronica's an artist, and artists are a little screwy sometimes. She'd never been in a real relationship before, and I guess she wasn't sure how to deal with it. What she needed was time to adjust, but she thought it was something else, like maybe she wasn't meant to be in a normal relationship at all. She was confused. She didn't understand the situation, so she ended it. Then she went off on some kind of artists' retreat. It's a shame because I think things would've worked out for them."

Faye sipped her Maibock. *Confusion. Shit, who isn't confused?*

"I knew her," Craig went on, drawing six mugs of Oxford Class. "I was working the night they broke up. She had a lot of nutty ideas about 'experience.' She thought she wasn't experiencing enough in life, and that's why she felt out of place around other people. She thinks experience is what will cure her confusion, but if she's not careful, she's going to end up *more* confused."

Faye felt equally confused. She hadn't wanted experience; she'd wanted love but what she'd gotten instead was a facsimile. It wasn't experience that had crushed her, it was finding out the hard way that a lot of awful things were easily disguised as truth.

The Maibock had her buzzing already. *Damn it, Jack,* she thought fuzzily. *Where the hell are you?*

Where the hell he was, exactly, and in no realm of legality whatsoever, was in the third-story apartment of one Virginia Thiel, also known as Ginny. The Dubbins nine-pin security lock had taken him ten minutes to tease open; he thought sure he'd be seen. But the hall had remained empty, by chance or by fate.

Wouldn't that be great if she hadn't gone, after all? he thought in the living room. He could picture the look on her face walking out of the kitchen—or better yet, the shower—only to discover a ragtag, unshaven Jack Cordesman standing stupidly with a set of lockpicks in his hand. It was a spacious, expensive pad, lots of good furniture, quality carpets and drapes, and one of those giant TVs where you could watch several shows at once. *Must be nice,* he humphed. *Rich bitch.* Veronica told him that Ginny made a hundred grand a year writing those things she wrote. Speculative feminism, the critics called her books. Tripe, Jack called them. He and Ginny had never really liked each other. Sometimes the three of them would go to the 'Croft, and Ginny and Jack would wind up arguing, which always amused Veronica. "You're an unkempt, monarchical pig," Ginny had once told him. "Monarchical? Does that word even exist?" he'd countered. "It's probably like the stuff you write about. Pure horseshit." "I'd kick you in the head if I wasn't afraid of breaking my foot," she'd come back. "Pound sand up your ass with a mallet, baby. How's that?" "Immature, uncouth, and hostile, which is about all I'd ever expect from a cop."

They were interesting arguments, at any rate. Jack found Ginny's invitation in a basket of letters by the phone. It was close to identical to Veronica's. Then he began his search. No purloined missives this time. Again, he didn't really know what he was looking for. He snooped around the kitchen counter, anyplace where she might've written something down when she called to confirm. *Ho! Contraband!* he thought. In a drawer under some address books he found a little bag of marijuana. *Shame on you, Ginny*. He could not resist. He emptied the bag into the drain and refilled it with an equal portion of McCormick's oregano from the spice rack. *See how high you get on that, honey.*

Next, the bedroom. This was irredeemable; he was *enjoying* it. Plowing through Ginny's privacy gave him a perverse thrill. No, this was definitely not ethical, but what was the harm? It wasn't like he was going to steal anything, or pull a whiz on the gorgeous beige carpet. Nevertheless, he imagined himself doing the most juvenile things: jumping up and down on the bed, moving the furniture around, writing "Kilroy was here" on the bathroom mirror. A few good squirts of whipped cream under the silk bedsheets would be nice. Or, hey, how about salt in the sugar bowl?

Time to grow up, he concluded. The underwear drawer revealed a surprising predilection toward panties of the crotchless variety. *Holy-moly!* he thought when he opened the next drawer. *Ginny's House of 1000 Delights*. The drawer contained vibrators, electric ben-wa balls, numerous prods, probes, and ticklers, and a few things that Jack, even in his wildest imagination, could not put a name to. They looked like alien appendages. One looked like the snout of a star-nosed mole. Another seemed to have tentacles. Jesus Christ, did women actually put these things into themselves? How could they keep a straight face? Last was a knurled black dildo over a foot long.

Jack had to strain not to laugh. *You learn something new every day,* he told himself. But next he opened the nightstand drawer, and groaned deep. A small night flask lay within; apparently Ginny wasn't averse to a nip in the wee hours.

Probably Scotch, Jack thought. Had fate placed the flask there, to test him? Had God? The flask's silver finish glimmered like a high sun. Jack watched his hand reach for it.

"No," he said. "I . . . will not."

He didn't touch it.

Beside the flask lay a small notepad, the top sheet of which was askew with Ginny's cramped handwriting. At the head of the page she'd written the name *Khoronos*.

Jack picked up the pad and read.

An address, followed by what seemed to be directions to someplace in the northern end of the county.

"All gone."

It was a familiar lament, and always a brightly horrific one. Being up felt great except when she realized that coming down meant staying down. The three grams she'd brought were gone. It hadn't even lasted three days.

Amy Vandersteen lay back and let the hot pipe fall out of her hand, just as her dreams had, and her life. *Yeah, all gone*, she thought. *Everything . . . gone*.

How long would her name last? A year? A couple of years? Her last movie had been a smash, and she had future deals for millions. So far, no one knew it was all a lie.

She couldn't work anymore, she couldn't focus. The things that had once meant the most to her—her craft, her *art*—had taken a backseat to her need. She hadn't even lasted a week on her latest picture; she'd broken down on the set. Cocaine-related psychomimetic shock, the doctors had said. The screenwriter and assistant director had been the ones who finished the film, not Amy. Amy had been at a rehab clinic in Houston.

She tried to quit many times, but time was circumstance, and circumstance always reclaimed her in the end. Her secret drug dependency loomed behind every door, around every corner—her future's shadow—waiting for her with a smile. She pretended she could handle it. But how much longer could she wear this mask when the mask was melting every day?

That's why she'd come here—to Khoronos' estate—to immerse herself in the convictions of her past and save her from the future. She thought sure that the sheer artistic *power* of

Erim's presence would embolden her, would give her the strength to stand up again and *create*.

Another dead end. Each time she fired up, she watched more of herself die. There was always a trade-off; the more she fed herself with the euphoric, hot vapors, the more completely her spirit starved.

Nobody likes me, she realized. The concession seemed so pitiful it was almost funny. But how *could* anyone like her? She wore her pretending like armor: no one must get to the real her. She wanted so much for Ginny and Veronica to like her; their closeness gave her strength—the cumulative power of womanhood—but even that was not strong enough to save her. Nothing was. Amy knew that now.

Nothing, she lamented.

Next, she was up. She was walking out of the house, into the backyard. She felt summoned by something, the need, perhaps, to be free of the mansion's walls, which reminded her of the walls she'd built around her life. The warm night's open space took the edge off some of her comedown. Suddenly she felt like running, breaking free into the beautiful gulf of night. *I'll run forever*, she thought. *I'll never stop. I'll run to the end of the world*.

The fantasy seemed nearly absolving.

"Over here."

Amy glanced to the back of the yard. A figure in white stood by the fence beyond the pool. It seemed to hover in place, an illusion caused by the soft moonlight floating on the water.

"Run!" the figure bid. "Follow me!"

The figure disappeared through the open gate into the woods. It was just a game, Amy realized. She didn't care. She ran after.

The dark path twisted through dense, tall trees. She felt blissful somehow, chasing a stranger through the woods. The moon lit the narrow path with dapples of light. As her feet propelled her forward, she thought of a steadicam scene in one of her movies. The determined protagonist in wistful pursuit of the truth. What a wonderful symbol! Chasing the pure white of revelation through darkness. To what would the mad chase lead?

The white figure blurred just ahead, vanishing around each bend. Who was he? Where was he taking her? These questions occurred to her but to no real significance. She was the protagonist, chasing truth. That's all that mattered.

Around the next bend, the figure was gone.

Where could he be hiding? Behind the trees? Amy slowed to a cautious walk, peering ahead. Another twist in the story. Suddenly the truth evades the steadfast protagonist, leaving her to wander amid the darkness of her own uncertainly. She'd been led deliberately to the point of being lost; now she must find her own way out. The symbol of every woman's plight: alone, in darkness.

She walked ahead one step at a time, watching, listening, her hands splayed as if feeling for trip wires. An owl hooted, and she nearly shrieked. Unseen animals rustled in the woods, sensing her presence. The protagonist as trespasser, delving into unknown terrains.

When she rounded the next bend, the kiosk appeared.

It looked like a latticework of crystal in the moonlight. Khoronos had shown it to her the morning she'd arrived. Was that who beckoned her now? Khoronos? The figure stood in wait of her, directly in the kiosk's center.

The end of the chase, Amy pondered. *The protagonist finds what she seeks at the end of her own darkness.*

Herself.

She saw *herself* standing in the kiosk, beautiful and naked in the moonlight. Radiant. Pure. Her smile was bright, like the sun. It was the Amy Vandersteen of the past, not the present. The real woman, not the slave. The tranquillity before the storm. The artist uncorrupted.

The words tolled like distant bells. *Before you can love others, you must learn to love yourself.*

This impossibility did not distract her. She shred her clothes as she crossed the kiosk's wooden floor, until she was standing before herself.

"Come to me," her past said to her present. The figure's arms opened to her. "We must free ourselves."

Was this a flashback? A hallucinotic jag triggered by years of drug abuse? She remained rooted in the moment's image, and its meaning. Nothing could be so important. Nothing in the world.

The final scene. Close-up of protag's face, eyes wide half in fear, half in wonder. She feels the summons, the space between them drawing in. This is the ultimate moment of self-awareness, where the woman of flesh becomes wed to the woman of spirit. At last the protagonist finds what she's been looking for. Her perfect self. Her womanhood undefiled.

"Kiss me," the image said.

Amy and Amy embraced. She felt a surge like electricity as her flesh made contact with her flesh. Her cheek brushed her cheek. Her hands caressed her buttocks, and her breasts pressed against her breasts.

"Save me," she whispered into her own ear.

At last the protagonist makes love to herself.

Their embrace tightened. Amy closed her eyes—

pater terrae

and kissed—

per me

her own—

terram ambula

lips.

"Aorista," the image croaked.

Amy's eyes shot open. She gagged as the foot-long tongue slid down her throat, and the penis, even longer, opened the moist rim of her sex and burrowed up straight into her womb. Her nerves pulsed like gorging veins, every muscle in her body flexing against the instantaneous avalanche of her own orgasms, and next she was lowered quickly to the kiosk's moon-drenched floor, and her legs were pushed back as the penetration deepened in and out of her flesh, each thrust giving her a new climax which hammered the breath out of her chest with sensations of pleasure she could never even have conceived, and when her suitor's own orgasm burst, endless, cold gouts pumping into her loins, all she could see was the face of this unholy deception, this ruse of night—

Not her own face at all.

It was a devil's face.

CHAPTER 29

"Jesus Christ!" Faye exclaimed. "Where have you been?"

Jack looked up from the kitchen table, startled. "I—"

"I've been sitting in that goddamn bar for hours." She set her briefcase on the table, less than gracefully, and sat down. "We didn't know where you were."

"I just got back," he said meaninglessly.

"From where? Another bar?"

"No," was all he said.

Lay off, she thought. *The last thing he needs right now is you yelling at him.* "I was worried, that's all," she said more quietly. Did that sound trite? Did that sound *girlie?* "I heard about what happened, Jack. About the case. I'm sorry. It's not your fault."

Jack shrugged. "Maybe it is, maybe it isn't. It doesn't matter. I was burned-out and out of control, and they needed someone to blame the no-progress investigation on when the press got wind of the case. Two birds with one stone."

"What are you going to do about—"

"About my drinking?" He smiled forlornly. "Quit. No choice. And, no, I haven't had anything today."

"I wasn't going to ask that," she said.

He held the odd, skewed smile and lit a cigarette. "There's this snide chump named Noyle running the case now. He'll probably abandon the ritual angle as a basis of the investigation."

"In other words, I'm out of a job."

"Looks that way. I'll find out tomorrow. Just give everything you've got to him, and that'll be it."

That'll be it. At least she'd gotten to do something different for a few days. "Craig said he saw Susan Lynn's murderers."

"Yeah," Jack acknowledged, "and he must've also told you that they were in the bar several hours but no one remembers their faces."

"Uh-huh. That's interesting, I found out some more stuff today. The aorists believed they were the devil's greatest disciples. Satan supposedly blessed the faithful. The sects even had litanies and prayers of protection that they recited before they went out and did their deeds. There's a lot of documentation that you might find amusing."

"Why?"

"From what you just said. Craig can't make a description of the killers, even though he was in the same room with them for hours. Remember our deacon spy, Michael Bari? He lived with the aorists for weeks, but after he escaped, he couldn't remember any of their names, descriptions, where they lived. He couldn't even remember which church they used for their rituals. There's a lot of similar testimony in the Catholic archival records of the late 1400s, when Rome made a serious effort to infiltrate the sects."

Jack tapped an ash. "Kind of makes you wonder."

"And there's more. Several of the Slavic cults, like the one Michael Bari infiltrated, worshiped the incubus Baalzephon, the demon of passion and creativity. Baalzephon seems to have direct counterparts in other demonologies, some dating as far back as 3500 B.C. You name it, the Aztecs, the Burmese, the Assyrian Ashipus, even the American Indians and the Druids—they all recognized an incubus demon who presided over human passion and creativity, just like Baalzephon. It says somewhere in the Bible that evil is relative. Well . . . they weren't kidding."

Jack seemed depressed now, either by the complexities of Faye's research or by the fact that he'd been dropped from the Triangle case. Perhaps she shouldn't even be mentioning it now. "Baalzephon," he muttered, indeed half amused. "The Father of the Earth. I wonder where these people came up with this stuff."

"It was all counter-worship," she said. "Stuff they invented as a spiritual revolt against their oppressors, the same old story told different ways down through the ages. Same thing as Santa Claus."

"Yeah, but Santa doesn't generally eviscerate women," Jack

pointed out. "What about this incarnation business? Did you find out anything more about that?"

"A little. The aorists paid homage to their apostate demons by sacrifice and incarnation—in other words, substituting themselves through surrogates. This gave the demon a momentary opportunity to be flesh on earth. Baalzephon's sects went further, though. They practiced sacrificial incarnation rites year round as a general homage. But once a year they executed a more specific rite that involved *selective* sacrifices. They believed that the triangle was a doorway, or something like an interplanar dumbwaiter. They'd do three incarnation sacrifices first, girls who would please Baalzephon specifically—passionate, attractive, and creative girls—then they'd sacrifice a fourth girl right in the triangle. This supposedly triggered a nonsurrogotic incarnation—"

"Baalzephon himself makes an appearance, you mean."

"Yes, to bless his worshipers in the flesh and to have intercourse outside the territory he'd been condemned to for eternity. This was the ultimate slight to God, a demonological loophole. The end of the rite was called the 'transposition,' where the fourth victim transposes into Baalzephon's space."

"You mean . . ."

"The fourth victim physically enters Hell through the impressa. I haven't found out exactly why, but one of the texts mentioned that Baalzephon likes to take a human wife on a yearly basis."

Jack winced. "This is some crazy shit, Faye."

"Sure it is. And the craziest part is that your killers are doing the same things that Baalzephon's sects did six hundred years ago. It's almost to a tee."

Jack brewed on it awhile. Then, perhaps unconsciously, he mumbled, "Devils."

"What?"

"We had a second witness, a dock bum. He said the killers leaving Susan Lynn's condo were devils. Not men. Devils."

"I wouldn't put much stock in a bum's observations."

"I'm not. It's just that this case gets freakier and freakier."

He was brooding again, rubbing his face in what he felt was *his* failure. But that wasn't all; Faye knew that. She'd known it the instant she stepped into the kitchen.

"But there's something else bothering you, isn't there?" she ked. "It's not just the murders, and your being dropped from e investigation. There's something else."

Jack looked up at her.

"Tell me," she said.

He told her everything then, and the details he'd never men- ›ned. He told her how this Stewie person had come to him ith his worries, how Veronica had seemingly disappeared. e told her about this "retreat" she'd gone on at some rich lettante's estate, and how he'd broken into Veronica's apart- ent, and a friend's, to try to find out exactly where they were. e told her about the directions he'd found.

"And you're going to go there," Faye said rather than asked.

"I don't know. It's not my business, really. I should just ve the directions to Stewie, let him go."

"You should go," Faye said. It was very abrupt. But what ould possess her to say that, to *encourage* this man, who she ›ssibly loved, to seek out a woman who had rejected him? ıe past always hurt—this Faye knew from experience. Per- ıps she felt complicit with him.

The following silence made her uncomfortable. An inkling ld her to leave. Just get up, say goodbye and good luck, and ave. But she couldn't. Veronica had left him. Faye would ›t, even if her presence meant nothing.

All she wanted was to do something for him.

What, though?

"What do you want out of life, Jack?" she asked.

"I don't know. A drink would be a good start."

"I'm serious."

Here came back the doleful smile, mirth in the face of defeat. have no idea. What about you?"

Faye couldn't tell him. She said good night and went to bed.

The brittle yellow streetlight from Main Street seeped into r room. She lay awake on her bed. What did she think she as going to do? The ceiling extended as a grainy, infinite rrain, just as her mind felt.

She heard Jack go up the stairs. She waited awhile, a half ›ur, perhaps, to give him time. Next, she herself glided bare- ot up the steps, her nightgown like mist about her body. She ıietly opened his door and stepped in. She skimmed off her ghtgown and felt licked by the tinted dark.

"Jack?" she whispered. She leaned over, shook him gentl He snapped awake, frightened for a moment, then gazed u

"Faye?"

"Shh," she said. "Don't say anything." She pulled the cove off. She sat on his belly and opened her hands on his chest

Oh, God. What now? What would he think of this? Had sh come in here just to fuck him? That might only make him fe worse.

Give him something, anything. Something he can't have an more.

Even in the dark his eyes shone plainly with uncertainty.

She ran her hands up his chest. "You can pretend," she sai

"What do you m—"

"You can pretend that I'm her."

His eyes stared up.

"You can pretend that I'm Veronica."

"No—"

"Shh." She took his hands and placed them on her breas "Pretend that I'm Veronica. Call me her name."

"No. That would hurt you."

She leaned down and kissed him. "I'm Veronica." Sh kissed him again and he kissed back. She reached behi and felt him.

Was this so false? What else could she do for him? Sure, was a fantasy that would be dust in the morning, but in th gift, if only for a night or only a moment, she could give hi back a sliver of the past he'd lost. She pondered the irony. was surrogatism in a sense, wasn't it? It was transpositio She was transposing herself with someone else, for him.

She kissed him more fervently now, more wetly. His pen felt hot, hard. "I'm Veronica," she whispered again. "Mak love to me, Jack. Make love to me like you used to."

She slid back on his belly and guided him in. The sens tion nearly shocked her, to suddenly be occupied by his flesh Should she pretend too? Should she pretend that Jack was h own dead love? The idea never crossed her. To Faye, he w. what he was in reality. He was Jack.

"I'm Veronica, and I still love you."

He let the fantasy take him then. He surrendered. "I love yo too," he whispered. He rolled her over in the bed, drawing h thrusts slowly in and out. She wrapped her legs around him once, and her arms. She liked his weight on her, and the steady movement cocooned within her limbs. She was shivering now, as the slow, precise thrusts grew more forceful.

Her impending orgasm seemed to hover, watching her. He moaned in her ear when she squeezed him with her sex. "I still love you, Jack," she whispered, and squeezed again as hard as she could, and then the delicious pressure in her loins broke and she came, and one more squeeze and he came too, spurting the gentle heat into her sex, whispering things, undecipherable endearments, and when he was done, when he had expended the last of himself into her, he whispered, "Veronica," and kissed her.

She had given him her gift. She wished she could give him something more real, but what else was there? This was all. She would give it to him again and again, for as long as he wanted. She would be someone else for him all night, and—

"Veronica," he moaned again.

—and she would not allow herself to cry.

CHAPTER 30

Creation often came to her as a trance, an autohypnotic removal of conscious things from the subconscious. Veronica thought of it as a veil, opened by the pure, raw energy of her muse. Frequently she remembered nothing of a day's work . . .

Like now.

"My God," she whispered to herself. "I . . . I'm done."

The painting was done.

It lay before her on the canted table, a découpage of melded colors murkily dark and vivid bright. *The Ecstasy of the Flames,* she mused. *The Fire-Lover.* The canvas encompassed everything she knew as an artist: the relief-like abstraction of the background and its dimensionality, the splotch-and-line details of the id grotto. She had re-created herself using photo-realistic techniques mixed with Braquesque expressionism. In her glinting nakedness, she looked real, yet more than real, more than herself. She'd painted not only her flesh but her spirit too.

The burning man stood by her side, wavering between pointillistic bright fire and cubist geometries. Something lurked beneath its fiery beauty, something she'd never quite seen in the dreams. Flesh, perhaps. Flesh made perfect by fire.

Veronica couldn't look away. The painting, her creation, *captured* her. She was looking at the work's point of juncture, where her own hand joined with the hand of the burning man. This was the painting's focal point, its thematic nexus. It rose to be more than the joining of two beings. It was the joining of ideals and spirit, of desire and passion. It was the joining of worlds.

"You're finished."

The sudden voice jerked Veronica's head around. It was horonos at the door, dressed in white and hair shining e light.

"I'm not ready for you to see it yet," she said.

"I understand. Your colleagues are also finished with their ojects. Tomorrow, perhaps, you will all show your creans."

"All right," she replied. Even though she was looking away w, the painting seemed to nag her, as if jealous for her atten n. "It was funny. I barely remember anything all day. It was most like I woke up and the painting was done."

Khoronos' eyes seemed brighter as he looked at her. "The ll of the Sisters of the Heavenly Spring," he said.

Dante, she remembered. *The Muse.* But he was right. This trenchment of creative focus felt like a higher state of con iousness.

Khoronos continued as if speaking above her, or addressing unseen entity. "There is synergy, Ms. Polk, between the tist's physicality and her spirit. The equiposition of both is e ultimate achievement. Most artists spend their lives lookg for this viaduct between body and mind. Most only touch on it. But great artists *live* in it, become *one* with it. As you ve."

"How do you know?" she countered. "You haven't even en it."

"I don't need to see it to see your triumph. All I need to e is you." The words drifted. "I can see it in your aura."

Veronica didn't believe in auras. This was just Khoronos' ay of telling her that her happiness was obvious.

"You have a beautiful aura," he said. "Such is the power creation, such a blessed state, yes?"

"Yes," she said, not quite knowing why. But it was. It was blessed state.

"I'm very proud of you."

Suddenly she wanted to cry. Did his acceptance mean that uch to her? All she knew was that for the first time in her life e felt she had truly succeeded, and she knew that she owed it him. She tried to look at him objectively. He must be in his fties, yet the wisdom of all those years had kept him young another more truthful way. He was beautiful—she could not deny that. He was beautiful the first time she saw him at th gallery. She'd stayed her attraction to him for so long. Perhap she felt inferior, or unworthy. That was it. She felt unworth of such a man of knowledge. But now she wanted him. Sh wanted him to come over to her right now and make love t her, to penetrate her at the foot of her creation.

She started to get up.

"No," he said. He knew. He knew what she wanted. Wa her desire that easy to see? "There are still some ruminatio that remain. Am I right?"

"You're always right," she said.

"I'll leave you now, but first I have a question."

She sat back down, looking at him in wait.

"It's preeminence that we're talking about, isn't it? Not ju great art, but *preeminent* art."

"I . . ."

"Ms. Polk, anyone can create a work of art that succeed But few can create a work that . . ."

Transposes, she knew. He didn't even have to say it.

His voice darkened. "Ms. Polk? Does your painting trans pose?"

She was shivering. "Yes. It does. I *know* it does."

This was the first time she'd ever really seen him smil Just the faint, if not sarcastic, half-smiles, only gestures c smiles. But this . . . He was smiling at her now, smiling wit her glory and her happiness. His smile made her feel bathed i sunlight.

"May I ask its title?" he said.

"*The Ecstasy of*—" But something severed her answer. She' thought about this for days, hadn't she? *The Ecstasy of th Flames* or *The Fire-Lover*. But these weren't titles, they we frivolities. At once she recognized that they were trite an stupid and inferior, not true titles at all.

She stared fixedly at the painting, and then she knew.

"It's called *Veronica Betrothed,*" she said.

CHAPTER 31

When Jack awoke, he thought he must be dreaming. He wanted a drink bad—certainly. Nevertheless, he felt wonderful. He felt . . . bright.

Faye was not in bed with him, but her scent lingered in the sheets. Whatever shampoo she used, or soap, made him dizzy. He pressed his face in the pillow and breathed. It was almost erotic. It was almost like . . .

Veronica, he thought.

Last night replayed in his mind like a forbidden film. She had let him pretend, to help him feel better, and that now made him feel bad. He knew that Faye liked him, and he knew that he liked her. But he'd used her to be someone else. He'd method-acted a lie. Feeling false was one thing he couldn't stand.

The shower purged him. The cool water took some of the bite out of his need for a drink. "I haven't had all I want," he said to the mirror, toweling dry, "but I've had all I can take."

He put on slacks and a decent shirt, and skipped the tie. Why should he wear a tie if he wasn't working? His enthusiasm slowed, though, as he descended the stairs. What would he say to Faye? He didn't even want to think about it. When he walked into the kitchen, she was hanging up the phone.

"Morning," he said ineptly. "Who was that?"

"I gave LOC your number," she said, and sat down to a cup of steaming tea. "They've been trying to locate a rare book for me, about the aorists. They found it."

But Jack didn't know if Noyle even wanted her on the case.

"It's what they call 'precaution printed material.' It's rare and not in good shape, so you have to make an appointment to see it. You have to wear gloves and stuff. My appointment's at noon."

"Before you waste your time . . ." Jack began.

"I already called that guy Noyle. He said, 'The county very much appreciates the expenditure of your time and efforts, Miss Rowland. However, your services are no longer required, and we've terminated the subcontract with your department.'"

"Asshole," Jack muttered. "I'd like to kick his prim and proper ass right off the city dock."

"I'm going to read the book anyway," Faye said.

"Why?"

"Curiosity, I guess. It would be like not finishing the end of a story. Oh, and some guy from the *National Enquirer* called. He wanted to talk to you about the 'Satanic Murderers.'"

"He can talk to my middle finger," Jack remarked.

"I told him you'd been kidnaped by aliens with Elvis tattoos and were presently indisposed."

"Outstanding," Jack approved, and started for the Mr. Coffee.

"And don't look at the newspapers if you're in a bad mood."

Asking first would've been redundant. His frown spread as he glanced at each paper. The front page of the *Sun* blared, "Ritual Slayings Plague Historic District." The state section of the *Post:* Satanic Cult Kills Three So Far in Bay Area. And the *Capital:* County Captain Fumbles Ritual Murder Spree. Three Dead in a Week.

Jack didn't bother outbursting; he'd done enough of that in Olsher's office. Instead, he sat down with Faye, and sighed.

"You forgot to shave," she observed.

"I didn't forget. I remembered not to. Why should I shave—I've been relieved of active duty. Shaving's a big pain in the ass. Women have no idea."

"Tell that to our legs and armpits. And what's this?"

She was holding up the $25,000 receipt Stewie got from the two guys who'd picked up Veronica's painting. "Stewie thought I might be able to get a line on where Veronica was by running the signature. Can't make out the name, though. It looks like Philip something."

"*Philippe,*" she corrected, pronouncing it *fee-leep.*

"Can you make out the last name?"

"Faux," she said. *Fo*. "It's French. And a little bit odd. *Faux* ieans false or fake. Some name."

Jack lit up and popped a brow. *Philippe Fake,* he thought. Stewie thinks he works for the guy who invited Veronica to ie retreat."

"What happens if you can't locate her?"

"It'll mean bad news for her career. Stewie's got a bunch of alleries wanting to do shows of her work. If you jerk those inds of people around you get a bad name for yourself. tewie's afraid her credibility will be damaged if he can't onfirm the shows, and he can't confirm the shows until he alks to her. And the funny thing is the phone number on ie invitation was a transfer through a message service to a ortable phone."

"That doesn't make much sense, does it? Why wouldn't this ich guy just use his home number?"

"That's what I'm trying to figure out," Jack admitted. He lanced at his watch; it was going on ten. "You're going to OC at noon? Let's get something to eat, then you can come o the courthouse with me."

"What do you need there?"

To see how far my lack of ethics goes, he thought.

It was only a two-minute walk to the City Dock. Jack got iis usual cop's breakfast: a big foil of fried chicken livers. Faye got a hot dog. They sat on the dock and ate, watching he boats.

He tried to look at her without being obvious. The morning it up her nearly waist-long hair. She was pretty in her silence and faded jeans. Randy had told him she was in her early twenties, but just then, with the sun on her face, she looked like a precocious teenager. He remembered how beautiful she was nude, how soft her skin felt, how warm she was.

"The aorists were very methodized murderers," she said.

"Huh?"

"Everything they did they did for a specific reason. Not like all this satanist stuff today, mostly disgruntled kids looking for a sense of identity. The aorists believed that faith was strength. Murder was a gesture of faith. They believed that the more severely they disserviced God, the more powerful they'd become in recompense from Satan."

"But I thought you said they worshiped *lower* demons."

"Yes, *apostate* demons is the term. Satan's brethren, Satan sons. They were like antithetical patron saints. It was all obla tory."

Jack ate a liver. "Faye, I don't know what oblatory means.

"It means that everything they did was a homage to the apos tate demons, which, transitively, was a homage to Satan."

Transitively, Jack thought.

"They were big on acts of offering is what I mean. Lot of the sects, particularly the ones that worshiped Baalzephon were fixated on this idea of transposition. It means one thing trading places with another. Transposition was the basis of thei offering. Murder for grace. Atrocity for power. They were also big on incarnation. Flesh for spirit."

All these big words and inferences made Jack's head spin *Apostates. Oblatory. Transposition. Jesus.* "I'm a cop, Faye you know, scrambled eggs for brains? Could you put all thi in police terms?"

"Sure. The aorists were hard-core motherfuckers."

"Ah, now, that I can relate to."

"The leaders of the sects were called 'prelates.' They supposedly had psychic and necromantic powers. You want to talk about hard core? These guys would think nothing of hanging a priest upside down by a meat hook through the rectum and gutting him alive. They'd force deacons to have sex with prostitutes, or sodomize each other on the altar, stuff like that. These prelate guys meant business. In fact, their final initiation was a self-mutilatory act."

"A *what*?"

"They cut off their own penises as an offering to the apostate," Faye said, and bit into her hot dog.

Jack tossed his livers in the waste can. "Come on," he muttered. He didn't need to hear any more of this.

They cut through Fleet Street to the State House, and went to the basement. "Office of Land Records," the milky sign read. When property was owned under a company name, you could sometimes find out if the company was legit by running the name through IRS. Jack's first big tip on the Henry Longford case, in fact, had come from this office. Longford had bought land as a business expense; the business had turned out to be a wash. The guy who appeared at the counter looked almost roverbial: heavy, elderly, balding, and he wore one of those anker visors. Jack could tell by looking at him that he might ot be averse to a little grease.

"You the recorder of deeds?"

"That's me," the guy said. "Whadaya want?"

I like him already. "I'm trying to locate the taxpayer on a iece of land."

"You gotta give me a liber number or a folio. That's the nly way I can get the plat number of the individual plot."

"How about the address?"

The recorder gave him the eye. "This a sham? If you got he address, whadaya need me for?"

"Actually I thought there might be a phone number in the ile. There's a dwelling on the plot. It's a friend of mine I eed to get ahold of. Can you help me out?"

"Look it up in the reverse directory."

"I already did. It's unlisted."

"If ya got the address, why don't ya just drive to the house?"

"This is easier. And besides, have you ever heard of the reedom of Information Act?"

"Sure, son. Write me up a standard request and I'll pro-ess it. Takes a week, sometimes longer if you piss off the ecorder."

"Come on, man. Help me out."

"Can't do it for ya, son."

Jack frowned. *Too many ballbreakers in this world.* This vas public information. "You think you could do it for Ulysses . Grant?"

The old man got the picture straight off. "No, but I might e able to do it for Benjamin Franklin."

"That's a big piece of paper, pal."

"So's a FOIA request. Your choice, son."

Jack gave the recorder a hundred-dollar bill and Khoronos' ddress.

"Course, there's no guarantee there'll be a phone number n the file. Might just be names and tax dates. And there's o refunds here." The old man held up the bill, brows raised. 'Yes or no?"

"Just get the file," Jack said.

"What are you doing!" Faye whispered when the man went n back.

"Lubing a palm to cut through some red tape. Every plot o land in the state is filed here, along with the name of whoeve pays the property tax. If there's a dwelling, there's usually phone number too."

"You're bribing a public employee, Jack. Aren't you i enough trouble as it is?"

Baby, there's never enough trouble, Jack felt like saying.

The recorder returned from the stacks. "Tough luck, son Like I said, no refunds."

"There's no phone number in the file?" Jack asked.

"No phone number. Just the taxpayer's name."

"I already know his name. It's Khor—"

"Herren," the recorder said.

"What?" Jack said.

"Fraus Herren, Line 2." The recorder scanned the ope file. "Funny, though. You say there's a dwelling on th plot?"

"Of course. They don't put addresses on vacant lots."

"I know that. But there's no construction date. Date of th building license should be here, and the closing date, tax dates When you put a house on a piece of land, the prop tax goes up All that should be here, but it ain't. Someone forgot to amen the file."

"Fraus Herren, you say?"

The recorder showed him the file. "Fraus Herren. Sound kraut. Lotta German developers buying up the waterfron around here."

Who the hell is Fraus Herren? Jack wondered. *Why isn't th deed in Khoronos' name?* "Thanks for your time," he grumbled.

"Don't thank me, thank Ben Franklin."

Yeah. He took Faye back out. "I just paid a ball note fo goddamn nothing," he complained.

But Faye was looking at him funny, shaking her head.

"What's the matter?"

"Jack, someone's really pulling your leg here," she said. "First you got a guy named Philippe Faux, and now you've got another guy named Fraus Herren."

"Yeah? So?"

"I already told you. *Faux,* in French, means false. Fraus Herren, that's German. You know what it means in German?"

"What?" Jack asked.

"It means false man."

False man, Jack thought. He got out of his unmarked and headed into the city district station. *Philippe Faux. Fraus Herren. Both mean fake.* It was almost like a deliberate joke, and the joke was on Jack.

Faye had left for LOC already. Jack thought he'd stop by the office and see how Randy was doing. He also wanted a little more time to decide what to do about Khoronos. *Should I go there myself, or just give Stewie the address and forget about it?*

Randy was hanging up the phone when Jack walked in the office. "This place hasn't collapsed without me?" he said.

"I miss the lingering aroma of Camel smoke," Randy told him. "Really. We've been grilling Susan Lynn's boyfriends all morning. Not a weirdo in the bunch, and they all had alibis that washed. Jan Beck came in earlier with the TSD workup."

"What's she got?"

"First place, the pubes. We got two different kinds of pubes. Unusually long, she said."

"Just like the first two," Jack added.

"Not like. They *were* the first two. The hairs matched and the semen matched. They also wrote the word—Aorista—twice this time."

"In their own blood, right? Not hers?"

"You got it. And the subtypes matched the first two 64s. In other words, one guy did Shanna Barrington, the other guy did Rebecca Black, and they both did Susan Lynn."

Jack poured coffee, contemplating this.

"And they really did the job this time," Randy went on. "It takes a lot to turn Jan Beck's stomach, but this did it. Says she never found so much jiz in a 64 in her life. Her whole repro tract was ruptured with it. Says the whole bed was a wetspot, and they gave it to her up the ass too. Beck was talking cc's; she said she pulled the equivalent of eight nuts just out of her tail. These guys left more wax than a twenty-man gang bang."

Jan Beck's stomach wasn't the only one turning.

"There's more," Randy said. "Beck thinks this is the last one."

"Why?"

"First two, the perps went out of their way to disguise themselves. They wore the black wig. Beck didn't find a single wi hair this time."

"Which means they don't give a shit anymore about bein recognized. And that means they're either ready to stop o they're ready to leave town, just like Karla Panzram said the would. But I don't think Susan Lynn is the last one. I thin there'll be one more murder."

Randy looked at him inquisitively.

"Faye, the state researcher, found out a lot more about th ritual protocol. These guys worship some medieval demon calle Baalzephon, some sex demon or something, an incubus, sh called it. Once a year this cult would try to incarnate Baalzepho by a specific rite. They'd sacrifice three girls, one for each poin of the triangle, then they'd do a fourth, to finish the rite. Every thing she's dug up so far syncs with what's already happened So that's my guess. There'll be one more 64 before these guy book."

"That's very imaginative, Captain Cordesman."

Jack knew the voice at once. How long had he been stand ing there listening? "Ah, Noyle," Jack said. "I almost didn' recognize you without your face buried in the commissioner' ass."

Noyle frowned in the doorway. "I'm a trifle concerned tha you haven't yet enrolled yourself in the county alcohol pro gram. Please do yourself a favor, Captain. Posthaste."

Posthaste. What a dickbrain. "Why'd you shitcan Fay Rowland?"

"Because her services are no longer integral to this case."

"They're not, huh? Well, what have *you* come up with besides handfuls of your own shit?"

"You're a very profane man, Captain."

"You're fucking right I'm profane, especially when a no experience little IAD weasel yanks my homicide investigatio and fucks up a week's worth of hard work. Faye Rowland foun out more about these assholes in three days than you'll fin out in a year of hobnobbing around, running rap checks o a bunch of dance-club scumbags and bar cockhounds. Don' you even want to see the information she's compiled on th aorist cult?"

"The aorist cult," Noyle repeated with a reserved smile. "I'v read your preliminary reports, Captain. They're quite . .

amusing. Fortunately we're a modern police department; we have no interest in devils. What we're concerned with are two highly dangerous chronic psychopaths, and we will proceed in the effort of their apprehension by following the standard investigative procedures, and maybe if you had adhered to the same standards, you would not have turned this case into the biggest embarrassment in the history of the department."

Jack stood up. Randy rolled his eyes.

"Listen to me, you little buttplug," Jack said. "These guys are not psychopaths. If they were psychopaths, we would've caught them by now. They're rational, calculated devil-worshipers. The only thing crazy about them is their beliefs, and the only way you're going to bust them is to research their beliefs."

"Sit down, Jack," Randy suggested.

"Their beliefs are irrelevant, Captain," Noyle said. "We don't investigate beliefs, we investigate crime and the perpetrators thereof. You might've solved this case by now if you'd spent more time on the suspects and less in the bars."

"There are no suspects, you idiot!" Jack yelled.

Noyle stepped back without a change of expression. "And I repeat. You are officially advised to enroll yourself in the county alcohol program."

"Posthaste, right?"

"That's correct, Captain. Posthaste. A police department is no place for a drunk."

Jack stood grinding his teeth. Noyle was wearing suspenders, the new craze. Jack was very tempted to give them a good hard snap.

Noyle left.

"You better watch yourself, Jack," Randy counseled. "Noyle is one guy you don't want to fuck with."

"He can bugger himself," Jack suggested, and sat back down.

"And you better take care of that rehab stuff too. He'll ax you, Jack. He's done it to a lot of guys."

Jack mumbled something not very complimentary under his breath. He couldn't argue, though. Randy was right.

"Beck left something else too." Randy picked up a chromatography analysis report. "Whatever you and Faye gave her to go on checked out."

"The tox screen?"

"Yeah. It turned out to be exactly what you said it was." Randy squinted at the writing in the comments box. "'Cantharadine sulphate, endorphic stimulant, derived via series-distillation of *Taxodium lyrata* tubers. Indigenous to central Europe. Produces aggregant aphrodisiac affect through hyper-stimulation of libidinal receptors. An oil-soluble colloid, will suspend microscopically in alcohol. Colorless, odorless, tasteless. No file in NADDIS. No record of criminal use in U.S.'"

"Great," Jack griped. "Indigenous to central Europe. You'll have to run a CDS trace through goddamn Interpol to find out where this shit's used. That'll take months."

"But what the hell is it?"

"Something like Spanish fly, I think, gets you horny. The aorists used it in the Middle Ages for orgies and rituals. Beck found traces of it in the bloodstreams of the first two 64s. It mixes with alcohol, she says. The postmortems said Barrington, Black, and Lynn were all in heightened sexual states when they died. That's how our guys picked them up so easy. They were probably putting this shit in their drinks."

"All this weird stuff"—Randy gestured at his desk—"and I don't know what to do with any of it."

"You know one thing, though," Jack cautioned, "and mark my words. You can bet there's gonna be one more murder before this is over."

"Here it is," the librarian said. "Be very careful; it may be the only copy in existence, and it's in bad condition. Turn the pages with the stylus, and I'm afraid you'll have to wear these gloves. The amino acids on your fingers will damage the paper if you touch it."

Faye donned the nylon gloves. "What about photocopies?"

"It's illegal to photocopy any Class D precaution printed material. You can photograph the pages if you have a camera. If not—"

"I'll use the copy machine I was born with," Faye finished, indicating her right hand. "Thank you for finding this. I'll let you know when I'm done."

The librarian left Faye to her cove. The book had been brought out in a lidded aluminum box, and rested in an acetate cover. It wasn't thick; it looked more like a brochure than a book. The binding had been removed to reduce page wear. Its faded title in black ink on red seemed to look back at her.

THE SYNOD OF THE AORISTS

No publication date, no copyright. The only printing information read: *Morakis Enterprises. Translated from Greek by Monseigneur Timothy McGinnis.* No author was listed either, and no contributors or bibliographic data.

The page after the title had a dedication:

To know God, one must first know the Nemesis.
This book is for all who seek God.

Faye Rowland opened the book and began to read.

CHAPTER 32

Ginny cranked out the last page from the Smith Corona XL that Khoronos had provided. Her story was done. It was only about 1,500 words, but she'd redrafted it obsessively. Even with her novels, it was not uncommon to rewrite eight or ten times. Art did not come easy for some; most of writing was rewriting. And to hell with all this word processor stuff. Ginny couldn't imagine writing with anything but a loud, clanky typewriter. It was the activity that spurred her, margin bells ringing, key clacking, the carriage whipping back and forth as her muse poured out of her fingertips. All her friends at her writers' group told her she was crazy not to own a computer. "Oh, but Ginny, you'll save so much time!" "I'm not interested in saving time, I'm interested in creating art," she'd come back. "Oh, but Ginny, it all goes on disk! You just push the print button when you're done! Laser jets! 640K RAM! 20-meg hard-drive! How can you live without one!"

"I will not sell my muse to technology," Ginny would then say, and if they kept it up she would politely point out that her books sold millions of copies while theirs sold thousands. To put it another way, Ginny was sick to fucking death of hearing about fucking word processors.

Her story was called "The Passionist." Eight hours of writing left her feeling like eight hours of road work; she'd proof it later. She drifted downstairs, blinking fatigue out of her eyes. Just past nine now, it was getting dark. No one was downstairs. She'd peeked in on Veronica only to find her dead asleep. As for Amy Vandersteen, Ginny hadn't seen her since yesterday.

She went out on the back porch and smoked. A cigarette after finishing a story was better than a cigarette after sex. The rush lulled her almost like pot and she looked dreamily up to the sky. The stars looked like beautiful luminous spillage; the moon hung low. Since coming here, since meeting Khoronos, she found beauty everywhere she looked. She saw wonders. Her vision had never shown her such things before.

She went back into the kitchen and microwaved a bowl of Korean noodles, which she found bland. She hunted through the spice rack for something to spark them up. Curry. Chili powder. Chopped red peppers. Below the rack, though, stood an unmarked jar. Ginny opened it and sniffed. The stuff looked like confectioners' sugar, but when she tasted some on the end of her finger, there was no taste at all.

"Try some," advised Gilles, who sauntered into the kitchen.

Ginny looked at him. *God, he's gorgeous.* All he wore were khaki shorts and a red sweatband on his brow. "It doesn't taste like anything," she said.

"It's like oysters. It makes you feel sexy. Try some."

Ginny giggled and did so. It still tasted bland, but it amused her the way Gilles was watching her, head tilted and arms crossed under the well-developed pectorals. "Where's everybody?" she asked.

"Erim and Marzen are meditating. They are very spiritual people. Spirit transcends flesh. Did Erim ever tell you that?"

"A million times," Ginny said. "Synergy. Transposition."

"Yes. Do you know what all that means?"

"I don't know."

"You will."

Even his weirdness was attractive. "What's that?" she asked, pointing to the fresh Band-Aid on his chest.

"My offering. I don't expect you to understand that."

His offering? Oh, he was weird, all right, but she didn't care. The magnificent body and sculpted face were what she cared about. When she turned to rinse out the noodle bowl, his hands were on her back, kneading her stiffened neck muscles, teasing them loose. "God, that feels good," she murmured.

"What does God have to do with it?"

"It's a figure of speech, Gilles. Jesus."

"Him too?"

His practiced fingers stifled her laugh. She wore no panties or bra beneath the sundress (Ginny didn't like constraints when she wrote; at home she sometimes even wrote nude); she could feel his contours against her buttocks as he continued to massage her neck. This was all too obvious, though she did not object. Why should she? "I want to touch you," he said then, and turned her around. *What a line,* she thought. Now she faced him, backed against the counter. She ran her hands up his chest and grinned.

"I want to touch you," he softly repeated.

She felt perfectly slutty raising the hem of her dress. His hand slipped over the downy hair at once, then lowered to investigate her sex. The long finger made her moist right off.

"So you've finished your story?"

"Uh-huh," she said. She was fascinated just watching, just looking down and seeing the hand play with her.

"What is your story called?"

"'The Passionist,'" she breathed.

"A title born of truth, of yourself? You are very passionate," he said.

Shut up, she thought. Had she subconsciously written the story for him? Her stories were allegories, her characters symbols of emotions. Perhaps she'd written the story for herself. *Anything we create is part of what we are,* she half thought as Gilles' finger probed. The last line was this: *Come away with me and my dream.*

But what *was* her dream?

The kitchen was dark. Ginny felt slick and hot. Had the white spice really turned her on? She knew it was Gilles. *Flesh,* she thought suddenly, and absurdly. She wanted his flesh, not his spirit. She was only being honest with herself: his passion could take a hike, for all she cared. She wanted his cock.

He took his hand away and put the finger in her mouth, making her taste herself. She lowered his khaki shorts. Immediately his *flesh* was hard in her hand. *That's all a cock really is,* she symbolized, amused. *A handle that women use to lead men through life.* She led him down to the floor by it. He stepped out of the shorts. Ginny pulled her dress up as Gilles arranged her on her hands and knees. "Like this?" he inquired.

"Yeah," she whispered, almost impatiently. The wan light from the living room was all that lit the kitchen. She could see the outline of his shadow above the outline of her own—she looked ahead as he inserted himself. The separation of images captivated her. She watched his shadow. He pushed her dress further up her back, then splayed her buttocks to penetrate more deeply. The angle and depth felt so good it almost hurt.

Ginny continued to think about things as he continued. She thought about love and lust. A few days ago she thought she might be able to love Gilles, but that seemed so foolish now. *Love* was foolish; it was an emotional play-act where the final exit was always the same: failure. Veronica had branded Ginny's ideologies as cynicism, but then Veronica was a head case to begin with; she wouldn't even admit she was still hung up on Jack. Love seldom worked. Wasn't Veronica proof? All love did in the end was tear people apart.

The notion that her ideals might be flawed never occurred to her. Ginny was at home with her ideals. Love had blown up in her face enough times. Men had used her, so now she would use them back, with her body and her looks. Seeing Gilles' shadow make love to her, without seeing his face, heightened the philosophy.

"You are beautiful," Gilles whispered. His hands gripped her hips. His rhythm picked up. He wasn't making love to her as much as he was probing her. *Probe me all you want,* she thought, biting her lower lip. *Just don't love me. If you love me, I'll burn you.*

His rhythm slowed a moment. Ahead, his shadow seemed downcast. Was he sad? Perhaps he had a lover somewhere, and he felt guilty now. Men could be such pussies. They'd realize their falsehoods and continue to be false anyway.

Then he said: "You are beautiful and you are true."

More passionist crap, Ginny thought. It frustrated her. The only way he could go on was to say something romantic. Did he think she was an idiot? She reached back and tickled his testicles, to goad him on. "Don't stop!" she whispered. Why was he hesitating? His shadow stood crisp and motionless in front of her.

"I'm sorry," he said.

"Sorry for what!"

He began again, thrusting much harder. *That's better,* she thought. Suddenly he felt huge in her, his penis like a stout plug in her sex, stretching her. He was getting her close now.

"You are very true."

Shut up shut up! She closed her eyes, closing out his shadow, to concentrate.

"But not true enough," he finished.

Ginny didn't hear him, too busy summoning her orgasm. Hence, she didn't see him either. She didn't see his shadow and how drastically it had changed. The widened shoulders and arching back. The large angulated head, and the twin protuberances like horns.

When Veronica woke, the first thing she saw was the painting. Now that she'd finished, her fatigue caught up with her; she'd slept all afternoon into the night. The clock read 9:30; her window framed full dark glittered with stars. She leaned up and stared at the painting, but remembered that she'd been dreaming of Jack. The images didn't mix. Her dream had just been pieces of them when they'd been together. She knew she should call him, at least to let him know everything was okay. But he was too reactionary, and jealous to the point of despair. Why reconnect herself to that? Stewie was another matter; he was business. She'd simply become too lost in everything—her work, her development, Khoronos—to remember to call him. He probably had all sorts of things lined up for her. Yes, she must call him, but . . .

Now that she thought of it, she could not remember seeing a telephone anywhere in the house.

When she'd originally called the number on her invitation, a woman transferred the call. It seemed a little funny.

A sense of emptiness followed her downstairs. Where did everyone disappear to so often? Downstairs was dark. She looked around the entire first floor but found no phone. *I'll ask tomorrow,* she concluded, and went outside.

The big pool lay still in the moonlight. She noticed the gate in the back fence open and decided a walk in the woods would be relaxing. You couldn't do this in the city; you couldn't go for a nice, quiet walk in the woods because there was no woods. Just throngs of people, traffic jams, and smog. Since coming here, Veronica had never felt so purged of the world.

But where will I go now? She strayed along the moonlit path. *Back home, to reality.* How long would Khoronos want them around? The estate was just a playground. Sooner or later she'd have to get back to her profession.

What would it be like when she saw Jack again? She hoped he wasn't moping over the end of their relationship. Ginny said that denial was actually assertion. But was it? Veronica felt convinced that getting back together with Jack would be a mistake. But—

I miss him, she realized.

The path opened into the little dell in which stood the white kiosk. She could just sit here and think, in the moonlight. She needed to think about things now that her work here was done. *Yeah, just think, just think about things.* She stepped into the kiosk—

—and froze.

The image seemed unreal. *I'm still dreaming,* she thought very slowly, and then the details of what she saw came quickly into focus. Veronica's throat shivered shut. Her eyes darted frantically, each revelation striking her like a blow to the head.

It was a corpse that lay sprawled upon the kiosk floor: a nude woman besmirched with blood. In the moonlight, the blood looked utterly black. A tremendous stain spread from the apex of the corpse's legs. The navel and sunken nipples looked like sockets, and the face . . . the face . . .

Veronica turned and ran.

—the face had been *eaten* off.

Her terror propelled her back down the path. Suddenly the woods seemed labyrinthine, insolvable. She thought in primal one-word bursts. *Murder. Help. Phone. Police.* She ran manic back to the house. Who was it? The corpse, bereft of a face, defied identification.

Up the wooden steps, across the deck. In the kitchen she stopped. *What! What!* "Somebody! Help!" she yelled, but the plea only echoed. She sprinted up the steps and burst into Amy Vandersteen's room. The room's tenant was not within. Veronica was about to run back out, but a few simple words locked her gaze. A lone sheaf of papers lay on Amy's writing desk.

Amy obviously had accomplished little of her project, too distracted by drugs. The pages were an attempt at some sort of an outline, a scene from a projected screenplay.

VOICE: All the truth that you can bear . . . is yours.
PROTAGONIST: What truth! Tell me!
VOICE: Look into the mirror. What do you see?
[Protagonist squints. Cut to a mirror, two o'clock angle.]
PROTAGONIST: Nothing.
VOICE: You're not looking closely enough.
[Cut to protagonist's face, then back to mirror. Mirror is empty.]
VOICE: Look closely and you will see the truth. Tell me what you see.
[Close-up protagonist's eyes. Zoom into pupils.]
PROTAGONIST: I . . . see . . . a man.
VOICE: Yes!
[Show flames in pupils.]
PROTAGONIST: I see a man made of flames.

A man made of flames? The similarity urged Veronica away from the desk. She dashed next to Ginny's room, not surprised that Ginny wasn't there. The manuscript, stacked neatly atop the typewriter, bore the title "The Passionist." She flipped to the last page and scanned the last paragraph of Ginny Theil's taut, clipped prose:

> touched her, and in that touch she saw all the love in the world. Flesh made perfect, all flaws purged by the fire. "I am risen," said the voice, but it was no human voice at all. The voice, like midnight, like truth, was incalculable. "Be risen with me."
>
> "But I'm not worthy!" she pleaded. "I've sinned!"
>
> "And I now absolve you, with fire."
>
> She openly wept before the flow of love. *I am risen,* she thought. Trembling, she reached out. His hand closed over hers.
>
> "Come away with me and my dream," said the man made of flames.

Veronica's heart wrenched in her chest. It was impossible. They'd all had the same vision in their dreams. The Fire-Lover. The man made of flames.

She was too confused to sort her thoughts. Then the words, behind her, rose in the air like a palpable shape.

"All the truth that you can bear, Veronica, is yours."

She shivered as she turned. Gilles blocked the doorway. "What have you people done?" were the only words she could summon.

"There's so much that you don't understand, but you were not made to understand. You'll see it all, though. In time."

"You're murderers," her voice wisped. She stepped back, and Gilles stepped forward. His muscles flexed beneath his tight, tanned skin as he moved.

He opened his hands. Suddenly his eyes showed only white. "I am risen," he intoned. "Be risen with us."

Madmen, she thought. Her instincts poured adrenaline into her heart, and she rushed forward. She tried to claw at his face, but his hands snapped up her wrists. She bit into his forearm. He didn't flinch. She bit down harder and felt her teeth grind against bone. He only winced slightly, holding her. Warm blood flowed into her mouth. Even when she bit out a collop of flesh, he barely reacted.

"Don't hurt me," he said. "We have a gift for you. It's a precious gift. Your transposition will show you wonders . . ."

She fought against his grasp, but his forearms, firm as steel rods, didn't budge. His grip on her wrists made her hands go numb.

"You cannot hurt me," he said.

Veronica squealed. Her foot lashed out and caught him directly between the legs. Gilles' hands snapped open—suddenly he was on his knees.

Veronica leapt over him, scrambled out of the room and down the stairs. Fleeing to Ginny's car would be pointless; she didn't have the keys and she didn't have time to look for them. She yanked on the front door but nothing happened. The dead bolt had no knob, just a keyhole. Locked.

She sensed the shadow that appeared on the landing.

She rushed back into the kitchen. *Get a knife!* She heard footsteps as she hauled open drawers, spilling their contents in a clang of metal. Her fingers closed around a fileting knife, when she noticed a lower cabinet hanging open. Immediately she noticed what was inside.

A phone.

It was a portable phone. A small whip antenna stood out of its handle, and a big battery pack was screwed into its housing.

A tiny yellow light winked when she turned on the switch, and the buttons glowed. Beeps resounded as she punched in 911.

She listened, panting. Nothing happened.

"God*damn* it!" she squealed. She'd never used one of these. She fumbled with the receiver, sensing the footfalls coming through the living room. A top button glowed SEND.

Before she could push it, she was screaming, rising, being lifted up by her hair. The heel of Gilles' bare foot slammed down on the phone and cracked its black plastic housing.

"You don't understand." His accented voice was clement, soft. Her scalp barked with pain. She whipped around—

"Veronica, please—"

She brought the knife across Gilles' face. Its blade sliced cleanly through one cheek and out the other.

He stiffened and let go. In silence he brought his hands to his pouring face and stared at her. The stare seemed to dare her. *I can't hurt you, huh?* she thought. Then she lunged again—

"Please, don't," he pleaded.

—and planted the knife into Gilles' left eye.

He stood shuddering. Blood flowed like a cascade down his chest, yet he didn't fall. His right eye held wide on her while the fileting knife jutted from his left.

And then, with resolute calm, he slowly removed the blade. Clear fluid ran down his cheek. The knife clattered.

"Please, Veronica. I won't hurt you."

She screamed again, a high keening sound, as the hand came around and grabbed her throat. Suddenly she was kicking, held fully off her feet.

"He won't hurt you," Marzen said very gently. "But I will."

The grip of the German's big hand tightened. Veronica gagged. Aloft, she seemed to be running on air, but soon her movements began to grow feeble.

Marzen's face looked up at her. Blank. Pitiless.

I'm dead, she managed to think.

The hand squeezed off all the blood to her brain, and down she went, into darkness.

CHAPTER 33

The fog of her thoughts sidetracked her all the way home. She'd read *The Synod of the Aorists* in its entirety, a tome as black as pitch tar. Its images seemed to peer at her like phantoms in the backseat. When she spotted the green sign, her exit—*Historic District, Next Right*—she nearly wept with relief.

Jack's car was not at the house. She drove around Church Circle, trying to listen to the radio. WHFS was playing a group called Strange Boutique. "Never throw away what could be true," the singer lamented in beautiful sadness. *How much have I thrown away?* Faye wondered. She did not pursue an answer.

She still felt confused about last night. Had she made Jack feel better or worse? Right now she wondered if she knew *anything*.

Big Brother Is Watçhing You, read the Orwellian sign in the bookshop window. Faye parked in the lot behind the Undercroft, unconsciously glancing about. Did she expect devils to be in wait? Black-garbed aorists bearing dolches in red hands? *Baalzephon is watching you,* she thought. Was there really a devil? Faye didn't believe in devils, only the ones man made out of his own imperfections. But the aorists were as devoted to truth as the Christians, avowing the same faith to different gods. Who could say that their acts were any worse than the Crusades butchering in the name of Jesus, the Templar Knights forcing conversion at sword point, and the mindless torture of the Holy Inquisition? Mankind pursued truth without ever really seeing it. Act for act. Evil for evil.

She scurried across the gravel lot. She needed to be around people, around life. Maybe she should get drunk and forget about everything. Relief embraced her the instant she stepped into the 'Croft. People, talk, laughter. Craig was expertly pouring four beers from four different taps at the same time. This transition, from the dark solitude of her research to this crowded reality, made her feel physically light.

"What can I do you for, Faye?" Craig inquired.

"Just water," she said.

Barkeeps had a knack for insistency. Craig brought her a bottle of the same strong German beer she'd had last night. "I asked for water," she complained.

"There's water in that," he said.

"Oh, well," she decided. At least if she got drunk, she could blame him.

"What's wrong, Faye? You look like you've just seen Death."

Not Death. Baalzephon. She ignored the comment. "Jack hasn't been in, has he?"

"Nope, not since last night."

Could he have used the directions he'd pilfered and gone to find Veronica?

"They're really giving it to him in the papers," Craig said.

"I know. It's disgusting."

"Why are they calling it the Triangle case?"

"Trines," she muttered, more to her beer. "It's a satanic emblem, a triangle with a star at each point. The killers drew them in blood at each murder scene."

"You'd think something like that could never happen in a town like this."

"This town is no different from any town in the world in any age," Faye responded too quickly. "It's got people. It's got beliefs. It's got good and it's got evil, and that's all you need."

Craig gave her a long look. "Any leads?"

"I don't know. I'm not even working on it anymore."

"So what are you gonna do now?"

She'd asked herself the same question a million times already. "Go back to my regular job. Go home."

"What about Jack?"

"I don't know," she said.

Craig's barkeep vibes sensed her despondency. "Cheer up. Sometimes things work out when you least expect them to."

"Yeah, right."

"And here he is now," Craig looked up and announced. "Living proof of the steelworkers' strike."

"Hilarious," Jack said, sporting three days' growth. The door swooshed closed behind him. "I saw your car when I was passing by," he told Faye, and took the stool next to hers.

"I—" she started to say.

Then he leaned over and quickly kissed her.

It was just a peck on the cheek, yet it nearly shocked her. Before she could even react, he was saying, "I've been looking all over town for Stewie. I've decided to give those directions to him. It's better that way. Whatever the problem is, he's Veronica's manager, so he should take care of it. None of it's any of my business really."

This information secretly overjoyed Faye. Did this mean he'd given up on Veronica for good? Faye doubted it, but it was a start. Circumstances often took time to come to grips with.

"But I'm still wondering about those names," Jack commented. Craig brought him a soda water with a lime slice. "Maybe it's just cop paranoia, but it's almost like this rich guy is using people to cover his tracks."

"Fraus Herren," Faye said. "Philippe Faux. And then the business with the phones."

"Yeah. It bothers me, that's all."

Faye reserved further comment. Why bring up subjects when the common denominator was Veronica? Faye felt jealous and subordinate to this woman she didn't even know.

"How'd it go at the library? You check out that book?"

"Yeah," she said, as the dismal images returned. "It verified the information I discovered yesterday. The aorists made random sacrifices constantly, but once a year they engaged in a special incarnation rite that specifically involved the trine—"

"The triangle."

"Right, and what they thought of as a transpositional doorway. The first three sacrifices served as a catalyst to the ritual. One for each star. These girls were supposed to be passionate and creative, to appease Baalzephon."

"The first victim was an art director, the second two were poets," Jack reminded her. "And they got around."

"Um-hmm. Very sexual, Baalzephon's cup of tea. Anyway,

the first three sacrifices were carried out by the surrogates, or surrogoti—highly trained spiritualists. That's what the Latin line is all about. 'Father of the Earth, walk the earth through me.' It was an incarnation summons. Baalzephon was an incubus. The surrogoti would invoke the demon transpositionally, trade places with him for a short time. They'd not only take on his physical likeness, but they'd become vehicles for Baalzephon's spirit as well. So it wasn't the surrogates themselves who were committing the precursory sacrifices, it was an incarnated aspect of Baalzephon."

"So the guys who killed Shanna Barrington, Rebecca Black, and Susan Lynn believe that it was actually Baalzephon who did it?"

"Yes. That's what they believe. But these were only partial incarnations. The full transposition came at the end."

"The fourth sacrifice you were talking about," Jack added.

Faye nodded, sipping her beer. "This fourth sacrifice was the most important, and today I found out why."

"I can't wait to hear this," Jack mumbled.

"The fourth was to serve as the ultimate gift to Baalzephon. She was usually selected out of several candidates."

"Selected by whom?"

"By the prelate. It was his job to choose the one who would best serve the demon. They often underwent intense spiritual training. Self-awareness was very important, not just women who were highly creative and passionate, but women who had a refined sense of 'self.' The prelate would take great care in selecting optimum candidates."

Jack jiggled the ice in his glass. "But that's what I don't quite get. Candidates for what?"

"For Baalzephon's wife," Faye said. "Baalzephon took a human wife every year. He was the hierarchical demon of passion and creativity, so his wives must be strongly possessed of both traits." Faye wasn't even looking at him as she recounted what she'd read in *The Synod of the Aorists*. "The sacrifice of the fourth woman effected a complete transpositional incarnation. The prelate would murder her with the dolch, directly upon a trine fashioned in some low place, like a cave or a quarry, or even a basement. This was the act that the first three sacrifices had led up to—the transposition. Baalzephon would open the trine and ascend, *incarnare*, or in the flesh. To stand upon the very earth that God had banished him from, and claim his bride."

Jack rubbed his eyes wearily. "This morning I told Noyle that there would probably be a fourth murder."

"I don't think there are any probablys about it, Jack. So far your killers have *duplicated* the original rite. Noyle would be stupid not to expect a fourth murder."

"Noyle *is* stupid," Jack said. "He's convinced the two killers are just a pair of crackheads or psychotics."

"There are at least three killers, remember. There's also someone out there who thinks he's a prelate, and you can bet that right now he's preparing for the fourth murder."

"Great," Jack said. "In a way I'm glad Noyle took me off the case; it's his problem now." He stood up, fishing in his pockets. Onto the bar he emptied a bunch of change, keys, and scraps of paper. *What a slob,* Faye thought. *But I still love him.*

"I'm out of cigarettes," he said, "and if I don't have one soon, I'll die."

"You might die if you *do* have one soon."

"Please don't confuse me with facts." Jack plucked quarters out of the mass of change, then disappeared for the cigarette machine.

Faye remained lulled on the bar, thinking. "Can I ask you something, Craig?"

"Of course." Craig was deftly juggling four shooter glasses around a lit Marlboro 100 in his mouth. "People ask me things all the time."

"Should I bow out?"

"I can't advise you on that one. But I can say that it never pays to give up." Craig spoke and juggled at the same time.

"You're a big help, Craig. I hope you drop those glasses."

"I've dropped many. How do you think I got to be so good?" Craig grinned. "Think about that."

Faye smirked at him. He was saying that fulfillment came through trial and error. She'd dropped a few glasses herself in life.

"But here's something for you to consider. There's a minor variation on the men's room wall, so you know it's true."

"Graffiti is the voice of truth?" she asked sarcastically.

"You never seen our men's room."

"Okay, Craig. What?"

He expertly juggled each shooter glass down to the bartop "A woman's got to do what she's got to do."

Faye's frown deepened. When she sipped her beer again she noticed a slip of paper Jack had removed from his pocket She blinked.

Then she picked it up and looked at it hard. The piece of paper was filled with scrawl, but right on top—

Jack returned, tamping a fresh pack of Camels.

"What . . . is . . . this?" Faye asked, the impossibility of what she saw stretching her words like tallow.

Jack glanced at the slip of paper. "Those are the directions I told you about, the directions to the rich guy's house."

"Rich guy," Faye repeated.

"Yeah, the rich guy. I already told you, the guy who invited Veronica to his estate for some kind of retreat. I copied them down when I broke into Ginny's apartment."

"You broke into Ginny's apartment?" Craig asked, incredulous.

"Don't ask," Jack said.

But Faye was tugging on his sleeve, urgent to the point of almost tearing his shirt. "Jack, Jack, listen to me!"

"Are you all right, Faye?"

"Shut up and listen!" She pointed to the word Jack had written above the directions. The word was *Khoronos*. "What's that? Why did you write that?"

Now Jack looked totally cruxed. "That's his name."

"Whose name?"

"The rich guy," he close to yelled. "I already told you."

"You never told me his *name*!"

"So what?"

"The rich guy's name is *Khoronos*?"

"Yes! Big deal! What's the matter with you?"

Her eyes leveled on him. "Like those other names, Jack. Fraus. Faux. They weren't names, they were words. Khoronos isn't a name either. It's a Greek *word*."

Jack tapped out a Camel. "What are you talking about?"

She paused to catch her breath. He didn't understand. "Let me ask you something . . . Do you have any reason to believe that Veronica's disappearance might have something to do with the Triangle case?"

Jack looked at her absurdly. "That's ridiculous. They're otally unrelated."

Then Faye Rowland enlightened him: "*Khoronos* is Greek or aorista."

CHAPTER 34

Logic was not a thing one generally considered during time of anguish—too easily usurped by emotion and, of course, poc judgement. In other words, Jack Cordesman began to *act* befor he began to *think*. Foot to the floor, he smoked and fumble with maps as he drove, drifting in and out of his lane. Ginny' directions were not difficult, yet he found difficulty in apply ing them to the county map grid. He felt something fightin against him.

Upon Faye's revelation at the bar, Jack was up and out *Impossible*, he thought. *Completely impossible*. But he was nc daunted by such formalities as common sense. She'd dragge at his shirt in the parking lot, yelled at him, tried to reaso with him, but for naught. "You can't go there by yourself! she'd shouted.

"Why not?"

"Those people are killers!"

"If they are, I'll deal with them," he'd stated very flatly.

"Let the police handle it!"

"I am the police. Besides, they wouldn't believe any of it anyway. Noyle? Olsher? No way."

"Take some people with you, then! Someone to back yo up!"

"No."

"At least let *me* go with you!"

"No," he'd said, and gotten into the car, closed the door, an driven away. He saw her shrink in the rearview as he pulled off She watched after him, standing in the middle of the street. Sh looked very sad just then. She looked crushed.

I'm a prick, he thought now. *I'm a cold, inconsiderate fuck er*. Now that he had a fair idea where he was headed, wisps of logic did indeed resurface. First, this could very well be a mistake and a tremendous overreaction. The odds were astronomical. Perhaps he'd written the name down wrong. Perhaps Ginny had. Second, even if it wasn't a mistake, Faye was right. Jack should have backup, or he should have at least tried to get some, not that his credibility these days was particularly convincing among his superiors. He was going off half cocked and then some.

The unmarked's tires hummed over the blacktop. The car devoured as much road as he could give it. He passed trucks and semi-rigs heading for the interstate; the long open fields to left and right blurred by. It was a pretty night, starry and warm. The moon followed him like a watcher.

What am I going to do when I get there? This was a sound inquiry. What did he think he was going to do? Bust down Khoronos' door? Infiltrate his estate like some black-bag commando? Was he the knight in shining armor traveling through hell and high water to rescue the damsel in distress. *Or am I about to make a prime ass of myself?*

And suppose these guys *were* killers? Killers generally had weapons. All Jack had was his Smith Model 49, a five-shot J-frame peashooter, and he had no extra rounds. In the trunk was a parkerized Remington 870 with a folding stock (which he hated because it kicked worse than a pissed-off mule) and an old Webley revolver (which kicked worse) that he only kept around because it was fun to take to the range. The shotgun would be difficult to maneuver in close quarters, and the Webley, though it chambered a big .455 load, was an antique. Big, clunky, and about thirty years overdue for a major breakdown.

He could only vaguely adjudicate the directions. At this pace, sixty-five, seventy miles per hour, he'd probably be there in ninety minutes. Khoronos was rich, eccentric, and obviously protective of his privacy. Jack envisioned a fortress rather than an estate. High fences, security windows, steel-frame doors. Jack could pick your average lock, but he couldn't touch tubulars (as were found on most alarm systems) and he couldn't do a pin-wired keyway. What if Khoronos had dogs, or guards? What if he had video? They'd be waiting for him, and they'd be ready.

But then the darkness crept back, a thousand years' worth. *Khoronos,* he decrypted. *Aorista.*

What if Faye was right?

They could be killing Veronica right now.

The ritual that never ends. At least if he died, he would do so at the hands of history, not some crack dealer or street scum.

He thought of Shanna Barrington, the black-stitched Y of her autopsy-section. He saw Rebecca Black lying crucified upon the blood-sodden bed, and the clean white walls blaring red satanic art. He thought of the sad poem Susan Lynn had written, the poem which had turned out to be her own epitaph.

He thought of the last time he'd made love to Veronica. He thought of the scent of her hair, the precious taste of her sex. He thought of the way she felt, so lovely and intense, so *wet* for him. He remembered what she'd said to him as he came in her, her voice a tiny plea, impoverished out of the desperation to communicate that which reduced all the words in language to utter inferiority.

Her plea was this: *I love you.*

Her love for him was gone now, he knew that, but he could never forget how beautiful things had been in the past, how important he'd once been to her.

And now these aorists, these *madmen,* might be killing her.

They won't kill her, he thought. His long hair blew in the window drag. *Not if I kill them first.*

His eyes trained on the endless ribbon of road, his hands firmly gripped the wheel. He lit a Camel.

He grinned maniacally.

He may even have laughed aloud when he whispered:

"If they so much as touch her, I'm gonna kill everything that moves."

CHAPTER 35

Aorista, Father! I am the aorist! Once more the great beautiful black bird descended, higher into the depths than ever. It felt sublime and bright in the magnificent, chaotic darkness, a black aura singing into the whisper of providence. It heard . . . *glorious* things. Portents and validities far beyond the total of all the knowledge of the world. These were the Father's whispers.

The bird sailed effortless over the chasms, each earthwork like a channel of steaming blood bubbling red as lava, and the thick smoke of baking fat the sweetest attar to the pitlike nostrils of its beak. Below, the ushers travailed, dividing twitching faces with stubby, nimble fingers, sloughing hot skin off the backs of the beautiful, unreeling entrails from plundered bellies in scarlet bliss. *Aorista!* thought the bird. *Aorista!*

Now it sat perched and watched, flexing its sleek black wings. Such honor to sit here, in the lap of truth. *You have honored me,* drifted the whisper. *So behold now all that awaits.*

Yes! Aorista!

Only then, in the darkled vision, did the great bird realize the place of its perch: the very shoulder of the Father.

Go.

—and so it did, soaring back through the apsis of the tenebrae, past the castellated crests of onyx and ebon fire. Back—

Aorista, Father!

—back—

Father of the Earth!

—and back, over the darkness of a thousand endless truths.

Baalzephon!
Back to the gift that lay warm in wait.
Hail!
Back to the blessed error of the world.

Veronica sensed the descent of motion. Her head bobbed with each step down. She was being carried to some low place.

When she opened her eyes she saw darkness tinted by dancing candlelight. A cloaked figured stepped away. Her carrier, too, wore the same garb; they looked like monks. Veronica tried to move, yet her limbs did not answer the command of her brain. She felt sluggish, drugged.

Her vision seemed to lag before her; she was naked in the arms of the sack-clothed monk. Where was she? And what was that, below her on the floor?

I'm not dead, she realized. And she remembered. The savage body in the kiosk. Gilles and Marzen attacking her. She remembered the German's big hand squeezing the consciousness out of her like water out of a sponge. They were madmen, all of them, but they hadn't killed her. Instead, they'd saved her for something.

What? What are they going to do with me?

And what had Gilles said earlier? Something about offerings?

Her cloaked bearer stopped. The flickering candlelight blurred her vision. All she could see were smears, suggestions of solid shapes submerged in dark. She squinted, tried to blink away the myopic tatters. What stood before her looked like a primitive chancel, a risen stone altar laid across stone plinths, and sided by iron candelabra. A crude red triangle had been drawn on the wall, where a cross might hang. On the center of the altar were a small jar and what appeared to be a black . . .

Knife, she realized in drugged terror. *It's a knife.*

Her carrier stopped beside the second cloaked figure. The candles sizzled slightly. They were black and crudely fashioned, releasing an oily fetor to the damp air. Veronica felt drenched in her own sweat, tremoring.

Then another figure entered the chancel.

Veronica stared.

The third figure faced the altar, murmuring something like an incantation. *He's praying,* she thought. It reminded her of

:r childhood. Church. The minister standing with his back the congregation as he spoke the offertory and raised the craments. But this figure was no minister, and it was not ead and wine that he raised.

It was the black knife.

It's Khoronos, Veronica realized.

"*Pater terrae,*" he whispered, though the whisper rang like metal bell in the dank, underground church. "Accept these eager gifts so that we may remain worthy in your sight."

"World without end," incanted the two others.

"To you we give our faith forever."

"Accept our gifts. Sanctify us and keep us safe . . ."

Khoronos turned, his hooded faced diced by candlelight. His nds clasped the earthen jar to his chest.

"Welcome, Veronica," he whispered very softly.

His cassock came unsashed.

Veronica screamed.

No penis could be seen between Khoronos' legs. There was ly a severed stump peeking out above the testicles.

"What should I do?"

Craig was starting to get addled. He poured two Windex ooters for a pair of dolts with glasses, then came back to :r. "How can I tell you what to do if you don't tell me what's ing on?"

"You'd never believe me," Faye muttered.

"Whatever he's off doing, don't worry about it."

How could she not worry? Jack was alone, against uncertain lds. "I'll call his partner, Randy."

"Jack can take care of himself," Craig said. He had three ps running and was mixing drinks at the same time, some- w without spilling a drop. "That's your problem, Faye. You ver have faith in anyone."

The statement slapped her in her face. "How the hell do u know!" she objected loudly enough to turn a few heads.

"I'm a barkeep, Faye. Barkeeps know everything." He inned, lit a Marlboro. "How can you expect to have faith in ople when you don't even have faith in yourself?"

Faye stare through the brazen comment. But was he right? hy couldn't she just have leave things be? Jack had to know hat he was doing better than she did.

Craig was jockeying; the bar was full now, standing roo only. Lots of rowdy regulars, and lots of couples. A row girls sat up at the bar, to fawn over Craig, and right next Faye was a guy in a white shirt writing something on a b napkin. Suddenly he looked at her. Faye recognized the sha tered look in his eyes. It was the same look she's seen in Jack eyes the first night she met him. It was the same look she'd see in her own for a year. Broken pieces. "My girlfriend broke u with me tonight," the guy drunkenly lamented. "I was goir to marry her."

"Sorry to hear it," Faye offered.

The broken pieces glimmered. "I still love her," he said.

Eventually two friends took him out of the bar; he was clea ly too drunk to drive. But he left the napkin he'd been writin on. Faye glanced at it. *It's a poem,* she realized.

It read: *My gut feels empty, my heart is black. I'd do an thing to have you back. So shall it be—you've cut the tethe but my love for you goes on forever.*

Faye could reckon this, despite the bad verse. For a yea her heart felt black, her gut felt like a bottomless pit of los Did Jack feel the same way now? Was that why he'd rushed find Veronica? Or had she really been tricked by murderers

She admitted the odds were just too wild. *But the name,* sh reminded herself. *The word. Khoronos.*

Craig frowned when some man with banged hair swaggere in. He wore boots up to his knees, and a black T-shirt wi an abstract picture on it. "Veronica Polk," the shirt read. "Th Pickman Gallery."

"Thanks for the nickel tip the other night, Stewie," Crai said. "The door's that away."

The guy shoved out a ten. "Just get me a drink."

Faye approached him. "Are you Stewie, Jack's friend?"

Stewie laughed. "Let's just say an acquaintance. *Frien* seems a bit of an overstatement."

"And you're also Veronica's agent?"

Stewie peered at her. "That's right. She disappeared la week. Jack was supposed to find her, but it figures he neve came through."

"Yesterday he found out where Khoronos lives," Faye sta ed.

Stewie's eyes spread over his drink. "How . . ."

"He's on his way there now."

Suddenly Stewie was frantic. "What do you know about it?"

"Everything," Faye said.

After that, she said a lot more.

"God*damn*!" Jack yelled. He was parked off the shoulder, otor running. The minute he'd gotten what he thought was right grid, he got lost. The TI-DM kept spitting out the ong frames.

Every county police vehicle now was fitted with a data onitor, a simple LCD system that was uplinked to the coun- mainframe. It sported a small screen and keyboard, and as manufactured by Texas Instruments. With it, an officer uld run an MVA or warrant check without having to wait r dispatcher processing. An officer could also run any street dress in the county and bring up the proper map grid on the reen. But so far Jack had punched up the address and locate- mmand three times and had gotten three different grids.

"Piece of *shit*!" he yelled, and smacked the wheel. He tered the address again and got another wrong frame. If e computer was down, the screen would say so. It could so be what they called a "bad lay"—some aspect of the rrain obstructing the radio relay—but that only happened in e snow or during a thunderstorm. Tonight, though, the sky as crystal clear.

It goddamn figures, he thought. There were some high for- t belts up this way, and some mountains. Maybe the signal as bouncing. He drove up to higher ground, then punched the address again. The screen flashed another wrong grid. gain, he felt thwarted, that fate or bad luck or *something* as deliberately standing in his way. *At this rate I'll have to quence the entire grid system frame by frame,* he thought, anting to be sick. Khoronos' address must be on a pipestem at was not on the paper map. But it would have to be on the mputer; the geographic survey was upgraded every day. So here the hell was it?

One more time, he decided. This time he got a notorious lay malfunction called a "slide"; the screen flashed an entire id *block*—twelve different frames in a few seconds. "Moth- less piece of shit!" he yelled. He wanted to punch the screen rip the whole system out and leave it in the street.

He lit a Camel and let his anger beat down. Then he glanc at the last grid frame.

Bingo. The screen logged the road he was on right now. T pipestem to Khoronos' lot sat just a hundred feet before hin

This is it.

He idled up. Here the residences sat back off the road. Lo driveways led deep into the woods, and a mailbox marked ea drive. Jack aimed his remote spot onto each one, checki the addresses. He could've laughed; Khoronos' address w skipped. *I do not believe this shit.* He backed up to the l marked drive and pulled in. As suspected, the driveway pr ceeded *past* the address on the mailbox.

"Dead End," a sign read.

"Uh-huh," he muttered.

He pulled past the sign, turned off the motor and the ligh and got out. By the trunk light he checked his Smith snub. T shotgun was loaded, five rounds of no. 4 buck. He slung it ov his shoulder. Then he loaded six .455s into the big Webley

He gently closed the trunk.

He tried to visualize himself. A suspended cop standing the dark in some guy's driveway in the middle of the nig with a riot gun slung across his back.

What am I doing?"

It was not too late to be reasonable. He could get back in the car, drive home, and proceed with this in a proper a professional manner.

Sure I could, he realized. *But I'm not gonna, so let's go.*

Jack began to walk up the dark road.

He didn't know if he was looking at a house or some arch tect's idea of a bad joke. *Frank Lloyd Wright would shit in h grave if he could see this,* he thought. Khoronos' house look like a futuristic castle: bright white, shutterless with guns windows, and configured of odd angels and lines. It stood o against the moon. The structure bothered him somehow, t trapezoidal tangents, the incongruency of its shape. Perha it was his imagination, but the more Jack stared at the stru ture's bizarre geometry, the more he saw the shades of the san occult glyphs left on the walls of three murdered women.

He skirted around the side. Most of the windows were dar Before the house stood a squat four-car garage. The doo ere locked but there were windows in the panels. He quickly hipped out his Mint-Maglite and shined it in.

More coincidence, or was this it?

First, there was no doubt that this was the right place. In the rthest bay he saw an orange Mercedes 450SL—Ginny's car. ext were two more vehicles: a white panel van and a long ack luxury sedan, a Lincoln or a Cadillac.

Stewie had said the two guys had picked up Veronica's paintg in a white van. Craig had seen a big black sedan pulling to the Undercroft the night Susan Lynn was murdered.

Again, he faltered. Neither Stewie nor Craig had gotten tag imbers or even partials, but he doubted that that mattered. ne decryption of Khoronos' name, plus the white van and e black sedan spotted by witnesses, was probably enough to t a search warrant that would wash in court.

But that would take a day, he thought. *And I don't have day.*

A high fence surrounded the backyard, beyond which stood e forest. The fence was painted glossy black. He couldn't e between the gaps. He saw no motion or pressure sensors the fence.

As stealthily as he could, then, he climbed over.

Now he was standing in wavering, lazy light. A large outoor pool filled the backyard; its submerged lights were on, hich vacillated upon the rear of the house. Jack froze, tried blend in with the fence as his eyes scanned the pool and e yard. He was alone.

No time like the present for illegal entry. He was getting to an expert at it these days. It was nice to know that even if did get kicked off the force, he'd be able to burgle houses r a living. He checked every window along the lower level. lore darkness. Next were a pair of French doors, any burglar's eam. He checked the lock on the knob, one of the better wik-Sets, but before he slipped out his pickcase, he turned e knob. *Some security,* he thought. The door was unlocked.

Then he did the next logical thing: he entered the house.

A line from the state annotated code seemed to haunt im: *Absent additional exigent circumstances, the officer must btain a warrant before entering any private residence without ositive consent of the tenant or owner.*

Jack stalled.

However, the officer may make a warrantless search of an thing, whether personal belongings, a vehicle, or a buildin, provided there is probable cause to believe it necessary to sav a life.

Fuck it, he thought.

He closed the door behind him, wiped down the knobs, ar walked in. He withdrew the Smith .38 and proceeded.

The downstairs search was effective and quick. He mac no noise and left no prints. Only a few lights were on. Tl entire lower level seemed a clash in design: colonial livir room, Victorian study, Tudor-style foyer. It was funny. H noticed no phones, no televisions or radios, or the like. H checked the kitchen last, large and contemporary. He stoppe stock-still.

On the floor lay a smashed portable cellular phone.

And something else. A puddle. Streaks.

Blood.

Still wet, he saw.

Now was when he should leave; things had added up to h legal favor. Khoronos' name, the black sedan, and now w blood. He should exit the house immediately, retreat to the ca and radio for help. As for probable cause, he could lie to th judge and prosecutor, tell them that he saw the blood from th outside, through the kitchen window, then he wouldn't have beat the shaky physical entry. He'd merely tell them he'd neve entered the house. But if he was going to do that, he'd have get out right now, before he might be seen. And . . .

He looked down at the blood.

It might be Veronica's blood.

He put the Smith snub in his pocket and unslung the sho gun.

It's time to stop fucking around.

He searched every room upstairs quickly and quietly. On room was the freakiest thing he's ever seen, a room made con pletely of mirrors. Jack didn't waste time wondering. The ot er five rooms were bedrooms. Veronica's was obvious: paint brushes, a smudged palette. A single painting set propped up dry. "Veronica Betrothed," she'd penned on the back frame and her name in the corner, "V. Polk." She'd painted herse in the strangest clarity, crisply naked yet stunningly abstrac holding hands with a figure of flames.

Jack could almost feel the heat just looking at it.

The other bedrooms were spartan and clean. In the last he und a typewriter and a story. "The Passionist" by Virginia hiel, but no Ginny to go along with it. *Where the hell is every-dy?* His temper raged. *The whole joint's empty.*

Then he heard a quick, muffled—

Thump!

Jack whirled, bringing the shotgun down and nearly releas-g his bladder. What he faced was a closed door. And again:

Thump!

Jack pointed the Remington straight at the door. His heart ammered. He popped off the trigger safety with his right index nger, and—

Thumpthumpthumpthumpthump!

—and nearly squeezed off a round at the start from the next ummel of beats. It must be a closet. Jack turned the knob, ulled and stepped back. He stood sideways, to offer as little rget mass of himself as possible, and the door keened open.

Jack lowered the Remington. A woman, bound and gagged, y on the closet floor. Bare legs squirmed, eyes bulged up om out of the dark. Jack stared. The woman was Ginny Thiel.

He dropped on his knee. "Don't make a sound," he whis-ered. "I'm going to untie you." Ginny went lax as Jack strug-led with her bonds. She wore a ripped sundress; blood streaked er legs. It was plain to see that she'd been raped.

They'd tied her up tight as a meat bundle. He finally got e gag off, which she'd nearly chewed though.

"Jack—

Jack pressed his palm across her mouth. "Quiet. Talk quiet."

She gulped, nodded.

"You're going to be all right now. Don't worry. But I need know what's going on.

"I . . . ," she murmured. "Khoronos, Gilles . . . aw, od . . ."

"What about Khoronos? Where is he?"

Tears flooded her eyes; she trembled at some recollection. Vhen he got the rope off her, she lurched forward and hugged im.

"Calm down." He pushed her wet hair off her brow. Her skin elt clammy, slick. It scared him the way she was shaking.

"Who else is in the house, Ginny? I need to know."

She stifled sobs into his shoulder. "All of them," she whi pered.

"Who?"

"Khoronos, Marzen . . . Gilles."

"Where's Veronica?"

"With them, I think," she sobbed.

With them. "Ginny, I've been through the whole house. N one's here."

"Basement," she choked. "The room with the mirrors."

But Jack had already seen that. What could an upstairs roo have to do with the basement? *She's traumatized,* he though *She doesn't know what she's saying.* He'd have to find it hin self.

"Listen to me. I'll get you to a hospital real soon, but I ha to find these guys first. So I want you to stay here. They thir you're tied up, so they won't come back. You stay here un I come for you. All right?"

She was still staring, half at Jack, half at memory. Even ually she nodded.

"Sit way back in the closet. Take this—" He put the Smi .38 in her hand. "You hear anybody come into this room, poi it up at the door. Hold it straight out with both hands. All yc have to do is squeeze the trigger. You hear me?"

She nodded again, looking at the little gun in her hand.

"Anyone opens this door that's not me . . . shoot."

He slid her back into the closet. If he let her go out to tl car by herself, she'd give his position away. Jack needed tl element of surprise, and he wouldn't have that with a delirio woman stomping about the house.

I'm wasting time. He looked at her, quelling his rag "Ginny, who did this to you?" he asked.

Despair replaced the terror on her face. "It was Gilles."

"What's he look like?"

"Young, big, short dark hair. He's French."

Gilles, huh? Jack thought. *Well, I've got something fc Gilles.* "How many others are there?"

"Those three. Gilles, Marzen . . . And Khoronos."

Gilles, French. Marzen, German, probably. Karla Panzra was right. Foreigners.

"Be careful of Marzen," Ginny warned. "He's younger, big ger."

Honey, nobody's too big for no. 4 buckshot.

"Sit tight. I'll be back soon, I promise."

Jack stood up, began to close the closet door.

"Wait, Jack. Marzen and Gilles . . . they're . . ."

"What?"

"They're not men."

"Just sit tight." He closed the door. *Not men.* She was half in shock, irrational. If they weren't men, what were they? *They're sick motherfuckers is what they are,* he answered himself. *And I'm gonna blow all three of them straight into next year.*

Jack brought the Remington to bear and headed back to the mirrored room.

CHAPTER 36

They lashed her to the floor, to iron lugs. She felt submerged in an utter blackness that was somehow beautiful and bright.

"*Pater terrae,*" she heard.

The three figures looked down. They'd splayed her over the Trine, her head at the top point, her feet at the lower two. Her lashed hands formed two more points. She was a human pentangle.

"Give us grace," spoke the Prelate.

"We are risen in thy grace," answered the surrogoti.

Sweat licked her naked body. The wavering candlelight looked far away, like dim stars. The darkness was showing her things—she *knew* now, and she was not afraid. She felt risen, too: her tininess and insignificance gently lifted to a higher stratum.

"Protect us."

"We beseech thee, in our love."

Love, she thought. She'd had love once, hadn't she? She closed her eyes and looked back on her life. Love? At least someone had loved her here. Greater love awaited, though, *infinite* love.

"Protect us."

The Prelate's voice sounded graven. Something was wrong.

"No one must interfere."

Interfere? She closed her eyes more tightly.

Then she *saw*.

She saw a man. The man was tainted yet radiant. He shined bright above whatever error she sensed. It was love that purged his taints. It was love that made him seem so bright in her mind.

"Kill him with these, if you must."

The Prelate was handing dolches to the pair of surrogoti. "Go," he bid.

The surrogoti turned and left.

But where were they going?

More confusion. She saw the man very closely now; he was walking through some image in her mind. It was not memory. It was not the past. The man she saw in her mind was Jack.

He was here. Now. He was coming for her.

"Flesh through blood. Body through spirit."

The Prelate knelt at the base of the Trine, between her legs. His aura radiated about his head like black sparks, like a halo made of twilight.

He raised a third dolch and kissed it.

He looked down at her then, in all his truth—

Truth? she questioned.

—but it was not truth she saw when she looked back.

She saw through it now, to the core of what it really was. Not truth at all, but a spurious replica—a fake behind a façade.

It was corruption. Total. Final. Black.

It was the antithesis of truth.

Veronica tried to scream, but no sound came out.

The Prelate grinned, a grin not of wisdom, but of perfect evil, and in a voice thick as smoke he began the Invocation to Baalzephon, Sentinel Apostate of Creativity, the Father of the Earth, which would be followed by the Final Rite of the Transposition.

Jack stood cruxed in the room of mirrors. Its bright silver walls enticed him to look at the thousand facsimiles of himself; he couldn't help it. He saw himself in the veins, disheveled, eyes propped open by weird fascination, and the Remington at port arms. Why had Khoronos built such a room? And what could it possibly have to do with the basement?

His reflection returned his confusion. But suddenly a darker reflection joined his own.

"So cometh the Vindicator?"

Jack spun, racking the shotgun. The reflections stifled him; it took a moment to pick the one that was real, and he knew that in that moment he could've been killed.

"We are risen," the figure said. "We never end."

A young man stood before him, in a black cassock and lowered hood. *French accent,* Jack thought. *Gilles.*

The young man's hand gripped a knife made of black stone.

"I have seen ages," he intoned, "and through those ages the inquisitors never change . . . But, then, neither do we."

Jack stared. *Someone cut this guy bad.* A blade had been riven cheek-to-cheek; it made his mouth look huge and phantasmal. One eye socket had been plugged up with tissues.

"Inquisitor. Leave while you still can."

"You're about six months early for Halloween, fella," Jack said. "Tell me where Veronica is or I'll blow your shit clear to gay Paris."

"You can't hurt us. We don't want to hurt you. Tomorrow we'll be gone, and your life will remain. You can't hurt us, believe me."

"I'm not gonna *hurt* you, pal, I'll gonna *kill* you. So start talking and maybe I'll decide to be a nice guy."

The figure took a step forward. The black knife glittered.

"Are you pure-ass crazy? One more step and I put a hole in your chest big enough to drive a bus through." Jack brought the shotgun up, eyesighting down the bead. This was the motherfucker who'd raped Ginny. Had he done the same to Veronica?

"Let's try one more time. Where's Veronica?"

The figure lunged, wielding the knife. Jack squeezed off a round, which slammed into the Frenchman's right elbow. The knife flew away with his forearm. Pellets cracked the mirrors behind the man; sprays of blood drooled down the glass.

Yet Gilles remained standing.

Jack racked up the next round. "What's it gonna be?"

"All the truth that you can bear is yours. How much, inquisitor? How much truth can you take before you see what you really are?"

Jack veered the bead to the figure's chest.

Gilles lunged again, reaching out with his remaining arm.

Jack put the next round into the kid's 5x, racked a third, and put that in the lower abs. The dual report slammed Gilles to the glass floor as if a pallet of mason blocks had been dropped on him. The floor spiderwebbed amid spatters of blood, and smoke rose as Jack appraised the broken corpse. *So much for him.*

Then he noticed the gap.

He racked up round number four. Behind the body, a panel seemed to lean open, a black seam in the room's silver glare.

Jack squinted. *A door.*

He nosed the Remington into the gap. A dark stairwell led down.

Veronica's down there.

He opened the door fully, took a step—

"Holy fuck!" he shouted, and squeezed off another round.

A second cloaked figure had lurched out of the doorway and grabbed the shotgun barrel. Ginny wasn't kidding when she said this fucker was big. He was *huge,* and worse, he'd taken the shotgun blast full in the gut and didn't drop. The guy's hands grasped the barrel and slide; Jack couldn't feed the next round.

Then the figure chuckled, levered upward, and tore the Remington from Jack's hands.

The fuckers must be wearing vests under the getups, Jack thought. His heart slugged when the figure broke the slide off the gun.

"Gilles vaz too merciful," the German said. "He gave you a chance to leave. I vill not."

"Fraus Herren," Jack muttered. He shucked the Webley and stepped back. "The false man."

"*Nein.* I am more real that you could ever know."

Careful, Jack warned himself. If they had vests, he'd have to go for a head shot, and that would not be easy with this big, top-heavy revolver.

Marzen lowered his hood and smiled. He withdrew an identical black dagger—a dolch, Jack remembered—and ran his finger along the cutting edge. Blood oozed from the German's fingertip, and on his own forehead he christened himself, drawing a crude inverted cross.

"I vill cut off your skin. I vill dig out your eyes and eat them. I vill feed your insides to my god."

"This is a *gun,* dickbrain," Jack pointed out. "It shoots *bullets.* That little nail file you got doesn't mean shit to me. I'll shove it up your ass after I blow your head off." But then he thought: *What the hell am I waiting for?* He cocked the Webley and sighted down on the German's head. Marzen didn't move—he just stood there, grinning. "I'll see you at your autopsy, pal," Jack said, and squeezed the trigger.

The glass room shook at the big pistol's report. It sounded like an ash can going off. There was one good thing about the Webley: when it hit, it hit like a runaway truck. The big hot-loaded .455 caught Marzen in the throat and blew him down the stairs. The dolch clattered after him.

How stupid can guys be? Jack wondered. They'd both just stood there and let themselves be shot.

"Jack, what the—"

Jack twirled, aiming the Webley.

Ginny screamed.

"Goddamn it!" he bellowed. "I told you to wait!"

She stood teetering. "I was scared. I heard shots."

"I just got done killing those two guys. And there's one more to go. Khoronos."

"Jack," she faltered. She held the Smith snub by the edge of its grip. The dried blood on her legs looked like tempera paint. "I told you, they're not men."

"Get out of here, Ginny. You're delirious—"

"They're devils."

Jack stared at her. The dock bum had said the same thing. Devils. He pointed to Gilles' corpse. "See that, Ginny? It's not a devil. It's a dead *man.* There's another dead man downstairs." He threw her the keys to his unmarked. "Go down the road and wait in the car."

He stepped over Gilles' corpse and headed for the opened mirror panel, but she rushed after him. "Don't leave me alone!" she pleaded.

He turned, infuriated. "Get out! I got no time to—"

—but what he saw as he turned paralyzed him. He saw Gilles' corpse lying behind Ginny. Then he saw the corpse . . . get up.

"Look out!" Ginny was in the way; he couldn't shoot. Gilles' hand snapped over her shoulder, grabbed Jack by the collar, and threw him to the floor. Jack heard the Webley slide out of reach.

Ginny's screams sounded like screeching tires. Jack rose to hands and knees, and looked up. Gilles had straddled Ginny on the floor, clamping her neck down with his one hand. *These guys aren't wearing vests,* Jack realized. The Frenchman's cassock hung open, showing meaty shotgun craters. And there was something else—

Ginny screamed and screamed—

My God, the thought poured across Jack's mind.

He was not looking at a man now, he was looking at a nightmare. The Frenchman's hand seemed cloven, taloned. And his face—

Sweet Jesus . . .

—was no human face at all. It seemed barely a face of any kind. Spheric yellow eyes glinted from the malformed cranium. The huge mouth protracted, full of teeth like cracked glass. Two stubs jutted from the runneled foreskull.

A devil's face, Jack thought.

The Webley had slid across the room, and he didn't see where the Smith had landed. All that lay between himself and the thing that was killing Ginny was . . .

The dolch. It glinted blackly just feet ahead of him.

But Jack thought he was going to be sick as he crawled for it. Ginny's machinelike screams burst out of her throat, flaying the air. They sounded mindless. The thing that had once been Gilles unhinged its wedged jaw. The bezeled teeth shimmered. Jack's hand landed on the dolch, and he lurched forward just in time to see the gaping maw close completely over Ginny's screaming face.

Her fists and heels pummeled the glass floor; her body twitched like electrocution. Teeth ground against bone and blood poured as the thing ate Ginny's face off her skull, like someone eating the icing off a cupcake.

Then a black forked tongue extracted the lidless eyes . . .

Jack plunged the dolch into the thing's knobbed spine.

Its howl blasted him across the room. Then the room exploded. Jack covered his head against the rain of glass, squeezing himself into a corner under the avalanche of sound—a tremor like a thousand screams in unison, which rose and rose—

And then stopped.

Then: silence. Like the silence after a bomb going off.

Jack opened his eyes. Ginny's bare feet twitched a few more times, then she died. Jack did not look at the sloughed red mask of bone where her face had once been. And the thing—

The obscenity in the black cassock was Gilles again. He lay skewed across the floor, dead.

Jack did not reckon this madness. Glass slivers slid off his back as he rose. He picked up the Webley and headed down the stairs.

They were narrow and dark. They turned at what must be the first-floor landing, and suddenly he detected light. It wavered dimly. *Candlelight*, he realized. *The basement*.

And he knew what to expect.

Marzen would be waiting, slightly more or slightly less than human.

The words turned about her head like quiet birds—"*Pater terrae, per me terram ambula*"—and then yes she thought she saw a bird a beautiful black bird rising like light from a chasm and something else even more beautiful rising behind it and then she heard more words smoking words I am Baalzephon, Father of the Earth. Be one with me and my minions, my love. Be with me forever.

The man made of flames took Veronica's hand and kissed it.

Jack picked up the German's fallen dolch on the first landing. Again, he did not even attempt to sew reality into the madness he'd witnessed. Perhaps he was mad himself by now.

The guns had only slowed them down, but it was the dolch that had killed Gilles. Jack stuck the Webley in his belt and gripped the black knife. It felt like sleek ice in his hand. It felt reverberant with some unearthly power.

He scanned down the stairwell. Nothing.

"Come on, you ugly fuck. I'm here. Come and get me."

But only silence hung in the stairs, and flickering light.

Then the tremendous weight slammed down on his back.

Jack's lungs voided. The thing had dropped itself from the ceiling of the staircase. Entangled with it, he rolled thumping to the bottom of the steps.

Pressure ballooned his face, the cloven hand latched to his neck. The candlelight licked Marzen's primeval visage. Dog-like jaws snapped twice, then it grinned. The light made a shadow of its horns against the wall.

Jack couldn't breathe, he couldn't even move under the muscled, inhuman weight. He felt encased in cement and smothering but somehow he was able to think: *I'm dying*.

The huge mouth spread wide, showing a black pit full of teeth. It began to lower to Jack's face. Its breath stank of all the evil in history.

Visions unfurled. Stars burst into bright colors and beautiful kaleidoscopes. Jack saw things then, as his mind blanked out. He saw love and graciousness. He saw wonder. He saw the old man Carlson trodding docks in rotten clothes, hungry and poor but *smiling,* each broken step a celebration of life. He saw Faye's sweet smile, the sun shining in her hair, and then he saw Veronica and all the love she'd had for him once. He saw all his flaws destroyed by the simple, bright light of joy and all the treasures of the world. Trees, the sky, starry nights and kisses—all these things and millions more in what would be the second before his death. Jack was dying now, at the filth-encrusted hands of an ageless evil, yet all he could see was jubilation. No, he was not scared, and he did not see devils.

He saw angels.

The roared deafened him. The ground beneath him shook like demolition as the incubus unloosed the bellow of its agony. Jack felt flattened by the tumult of noise; the taloned hand came away from his throat and the crushing weight sidled off him.

Gagging, he opened his eyes. Blood pulsed back into his brain and he could see again. Jack was alive, but Marzen lay dead at his side, the black dolch buried to the hilt in his belly.

I'm still alive, Jack thought.

He got up and turned.

A figure stood like a chess piece at the end of the light. It was waiting for him.

"Khoronos," Jack said.

"Inquisitor. Welcome to the temple of my god."

Jack stepped up, drawing the Webley from his belt. "You're not like them, are you?" He pointed the revolver at the figure's cloaked head. "I know you're not."

"The flesh falters, but the spirit goes on. No, you needn't a dolch to kill me, inquisitor. Kill me with your guns, your crusader's tools. Kill me with your prisons, your poison gas, and your electric chairs. You may kill me with your bare hands if you like. It hardly matters."

Candlelight glistened on the lean face. The candles sizzled. Khoronos stood perfectly still and did not blink. His smile looked like a concession, a lament.

"Where's Veronica?" Jack demanded.

"Instead of fighting us, why not join us? Be one with us in the temple of our god. We never end, inquisitor." The clement voice drifted. "Infinity can be a beautiful thing."

Jack's heart felt dead. "Where's Veronica?"

"She's gone," Khoronos said.

His hand bid the floor. All that lay within the shape of the Trine was a large pool of blood.

"She is with the Father now, the Father of the Earth."

Baalzephon, the word whispered in Jack's head.

Khoronos spread out his hands and looked up. Only the whites showed in his eyes, and a gentle smile touched his lips.

"Aorista," he said.

Jack dropped the Webley's hammer.

In this bizarre transition of bullet to flesh, Jack heard only a bang that seemed far away. A flash popped. Khoronos' face split in the sack hood. The bullet mowed him down like a tall weed.

Footsteps pounded behind him. Stewie and Randy and several uniforms burst into the basement. But Jack didn't see them, he didn't care. They seemed to sense this and stayed themselves to give Jack room.

Jack approached the Trine.

Khoronos lay dead on his back. Blood leaked from his cracked head within the hood.

Jack knelt at the Trine.

He put his hands in the blood—Veronica's blood. It had no heat in it at all.

Goodbye, Veronica.

He brought his hands to his face and began to cry.

EPILOGUE

On that night, while Jack had been infiltrating Khoronos' phantom house, Stewie Arlinger had called Randy Eliot after having listened to Faye Rowland's strange tale of sacrificial rites and encrypted names. Randy had easily pinpointed Jack's location by instructing the duty programmer to recall the map grids that Jack had run through the data monitor in his vehicle. That's how they'd found him.

Two days later the papers and the news had everything. "Suspended Cop Nails Triangle Killers," the *Post* read. The police would never successfully trace the identities of the ritualists; Khoronos, Marzen, and Gilles were just names on three death reports, names without backgrounds, without lives. Jan Beck of the county police Technical Services Division easily linked the forensic evidence of the first three murders to the alleged perpetrators. The case was closed.

The body of Veronica Polk, however, was never found.

Jack did the rehab thing, if only to prove to himself that he could. He would never drink again, and, though at first it troubled him, the fact quickly diminished to insignificance. He still went to the bar, though, but drank soda water with a twist. It proved a fascinating perspective: watching a bunch of other people get drunk while remaining sober himself.

After a time, he began to think about things. He thought about love. He would always love Veronica and her memory, but he also knew that she was dead, and that the past was the past. Part of himself would mourn her for the rest of his life, but the other part would go on.

The aorists believed that time was inconsequential; whatever truth was, it went on without regard to duration. But Jack knew that this was not applicable. Time, in actuality, was short. He asked Faye to move in with him, and she did. She quit the state and got a better job with the county library system. He spent $1,400 on an engagement ring ("Ouch!" he'd remarked when the saleswoman informed him of the price); however, he hadn't yet summoned the courage to give it to Faye. He didn't know what she would think, or even how she might react. He didn't know if he was moving too fast. He knew that he loved her, though, so at least he knew something. Perhaps he would give her the ring tomorrow. Perhaps tonight.

"Here are the ballistics reports," Jan Beck said. She plopped them on Jack's desk. Randy offered her some coffee, but she politely declined. "I'd rather drink embalming fluid than Captain Cordesman's coffee."

"Sure," Jack said, "but embalming fluid doesn't have caffeine, and what the hell do I want with the ballistics reports?"

"It was your case," she answered, "so you can stow them. I just do tests. I'll tell you, though—I have new faith in the .38 standard-pressure round."

"What do you mean?"

"It did a job on Khoronos' head."

Jack laughed. "Some forensics expert you are. It wasn't a .38, it was a .455 metal jacket. Most gunshops don't even carry them anymore; the rangemaster loads them for me special."

"You're pulling my leg," Jan Beck said. "A .455?"

"That's right. I fired it out of an old Webley."

Now it was Jan Beck's turn to laugh. "Then you missed. The bullet I pulled out of Khoronos' head was a .38 semijacketed wadcutter. I figured you shot it out of that little Smith snub of yours."

Randy was frowning. "Jack didn't shoot Khoronos."

"Sure I did," Jack said.

"Don't you remember? After I tagged your location with the duty programmer, I brought a bunch of uniforms out to Khoronos' house. Stewie went with us. When he and I were searching the upstairs, he picked up your .38 snub in that room with all the broken glass. Then we found the door that led to the basement."

Now Jack was thoroughly confused. "What are you talking about?"

"Stewie shot Khoronos," Randy informed him. "Not you. He shot him with your .38."

"Are you sure?"

"Of course. I was standing right next to him."

Jack didn't see what difference it made. Nonetheless, it bothered him. He expressly remembered dropping the Webley's hammer and seeing Khoronos go down. When he went home for lunch, he called Stewie's office but his receptionist said he wasn't in. Then he went upstairs and looked at his guns. He hadn't cleaned them yet. He opened the Webley's receiver; the round over the barrel port would be the one he'd shot at Khoronos. He took the round out and saw that the percussion cap was dented, which meant that the firing pin had struck. But the big round-nosed bullet was still implanted in the casing.

A dud, Jack realized. This happened sometimes, especially with odd reloads. A bad primer wouldn't ignite the powder. *Goddamn thing never went off,* he thought.

Next, he opened the Smith snub, the gun Randy claimed that Stewie had picked up in the mirrored room. Jack hadn't fired it that night, so it should have five unspent cartridges in the cylinder. But there were only four; the casing over the barrel port was discharged, empty.

How do you like that? he thought. It *was* Stewie who shot Khoronos.

Faye's briefcase sat opened on the kitchen table, full of all the research she'd done on the aorists. A yellow legal pad had been top-marked *Synod.* Apparently she'd transcribed some text by hand, for the pad was lined with her script.

Jack didn't bother reading any of it. Why should he? The case was closed. The last line however, read: *He who shall slay the Prelate shall become the Prelate.*

"Cash or charge, sir?"

"Cash," Stewie said. He had plenty of that now, and he always would. *He bestows treasure upon the faithful,* he mused. Los Angeles seemed perfect. Lots of artists, lots of creative women. Initiating two new surrogoti would be easy. An artsy town like that? *Piece of cake,* he concluded.

"Smoking or nonsmoking?" inquired the girl at the ticket counter.

"Nonsmoking, please."

"Name?"

"Pardon me?"

"Your name, sir? For your boarding pass."

"Oh, yes, of course. Khoronos. Stewart Khoronos."

The flight was quiet, comfortable. Stewie particularly liked the window seat. He looked out the tiny window, gazing in awe upon the world which awaited him.

He pressed his hand to the glass and whispered this:

"Aorista."